EVERYBODY'S BROKEN

If you are reading this book, I have prayed for you.

There is no better Life Coach than God. By His grace, every minute we overcome is a training field. Think of these minutes as practice for the really tough days and as they say, fight like a girl!

FAY LAMB

Everybody's Broken

Amazing Grace Book Three

FAY LAMB

W
Write Integrity Press

Everybody's Broken
© 2016 Fay Lamb
ISBN-13: 978-1-944120-20-7
ISBN-10: 1-944120-20-3
Ebook ISBN-13: 978-1-944120-19-1

All rights reserved. No part of this publication may be reproduced or transmitted in any form or by any means without written permission from the publisher.

This book is a work of fiction. Names, characters, places, and incidents are either products of the author's imagination or used fictitiously. Any similarity to actual people and/or events is purely coincidental.

Scriptures are taken from the Holy Bible, King James Version by public domain.

Published by:
Write Integrity Press, PO Box 702852, Dallas, TX 75370

Find out more about the author, Fay Lamb, at her Facebook page or at her website: The Tactical Editor

www.WriteIntegrity.com
Printed in the United States of America.

Everybody's Broken

Dedication

As a child, much like the characters in this book, I had a grandmother who had a world full of treasure at her fingertips, and she gladly shared her bounty with me.

This book is dedicated to my six precious grandchildren: may they unearth their own grandmother's treasure and understand all the love that she bestows with it.

For Jacob, for Kaylee, for Emilee, for Micah, for Abigail Fay, and for Kellan ... may your lives be filled with journeys and wonder, and wherever you travel, may you know that Mamaw believes no one could love you more.

Fay Lamb

Acknowledgements

When I start a story, I never know the adventures my characters will embark upon. In *Everybody's Broken* I soon learned that every character had a surprise for me. Thus, the story became a very complex one.

At the end of the journey, as most writers who seem to mostly wing it find, there is a bit of confusion as to whether plot and plot twists come together.

Enter the three best voluntary readers, proofreaders, editors and one new editor who are the best imaginable. They went on this journey before I sent it to you,

An author can often envision the journey, but the curves give us problems. So, I want to say a special thank you to Kristen Hoegrefe, Sharon Hardin, Patricia Dyer, and Marji Laine for their invaluable assistance in checking for and elimination of the plotholes, pitfalls, and the sudden stops that often keep a story from being enjoyable for the reader.

Everybody's Broken

Chapter 1

April 15, Bodacious Cove, Florida

God had betrayed her.

Abra Carmichael brushed at a solitary tear trickling down her cheek. Carmichaels didn't show their emotions in public; she hadn't given God the satisfaction of seeing her display them in private either. Not again, not after He'd crushed her, as if she were no more than a pesky gnat buzzing around Him with desperate prayers she'd whispered into His ear.

God wasn't resurrecting her husband, Beau. He'd taken a gunshot to his head. Unidentifiable if not for his uniform and the wedding band he wore.

Her brother, Finn, had disappeared from the murder scene, taking with him her twin five-year-olds. She needed Finn to be alive, to have her boys with him somewhere.

Two elderly, beloved residents of Bodacious Cove came to stand in front of her as she sat in the church pew.

Though it took every ounce of effort, Abra stood. If Pap were alive, he'd chide her if she didn't. "Ms. Mercy, Mr. Zeb, thank you for coming." She held out her hand.

Zeb wrapped his big paws around her upper arms and squeezed.

Mercy took Abra's hand in both of hers, as if Abra had become an orphaned child. "I'd ask you how you're holding up, gal, but I know you Osteens: strong as you are kind."

Abra fought back emotion. She wasn't strong, and she hadn't been kind through this ordeal. "Thank you for saying so. I appreciate your help with the search party, taking care of their needs."

"And we'll keep doing it until those little ones return."

Her world tilted for a second, and Abra reached for the back of the pew. She should have eaten this morning, but an empty stomach was better than losing anything she placed into it.

"You sit, honey," Zeb said. "We love you, love Finn, and those little rascals." He winked at her. "Beau was a good man. I planned to put his name in the running after Chief Herman's retirement."

Mercy and Zeb moved away.

Abra sat hard on the seat. She'd never tell them Beau hadn't wanted to become police chief. "Someday, maybe when the kids are grown, but then I'd have you all to myself," he'd said more than once.

Happy one day. Dead the next. She inhaled and let out a stuttering breath.

The cloying aroma of the floral arrangements surrounding Beau's casket gave her a headache. The drone of hushed tones didn't help either. The good folks either sorrowed with Abra or cast sharp glares of doubt her way, each undermining the façade of composure she'd constructed over the last two weeks. She needed her best

Everybody's Broken

friend to step across the sea of division and wrap comforting arms around her. But Mazzie Harris hadn't arrived.

Instead, Chief of Police Loyal Herman came to stand in front of her. Even without looking up, the garish pinky ring he wore gave him away. He sat and patted her hand. His touch wasn't as comforting as Mercy's had been, and Abra pulled from his hold.

He smelled of muscle liniment and the spearmint gum he constantly chewed. "How are you doing?"

Abra meant only for her and Mazzie to sit here. He hadn't been invited to the front row, but here he was, making himself the master of ceremony.

Chief Herman ran his hand across the slick part of his balding head. A fringe of dark hair encircled the empty space.

Abra's hands trembled in her lap, a sign her defenses would burst if she didn't shore the breach that her anger at Herman caused. She clenched her fists. Why wasn't Mazzie here? She'd promised to arrive before the crowds showed.

Mazzie: her stronghold, standing up against the hours of interrogation they'd both endured. Investigators had separated them, placing each in a different room, bombarding Abra with questions: where had they been the day Beau had been killed? Did either of them own a gun? Did they have reason to believe anyone held a grudge against Beau? Against Finn? Had Beau and Finn argued prior to Beau's death? Could Finn have been involved in anything that could have gotten Beau murdered? Why would Finn leave with Abra's children? Could it be he was aware of abuse? Could Finn believe the boys needed protection from their mother—protection Finn hadn't afforded Beau?

Horrible questions meant to disarm and entrap.

Abra told the truth. Her answers never changed. She

doubted Mazzie offered any different.

She had not killed her husband nor conspired with Mazzie to kill Beau.

The chief was one of Pap's best friends. He, of all people, should have stopped the ludicrous speculation surrounding any part she or Mazzie might have had in Beau's death. The divide between her husband's employer and Abra widened with each new day, and she didn't want to close that gap now. "Mazzie will be here soon, Chief Herman. You're in her seat."

"Abra, you can't be upset with me for pushing the funeral forward. After the autopsy and the gathering of evidence, I wanted to give us time to locate Finn and the boys, but the town has to heal. We've never experienced such a tragedy."

Abra put her fingers to her lips. Unkind words dangled at the tip of her tongue, but she'd not thought through them. They would remain unspoken. She took a deep breath. "My boys won't have this opportunity to say good-bye to their father. What about their healing?"

The chief looked at his hands. "Honey, after two weeks, I think you and I both know the boys aren't coming home."

"The boys are with Finn. I'm sure he has a reason for not bringing them back to me."

Herman leaned toward her. "Or for not calling to tell you where he's staying. His silence can only mean two things, and neither one of those is good for you, for Finn, or for your sons." He spoke only loud enough for her to hear. "I'm not your enemy, Abra. You've been cleared in Beau's death."

"But Finn ...?" This wasn't the time to talk about it, but she needed to know.

"I'm sorry, but unless this case takes a drastic turn, finding Finn's body is the only thing that will clear him ... at this point." He stood.

Abra lifted her shoulders, pressing her back into the cushion of the pew, fighting a flow of tears. She wouldn't cry. She forced herself to meet his eyes. "Thank you, Chief, for your faith in my family. Pap would have a lot to say if he were alive."

The chief shook his head. "Your husband died a hero. Let's put our differences aside and celebrate his life and mourn his death."

She jerked her gaze from his. Trouble was, staring at the cross above the baptismal pierced her with the pain of God's rejection equally as much as lowering her gaze to the closed casket where inside lay the lifeless body of the man she loved. Even the picture of Beau in his dress uniform, his green eyes twinkling, and his crooked smile hinting of tantalizing secrets, threatened to undo her. Despite the picture, the memory of identifying his body by the things he wore, by what had been left of him, would not leave her the peace of seeing her husband as he was in the photograph.

The first officer in the town's history to be killed in the line of duty, he'd be laid to rest with full honors.

She turned toward the foyer to search for Mazzie, ignoring the mixture of condemnation and sympathy from those clad in the dress uniform of several surrounding police forces and from those dressed in the dark clothes of civilians who mourned. Until the case had closure, some might always doubt her innocence.

Everyone's attention shifted toward the foyer. Morning sun streamed into the sanctuary from the glass enclosed foyer. Abra covered her tired eyes to shield against the glare.

A hush fell over the crowd as two men and a woman entered through the double door entry of the sanctuary. One man had his arm around the woman's waist. The other man talked quietly to someone who pointed at Abra. The man turned and searched in her direction.

Abra's heart hitched as whispers began to build. She looked at the coffin, tempted to run and make sure Beau was not inside, that God had not given up on her, that her husband was alive. Somehow, someway her identification had been wrong.

An usher hurried the three newcomers down the aisle toward Abra. She stood, joy rising inside her. This had been a horrible joke. Beau was here. Peter and Paulie had to be with him.

"Beau …" Her husband's name lilted from her lips like a ghost lifting from other-worldly fog.

An intense azure gaze, framed in dark lashes, locked with hers.

Blue.

Not green.

She blinked and stumbled backward. God had definitely abandoned her. She'd never see the twinkle in Beau's green eyes again.

"Shane," the man beside the woman whispered, "you startled her."

Shane winced. "I'm sorry."

"Welcome." Pastor Dreyfus approached, scratching his silver hair. "Young man, you must be a relative to Beau."

The man nodded. "Shane Browne, Beau's cousin." He nodded toward his companions. "Beau's sister, Randa, and her husband, Dalton Rylander."

Abra had heard about Dalton but not from Beau. Finn met both Dalton and Beau at the University of Georgia, and Finn had never shared how closely Dalton and Beau were related.

Beau never talked about anything or anyone from his past. He'd asked her to walk beside him in faith, and she'd done so. Someone or something in the life he'd left behind had hurt him, and Abra had done everything she could to make that pain go away, including pretending it never happened. As far as Beau had been concerned, his life started when he came to visit Finn in Bodacious Cove, met Abra, and decided to stay. Finn had to have known, but her brother was good at keeping secrets. And when, as a child, Abra had asked someone things they didn't want her to know, that person had left town, never to be seen again. Little girls didn't get over rejection so quickly, and Abra doubted she ever would.

But for Beau and Finn to keep Beau's family a secret from her ...

Randa ran a hand through her blond waves and looked to her husband, her eyes so remarkably similar to Beau's.

"Abra, Chief Herman contacted Beau's former employer, our sheriff, a couple of days ago about Beau's death," Dalton said. "Otherwise, we wouldn't have known. I'm aware Beau didn't mention us to you. He told me that when I last spoke to him. We're here to offer support, to help in the search for the boys and Finn, and to mourn with you."

How many more of Beau's secrets would she learn before this tragedy was behind her? She hadn't even known he'd once been a deputy in some place he'd never mentioned.

She never dared ask.

Because losing him had been her greatest fear.

Her gaze fell on the coffin.

Fear had been a waste of time. "What's going to happen will happen." Beau always said. "Don't waste time on worry, sweetheart. Plan a little; live a lot."

"We're sorry to intrude." Shane must have misread her silence. "If you want us to sit somewhere else ..."

She forced the words up from within her broken heart, past her closed throat, and into the air. "Please. No. Sit with me. We're family." She scooted down to sit in the middle of the pew, leaving room for Mazzie. Randa sat beside her, Dalton next to Randa, and Shane on his other side. Dalton laced his fingers with his wife's.

Abra envied the gentle squeeze he gave.

The pastor stepped to the podium. "We're about to start. Take your seats everyone."

She straightened and prepared to shut off her emotions. The only way she knew how to survive the formality her husband deserved.

Randa leaned close. "I'm sorry we didn't meet before this."

Abra took a deep breath. She released it, but somehow, it didn't want to flow. She gave a nod of assurance that she understood Beau's sister's attempt to lighten the overwhelming situation.

Randa reached for her hand, and though Abra resisted, her newfound sister-in-law held to her tightly.

Another commotion began to stir, and Abra turned. In the opposite aisle, people stared toward the foyer. On her side of the aisle, necks craned for a better view. Abra looked to the pulpit for an answer from the aging preacher.

Pastor Dreyfus's eyes widened. He cast a glance her way as he rushed from the podium. "Praise You, Lord. Praise You," he muttered as he hurried to the back.

Mazzie entered the sanctuary, hurrying down the plush carpeted aisle of the church.

Gasps filled the sanctuary. Then muffled cries.

Mazzie held out her hand toward Abra. "Come with me."

Abra stood, skirting Beau's family, and moved back down the aisle, her steps unsteady, her heart pounding, unable to comprehend the unfolding events.

Mazzie linked her arm with Abra's. "Honey, God loves you. He really does. Beau's gone, I know, but ..." she pointed ... "they're still here."

Abra stopped. She covered her mouth with trembling

hands. "How?"

"Does it matter? They're alive." Mazzie reached and squeezed Abra's hand and looked toward the foyer where Abra's five-year-old boys clung to the elderly pastor.

Abra fell to her knees, opening her arms. Great choking sobs poured from her as her twins—the only part of Beau she had left—ran into her embrace.

Abra dragged her tired body over the threshold of her home, the boys clinging to her and Mazzie standing beside her. After the funeral, Abra handed her newly discovered brother-in-law, Dalton, the key to the house, gave him directions to the seaside estate, and left Beau's family to handle those who planned to come by for a meal fixed by the ladies from her church. The Bodacious Cove Police Department left her no other recourse. If it hadn't been for Mazzie's insistence, and Trace's agreement, that they be allowed to lay Beau to rest first, Herman would have had them all miss the funeral.

While Abra made the arrangements for Dalton to oversee things at home, Detective Trace Bastion, following Chief Herman's directive, stood close, hovering, twisting the high school ring he should have separated with long ago.

How many times had Abra chastised Beau and the boys when they laughed at "Detective Trace," as Beau said they were to refer to his friend, as Trace continued his habit? Abra always hated seeing the confusion and possible hurt on the otherwise straight-laced officer's face. But men were little boys at heart, and teasing was a part of a never-ending rite of passage, as far as Abra could determine.

As soon as he could, Trace had escorted Abra,

Mazzie, and the twins to the hospital emergency room for the boys to be seen and evidence sought.

The doctors found no signs of abuse. In fact, the only injuries they discovered were tiny cuts on their faces, all but healed in the two weeks since their disappearance. The doctor surmised they were caused by small shards of glass, something neither boy would deny or confirm. Both assured her—and apparently, the case worker and the police—that they hadn't been hurt. They refused to speak when asked about their father's death or Finn's disappearance. Maybe their minds shielded them from the horror they must have seen, pushed it back to some crevice that hopefully would never seep forward.

After the boys' examinations, Trace transported them to the police station where they'd undergone questioning.

Now, standing in her living room filled with the fine people of her town, Abra pulled back her hair, holding it at the top of her head. She sighed. Didn't these people realize she'd be tired and want to spend private time with Peter and Paulie? All she desired was to climb the stairs and crawl into her bed with a twin on each side and have them argue over which story she would read first. A moment of normalcy amid the chaos of the last weeks. Would it be normal, though, without Beau sitting on the other side of the bed, waiting to carry one of the boys to their room while she lifted the other?

The thought jolted her. Everything she and Beau had done together—parenting, keeping the home, running her business—God had left her to do them alone now.

Mazzie touched her arm. "You okay, Abracadabra?"

Abra ignored the use of her full name and the question. She suspected Pap, always a man of contradictions, had given her the name because of her October 31 birthday; however, Halloween was never celebrated in the Osteen house—at least not as Halloween. And Abra hated the ridiculous name.

Everybody's Broken

Mazzie leaned forward. "Abra?"

Abra took a deep breath. "No. Not really, but I can't think about it now."

Her faith had been so weakened during those lonely days and nights that she'd lost all hope of holding her boys in her arms again. The tears gathered in her eyes.

Gratefulness welled up inside her, and Abra gave a silent nod to God for His compassion and pushed her bitterness aside—for the moment.

The boys' safety could only mean one thing: they'd been with Finn. Again, they'd remained close-lipped when speaking to officials trained in getting such information; and, according to Mazzie, her interrogation came with an accusation by Herman that she was somehow influencing the twins. He'd even gone so far as to say they'd been with her over the last two weeks.

Nonsense. Mazzie would never do that to her. Besides, where would she have hidden the boys? Both Mazzie's home and the mortgage title agency left to her by Pap had been searched without need of a warrant. Mazzie wanted the murder solved as much as Abra.

"Hey." Dalton met her. "We did encourage folks not to wait around, but most said they wanted to give you a hug and then leave."

Shane bent down to the boys' level. "If it's okay with your mommy, Uncle Dalton and I would like to go see the beach. Wanna show it to us?"

Paulie held tighter to Abra.

Peter stared at Shane. "Why do you look like Daddy?"

Shane gazed up at her with those blue eyes. He might resemble Beau enough to confuse a woman in shock or those who didn't know Beau well, but she'd never confuse him for Beau again. Besides the difference in eye color, Shane's hair was black except where the sun had lightened the edges to burnt amber. Shane's chin wasn't as pronounced as Beau's, and he stood a tad shorter than Beau's six feet. They did share the identical crooked smile, though.

"Well, your daddy was my cousin. I've been told we took after our Grandmere—your great grandmother." Shane's voice was deep and warm, almost hypnotic, as if he wanted to wrap the boys in safety simply by speaking to them.

Beau had always been gently commanding with his family and friends, but suspected criminals got the full force of his intent when he ordered them to do something. Mazzie called him Sarge, and Beau pretended to hate the nickname, but Abra had seen him smile a time or two when they'd verbally sparred.

"So, what do you say?" Dalton asked.

Peter shook his head, and Paulie did the same.

"If you change your mind about hanging with us, and you still don't want to go outside, we found a box of Legos, and Dalton and I once won a contest. We made a street that looks like one where we live."

"Huh-uh," Peter said.

Abra started to correct him, but after his long day, one bad-behavior pass was warranted.

"Uh-huh," Dalton narrowed his eyes. "I got pictures. I'll send them to your mom to prove it."

"Can you build a pirate ship?" Paulie tugged on Shane's suit coat.

"Nah, not Shane, but I can." Dalton answered. He stood tall and straight, arms folded across his chest, and with a slight turn, looking out over the briny sea through Abra's front window, took on the essence of a pirate captain.

Shane studied the boys. "Paulie, let's you and me be a team, and challenge Dalton and Peter. Whichever one of you helps to build the best pirate ship will get a new Lego set. Aunt Randa and I own a toy store, and we get the best."

"Who's gonna judge?" Peter asked.

"Me, silly." Mazzie grasped the necklace of pearls dangling around her neck and swiveled her hips from side to side, causing the bottom layers of her black dress to sway with her. "I'm very judgmental. At least that's what I've been told." Her friend brought out her best Southern accent for their guests, a hint to Abra that she was hiding her pain.

Abra laughed. "Yes, you are."

"Okay," Paulie tugged Shane's arm.

As the men allowed the boys to drag them away from the well-wishers, Abra mouthed her thank you. They were only boys, and they didn't need to be wrapped up in the duties of grief.

Her guests, who'd apparently given her a two-minute reprieve, now headed in her direction.

"Chin up," Mazzie whispered as she moved past. "I'll play defensive back, darlin', and make a few interceptions for you."

Abra would have laughed again if the last one hadn't left her weary to the bone.

The townspeople who'd come to her home were friendly folks who'd always believed in her. True to their word, they filed past with hugs and "I can't know how you really feel, but I know a little about grief" sentiments.

Mercy and Zeb were the last to leave. Abra caught their departing glances and nods to Mazzie but dismissed it as secret code for "she needs you."

With the house empty of everyone but Mazzie, the boys, and Beau's family, Abra pushed herself to start cleaning up the mess.

Randa worked silently along with her, putting food into containers and cleaning the dishes. When everything was done, Abra leaned against her kitchen sink. "The maid will be happy that she didn't have to tackle the cleanup, I suppose."

"A maid?" Randa took a seat at the table in the nook by the window.

Abra tensed, waiting for some judgment from her sister-in-law. "We have a lady who comes in Monday through Friday."

"I'd hire one, but I'm afraid that cleaning up after Dalton is a million-dollar job." She smiled. "Is there anything else I can help you with?"

"You've been wonderful."

"It's the least I can do." Randa strummed her fingernails on the table, once, twice. Then she stopped. "I'll never understand why Beau left us and didn't return, but I learned enough from your friends and neighbors to know that he was happy here with you." She grasped Abra's hand with both of hers. "There is no way to adequately thank you for loving him."

"I'm sorry that our first meeting is during this tragedy. I don't understand—"

"Just between you and me," Randa interrupted, "once upon a time, Beau was the big brother I adored, but I ended that." She shook her head and turned those green eyes to Abra. "He was the best big brother I could ask for. Treated Shane as if he were our brother." She swiped at a tear and looked to the ceiling for a long moment.

Tears dry, she returned her attention to Abra. "I'd give all I have to talk to him one more time. I've longed for him greatly, especially over the last couple of weeks. Sad, isn't it? Even if I could have found him, he was already gone."

Abra thought there weren't any more pieces of her heart that could break. Tears filled her eyes as she cried against her newfound sister-in-law.

"Mommy! Mommy." Paulie ran to her. "Mazzie says it's a tie. That's not fair. We need another judge."

Abra pulled away, wiping her eyes. "Oh-ho-no,

young man. I've never won an argument with that woman, and I doubt anything will change today." Abra pinched his cheek. "If Mazzie declared it a tie, a tie it is." She looked to the clock on the wall. "It's been a very long day. Let's get you upstairs, in the bath, and ready for bed."

Paulie hung his head and walked away, his body swaying.

"What did Daddy say about that?" Abra asked then closed her eyes. She'd given Peter a pass. She should have let his silent sass go without altercation.

"That attitude comes in actions and not just in words," Randa's answer came with a half-laugh, half-cry.

Paulie swung toward them. "You knew my daddy?" He lopped back.

"He was my brother. Our grandmere used to say that to us when we were little."

Paulie studied Randa as if for the first time. "If you're my daddy's sister and Shane's my daddy's cousin, how come I've never met you?"

"Paulie!" Abra corrected. "Apologize."

"Sorry." The boy lowered his head.

Randa reached out for Paulie's hand.

He peeked up at her.

"You asked an honest question. I've been at home with Uncle Dalton and Shane. We live in another state. Your daddy was here with you and your mommy, and we just never got the chance to come and meet you." She placed a kiss on the top of Paulie's head and stood. "And I'm so glad we did. Because with your daddy in heaven, I'm going to miss him, but your daddy always gave good gifts." She cut a look toward Abra. "And this time, he's given me a family that will always remind me of him." She led Paulie from the room.

Paulie looked up at his aunt as he held to Randa's hand, leading her to the arena of the great pirate ship contest. A bright smile covered his face.

Peter wouldn't be that easy to win over. He was the fierce protector like his father. Paulie was the nurturer. Abra suspected he'd inherited that from his Uncle Finn. He definitely hadn't gotten it from her.

Abra leaned forward, her hands covering her face, and wept. With the protector and the nurturer both gone, what were they going to do?

Chapter 2

Shane tipped the glass of iced tea to his lips and stared out the window to the ocean beyond the darkening sky. In the reflection of the glass, he could see Mazzie sitting on the couch with Dalton. Randa sat in the silence that was now becoming all too familiar since her doctor's visit a few weeks before. Something had happened, but she wouldn't share it with him. In time, Shane hoped Dalton would trust him with the truth. Shane offered his cousin a heartfelt smile.

Randa's lips moved slightly but didn't curve, as if she was too weary to move a muscle.

Dalton worried his lip the way he did when something burdened him. "You haven't heard from Finn?"

Shane turned back to the conversation. He didn't have to be a lawyer to know Dalton was badgering the witness.

Mazzie wasn't talking.

"Mazzie, you have no information?" Dalton

continued his interrogation.

Shane never met Finn Osteen, but the missing man had been a good friend to Dalton, Beau, and Beau's ex-girlfriend, Jasmine. They were the Five "H" Society: Handsome, Hillbilly, Helium, High Jinx, and some clown they named Hound Dog. Shane was surprised he could remember those names through the fog of alcohol and drugs his life had become during Beau's college days.

Shane met Hound Dog once or twice, but he'd forgotten the man's real name. He'd followed Beau, *Hillbilly*, Jasmine, *Helium*, and Dalton, *Handsome*, to town during college breaks. The dolt enjoyed Grandmere's Southern cooking and hospitality a little too much as far as Shane was concerned. Finn, *High Jinx*, never visited with the others during those breaks, but Shane heard enough about Abra's brother to know he was different from Beau, someone he didn't think would fit in well with Beau and Dalton's studious, no-nonsense crowd. At this point, Shane couldn't say that he'd ever really known his cousin at all, and the truth stung him like the catfish barb Beau dug out of Shane's foot when he was six.

"Nothing?" Dalton's anguish gained Shane's attention.

Mazzie stared at Dalton for a long while as if weighing her answer. "Nothing," she whispered as if those two syllables had cost her too much.

Beau's leaving their hometown of Amazing Grace had left a big wake, one that threatened to overturn the boat of life he'd placed them all into. Mazzie's answer proved that. Beau's death was no different. If Shane understood a little bit of the conversations he'd heard between Abra and Mazzie, Finn was more than Abra's brother to the beautiful southern belle. Having someone you thought would always be there for you vanish without a word was a pain that no one should ever have to go through, whether it happened six years before or only a couple of weeks ago.

A wispy form flowed down the grand staircase in the foyer of the home, catching Shane's eye.

Abra had ventured upstairs several times now, checking on her sons. The taffeta black skirt she'd worn all day reached to the bottom of her knee. She'd long kicked off the stilettos she'd worn for the funeral, but whether barefoot or in high heels, she moved with grace.

Shane placed his thumb and forefinger against his eyes and rubbed. The thoughts were the result of the long day and all the questions that still weighed upon him. Certainly, he wouldn't look at Beau's widow that way under normal circumstances. He couldn't remember any woman who'd caught his eye since his sobriety and definitely not since becoming a single father.

Randa patted his shoulder. He hadn't seen her approach.

Abra stopped and looked at him. "Are you okay? You look pale. If you're tired ..."

He shook his head. "Thank you. I'm fine. Just missing my little girl."

"I'm sorry. I didn't realize you'd left your family to attend the funeral. Your wife and daughter would have been more than welcome."

He forced a smile. "No wife. Never has been. Just my daughter and me."

Her eyes widened. "Oh ... I'm so sorry."

Randa placed her hand on Abra's arm. "Shane's very secretive about Taffy's mom. Won't even tell us who she is." She turned back to Shane with a snarky smile. "There are times when he can be as good as Beau about keeping secrets."

Shane narrowed his eyes at his cousin. Randa was hurting if she lashed out in sarcasm. He forced himself to look away and to give his attention to Abra. "My thoughts about Beau are traveling to places they don't need to go."

Abra nodded as if she understood. "Anger. I get so mad at him for leaving me. Then I'm ashamed because I know he wouldn't have left given the chance."

"Don't be so sure about that."

Abra backed away from him but not fast enough for him to miss her wince.

Well, even if he found himself attracted to Abra, his attitude would close that door and lock it up tight.

"Shane!" Randa scolded him then softened. "I'm sorry for what I said. I think we're all feeling lost without Beau."

Still, Shane hated this person he'd become as the long day drew to a close: edgy, vindictive, envious, raging with the anger Abra thought she could understand.

Shane inhaled deeply. "Abra," he let her name rush outward, "I'm sorry. Beau was important to me, and I have to think this is my grief speaking."

Abra pressed two fingers against her lips as if afraid to speak.

He'd done that to her.

He needed to change the subject. "I saw a workshop in your garage. Beau never lost his love for carpentry, did he?"

"No, he didn't. He crafted most of the furniture here with Pap. Our clients were so impressed they paid some good money for Finn and me to place them in their homes. We're interior designers." She smiled at what seemed a happy memory. "Beau complained that Finn and I didn't give him any rest, but he loved spending time in that workshop."

"Pap was your dad?" Randa asked.

Abra nodded. "He and Beau shared a love for woodwork. Pap started out as a carpenter, worked his way through college, got his degree, and ended up in construction and then real estate. Pap just couldn't

Everybody's Broken

comprehend that Finn and I were made of different stuff. We liked to put design into what he liked to build. Beau was Pap's answer to prayer." She looked upward and dabbed at her eyes, her lips trembling as she spoke. "And behind their backs, Finn and I agreed that God answered our pleas when Beau became that son who shared Pap's interest from politics to carpentry to golf."

Her nervous rambling would have made Shane laugh if not for the sorrow in her blue eyes.

She ran a hand through her dark tresses and turned from him. "Pap put a lot of money into this once empty scrap of beach and turned it into a lovely little town, don't you think?"

"The place is as nice as Beau claimed," Dalton said.

Randa cleared her throat. "You mentioned that earlier, Dalt, but you never told us Beau contacted you. How long ago?" Randa sat on the sofa directly across from her husband in this house expertly decorated to showcase elegance and relaxation. She crossed her legs, kicking her right leg back and forth, much like an annoyed cat would twitch its tail.

"A few weeks before he died. He asked me to prepare a trust that would easily put to rest any legality for Abra in the event that something happened to him."

Abra gasped. "He thought he would die?"

"He said time had come for him to get serious. He explained he'd never told you about us."

"And did he explain why?" Randa demanded aloud what Shane's heart prayed Dalton wouldn't reveal.

"No, babe. I asked. He wouldn't tell me. Said it had nothing to do with us and everything to do with him."

Shane let out the breath he'd held and kept silent. Beau had hated falsehoods, but Dalton proved Beau had lied like a professional—unless Dalton was keeping the truth from Randa.

Shane stared into the remaining iced tea until a tender

touch on his hand drew his attention away. He released the glass to Mazzie, who offered him a sincere and friendly smile before taking the glass into the kitchen.

When she glanced back at him from behind the counter where she remained, Shane understood. Mazzie knew something—whether about Beau or Finn, he had no idea. Her smile vanished, and she swiped a tear from her cheek. "Abra, honey, I have to go now." She reached for her purse on the counter and swung toward the back door. "I'll see you and those precious kiddos tomorrow morning."

Abra had barely reacted when the door closed behind her friend.

"She and Finn were very close," Abra said. "She's as worried about him as I've been."

"There's no way that Finn could have—?"

"No, Randa!" Dalton stood. "No, babe. If you knew Finn ..." he gave a half-laugh "Right, Abra?"

The two shared a tender gaze before Abra nodded. "Finn is so mild natured. He wouldn't handle a gun. I've never known him to hold a grudge."

"Besides," Dalton sobered, "I had a long talk with Chief Herman."

"What would he tell you? From what I hear he casts suspicion upon anyone who breathes." Randa narrowed her eyes at her husband. "Don't you dare claim attorney privilege."

"My client is dead." Dalton paced. "First of all, yes. Beau indicated something had happened here that had him fearful for his life." Dalton looked to Abra.

She lowered her head. "Mazzie will tell you Beau thought Pap was killed unintentionally. Beau never told me his suspicions, and I don't want to get into it."

Dalton shrugged at Shane. "Anyway, Beau said someone wanted to purchase The Gray Lady. A local realtor called him. Beau wasn't happy about it, but he kept a carrot dangling in front of the potential buyer for reasons he didn't reveal to me. At the same time, he changed his will to a trust, and he left the old gal and everything in it to Abra. He stressed to me that he didn't want her sold."

"The Gray Lady?" Abra jerked her gaze to Dalton.

"Our grandmother's place," Randa explained. "Beau inherited it. Shane's mother left her house next door to Grandmere's place to me. Beau had already given Shane his old watermill house."

"Watch what you're calling old. I put a lot of sweat equity into that place compliments of Beau Carmichael." Shane smiled then sobered. "Who asked the realtor to contact Beau?"

Dalton shrugged. "All I can tell you is that Beau believed, for a reason he refused to reveal, that the person who wanted to buy the house was somehow related to something that happened here. I'm assuming now that he meant Abra's father's death." He looked to Abra.

Abra stood with her fingers against her lips, no words parting them.

"How could Abra's father be connected to The Gray Lady in anyway at all?" Randa asked.

"Beau was selective in the information he doled out," Dalton said. "I get the idea Finn knew more than I did, but we were both sworn to silence—me by ethics and Finn by promise."

Abra swayed back and forth, fingers still pressed to her lips, eyes wide.

"The good news is they've ruled you out as a suspect." Dalton winked at Abra. "That'll make tomorrow a lot easier."

"Tomorrow?" Abra balled her hands into fists. "They aren't going to badger me about Finn again. If they weren't so hot to close the case, they'd have known from the beginning it couldn't be either of us. Mazzie either.

We loved Beau." She sank into a chair.

Shane straightened. "Is Finn their only suspect?"

Dalton shook his head. "Nope. They have another person in their sights."

"Who?" Shane demanded.

"They received a tip yesterday after the funeral and found a gun they believe might have killed Beau. The serial number allegedly matches that gun stolen from your grandmother many years ago, taken from the home she left to Beau, the home he'd previously left to you in a will that has now been canceled by his recently revised trust."

Shane shook his head. "I never saw that thing."

"They'll have to do ballistic testing," Abra offered.

Shane ignored her. "Don't tell me …" He moved closer to Dalton.

Dalton tilted his head and raised a brow. "You're now their main suspect, buddy."

Everybody's Broken

Chapter 3

Shane leaned forward, elbows on the table, hands clasped in front of him, and his head resting on them. Detective Bastion paced back and forth in an interrogation room Shane guessed doubled as a closet, the space only large enough for a heavy square table and two chairs. Claustrophobia alone might make some people confess to crimes they never committed.

Shane sat in one chair, pressed tightly against the wall. Dalton had been smart. He took the chair in the corner, which afforded him more room, his legs straight, ankles crossed, and arms folded over his chest.

Dalton's phone, on the table, buzzed, and he sat up to tap the screen and read his text.

Bastion continued his short walk back and forth in front of them.

When Beau had worn his deputy sheriff's badge, he'd never let it add an ounce of arrogance to this demeanor. A commanding presence and an I-mean-business attitude, yes, but never insolence. Bastion carried his inflated ego around as if the badge entitled him to it.

Dalton seemed not to mind. After returning a message, he leaned back again.

Yeah, Dalton's type of arrogance was laid-back and not in your face, and his nonchalance comforted Shane. Hidden behind that mask of indifference was a legal mind like no other.

The silence had stretched long enough between Bastion's last question and the nod Dalton now gave Shane, telling him to answer the interrogator.

"I did not kill my cousin. I have not seen him in over six years. I did not know that he had taken me out of his will to give Grandmere's house to Abra. I didn't even know I was in the will. I don't care about the place. I have my own—given to me by Beau—and my daughter and I are happy there. I always thought he planned to return home and settle down. He loved the house. Grandmere made no secret to any of us that the place would be Beau's one day, and there isn't an ounce of envy in me in that regard."

"But this home has been in your family for generations. Your cousin left it behind."

"And the house meant more to Beau than it meant to me or even to Randa. Dalt surprised me last night when he said Beau had received an offer for him to sell. Homes like Grandmere's take a lot of upkeep, as we've found out since Beau left. My cousins ..." he waved toward Dalton to include him in the relationship "... and I have split the costs of maintenance for six years since we had no idea where to find Beau. I'm glad he left it to his wife and his sons."

Bastion leaned forward, hands on the desk. "You've seen Abra's house. Do you think she needs some dusty old place in Hickvilles, North Carolina?"

Shane shook his head. "The town is Amazing Grace, and you haven't seen the house. Maybe you think Beau married Abra for her money." He met Bastion's stare. "He didn't."

"Shane, answer the questions. That's all," Dalton counseled.

Shane leaned back hard. "Fine. No. I didn't kill my cousin for a house I never wanted to own."

Bastion leafed through a mess of a file in front of him and stopped at one page, smoothing it down but not looking up.

Shane bristled. "I hope you're not holding Abra and the boys here again. They've been through a lot."

"Don't worry about them." Bastion studied his paper while twisting a ring around his finger. "I'm sure your lawyer told you she's been cleared."

"And I suppose you thought the boys would tell you I did it. That's why you have them back here again. It isn't right, you know. Those two have been through enough."

"Shane, Abra went home." Dalton pointed to his phone. "Randa says they're waiting for us to join them on the beach. The boys are asking for you."

Bastion tilted his head. "You've made fast friends with them, huh?"

"Detective, Shane has been in Amazing Grace. He owns a business with his cousin. He's also a musician and a well-known songwriter. He performs at venues all over the area. I have witnesses that can place him at any given place in our vicinity at any time you need. Shane never met those boys until yesterday at their father's funeral."

"How do you explain the gun, Mr. Browne?"

Shane glanced to Dalton who nodded once again.

"I own two guns, and they're both locked away in my home right where they've been. I told you, my place is in the woods. I use my rifle or my 1911 only if something wild gets too close to my house or to my daughter and me when we're hiking. I shoot in the air to scare whatever it is away. I would never kill an animal needlessly. I film them. I'll gladly produce my weapons."

"You know I'm talking about the gun owned by Elizabeth St. John, your grandmother. The one she reported stolen several years back."

"Several?" Dalton half-laughed. "We were in college when that occurred. I remember because Shane's mom pitched a fit knowing Mrs. St. John kept a firearm in her possession, let alone had it licensed and claimed to know how to shoot the eye out of a charging chipmunk at fifty paces."

Shane shook his head. Grandmere. A little bit hillbilly and a lot of Southern matriarch.

"Did you steal that gun, Mr. Browne? From what I hear you had a rough period during high school and afterward. Drugs. Alcohol. A charge of possession."

From the corner of his eye, Shane caught the jerk of Dalton's head that almost gave away his sudden lack of indifference. "Mr. Browne's past has nothing to do with your investigation," Dalton said, his eyes nearly closed as if bored with the interrogation.

"Mr. Rylander, you might be from North Carolina, but even you have to know that a Florida court would consider Mr. Browne's past germane to the proceedings."

Dalton didn't move from his relaxed stance. "I don't know what the *Germans* have to do with this, but I've never lost a Motion in Limine. Shane's juvenile record won't be a problem for me or any Florida attorney that we'll have to hire if you insist on charging him with a crime you cannot possibly prove he committed. I doubt any prosecutor would try this sad trick you're trying."

How Dalton pulled that off without a guffaw, Shane would never know. Shane leaned forward and stared at the floor to keep from busting out in laughter.

Bastion remained stock-still for several moments.

Shane peered up at him.

The investigator's gaze rested on Dalton. He gave a

slight nod Dalton's way. Then he turned toward Shane. The man flinched then ran a hand over his hair, before resting it at the base of his neck.

Shane cast a wary glance to Dalton who shrugged.

Bastion leaned on the table, glaring at Shane. "So, did you steal your grandmother's gun to buy drugs? Get it back? Kill your cousin?"

"I have never seen the gun, only heard about it after Grandmere reported it stolen. The whole affair was a big to-do in our town. Grandmere and her gun ownership against my mother who abhorred weapons. Everyone had an opinion, and no one considered me a suspect. I've made mistakes. Stealing or murder might be the only two I've never made. I was always taught that if something didn't belong to me, I didn't touch it. The person you're claiming I stole from is the one who taught me that. The stupid thing was ..."

"Shane." Dalton's tone laid a cement block in front of Shane's motoring mouth. Shane slammed it shut.

"How about the drugs and alcohol? Still a user?"

"I have a daughter, Detective. She's my life. Beau helped me get clean, and I haven't disappointed him." Though Beau probably thought he had. That's the only reason Shane could understand for Beau leaving town without a word even to Randa while Shane attended the Country Music Awards in Nashville and brought home his first award for Song of the Year. Shane had dedicated it to Beau in his acceptance speech. He doubted Beau had heard.

"Your daughter, Taffeta, her mother abandoned her."

Shane jumped to his feet, nearly upsetting the table. "Taffy's mother loved her. That's why she left her with me."

"Still a mother who could leave her child ... one of your drug-addicted girlfriends?"

Shane took heavy breaths, willing the temperature on

37

his rage down several degrees. "Taffy's mother is dead. She died a few months after Taffy was born. She never used drugs or alcohol. She graduated college at the top of her class."

"Suicide or foul play?" Bastion lifted his brow as if he suspected the latter.

Dalton's gaze pierced Shane. For a while, Shane had thought Dalton had repeated information he'd received from Beau, but Shane doubted Beau knew this truth. If he had, Beau was definitely not the person he had seemed for so long. And the hint of shock on Dalton's face showed he'd never put some of the pieces of the puzzle together. Until now.

Shane sat, the action giving his anger time to ebb. "She's dead. Let's leave it at that."

"I asked you. Was it suicide?"

His anger revved again. Did this guy actually think he'd killed Taffy's mother? "That's the word we received via our sheriff who learned it from her father. Is there any reason to doubt that information?"

Bastion closed the file. "All right. That's all for now. You can leave. Go to your little beach party."

"Sir." Shane stood and straightened to his full height, no longer intimidated by the bully cop. "A member of our family was buried yesterday. His sons are grieving. Whatever we're doing on the beach is none of your business, but if it is a party, it's because those boys need a distraction from the interrogation your department gave them yesterday and today."

"We planned to leave town tomorrow." Dalton took his time to stand. "Any reason we can't?"

"Long as you stay where I can easily have Mr. Browne arrested." Bastion didn't take his eyes off Shane.

"You find probable cause, and Sheriff Daniel Dixon won't have trouble finding me or putting my hands in the cuffs." Shane glared at the arrogant man.

"I'm sure he won't have trouble finding you. He's arrested you before." The smile that tipped the officer's mouth curled Shane's fists.

"Shane, wait outside," Dalton ordered.

"I'm not—"

"Wait. Outside."

Shane moved to the door. He flung it open, nodding to the police chief staring into the tiny one-way mirror. Then he moved down the long corridor, past the prisoner handcuffed to a bench. A kid, really. No older than Shane had been when Beau pulled strings with the sheriff's department where he worked to get Shane released into his custody. Without a word, Beau had driven to the old mill property Beau's father had purchased before his death. Beau put Shane to work, teaching Shane as they renovated the unique old place. Beau worked him from sunup to sundown, allowing Shane to take Sunday's off to attend church and rest up for another grueling week.

How many cousins would take a leave of absence from a job he'd just gotten with the sheriff's department, fresh out of college, to corral a wayward family member? Beau jeopardized his career to get Shane straight, and in doing so, he'd given Shane something valuable, something he'd never be able to repay.

Shane pushed open the front door of the police station. The Florida heat blanketed him. He hated this place, couldn't wait to be home in the mountains with his daughter. Florida was nothing but a wide expanse of sky. Nothing broke the plains or the vastness of the ocean.

And he'd never been away from Taffy since the day he'd first cradled her in his arms, looking down at the downy brown hair and the pretty little eyes that stared up at him with what he claimed was a wonderment that mirrored his own. The fear of traveling with her on a plane, of learning to care for her, had all been vanquished at the little quirk of tiny lips. Tears had filled Shane's eyes, and when he looked at the mother who so lovingly tendered the babe into his care, her face was a flood of emotion. He offered to hand her child back to her.

"No. Love her and bring her up, Shane. You were brought up well. Only promise me that my little girl will always be happy."

He hadn't let go of Taffy that day, and he doubted he ever could. He missed his daughter, but she was safe spending time with a school friend.

Shane sank down on a bench in the hot sun. He leaned forward and covered his eyes, unable to stop the sobs that poured from him.

He hadn't cried when he'd learned of Taffy's mother's suicide. Hadn't mourned Beau's death—not really—and he hadn't absorbed the truth that his cousin and best friend, Randa, was booting him out of her confidence, refusing to share with him what she'd learned at her visit with her doctor. She probably knew—Dalton had most likely given her the real reason Beau had abandoned them all. Randa might never trust Shane again.

The sorrow he'd held dammed inside and the homesickness for his daughter raged like a flooding river.

"You okay?" Dalton sat beside him.

Shane took a moment before nodding his head. He wiped the back of his hand across his eyes.

"Before you ask, he wouldn't reveal his source. I have a thought that maybe under duress Abra repeated some things Beau might have told her."

Shane shook his head. "No. Beau didn't know about ... Taffy's mom."

"Other than the obvious reason ..."

Shane straightened. "And what would that obvious reason be?"

Dalton stared at him for a long moment. "Stealing your cousin's girl. Beau wouldn't take kindly to that, would he?"

"Beau left his girl behind long before I got involved."

"Any reason you never told us?"

Shane stared out at the asphalt parking lot and Highway A-1-A beyond it. "No one's business."

Dalton slapped Shane's shoulder. "I admired you for changing your career plans to take care of Taffy. I never suspected you and Jasmine ..."

"I never claimed to be a saint, Dalt. And I didn't change my career. Raising Taffy saved me from that lifestyle."

Dalton started toward the parking lot, and Shane followed. He stood by the passenger door waiting for Dalton to unlock the car. Instead, Dalton leaned his arm against it then jumped back. "Hot."

Shane laughed. "Yeah, Einstein, ya think?"

"You're right. Beau said he never told Abra about us. Finn knew about us and where we were, but Beau wasn't one to betray family confidences, and Finn isn't one to break a promise. I'm sure Beau knew nothing about you and Jasmine, as sure as I am that he would never share your past struggles with anyone."

Shane took a deep breath. Dalton hadn't put it all together—not yet anyway. "What are you getting at?"

"Someone told that detective some pretty intimate stuff about you, stuff no one could know. Unless you've told someone besides us, and I know that didn't happen. You and Beau, man, you've always driven me crazy with your silences." Dalton raised his hand as if planning to hit the roof with his fist but pulled away. "Bastion's source had to know Beau—or you—pretty well, don't you think?"

"No one could know what that detective learned. Randa wouldn't share our past troubles. And she doesn't know Jasmine is Taffy's mother. Taffy was a surprise to Abra when I mentioned her last night."

Dalton clicked the door opened. "Can you think of

anyone in our pasts who'd want Beau dead?"

Shane sat inside the car. "Magda Moxley embroiled Beau in that internal affairs investigation before he left. She's never sober enough to concoct something like that on her own."

"She was sober when she made the charge, a disgruntled prostitute trying to get even for an arrest, who later recanted. Sheriff Dixon always said if Beau returned to Amazing Grace, a job was waiting for him. I suspect he's known Beau's whereabouts. He had to give the recommendation for the force here."

"Start the car already." Shane frowned. "It's a hundred plus degrees with these leather seats."

Dalton turned the key.

Shane flipped up the AC and turned the vent directly toward him.

Dalton faced Shane. "I'm going to tell you something, and only because I want you to rest easy. I don't know how they found that gun at the same time we arrived here, but I'm very sure it wasn't the murder weapon."

"Tell me something I don't know."

"Whoever planted the evidence did a sloppy job. Bastion doesn't even have enough information to keep you in Florida. I get the idea the interrogation wasn't his idea."

Shane let the information soak in. "The bulldog who pulled things out about my past that I thought no one knew but me, he's not serious?"

Dalton backed the car out of the spot. "Shane, the man has to know that simple handgun Grandmere sported is nowhere close to the caliber that killed Beau." He pulled to the stop sign at the parking lot exit. "Now, the pistol you have at home—the one Beau bought you—if they had it, you'd be in jail until the ballistics test returned. Are you sure it's in your house in North

Carolina?"

"When you called, I'd just gotten off the trail with Taffy. I took out the cartridge, made sure the chamber was clear, and tucked the magazine in its usual place, and the gun is in my safe."

Dalton pulled out onto the road.

"What's this about, Dalton? Do you know?"

"I can't make sense of it. Why try to poorly implicate you? It's as if they want us to run."

"So they can get to Abra and the kids?"

Dalton didn't speak for a few minutes. Then he turned to Shane. "I'd rest better if she'd agree to spend a couple of weeks with us."

"Time away would be good for the twins. They're closed up. If Finn killed Beau—"

"That didn't happen. Those boys aren't talking for a reason. Trauma? Threats against their mother? Something they learned that has to do with their father?"

"You said Beau claimed Abra's dad was accidentally killed. I got the idea she wasn't willing to talk about it."

"All Beau said was that he was the intended victim, not Abra's father."

Shane pushed his shoulders down, feeling the strain of tension. "Abra and the boys could be in trouble."

A loud boom, followed by another, met with crashing glass. Dalton fought to maintain the wheel, but the car swerved from one side of the road to the other.

The car bumped along until Dalton managed to straighten the wheel and pulled off to the side of the road. "Stay down." He pushed at Shane as he also sought cover.

Shane yanked out his phone and dialed 9-1-1. "Bodacious Cove, Florida. Yes. A-1-A. South of the police station. Shots fired. Tire blown and windshield shattered. Not sure if the shooter has fled."

Dalton peered upward. "There's a crowd gathering. We're in front of Bodacious Cove's Burger *Dive In.*

"Are you okay?" A heavyset older man peered through the glassless windshield. Shane recognized him from the funeral and at Abra's afterward. Zeb.

"We heard the shots. You boys ain't running no pot through here, are you?" Zeb lifted one bushy eyebrow.

"No, sir," Shane answered.

"Saw you pull out of the police station. Sure you ain't in no trouble, boys?" the old man badgered.

Dalton leaned his head against the steering wheel. "No, sir. We ..."

"Zeb, leave them alone. They're Beau's family."

"Can't be too careful, Mercy," the old man said.

Shane pushed open his door as sirens neared. Sweat poured down his back. "I'm in hell, and it has nothing to do with Florida," he muttered as he slammed the door.

Shane opened the front door of Abra's house.

Dalton skirted around him to catch a hysterical Randa in his arms, and Shane locked the door.

While Abra stood looking on, Paulie ran to Shane, wrapping his arms around Shane's legs and holding tight. Shane allowed him to cling there for a moment. If only he could hold Taffy in his arms right now.

If something had happened to him, his little girl ...

He shook that thought away and stooped down to hug the frightened child.

Peter touched Shane's shoulder. "Paulie gets scared. He thought you were gone ..." he swallowed hard "... like Daddy."

Shane pulled both into an embrace. "I'm fine, guys. Just fine."

"But he shot at us, too." Paulie's words were only a whisper.

Everybody's Broken

Peter pinched Paulie.

"Ouch!" Paulie pulled back. He glared at his brother and then leaned in to wrap his arms around Shane's neck.

Shane tweaked Peter's nose. "It's okay." Then he gently tugged Paulie away from him. "We're fine. Uncle Dalton's fancy rental car is a bit messed up."

"Aunt Randa was afraid and Mommy ..." Paulie's green eyes filled with tears. "I bet she was afraid when Uncle Finn called about Daddy, too."

Paulie trusted Shane. That was a good start to getting the boys to open up to him. "I'm sure she was, kiddos, but that's behind her now. I saw her face at the church yesterday. Her fear turned to joy."

"Trace advised us to stay inside away from windows." Abra closed the curtains, hiding their view of the ocean.

The boys' gazes fixed on Shane.

He stood, keeping his hands firmly on their shoulders. Peter pulled from his touch and moved to stand beside his mother. Paulie did the same, each continuing to watch him.

The front doorknob turned, jiggled, and then a bang rocked Shane.

Abra pulled the boys back with her.

Dalton held up his hand. He peered through the peep hole. Then he opened the door.

Mazzie hurried inside.

Dalton closed and locked the entrance.

"My goodness, Abra. I go on an errand to feed ya'll, and I have to hear about the accident from Mercy Tuttle at the grocery store. The way she rambled before Zeb told me everything was okay ..." Mazzie moved inside and plopped down on the couch.

Shane hid his smile. Despite her lack of forthrightness, he liked Mazzie. She was the consummate picture of a Southern beauty queen. Petite and pretty with high cheek bones, just enough makeup to let a guy know she cared about her appearance, and the sass in dress and style that probably drove Finn Osteen wild. The accent she carried seemed a little overdone, but it added to her charm.

And now the queen was playing out the drama. "You better never let me hear such horrible tidings secondhand." She waved her hand in front of her face as if to cool off, though the house, compared to the temperature outside, was comfortable.

Abra moved to the couch and leaned over her friend. "And the groceries you went to buy …?"

"I threw them in the trunk of my car. They're scattered all over the place. I heard them rolling around. Might have even cracked that bottle of Hellman's. My goodness, I was so shocked, I used the front door." She stood. "We can bring them in."

Shane eyed Dalton, who nodded and headed toward the door.

"No!" Randa reached out for her husband. "No baby," she said more softly, holding to Dalton. "I can't lose you, too."

Mazzie patted Shane's shoulder as she walked by. "Ain't nobody going to shoot at me."

Before he could protest, she was out the door.

Shane followed her, Randa's protests ringing in his ear, but he couldn't let the woman go outside alone.

Mazzie opened the trunk of her Audi, which she'd backed into the drive. Scared enough to forget about the front door but not so frightened she couldn't back in? He eyed her as she pushed the button and the trunk opened. Sure enough, the packaged food had fallen out of the bags and scattered everywhere in her trunk.

Shane leaned inside and gathered the items, putting them in bags. Mazzie reached in and grabbed the intact jar of mayonnaise. "I only said that because Abra wouldn't

Everybody's Broken

have let me come outside to get these either."

Shane stopped his bagging. They were both from the South, but the woman was speaking Greek to him. "What?"

"Well, honey, no self-respecting Southerner is going to let a jar of Hellman's go to waste, busted or not. Whatever the danger we find ourselves in, the Hellman's must always come first." She lifted her eyebrows, her expression stoic until her lips twitched.

He laughed, and she joined in.

After they'd gathered the five bags, she held to the car's trunk door. "You gotta get 'em out of here."

"Dalton's going to talk to Abra." He reached up to pull the trunk down.

Mazzie resisted his tug. "Listen to me, Mr. Browne. That brother-in-law of Beau's has to know that Abra and the boys are in danger, whether they're pawns, marked, or simply caught in the cross-hairs. That girl, her brother, and those little angels are the only family I have left in this world. Pap treated me like a daughter and Finn ..." She looked away for a long moment. "Finn is the only man I will ever love." She closed her eyes tightly then stared him square in the eyes. "Honey, I think that all ya'll have to get out of here."

When he blinked, she shook her head. Might as well have called him an idiot. "That cousin of yours. He had his secrets. I told him more than once to tell them to Abra, but he wouldn't do it, and I suspect ..." She shook her head. "What he didn't tell any of you might just get ya'll killed." With her bags in hand, she slammed the trunk and turned toward the house.

Shane blocked her from opening the door. "So, why don't you tell me what I need to know to protect us from whatever Beau mentioned to you?"

"I don't know what you're talking about." She pushed to get by him.

He refused to move. "Beau, or maybe it was Finn, told you something, and for some reason, you think it's breaking some Southern code to let us know what it is."

She leaned against the door. "He wanted me to look after Abra and the boys, but he didn't want to trust me with what was going on—said he couldn't put the pieces together, and an unfinished puzzle could look like a lot of things it wasn't meant to be."

Shane nearly dropped the weight of groceries in his hand. The words Mazzie had spilled were Grandmere's words—something she'd say about Shane's mother. The truth was without all of the puzzle pieces that friends on the outside weren't aware of, Grandmere and Mom looked like two women who should have always been at odds. Instead, they were best friends even when fighting over Grandmere's gun rights.

Mazzie stopped fighting for entrance. "What is it?"

"How did you and Beau get along?"

"I loved him like a brother, not that most people would have known. We squabbled a lot. Play mostly, but he was a hardheaded son-of-a-gun, and he could ruffle my feathers."

"Someone on the outside might think you weren't friends?"

"Lots of people thought so. Why do you think I was one of the first suspects Herman pulled in for questioning?"

Now that surprised Shane. "I have no idea. Tell me."

"I tackled Beau out in front of God and everyone about a month ago."

"Tackled ...?"

"Yeah, tackled. I dove right under that volleyball net at the church picnic. Took his feet out from under him and made him eat beach sand. He nearly choked before Abra and Finn pulled me off of him."

Well that was a good one. Shane leaned against the

Everybody's Broken

door. "And what did Beau do that got your dander up so high?"

"He spiked a ball right into my face. On purpose. He apologized when we were alone later, but we sure put a damper on the festivities."

"Beau was raised better than that," Shane challenged.

"He did say he had his reasons, and he was sorry he couldn't say more. Told me he cared about me and begged me to forgive him. We talked when we were together, but as far as anyone outside of the family knew, he was still angry with me."

Shane smiled. Beau being knocked off his feet and fed sand by a southern belle did paint a funny picture.

The frown on Mazzie's face spoke volumes. If she wasn't carrying the grocery bags, her hands would either be fisted on her slender waist or wrapped around his neck. "Let me spell this out for you. I love Abra, but she's a peacemaker. Her daddy was big and boisterous, her brother meek and creative. Finn admired Pap, but they clashed often. Abra loved Beau, and that love was made easier because Pap and Beau were close. That relationship took a lot of pressure off Finn. Pap had a son-in-law who liked to play golf, who loved working with wood. Abra and her brother collaborated creatively without any friction from Pap, and we were all one big happy family. I took Beau at face value. When I accepted his apology, he confessed Abra wasn't very strong, and she and the boys would need me."

"That still doesn't tell me why Beau would share secrets with you even if he didn't quite tell you everything. He always kept things to himself."

Mazzie took hold of the doorknob as if to keep anyone from exiting. "Finn and me, we loved seeing Abra so happy with Beau, but even before that day when he bent so low as to give me a black eye, I knew his secrets had already brought something down on us. He destroyed the life we all loved."

Shane studied her.

Mazzie glared back at him, but she remained quiet, though tears began to gather in her eyes.

"What happened? What do you think Beau caused?"

"Pap was poisoned." She swiped the tear away. "He fell face down in the sand trap of the eighteenth hole of his crowning achievement—the Bodacious Cove Golf Course."

"Abra doesn't seem to believe that."

Mazzie glared at him. "Because she doesn't like the hard truths. She won't let herself believe it, but you can ask Bastion."

Shane almost laughed. "Believe me, if that man thought Abra's father was murdered, I'd somehow be a suspect. He'd have questioned me."

"They never officially opened an investigation."

"That makes no sense. There has to be a coroner's report. His death certificate would state the cause."

"Did you hear me? Pap fell over in a sand trap. Golfers don't have to be very athletic and fit, especially when they have a souped up golf cart like Pap's. The inept coroner ruled it a heart attack. Beau never told anyone otherwise, but he discovered something."

"What makes you think Beau was the reason Mr. Osteen was killed?"

"Beau swore me to silence, but now that he's gone, I can tell you."

Shane braced himself against the door, the impending news weighing him down more than the groceries in his hand.

"Because," Mazzie whispered, "Beau and Pap each had a soda, but while on the course, Pap didn't pay attention. Beau teased him when he drank from Beau's opened can because Beau had already opened and took a swig of his. Pap's was still unopened, and Beau told him to keep it. He didn't want Pap's germs. When Pap keeled over, Beau being Beau ..."

"Suspected foul play."

"And because he imagined the poison was meant for him, Beau kept things quiet. He had the contents of the can tested."

"And ...?"

"SUX."

"What?" Shane's patience wore thin in the heat.

"That's short for some medication I can't pronounce. Beau said it paralyzed Pap's muscles. He didn't pass out. Shane, he was alive and gasping for every breath he took as his muscles froze, suffocating him, and they were too far out from the clubhouse to get help to him in time."

Heat was no longer a problem. Mazzie's words chilled Shane to the bone.

Everybody's Broken

Chapter 4

Abra checked on the boys one last time before heading downstairs. Beau's family would be leaving tomorrow.

She wouldn't rest until they were safely on their way. Beau's secrets had caught up with him.

And they seemed to involve his cousin somehow.

Earlier in the day, Loyal Herman had come at her pretty hard, telling her Shane's secrets, things she hadn't thought necessary for her to know until he and Dalton were nearly killed. She couldn't very well turn Beau's family out, but she sure wouldn't relax until they were on the road.

Then life could return to as normal as possible. Going back to the office would be hard. Her last sight of Finn's smiling face had been as he'd herded the boys out to meet Beau for lunch on that forever life-changing day. When Beau left home two hours earlier, he'd promised to be home for dinner.

She'd get through it. After all, even filled with the ghosts of her father and her husband, this was home. If memories became unbearable, she could move to Finn's bungalow.

A week after the police department had practically torn it asunder, Abra and Mazzie had pieced it back together, lowered the AC to protect Finn's fantastic artistry hanging on the walls in frames he'd built himself, cleaned out the refrigerator, and secured the place. Mazzie insisted upon closing the hurricane shutters on the house and Finn's cabana.

Abra held to the banister as she made her way down the stairs of her own home. Randa and Shane sat together talking. Shane messed his cousin's hair, and she smacked at him.

Abra smiled. Despite what Herman had told her, she actually liked having them around. Randa reminded Abra of Beau. Practical, level-headed, holding things close. Something was wrong between her and Dalton, but Abra hadn't figured it out. When Shane had called about the shooting, Randa had nearly fallen apart with worry for her husband and her cousin.

Abra crossed the foyer at the bottom of the stairs.

Randa and Shane separated to give her room to sit.

The drapes remained drawn. She couldn't remember a time when she'd had to do that, especially on nights when the moon, unfettered by clouds, illuminated the foam of the waves.

"Abra." Dalton moved out of the kitchen, holding a plate filled with his third hamburger of the day and a handful of chips. "We'd like to talk to you."

She couldn't imagine what they had to tell her, but Mazzie said they'd be discussing something, and she begged Abra to take them seriously. "I'm listening." She ran her hands over the denim of her jeans and stopped, staring down at her wedding set.

"We'd like you and the boys to follow us home tomorrow."

She almost laughed aloud. Instead, she remembered

Beau's helpful advice. She pressed two fingers to her lips and shook her head, taking several seconds before she lowered them. "Bodacious Cove is our home. I can't leave—not until I know my brother is safe."

"That's just it." Randa reached for her hand. "At first, we thought maybe this killer was after us. We can't think why. I mean, I don't know why anyone would set out to kill Beau. He had no enemies." She bit her lip. "Well, at least not anyone who could do what was done."

Abra tilted her head. "But he had one ...?"

Randa's lips trembled. "Our town prostitute. She accused Beau of ... inappropriate behavior ... during an arrest."

Abra stilled. Even as close as Beau and Mazzie had become—like brother and sister—he always kept a respectful distance. He'd give Mazzie a brotherly hug, but not if Abra wasn't there.

She couldn't stop the quirk of her lips. The only time her friend and her husband had serious bodily contact was the day Mazzie unleashed on him during a volleyball game. Oh, boy, had that been the talk of the town, and it set Mazzie up right well for the town to think she'd been involved in Beau's murder. The town, though, hadn't been privy to the antics once they arrived home, and Abra sprayed them both down with the cold water from the outside hose.

No. Mazzie and Beau had been very good friends.

"Oh, he didn't do it," Randa said.

Abra shook her head. What had they been discussing? Yes. Beau. And a prostitute.

"She recanted," Randa said. "But only after Beau left Amazing Grace. I suspect Sheriff Dixon contacted him, or he wouldn't have wanted to get back into law enforcement. That's the way he was."

Abra gave Shane her full attention. "Did you have any enemies that could have gotten Beau killed?"

Shane didn't blink. "No."

"Chief Herman told me about your juvenile record. Told me about your daughter's mother. That she was dead. He said suicide, but I got the idea he thought that wasn't the cause. Her family wouldn't hold anything against you?"

Randa gasped. "Shane, you never told us anything about Taffy's mother, not even who she is."

Oh, Beau, I've done it again. Abra covered her lips a little too late this time. She dropped her hand. "I'm sorry, Shane. I thought they knew."

"Randa, all Abra needs to know is that Taffy's mother's family isn't a consideration in this," Dalton said.

"How could they not be?" Randa stood. "If someone had taken a child away from me, I would be heartbroken. I might be suicidal, too."

"I didn't take Taffy from her mother, Randa. She gave her to me," Shane said.

"Why?" Dalton asked the question.

"Because I was the better one to care for her. She asked me to raise Taffy, and that's all you need to know. Any of you. Taffy is my child."

"You had to have known how hard it was for this woman to have carried your child for you when you obviously didn't care anything about her."

"Randa, you need to stop. Your pain is skewing the way you're looking at Shane's actions. Taffy's mother obviously trusted Shane enough with their child."

Shane lowered his head. "Taffy's mother called me. She told me about the baby. I flew to where she was. My name was on the birth certificate. She kissed Taffeta Antoinette Browne—the name she gave her, by the way—and lifted her into my arms. Taffy's mother took care of all of the legalities. I left the hospital with the agreement and the order giving me full custody. When I arrived home, I tried to reach her to tell her Taffy and I were doing fine, that you were helping me learn to be a good father, but her number had been changed."

"Who was she?" Randa looked up, her gaze pleading.

Shane glanced from Dalton to Randa.

Abra had to turn away. She'd started this with words that she hadn't checked.

"I'll tell you someday but not now. Not anytime soon. You'll just have to trust me. Everything I said is the truth."

"Except what you're omitting to say," Randa accused. "Didn't you learn anything from Beau's mistakes? He's left us all hurting here," she cried.

Abra pulled the distraught woman into her arms. "I'm so sorry for repeating things that weren't meant for me to hear in the first place. Herman spelled it out as if it was common knowledge."

"He's a terrible man."

"Just ask Mazzie." Abra forced a smile into place. "She keeps a list of all the reasons he needs to be removed from his position, and she's planning to run for mayor to make it happen. You don't ever want to be on the bad side of Mazzie Harris."

Randa wiped her tears. "Yeah, I can see that."

"Can you imagine what growing up with her was like?" The conversation had moved away from the edge of the precipice the family was about to tumble over. Abra breathed a sigh of relief.

"Mazzie wants you to go with us," Shane said. "She's sure you're in danger here, and she wants you and the boys safe."

Time to grow a backbone—even if it was to stand against her best friend. "I said I'm not going. Whoever did this, sent the boys back to me. Why would they do that if they planned to ..." she shuddered at the thought. "No. Whatever brought this on, whatever Beau was involved in, had to have happened before he came here."

Shane started to say something, shook his head, and clamped his lips together.

"What about Finn?" Dalton asked.

"Finn is okay."

"No," Shane said a little too quietly. "Whoever shot Beau also shot at the boys."

Abra stared, waiting for more.

Dalton nearly dropped his empty plate. "How ...?"

"Paulie let it slip. I got that much out of him, but Peter's pretty tight-lipped. He wouldn't let Paulie say much else. Whether Finn's alive or not, we don't know where Beau's killer is. Where's the vehicle the boys were in?"

"Why would they tell you and not tell me?" She shook her head. "Finn is not a murderer, and he's fine. You're just saying this to get me to agree."

"I think you have me confused with the fellow Bastion wants you to believe I am. Those boys are attached to me whether you like it or not—whether I like it or not. I look like their father. The reason they told me is apparent. They had faith in Beau. Now, what you need to decide is whether or not you're going to trust me when I say you and the boys will be safer with us from whatever stupidity Beau started here."

"Shane!" Randa slapped him.

Shane stepped back, his hand over the spot where the skin on his cheek had already reddened. "You go or you stay." He turned a hardened glare at Abra. "I have a daughter to protect. We're leaving in the morning with or without you."

Abra couldn't sleep. She paced her room, departing only to check on the boys.

How could she leave Bodacious Cove? Pap had developed this little spot of heaven, had created a hometown as a playground for her and Finn. How many children had such a legacy?

She also had a business to run, clients to appease. They'd waited on her grief long enough.

But it wasn't like she needed the money. The interest gained from her half of the inheritance from Pap was enough to run a small country quite well. Pap had taught her to work, though, and Carmichael and Osteen Interior Designs was the only way she could see to push past her grief.

Besides, Finn would reach out to her soon.

Shane had been right in one thing. The twins trusted him if only because of his resemblance to Beau. Without Shane here, would they open up to her, or would they keep their secrets?

And the memories of Pap and Beau. Were they better left here alone for a while so that the boys could pull away from them, not forgetting the love they'd shared, but losing the bad stuff, especially their last look at their father and possibly Finn?

Abra still had the memory of Pap's hearty laugh as he'd headed out the door with Beau to play a round of golf, Finn's smile as he waved good-bye, and Beau's last kiss on her lips and the twinkle in his eye as he'd left for work that morning. She tried to focus on that moment and block out the time of horror in the morgue. She refused to look at what was left of his head. She'd stared at his uniform and the bloodied *Carmichael* on the nametag and, finally, at the simple gold band he never took from his finger.

Now, she thought about falling on her knees and asking God for direction. No. Annoying Him with the buzzing of her prayers wouldn't be right. She'd go downstairs and dig into some ice cream. That would help her to think.

Her bare feet plodded onto the cold tile at the bottom of the stairs as she made her way into the kitchen. She had always been a midnight snack thief. Beau once teased that her snack alarm went off at the same time every night. Mazzie had confirmed it, and they'd howled with laughter.

She opened the freezer and reached in for the chocolate ice cream, thought better of it, and grabbed the vanilla. A float sounded like a good idea. She set the box on the counter and opened the refrigerator.

A noise at the window over the sink startled her.

She held her breath and made herself ignore her fear. She reached for the soda bottle. Once she sat it on the counter, she opened the cupboard next to the fridge and pulled out a glass. Only then did she give a slight glance to the window.

Nothing.

Just her imagination or a bug seeing the refrigerator light and hitting the window. Her body unwound like a tightly twisted rubber band once released.

She pulled the ice cream scooper from the drawer and after tugging open the carton, she dug in, filling the glass with the ice cream and pouring the soda over it a little at a time, letting it settle between the cracks left in the ice cream.

Still holding the soda bottle, she brought the float to her lips for a taste of the soda foam that bubbled to the top. The best part.

Another sound at the window strengthened her resolve not to look. Stupid bug. Go away and bother someone else.

She put the ice cream back into the freezer and leaned back against the counter, tipping the glass to her lips. Some white, at the edge of her vision, caught her attention. She jerked her gaze toward the window. A large

Everybody's Broken

piece of paper stuck to the glass. A crooked piece of tape holding it there.

The sight drew Abra forward with all the anticipation of passing a bad accident on Interstate 95.

An enlarged photo showed Beau lying dead at the crime scene, blood pooled around what was left of his head.

She moved even closer.

Finn's truck sat in the background. His vehicle hadn't been found at the scene. From inside the cab, the boys peered through a hole in the passenger-side window. Around the hole, cracked glass clung together. Behind the boys, Finn's body drooped over the steering wheel.

Someone unseen snatched the photo away from the window. "You and the boys are next, Abra!" The voice was deep, unreal, and unrecognizable as either man or woman.

Abra dropped the glass in her hand.

A scream rang through the house, continuing until Randa wrapped her arms around Abra and stopped her from filling the air with her terror.

"He's dead. They're both dead. Oh, dear God, why?" She pointed toward the window. "A picture. Beau ..."

"Abra," Randa whispered. "You woke the boys."

Abra stepped out of her embrace. She reached for her kids, bending and tugging them close. Now, at least she shared the same last horrible memories of the sight of their father and their uncle.

She sobbed against their tiny bodies, feeling them cry, too.

Dalton said something into his phone and hung up.

Shane ran outside and returned, shaking his head.

"Sorry, Mommy. Sorry." That it was Peter crying out the words shocked her.

She pulled back. "How did you get away? Tell me? Did he bring you home?"

61

"He said not to tell you anything because he'd hurt you or kill you." Peter trembled.

"He said you weren't who he was after, and if we said anything, he'd kill us," Paulie whispered.

"Who said all of this to you? Have you seen him before?" She looked from one to the other.

Her oldest twin clamped his lips together. Peter would never cave. The truth had to come from Paulie.

"Honey, we have to know. This person, he killed your daddy. Your Uncle Finn ..."

Peter again shook his head.

Paulie pushed in front of him. "He didn't kill Uncle Finn. Uncle Finn is the one. He told us to stay quiet."

Abra fell back as if shot by the bullet that killed Beau. Her mind raced for a way out of this nightmare maze that led to her brother's indictment for her husband's murder, for the kidnapping of her children.

Not Finn. Never. Nothing they said sounded like her lovable, easy-going brother.

He and Beau were best friends.

She'd seen Finn slumped forward in the truck.

"Abra," Randa touched her arm. "Let me get the boys back to bed."

Abra nodded to the kids. "Mommy's okay. You go with Aunt Randa."

As her sons followed Randa up the stairs, Abra paced. Something wasn't right. "The picture, if Finn did this, then who took the photo, and why would Paulie implicate Finn? They were so close."

"You asked the right question." Dalton pulled on his lower lip. "Who took the picture?"

"Could he have killed Beau and committed suicide?" Shane asked.

"We're back to the picture again. Finn couldn't be in both places. And explain how the boys got to Mazzie's house two weeks later." Dalton clenched his jaw and released it. "Abra's right. Something's not adding up here. The boys' thoughts are muddled. Who is the *he* they're talking about and in what context?"

Dalton came to stand in front of her. His gaze pierced Abra's. "I would love to question them, but I want the truth. Right now, I'm not sure what happened. They know, but what they're processing isn't making sense in any way. We need to let them work through this, let us know a little at a time. We need to take the bits of truth they give us and piece them together. The police will eat away at whatever that truth is, and they'll twist it away from us if you stay here."

Abra nodded her understanding. Peter and Paulie were hurting and confused, but what should she do with what she'd learned?

"You did the right thing, calling the police," Shane insisted.

Abra pulled her hair tight and then released it, trying to think clearly. She couldn't share what she'd learned from Paulie to the department, not with the way her family had been treated thus far.

She fell into the chair in the nook and stared into her hands. "I don't know. Finn, I don't know."

The kitchen door opened and slammed. Mazzie bent down beside her and touched her face. "Abra?"

Abra blinked.

Beau's family backed out of the kitchen.

"Herman or Bastion will be here any minute." Mazzie turned on the balls of her feet and looked behind her. Then she swiveled back to face Abra. "Listen to me," she said. "You're in danger here."

"The picture. There was a picture in the window." She pointed.

"Honey, if there had been a picture, I'd have seen it."

Abra blinked again and looked at the overturned float on the floor, the soda spattered all around, and the melted ice cream. "The thing was taped to the glass. Beau was on the ground dead. The boys were in the car, crying, and Finn was draped against the steering wheel. I don't think he was alive. He couldn't have killed Beau. He was a victim." She clung to Mazzie.

"Of course he was."

"Paulie's confused. Whoever took that picture shot Beau and Finn. The boys have to know who it is. Why would Paulie say Finn told them to keep it quiet?"

"And if Finn was dead, he couldn't have told them anything, now, could he?"

"But the boys seem so sure. What if he did? What if he told them before he killed himself?" Abra started to get up, but a wave of dizziness toppled her back. Confusion pulsed around her, the truth somehow out of her reach.

"Finn didn't take any picture. You said he was in the truck." Behind them, Dalton cleared his throat.

They looked to him.

"Leave that conversation out of what you tell the authorities; give the boys time to talk to any of us. Anything that comes from them to us will be told in a safe environment, not with police badgering them. Can you do that?"

The confusion in her mind was a vortex, sucking her into a world of doubt, a place where the answers had to be, but Abra had to search for them, to find them. "But should I keep this from the authorities?"

Dalton's face blanched white.

"I'll handle this," Mazzie told him then turned and grasped Abra's hand. "Finn didn't kill Beau. You have to trust me on this one. For goodness' sake, think of what you're saying. The boys were frightened half out of their minds. They're so young. What they don't remember, their brains will make up for them. Dalton's right. Give the boys time to tell the truth."

"Peter and Paulie aren't going to lie about something

like that. They adored Finn. Maybe Finn shot at Beau, and Beau fired back to protect his sons. Then Finn got the final aim and killed Beau."

"Beau Carmichael do something as careless as fire a gun in the direction of his sons? Suppose Finn could kill the man you love. Tell me how he got out of that truck and snapped a pic of himself in the vehicle at the same time. Convince me, and I'll stand aside and let you tell the authorities everything." Mazzie shook her. "But you better listen to me and listen good, because they aren't going to give us much more privacy."

Abra blinked. "You answer me this Mazzie Harris: who brought my children to you before the funeral?" Something niggled at the edge of Abra's mind and worked forward. "Dalton called the police. How did you get here so quickly?"

Mazzie widened her eyes and clamped her mouth shut.

Abra waited for the wrecking ball of betrayal to crash against her heart.

Mazzie's fingernails bit into Abra's skin. "You're going to have to trust me on this one. Don't make me lie to you."

"I want answers. Those are my children. Beau was my very-much alive and wonderful husband. Now my life has been turned upside down."

Mazzie spun away from her and walked back. "Now you want to take your head out of the sand and ask questions. Now, really?"

Abra stood and grabbed her friend by the shoulders. "Yes. I need for you to tell me. How did you get my boys?"

Mazzie narrowed her eyes and shrugged from Abra's hold. "He left them on my porch. I opened up my door, and there they were, all dressed and ready to attend their daddy's funeral."

"He? Who's he? The boys didn't tell you who left them?"

Mazzie didn't speak for a long moment. Then she heaved a sigh. "No, Abracadabra, they didn't tell me."

"The killer left them there without waiting for you to answer?"

"Now, that would make a lot of sense, wouldn't it? I'd open the door and see the killer's face. No, the killer was not on my porch with Peter and Paulie. In the words of Scarlett O'Hara and without meaning to take the Lord's name in vain ..." she raised her right hand "... As God is my witness, I did not see the killer on my porch, and here's something else for you to think about ..." Mazzie's eyes filled with tears.

"I'm listening."

"Finn didn't kill Beau, and if you tell the police he did, you'll never be able to take it back. Finn's life won't be worth a throbbing hangnail, and I'll—I'll never talk to you again. I mean it." Mazzie swiped at her cheeks. "Finn is mine. I love him, and if you open your mouth and take him from me ... Right now, I don't know where he is, what he's doing, if he's alive, but I do know he didn't kill Beau, and if you say otherwise, even if he has the chance to forgive you, I never will. Do you understand me?"

Abra brushed strands of wet hair from Mazzie's face. Then she got to her feet as the doorbell rang. "Wash your eyes. If they see you crying, they'll know something's up. Tomorrow, the boys and I are packing and leaving town. You want me to trust in Finn, I need you to hold down the fort. Close the office, whatever it takes. Tell our clients I had a nervous breakdown, and I'm not coming back for a while. You take care of all of our accounting. You can shell out refunds with interest. I don't care."

Mazzie wiped her eyes quickly. "Don't I always take care of you and Finn?" She laughed.

"Maze?"

"Done. Done. Done. And Done."

"And you watch your back. Finn would never get over someone killing his girl."

Mazzie laughed and new tears sprang to her eyes. "Great! Just great, Abra. Now, what am I going to do?"

"About what?" Bastion thundered into the kitchen. "What's going on here, Abra?"

"You know, I was walking in my sleep. I had a nightmare. I thought I saw something I couldn't have seen. I was just telling Mazzie I'm going to leave town for a while."

"She's going to stay with Beau's family for a bit." Mazzie poked Bastion in the chest before walking past, turning her head as she reached the kitchen's edge. "Bottom line, bottom dweller, you're not needed here."

Laughter erupted from the living room, and Abra had to turn away.

"Abra, I don't think I have to tell you to stay in touch with the department. We might have news, and you and the boys might be needed for future testimony if we find the killer."

Abra started to put her fingers to her lips, but his words had placed everything into perspective. She wouldn't hold her punches this time. She had something to say, and she was going to say it. "Let's see, Trace Bastion. You, or maybe it was Loyal Herman and you were only following orders, had me pegged as my husband's killer. Mazzie was dragged into your net. You thought Finn could be the murderer until Shane came into your line of sight. How many more people are you going to finger for this crime before you give up the easy route and start digging in and finding the person no one here could possibly know?"

"I'm working as hard as I can to bring this person to justice."

"Do you still think Finn had anything to do with

Beau's murder?"

"Finn is a victim. You may not believe me, but I've never thought of your family as my enemy. My emotions aren't on my sleeve, but I cared about Beau. We worked together in a dangerous job. I want to find his killer, so yeah, I'll look at anyone and everyone I think it could be. And ..." He leaned toward her, his lips touching her ear. "... getting out of the cove is a smart move."

Abra stepped back and stared at him. "Even if ..."

"I don't need a ballistics expert to tell me the ammo from that small handgun produced by an anonymous person couldn't have killed Beau. I can't think of a reason for it to be produced except to run Beau's family out of town or to hold up the investigation. I don't need a psychology degree to know when a man isn't lying. I do know that you need to get away from this town until we discover who hated Beau enough to kill him and shoot at Finn in broad daylight in front of your sons."

Abra paced away from him and back. "You're saying Shane might have been framed?" she whispered.

"I know he was. I was fed information that I'm certain no one should have known. I saw it on the guy's face. The lawyer, the only time I saw him fazed by my questioning was when I asked Browne things that I got the idea no one knew but him."

"And that proves his innocence ...?"

"I did some digging after your father's death. I forced Beau to tell me some things, and part of my questioning centered on what I knew. Honestly, I don't think Beau shared everything with me. Believe me, though, if Browne had been our murderer, he would have caved. The guy cared about your husband. They all do. I know they'll care for you. Let them."

"I don't understand." Abra ran her hand through her hair.

The always straight as a board detective hunched

Everybody's Broken

over, staring at the notepad in his hand. "Your dad paid my way to college. Did you know that?"

Abra shook her head at the question and the conversation's abrupt change in direction. She'd known Pap had done lots of kind things, but he was never one to do and say. She believed Bastion, though. Pap had paid Mazzie's way to school, too. They'd applied, and when the acceptance letters arrived from their first choice of school, Pap took the information from both of "his" gals, and did all that a father would do to send them off in style. He didn't have to tell anyone that he thought of Mazzie as his kid. The world saw it in his actions.

"Dashell said my father was one of the finest men he knew," Bastion continued. "Dad died too soon, he said, and Dashell wanted me to know that a man of integrity always had faithful friends. I owe your father, as I see it. Since he's not here, I'll do everything in my power to bring Beau's murderer to justice. Dashell's murderer, too. I think they're connected. And I want to prove that I am a faithful friend to Dashell, to Beau, to you."

Abra bristled. She would never believe anyone could kill a lovable old soul like Pap. "I'll keep in touch, Trace. And when you call me and tell me you've found Beau's murderer, I'll come home and testify to what I know." She slipped her arm through his, leading him toward the door. "Don't mind Mazzie. She loves Finn, you know."

"She never could see me past him."

Abra stopped at the door. "Thank you, Trace. I'm sorry for my big mouth, but I'm not sorry that it got me to see things your way."

He nodded and ducked out the door.

When Abra turned, Mazzie was standing beside Dalton holding something in her hand. "You looked awful chummy."

"Well, he shared his heart, Mazzie, and you know what a sap I am. I'll do anything if someone does that."

Mazzie tilted her head for a second. Then she held out the object. "Dalton just pulled this out of his pocket. Finn has one exactly like it."

Abra took the keychain with the black "G" of the Georgia emblem surrounded by the brilliant red. She turned it over and read the inscription. "Handsome, huh? That's pretty arrogant."

Randa laughed. "They had this silly Five H Society thing where all of them had nicknames that started with the letter H. Dalton was Handsome."

"You've seen Finn's." Mazzie said. "Hi-Jinx. Great description for him." Mazzie smiled.

"Beau was Hillbilly," Dalton added.

A pound of hurt crashed down upon Abra. She fought to stand her ground and not flee. Beau had never told her about his club, nor had she ever seen his keychain. Finn had said it was something silly he'd done in college.

Lies. And every one of them jagged and sharp, ripping emotional flesh.

"There was another guy." Shane snarled. "Hound Dog."

Dalton nodded. "Never so glad to be rid of someone in my life. Couldn't shake him until after graduation."

"And Jasmine." Randa snapped her fingers. "What was her nickname?"

"Helium," Shane said. "Because she was always so flighty and happy."

"Even though we heard ..." Randa turned to look sharply at her cousin ... "she committed suicide."

Everybody's Broken

Chapter 5

Monday, October 17, Amazing Grace, North Carolina

Jebediah—Jeb Castor—that's how they'd know him. He decided that before he signed the lease on the old house.

Before then, he'd only been in town a few weeks, laying low at a local low-rent motel before his money began to run thin. That prompted him to find a place to stay until things in life began to make sense to him again.

As if they ever would.

He pushed open the door to the law office and walked up the stairs despite the pain each step rippled through his head.

Inside, he smiled at the pretty young receptionist and rubbed his icy hands together.

He needed gloves. He was not a cold weather person, and preparation was not a part of his makeup. Never had been. Anyway, who would suspect a freezing cold drizzle in the middle of October?

But such was his lot. His fair-weather life had collided with a foul storm front.

"Yes, sir?" The young girl smiled. "May I help you?"

"I'm looking for Dalton Rylander?"

She shook her head and clicked some keys on her computer. "He's in court, and I don't have an appointment on his calendar."

"I'm an ..." He started to tell her he was an old friend, but decided against it. They needed to keep their stories straight. "Do you know when he'll be back?"

"I expect him any minute. The hearing was only slotted for ten minutes."

Dalt could cause a lot of havoc in a courtroom given only five minutes. No telling what would happen in ten. "I'll wait."

"Not a problem. May I get you some coffee or something else to drink?"

"Coffee sounds wonderful." He nodded. "Cream and sugar."

She left him and returned promptly with a coffee mug. "You're obviously not from around here. You have to be freezing."

"A little, yeah." He nodded and took a drink.

Horrible slop. Made by Dalt, no doubt, yesterday or maybe the day before. He choked it down. Anything to put warmth back into his body.

Next stop, a consignment shop to buy a coat for this dead of winter. Well, it wasn't winter yet. But his autumns had never been this frigid. This weather might as well have been a subzero cold front in the depths of January.

His hand holding the coffee trembled. He grabbed the cup with his other hand and opened and closed the fist on the offending one.

The receptionist had gone back to her work and didn't notice.

He sat down on the sofa in the nicely arranged waiting room. Of course, the office could use some work, but it fit Dalton's personality, with its dark wood and even darker wainscoting and walls painted a light green. The receptionist sat in an alcove to the right of a hallway. Across from her, its beveled glass facing Jeb, was most likely a conference room that doubled as a law library. At the end of the hall, was an informal kitchen area, and somewhere in that direction, Jeb would probably find Dalton's office, not much different from the rest of the place.

Jeb laid his head against the straight back of the 50's style couch and stared up at the metal tray ceiling with fleur de lis designs pressed into them.

"A long time ago, this place was a nefarious business," the receptionist said.

Jeb lifted his head.

She didn't stop her typing. "If you get what I'm saying."

Jeb smiled. "A distinctive touch. All you need is Sam Spade printed on the window and you'd have a Bogart movie scene." He finished his coffee and leafed through a magazine. Somewhere in the office a clock ticked away the seconds, which blossomed into minutes, and a minute that was about to reach an hour when the door opened.

"Chrissy." Dalton entered and held up his hand.

The receptionist high-fived him.

"Won my motion. The state dropped its case against our habitual cat burglar, who promised me he will steal no more felines. He'll trust the owners to care for their pets."

"Dalton ..." The girl pointed into the waiting room.

Jeb stood slowly, getting the feeling back into his left side.

Dalton turned. He tilted his head.

Jeb had grown out his hair, and he'd let the growth on his face remain shaggy and unkempt as much as he could stand it. Nothing long. He wasn't a Louisiana hillbilly, not that he held anything against that sort. He only wanted to maintain a little of the style he'd been forced to lose along with everything else that might distinguish him as the person he'd once been—the one he would never be again.

Dalton started to speak but shook his head instead. In silence, he walked toward Jeb.

A soft sob escaped Dalton. He wrapped Jeb in a tight embrace that sent pain everywhere Jeb's damaged nerves allowed it to travel.

Pulling away, Dalton cleared his throat and motioned for Jeb to follow him. He pressed his palms into his eyes. Then he cleared his throat again. "Hold my calls," he told Chrissy. "No one comes in my office." He backed up. "Tell Randa or Shane I'll get back to them."

Jeb followed him to the room at the end of the hall.

Dalton moved behind the heavy, darkly wooded desk and leaned his hands upon it. He lowered his head. "Thank God. Thank You, God."

"Love you, too, man."

Dalton looked up and charged around the desk again. He grabbed Jeb by his shirt, drawing it together at the neck. "Why? Why did you do it?"

Jeb stepped back, but Dalton held firmly, pulling him within inches of his face. "I don't know what to do with you? This was never part of the plan. Never."

"I blew it." Jeb pushed away from Dalton's hold.

"Abra's here. Been here since the funeral." Dalton made his way around his desk.

If he'd known, he wouldn't have lighted in this little hick town. Surprisingly, he'd been able to stay out of sight. Now, he had nowhere else to go. The doctor he'd found in Georgia told him he needed to convalesce. He might suffer some pain, but the doc expected a full recovery.

Dalton moved to the window and stared outside. "Something isn't sitting well with me. I think Abra needs

Everybody's Broken

to stay here."

Jeb looked beyond his friend and shuddered at the gloomy clouds shrouding the mountains that surrounded the town. "So do I." He rubbed at the numbness in his hand. "How are they?"

"Same as all of us. Shattered. If Randa ever suspects my hand in all of this, I'm going to lose my wife. Things are tough for us right now. If Randa doesn't leave me, Shane will kill me. Either way, sooner or later, I'm going to lose her." Dalton turned. His gaze rested on his desk and not on Jeb. "I'm sorry. I've held those thoughts in for so long. I didn't mean to burden you."

"This is my burden, too, you know. Randa and Shane never have to know of your involvement. Abra either. So you know, I'm going by Jeb." He half-laughed. "The old man was an odd one for names. But I guess using my middle name comes in handy for fitting in around here."

Dalton huffed. "Do you have a place to stay?"

Jeb nodded. "Not the greatest, but it's off the beaten path."

The new landlord had said the place sat in a holler, whatever that was. Jeb was thankful it had running water.

"It isn't much," he said, "but I took a walk up a little ways, and there's a nice rustic home—a converted watermill."

Dalton closed his eyes. "Sits up on the mountain just a bit? Walkway over a creek?"

"That's the one."

"Shane's place. Don't tell me you're in the old shack at the bottom of the hill."

"Okay, I won't tell you." Jeb sat and stretched out his left leg. The walk he'd taken earlier hadn't been as good for him as he thought it would be. He leaned forward and rubbed tired eyes.

"Shane and Abra do a lot together. She'll be by your place sooner or later." Dalton smiled. "Parents without benefits, Randa and I call them. They're good together. If they ever notice, watch out."

Jeb didn't want to hear any of that. Life was moving on without him, and he hated it. "I wanted you to know I'm here. I'll make myself scarce."

Dalton stood in front of him. "Showing up here probably isn't your brightest idea."

"Well, neither was the last plan we hatched, but I'm all out of schemes." Jeb rubbed the back of his neck where the pain usually rested. "I need some work, not only for the money, but to keep these infernal memories from flooding in. Any ideas?"

"With all the talent you have to access? Use it." Dalton returned to the window. He stared below then turned with a smile. "It might be tricky, but the town used to go all out on seasonal decorations. As downtown merchants, Randa, Shane, and I have tried to get some interest going, but a downward economy results in less creativity and thus less sales. Several merchants did nothing this year. Randa's running behind schedule. Someone like you, who comes in and offers to do something in that arena for low cost might make a go at it. Someone spreading the news to the local papers and some quality in the jobs might bring in more business, and the circle of economics might keep you busy."

Jeb nodded. Dalton could have majored in any degree. The man was intelligent, quick on his feet. "*Tricky* is the right word, but I'll give it some thought. I have no access to anything I left behind."

"I've watched you turn cardboard into props worthy of a Broadway stage. I'll front you any cost for supplies. Pay me back when the jobs are done. Throw my name around. Believe it or not, people respected me as much as they did Beau once upon a time." Dalton offered Jeb a tired smile. "Whether I deserve it or not, I still have it. Yeah, it'll be tricky, and it probably isn't very smart. Still,

I'm glad we're all here."

"No, we're not." Jeb closed his eyes. "I don't know about you, but there are a few key people in our lives who are missing. I messed up, Dalt. Bad."

Dalton's shoulders seemed to bend with unseen weight.

"We're still fighting an invisible foe."

Dalton nodded. "He thought he had it all figured out."

"I thought he did, too, but I have my doubts."

Dalton raised his arms out to his side. "We did what needed to be done. Let's hope this time it goes better for us than it did before. The mastermind of our brilliant plan is gone, and he left his two stooges behind."

Abra longed to roll down the window and feel the fresh air on her face. The winding road to Shane's was one of her favorite places. Who would have thought that in only six months, she'd be used to the mountains?

The only thing she wasn't used to was the cold that seemed to come from nowhere. Sunny and mild one day, raining and misting now. And Randa told her there would be lots of snow coming. Something about the amount of fogs that laid low on the ground during August. Then Randa said she'd watched a black squirrel playing in her yard. The dark rodent was supposedly a sign of a harsh winter. Abra wasn't sure if she could believe Randa, but she had been sure to buy some especially warm clothing for the boys.

Despite the gloom of the day, Shane had encouraged her to drop off the boys for a hike up the mountain since Abra had volunteered some office time at the church she had been attending with the family while in Amazing

Grace. The poor pastor operated without a secretary, and every Monday afternoon, she gave him an hour or two of her organizational skills while Shane had all the fun. Usually, Shane picked all the kids up from school, but Taffy had an earlier dentist appointment, and he'd checked her out.

"Maybe we'll see Bumblebee today," Paulie whispered.

"Shu-ut-ut up," Peter hissed.

"Buzz, buzz," Abra peeked at them in the rearview mirror. "Is that what Shane and Taffy film for their music CDs and DVDs? Bumblebees?"

"Shane films lots of animals. Last week we got to watch two otters play in the stream at Mount Tabor. It's really not a mountain. It's a place where the mountain levels out to one side, but it's higher on the other. The stream roars down. Shane owns it."

"The mountain or the stream?" Abra winked at them in the mirror. Then she gave her attention back to the road. The old ramshackled home that marked the turn to Shane's place was just ahead.

"Daddy gave it to Shane. It belonged to our grandpa who died before we were born. Shane doesn't let people on the land unless he knows them 'cuz they'll hurt the animals. He only allows nice people who don't want to kill them," Paulie announced.

"Uncle Dalton calls Shane a tree-hugger." Peter snickered.

Abra laughed. "He's teasing." She negotiated the turn, traveling alongside the old home.

A figure on the crumbling back porch startled her, and she hit the brake momentarily. Shane had said the place was empty, that the old man who'd once lived there leased it out sometimes, but he wouldn't fix it up.

When the lane to Shane's house curved, Abra looked back.

The guy was no longer there, but a beat-up older model car was parked in the back on the other side of the porch.

"You listen to Shane today, and stay close to him."

"We do." Paulie bounced in his seat. "Shane said that we couldn't come with him and Taffy if we didn't. He doesn't give chances anymore. He said that hiking was fun, but we had to be serious until he said we could play."

Well, that made Abra feel better. Not. But Shane had been making a valiant effort to keep the boys from feeling fatherless. Since school started in August, they had attended every school event together, whether for Taffy, who was a year ahead, or the boys.

"Then don't mess up. You hear me?" She pointed her finger in the air.

The boys nodded.

Abra pulled into Shane's yard, parking behind his SUV.

Shane and Taffy stood beside his garage, checking over their equipment. Both waved as the boys rushed from the car, and Abra made her way to them.

"Hey." Shane nodded. "You look nice. Trying to catch Pastor Moxley's eye?"

At first, Shane's humor had caused trouble between them, but she'd gotten used to it. She gave her best imitation of Mazzie, twirling around, arms open to show off the tan shirt under a navy jacket and the steam punk belt buckle with raised gears. She'd bought the accessory from Antiques by Grace where she'd also been finding and hoarding decorations for the boys to help her with over the weekend and some for the church Harvest Festival as well. "No. Only yours."

He straightened and looked her up and down. "You got it."

Taffy giggled, and the boys faked death.

Shane laughed and held out his fist. Abra bumped it.

She opened her mouth to speak.

"Be careful," Shane got the words out before she could.

She half-nodded, half shook her head, probably reminding him of a bobblehead. Not what she intended. "You, too. You have precious cargo with you." She pointed to the three rug rats.

"I'll have them home by dinner time. Why don't we bring us something to share?"

She loved this guy. Well, not like that, but, man, he was good to her. "That sounds great."

"So, if we catch a trout or bag a rabbit ..."

She skidded to a stop then realized he was joking. "No wildlife, Mr. Tree Hugger."

He laughed.

She turned but swiveled back, pointing through the thicket to the house on the road below, which would probably be invisible during the summer, but with the foliage beginning to fall, she could see the dingy white. "You have a new neighbor ... renter or vagrant. I saw him on our way up."

Shane stared through the trees for a long moment. "I'll check into it. Thanks for telling me."

Abra waved as she moved back to her car. "Have fun!" She sat inside and watched as Shane handed each of the kids a backpack then hefted his own onto his shoulder. He reached inside the opened garage and lifted out a rifle.

She wasn't sure if that comforted her or scared her to death.

Chapter 6

Abra dusted the flour from her face and looked at the clock fixed on the far wall of the kitchen's nook. Two more hours before school let out and five minutes for the cookies to bake. The casserole for their dinner was ready for the oven, and she had nothing else to do in the large house Beau had left to her. And it was only Tuesday. Three more days of complete boredom until the weekend would deliver her kids to her all day Saturday, and they'd be together with Beau's family at church on Sunday. Worship, like volunteering, was a habit she couldn't break. Although she went to His house without giving much thought to the process, she still felt as if He was never home—at least for her visit.

As far as The Gray Lady, even after all this time, she hadn't been able to bring herself to explore the place. Other than the boys' room that they insisted upon sharing, her room, the kitchen, and the solarium, the house remained untouched—at least by her and the kids.

Abra wiped her hands on the dishtowel and made her

way to the central hall. If she went to the front of the house, a vertical foyer connected the living room and formal dining room. A stairway against the living room's wall, led to the upper story. Across from her was the library Randa declared her grandmother's pride.

Abra turned away from it, yanking against the memories of Beau's love of literature, which would pull her inside. Instead, she moved into the solarium at the back of the house. A figure standing by the full-glass door shook Abra to the core. Then she laughed.

"How do you manage to step in here each time before I knock?" Randa asked as Abra hurried to let her in.

Her sister-in-law had a dishtowel draped over her left shoulder.

Abra wouldn't admit that she spent most of her time in this room. "Pure coincidence. I'm counting down the minutes until I fetch the kiddos."

"That's why I'm here." Randa smacked at the cloth and yanked it off. "I lose so many of these things."

That was true. At least once a week, Abra washed and sneaked all the towels Randa left back to Randa's kitchen.

"I have to go to the store a little later. Shane has a decision he wants to talk over with me, and he wondered if you'd pick up Taffy with the boys."

Abra smiled. "Sure. They can do their homework and play here until Shane comes for her." She motioned to the backyard and to the overly large and adventurous jungle gym Dalton and Shane had insisted on building for the children.

When Taffy visited, they ran between the two houses, compliments of a gate Randa had announced with tears in her eyes had waited a very long time for kids to push through. "Pretty soon the path will be worn once again from the solarium to my back-porch door. I can't wait."

Already, the grass had begun to wear away.

Randa sniffed the air. "Do I smell oatmeal cookies?"

Abra smacked her head with her hand and hurried back through the house. She yanked open the oven and pulled out the treats, releasing a rush of breath. "Thank you. Another minute or two, and I'd need to trash 'em. The boys are just like me. They eat nothing once it's burned past a certain point."

"Not me. The blacker the better." Randa winked. "At least that's what I tell Dalton whenever I ruin a meal."

Randa's light banter belied an undercurrent that ran between her and her husband, something that parted them like a raging river on occasion and at other times brought them together as tightly as Florida's love bugs in the rising heat of day. Shane seemed to have stumbled on the outside of the current, but on an opposite shore from Abra. He had to know what bothered the couple. Abra didn't have a clue, and she wasn't about to ask. If Randa ever told her, she'd be there for the couple, the way they had been for her since they'd met.

Abra used a spatula to lift the cookies from the pan and place them onto her cooling rack.

Randa sat on a stool at the counter and picked one up, dropping it quickly onto the marble. "Duh!" she laughed at her mistake.

Once a day, Randa uttered that word. When Abra returned to Bodacious Cove, she'd miss her sister-in-law's easy ways almost as much as she missed Mazzie's audaciousness.

"You okay?" Randa asked.

Abra stopped short of a nod. Randa had become her friend, and though Randa wasn't sharing her burdens, without Mazzie here, Abra needed a sounding board. "I heard the noises again."

Randa stopped, cookie midway between hand and mouth. "Like the other day?"

Abra lowered her voice. "It sounds crazy, and I know

you only want me to feel secure, but it isn't the house settling like you suggested. It's not rats or other rodents. Last night, I heard a voice. Muffled, distinctive."

"One voice."

"One voice." Abra opened the refrigerator and took out the milk. She dropped down the dishwasher door, took out two glasses, poured them both some milk, and then picked up her own cookie. "But it seems to be carrying on several different conversations."

Randa pushed the cookie into her mouth like a kid.

Abra laughed as her sister-in-law chewed for a bit.

Randa swallowed and drank her milk. "Explain what you mean by different conversations."

"The voice is the same, but let's say you and Dalton are here with me. I talk to you and then I talk to Dalton. I engage with you both differently."

"I'm not sure that I get what you mean."

"I'm sounding crazy, but last night I went in to the boys' room, locked the door, and slept on the floor between their beds. I didn't hear it quite so loudly in there."

Randa brushed the crumbs from around her face and downed her milk. "Why don't you come with me to the store when I leave? You can pick up the boys and Taffy at school when it's time, come back to the store, and Shane can walk you home and take a look."

"I haven't been afraid during the day. I'll be fine." Abra moved around the counter and embraced Randa. "Thank you for being my friend. Coming here was a good thing. Even with noises and voices, I feel the boys and I are safe, and we're surrounded by people who lo—care for us."

Randa continued to hold Abra tightly. "While I do care for you, I have grown to love you, too."

The doorbell chimed a song that always reminded Abra of Big Ben, though she didn't think the large

Everybody's Broken

London clock could be nearly as loud.

She made her way to the door and peered out the peep hole Shane had installed. She unlocked and opened the door to the friendly older mailman she'd met on many days during his route—mostly as he walked by while she sat on the porch. Very little mail—except for the utilities for The Gray Lady came Abra's way. "Morning, Mr. Hollister."

"Morning. I have a package and an envelope for you."

Abra glanced back to where Randa peered out of the nook's entrance.

"Something wrong?" Mr. Hollister asked.

"No. I'm not used to getting more than junk mail and bills here." She took the small box with no return address. But the larger manila envelope caught her eye, and she smiled. "Of course. It's from a friend." The large envelope was from Mazzie. The box probably contained something Mazzie thought she would like to have here with her or gifts for the boys.

"You have a good day now." Mr. Hollister saluted her as if she were a general.

Abra closed and locked the door, the action second nature to her now. "From Mazzie." She held up the envelope. "I'll open them later." A long time ago, she'd have ripped into a package with her name on it. But now, even mail from Mazzie reminded her of the letters that she, as a little girl, longed to receive—the letters that never arrived. She missed Mazzie so much, and opening them now would bring up feelings better left deep inside until she could deal with them and not choose to run back to her best friend. She tossed the packages on top of the nook's desk.

Randa chewed another cookie then licked cookie bits from her fingers. "Well, I managed to leave some for the crumb snatchers." She winked. "I better get myself ready to head to the store. Maybe we'll see you there."

Abra nodded. She probably would. The boys never tired of Count It All Joy Toy Store. Though Taffy sometimes acted as if she'd long grown bored by it, one mention that her daddy was there, sent her scurrying for the walk.

Abra followed Randa to the solarium door and locked it as Randa crossed the yard. Then she stood looking out the floor to ceiling windows that made up the room.

For the last couple of days, intermittent dreariness mixed with gleeful brightness. Now, the sun shined on raindrops atop the leaves on the maples, turning the scenery from dank to sparkle.

Hopefully, they'd have sun this weekend for their decorating. Peter wanted the scary factor, but Abra and Paulie had overruled him in a two-to-one vote. Abra had enough scary moments to last her a lifetime.

She smiled. Though Pap issued a mandate every year that they would never celebrate the pagan holiday, preparations would be underway for the awesome parties he would throw for her October 31 birthday—big festivities, where children were invited to dress in tasteful costumes and the fun was more like a fall festival than a horror fest. As she'd grown, the party had taken on epic proportions, the house filled with teenagers and adults dressed in costume. And no one dare show up in demonic garb or obscene outfits. If so, they faced the wrath of Pap Osteen—and no one would risk that.

The smile faded, and Abra fought against tears. This year, the only person around who would remember her date of birth would be Mazzie. That was a good thing, though. The church she attended with Beau's family hosted a Harvest Festival, and she and the boys would have fun. She'd even volunteered to help with decorations.

What would she have done if she'd known that last

year's birthday would be the last she'd have with Pap, Finn, and Beau? That this year, Mazzie would be six hundred miles away?

She stomped her foot on the tile floor. "No," she said. She wouldn't cry and give in to the pity party that daily knocked at her door.

Time to move on.

Abra turned to head back into the hall, but a shadow caught her eye at the edge of the detached garage on the other side of the ivy-covered fence—another part of the property where she seldom ventured. With the surrounding fence and the long walk through the yard, she'd chosen to forego use of the garage and park in the front driveway. She peered through the ivy, making out the large garage, but could see nothing.

She shook the crawling fear away from her and moved inside, pulling closed the French doors she usually left open. She locked them and looked outside once again.

The yard was empty of everything except her imagination.

Shane restocked the shelf of small stuffed animals rifled through by a group of vacationing children. He picked up the box at his feet, thankful that all he had was one child, and now often, he cared for three. Hiking with three children had been a little harder than he'd imagined.

Peter and Paulie learned quickly, though. Shane supposed Beau had taken them camping on occasion, though the boys never talked at length about their father or their Uncle Finn. And that bothered Shane.

He stuck close to them because he suspected the boys needed him in their lives, a buffer from the grief that could turn them in a wrong direction. Beau might have abandoned Shane and Randa, but Shane couldn't stand by and watch Beau's boys self-destruct the way Shane had after his father's death.

And no one had lost hope that they would open up with the truth soon.

"Let me know if I can help you with anything," Shane called to two women meandering through the large selection of toys and games.

"We will. Thank you," one called back to him.

The store's sing-song bell alerted Shane to the entrance of someone new.

Jeb Castor waved as the door closed behind him. He held the same sketch pad he'd brought with him earlier when he inquired about work.

"Randa should be here in a while," Shane said.

Jeb nodded and turned away. He stared at their store window then down at his sketch pad once again before pulling a pencil from his back pocket and scribbling. Then he placed the eraser end of the pencil to his temple.

Shane went through the curtained entrance to the storeroom to return the empty box. When he returned, Jeb stood behind a shelf, his eyes focused on the door. Shane approached and shook hands with the town's newest resident.

The door swung open with the tune, and Randa rushed in. "Been busy today?" She pushed her purse under the counter, as she always did out of habit.

"Usual traffic and sales," Shane advised. "Randa, I'd like you to meet Jeb Castor. He's new in town, a friend of Dalton's who sent him our way. Jeb has a unique proposition for us."

Randa stared from Shane to Jeb. "I can't imagine."

The two shoppers approached the checkout counter.

"Why don't you and Randa meet in the office? I've already heard the offer. I'll wait on these ladies and watch the store," Shane said.

"We can meet over here." Randa motioned toward the corner of the counter behind the checkout. "Is that okay, Mr. Castor?"

The man ran his hand through his dark hair badly in need of a trim then over the scraggly facial hair. His gaze moved toward the door as if anticipating someone's entrance.

"Was Abra okay with picking up Taffy for me?" Shane asked.

"As always," Randa smiled. "She might bring them by, but I suspect they'll want to play for a bit. Mr. Castor, I'm intrigued. What do you have for us?"

Jeb opened his sketch book. "I've been visiting stores on Main Street. The decorations are a bit on the skimpy side, but I can bring some magic to the season. I ran into Dalton, and he said that if the merchants like what I do for autumn, maybe I'll get some work for Christmas. I'd like to show you some ideas I have for window displays. Of course, when the season's over, I'll clean up any paint and materials. I have some ideas for your two front windows."

Shane said good-bye to the customers then stood beside Randa as she reviewed the sketches Jeb had clearly taken time to prepare.

When Randa looked up, she smiled. "If you can pull this off, Mr. Castor, that would be fantastic. What will you charge?"

"Call me, Jeb," the man said as he opened the back of the sketch book and leafed through some papers tucked inside. He pulled out a handwritten estimate with the store's name written upon it. "Like Shane said, I'm new in town. I need to prove myself. I'm giving everyone a discount. I'll front the money for the supplies, and when you're happy with my work, I'll collect my pay."

Randa shot Shane a look. "No." She handed the paper back to Jeb.

Jeb stepped back without taking the estimate. He

winced with the action but recovered quickly before Randa could notice. "Do you honestly believe I'm overcharging you?"

"It's not that." Randa waved the paper. "I can't pay you this little to do that much."

Shane smiled. That was Randa: always looking for fairness in every situation. He loved her sense of fair play and her ability to love him despite the fact that his dreams had come true, and hers hadn't yet. His dreams, in the form of his daughter, had to challenge Randa each day. For some reason, she and Dalton hadn't started the family Randa always talked about when she was dating Beau's best friend. They seldom mentioned anything about kids these days.

"How about this?" Jeb said. "I do the work. You don't like it, I get nothing. You like it, you pay me what you think it's worth?"

"That I can live with."

"The store owners I've talked with like my idea of a Saturday reveal, bringing in customers and tourists. So, I'd like to cover the windows while I work. Yours is the last store I've signed. My plan is to do the prep at home and to add any painting on the outside at night after the stores close. I'll bring everything and dress the window at your convenience, but I'd prefer to work after store hours. Since yours is the last store signed, I'd like to work here Friday night."

Randa returned her attention to the pad and Jeb's renderings. Then she handed it back. "Yes, I like this one, but only because it captures a child's view and not that creepy stuff people want to bring into it these days. "After Halloween, I'd like that one changed to another autumn theme perhaps thanksgiving to match your theme for the other window. And again, you'll be paid what you deserve."

"And I'm sure you'll let me know what that is," Jeb

teased.

"Most definitely." Randa held out her hand.

Jeb shook hers and then Shane's. "Friday night, I'd like to arrive a little early and cover the windows. Then I'll stay after closing. I can understand if you'd like to be here. The good news is that you won't have to have your windows covered as long as the other stores." He picked up his things and walked toward the door, limping a little.

"Are you all right?" Shane asked.

Jeb didn't turn. "Old injury acting up. Thank you, folks."

"Before you go, would you like us to pay the cost of the materials?" Randa asked.

"I'll get it from you on Friday. I'll be picking up a lot of stuff, and I'll need to determine each store's share of the bulk materials."

"Well, if you under estimate, you be sure to give me the receipt, and I'll reimburse you." Randa pointed.

Jeb left, and Shane hugged her. "You are the best."

"There's something about him." Randa pulled from his embrace. "Can't put my finger on it."

"A little scruffy, maybe," Shane offered.

Randa busily cleaned the counter and straightened all the minimum priced merchandise they kept there to catch a shopper's eye at the last moment before checkout. "You go see Taffy. I'll close up in about an hour. If you're still hanging around, I suspect Dalton and I'll see you for dinner."

"A free meal and one I don't have to fix. You're on. Anything I can do to get things ready?"

"Nope. It's in the crock pot, and the table is already set. I'm efficient if nothing else."

He started for the door.

"Shane?"

"Yeah?"

"Did you say Jeb was a friend of Dalton's?"

Shane reached for the door and opened it for a customer who was entering. "That's what he said? Something wrong?"

"Don't you think it funny Dalton has a friend we've never heard about?"

Shane did, but worrying her was the last thing he wanted. "Jeb lives at the old Saltsman cabin below me. I've seen him around, but I never got the chance to say hello. Talked to Saltsman. He said Jeb's down on his luck. Injured a few months back."

"That old place isn't fit for anyone to live in." Randa opened the cash drawer and started counting out the cash for deposit on her way home.

"I'm sure we'll get the scoop at dinner. See you then." He pulled open the door and stepped into the cool autumn air.

He stopped outside the door next to the toy store and looked through the glass and up the stairs to Dalton's office door.

Taffy was with Abra, and they hadn't made it to the store. Surely, his daughter wondered where he was.

Any questions he had for Dalton could wait until later.

Everybody's Broken

Chapter 7

Abra had fallen into her own personal *Groundhog Day*. She'd retrieved the kids from school yesterday so that Randa and Shane could have a meeting. Shane told her the Main Street stores were hiring a vendor to decorate the store windows. If only she'd thought of that.

Before school this morning, Taffy had asked to be allowed to come home again with Abra and the boys. Shane had swallowed hard at Taffy's request, and he'd nodded before rushing off, leaving Abra alone in the schoolyard as their children made their way to class. Abra suspected Shane and Taffy were separated very little, and his little girl's independence was tough for him.

Now, Abra stood in the solarium, a cup of tea warming her hands. Outside, Paulie and Taffy climbed up the slide. From the bit of imaginary play Abra heard, Taffy had deemed it a mountain, and they were seeking outlaws hiding in the woods.

"I'm going to get you, you mangy varmint!" Taffy's Southern twang hit the air at the same time Abra took a sip of tea. She fought to keep from coughing.

How many times had she stormed the beaches of Normandy with Finn, and how many times had he refused to join her and Mazzie in a tea party? In their teenage years before college, all found common ground with beach volleyball and surfing. She lifted her cup to the air. "Here's to you, Finn, wherever you are."

Peter stood alone, looking at something inside the vine lining the back fence. He pushed his arm in and drew out a piece of paper.

Curiosity pulled Abra out the door. "What did you find?"

Peter looked at it and shrugged, crunching it in his hand, his fist clenched around it. "Nuthin'."

"Probably one of our ornery outlaws got caught in the branches and tore their raggedy clothes." Taffy twirled down the pole from the top of the slide.

Before Abra could reach Peter, he tore whatever he had into tiny pieces, looking briefly at Abra before jumping out of Taffy's reach. "I'm the outlaw. I've been with you all this time, and you didn't even know it. Now what're you going to do?"

"You're not an outlaw!" Paulie shouted. "Outlaws are bad people. They're killers."

Peter stopped in his tracks and turned to his brother. "I'm only playing."

"We want to arrest the outlaws." Paulie scuffed his tennis shoes in the lush grass. "So they can't kill good people like Daddy."

"We want to kill 'em." Peter's eyes narrowed, and his nostrils flared as his breathing deepened. "And cut out their hearts." He hugged himself. Tears ran down his face.

Abra dropped the cup and ran to him. Peter never cried. Like Beau, he buried his emotions deep inside. She fell on her knees at his side, and he wrapped his arms around her neck. "Daddy, please come back. Please. I want Daddy! I want Daddy." His scream pierced Abra's ear. With each of his cries, Abra's heart rang with *I want him, too.*

Paulie fell against Abra, and she tugged her arm out and wrapped him in the embrace. "Uncle Finn ..." Paulie whispered.

Abra closed her eyes tightly, and when she opened them, she met the green-eyed gaze so much like Beau's and the twins'.

Taffy swiped the tears off her face as if they were a nuisance. "I'm sorry. I made up the game. I know I shouldn't of."

Abra opened her arms wider and drew the little girl into the circle. "You didn't do anything wrong," she said. "I'm all for catching outlaws hiding out in these here hills." She leaned back. "Who's with me?"

The kids stared for a moment. Then Paulie laughed. "Mommy's playing. Mommy's good at making stuff up." He pulled Taffy with him, the moment of emotion passing as quickly as it had come upon her younger twin.

Peter, though, looked back at the bits of paper he'd left scattered on the ground. "I'll pick it up." He moved like a man on death row, bending and picking up the shreds. Then he walked with dragging steps to the trashcan, lifted the lid, and let them fall inside. His gaze strayed to the bushes where he'd gotten the paper.

"Mommy," Paulie called. "We're going after Billy the Kid. You gotta go up and around the mountain, and we'll meet you on the other side."

Abra held out her hand to Peter. "What do you say? Think we can find old Billy before they do?"

A wide smile was Abra's reward. He took her arm and pulled her after him.

Shane entered Dalton's office.

Dalt's legal assistant, Chrissy, motioned Shane back toward Dalton's door.

Shane knocked.

"Yeah," Dalton called.

Shane entered. "Got a minute?"

Dalton looked away from his computer. "Sure. Just doing some research for a hearing next week."

Shane took a chair without waiting for an invite.

"What's up?" Dalton stretched back, his hands laced behind his head. He yawned.

Shane couldn't help but yawn, too. "Do you know Jeb Castor?"

Dalton flinched.

"Yeah. I talked to him a day or so ago. Why?"

Shane studied Dalton. Something wasn't right. "A legal case? Something that should concern Randa or me if we hired him to do our window display?"

A slow smile slid across Dalton's face. "No. Nothing like that. He's an artist. He was injured recently. A setback to his career."

"That's why he has tremors and walks with a limp on occasion?"

Dalton nodded. He leaned forward. "He's down and out. Nothing to concern you."

"I know attorney-client privilege, but he didn't seek you for any criminal law advice, did he?"

Dalton turned his head to the side and back to the middle "Didn't seek my legal advice at all. We have nothing to worry about."

"He said you were a friend of his. Exaggerating to get the job?"

"Well, in Amazing Grace, we pride ourselves on being friendly to strangers. I told him to use my name."

Good enough. Shane's worries were vanquished. "Any news on the investigation, or am I still considered the prime suspect in Beau's death?"

"They aren't going to contact me, because their evidence didn't hold up. Abra might have heard. Have you asked her?"

Shane never brought up Beau's death to Abra. "So you think I'm in the clear?"

"Everything's good so far."

Shane opened the door. "I guess that should comfort me."

Dalton chuckled.

"What?" Shane spun around.

"I was just thinking. I'm glad I wasn't in that first will. I'd have a fool for a lawyer."

"Ha-ha. You're just jealous he didn't think to leave you the big toy in The Gray Lady's garage."

Dalton sobered. "Abra's never had any interest in venturing back there."

"She said she hasn't gotten up the nerve to delve through the house yet. Feels as if she's invading a life Beau never intended her to see. All the same, the thing needs to be driven. Letting it sit in there is worse than running it all over the place. You might want to tell her about it. If she doesn't want to drive it, you and Randa should take it for a joyride." Shane stepped into the hall and headed toward the exit. "I'll see you at dinner. Abra's got Taffy again today. I need to go."

Shane knocked on Chrissy's desk as his usual goodbye and reached for the office door.

The knob turned in his hand. Shane stepped back as Jeb entered. He looked as pale as a full moon against a dark sky. "You okay?"

The man nodded. "I came to see Dalton."

"Jeb," Dalton worked his way around Shane. "Come on back. I've had lots of visits today. See you later, Shane."

"You're sure? You're okay?" Shane pressed. He

started to tell Jeb where he lived, that he was available if the man needed him, but having a stranger near his daughter—not an option.

"I'm fine," Jeb assured. "Just a friendly chat." The man walked with Dalton down the hall.

Shane watched until they got out of sight. Then he shook his head.

"They're old friends," Chrissy offered. "You should have seen Dalton the first time Mr. Castor walked through the door. You'd have thought someone had been raised from the dead."

Shane didn't move.

"Oh, Shane. I'm sorry. That was awful of me after Beau ..."

Shane raised his hand. "No need to sign up for sensitivity training, Chrissy." He pushed a playful tease into his voice. "I didn't think anything of it. Besides, you work with Dalt. You're bound to pick up his habits." He winked and took his leave.

Outside on the landing, he lost the smile.

Dalton had lied. That wasn't like his cousin-in-law. Oh, he was very good at keeping secrets. That trait came with his job, but the secrets were always for his clients. He used secrets tactically, bringing the bombshells into court. He never lied to his family.

At least as far as Shane knew.

He opened the door, intending to barge back inside and into the meeting to demand the truth.

He stopped.

Dalton was too good a lawyer to betray whatever was going on.

"Something wrong?" Chrissy looked up from her typing.

Shane shook his head. "No. I'll catch you later." He hurried out the door.

Outside the sun peeked out from behind an October

cloud. Shane turned toward the toy store next door.

Again, he held back. Randa and Dalton's relationship was already strained. He wouldn't add to it needlessly. Shane wanted to see his cousin and her husband in sync once again, talking about their future and the children they were going to have.

He walked down Main peering into the few shop windows that were not already covered to hide Jeb's designs. The man might have some handicaps, but he was getting work done. The number of windows covered with brown butcher paper and the artistry painted on the windows were a testament to that and to the town's reputation of helping the down and out.

The day before, Randa had contacted their neighbor stores all along both sides of the historic district, and organized each store's unveiling one after the other, allowing the window shoppers and potential customers to follow a route. *Count It All Joy* would be the last store to reveal.

Randa planned to offer apple cider and cookies, and Shane would perform. Abra had gushed over his gold records on display in his home studio, but he'd been embarrassed to sing any of the goofy stuff he and Taffy wrote for kids. Saturday would probably confirm him as a fool in her eyes.

At the end of the block of shops, Shane waited for the jaywalk bird to chirp. When it began, the lighted man walking in the post indicated he could safely make his way over. Shane stepped into the crosswalk.

The revving of an engine brought him to an abrupt stop. He turned as the car raced toward him.

Step back. A voice in his head screamed, and he obeyed.

The vehicle had been close enough that a rush of air had swirled around him.

The jaywalk bird stopped its squawking, but Shane

stood and stared at the speeding car.

"Looked to me like the guy was aiming for you," a woman commented as she moved around him.

Shane started down the side street and cautiously across another block that led into the neighborhood where he'd grown up in the house beside his grandmother's old place.

Melancholy filled his soul. He missed Grandmere and her sense of adventure. She always shared tales about grand things. In the end, the simple truths she conveyed about the treasures she wove into the stories came down to the priceless things in life people missed every day.

Grandmere had more treasure than all the kings of England, at least that's what his mother used to say. Beau had always been Grandmere's favorite, but when she'd passed not long after they'd lost Shane's mom, Grandmere had left them all pretty well off. Momma had willed Randa the house. She'd mentioned it to Shane when she made the decision, explaining to him that Randa and Beau's father—Momma's brother—had helped her keep the place when Shane's dad lost his job, his will to live, and sometimes, his desire to even care for his children. Shane couldn't have been happier for Randa who needed to feel as if the house had always been her home. Losing her parents so early left a void Beau could never fill and one Shane had failed to cover as well. He hadn't really understood what Randa was going through until he'd lost his father, then his mother, and his grandmere all too quickly one after the other: Dad to an overdose of sleeping pills taken with too much whiskey, Momma to a broken heart, and Grandmere, they said to old age.

Beau inherited Grandmere's place, and Shane had the land and the watermill Beau's father had left to Beau— the same land he made Shane clear, the same watermill Beau worked with him to renovate into a beautiful home.

The place had been showcased in one of those stylish house and garden magazines after his notoriety as a top songwriter caught their attention.

Grandmere had left Randa and Shane a little more money than she'd left Beau because The Gray Lady came with everything inside of it. That was the old Southern matriarch's golden rule when it came to her grandchildren: she gave to them equally, especially of her love, even when she had her favorite. Shane suspected the woman looked over her investments carefully because she wanted to leave something for each grandchild.

Taffy's earnings from the profits of the children's CDs and DVDs they made from their filming during hiking, and the songs they created together were being set aside for college. The songs he wrote for the inspirational and country markets, along with the split in profits from the toy store paid his bills. The rest of Grandmere's inheritance pretty much gathered interest.

As he neared The Gray Lady, the sounds of children's laughter filled the air. He closed his eyes, remembering the games of tag and hide and seek, the roughhousing with the water hose, and Grandmere's dog, Tippy, nipping at their bare feet as they played in the lush, green grass.

Grandmere's legacy lived on.

He picked up his pace and climbed the front steps to the old place. He moved to the left, his tennis shoes slapping against familiar wooden planks. On the far side, he stepped down onto the concrete sidewalk and neared the outer gate ... close to the entrance into Randa and Dalton's yard.

"Billy the Kid, you come out of that-there drinking hole, and you face us like the mangy dog you are." Abra stood on the top of the slide, her eyes shaded from the sun. She peered across the yard. "You hear me, Billy. This here running is done. We've come to take you in to pay for your crimes, you horse thief." She stared for a very long time over the hedges that shielded the house from the detached garage. Then she shook her head as if clearing her mind. "Come on out, Bill. We have you surrounded!"

Shane leaned against the chain-link fence. He'd watched her the day before as the kids sat in a circle and Abra paced around them, taking her time, "Duck ... duck ... duck ... duck ..." After three turns, she worked her way around to Taffy and slowly bent down. "Goose!" she had called, and Taffy ran after her, chasing Abra around as Abra zigged and zagged, finally letting Taffy tackle her. Then, as now, Abra's guard was down. Shane stood lost in the beauty of her playful spirit.

A fleeting fancy danced in his mind. Could he ever catch their imaginary play on video and set it to music?

He'd consult his business partner. If Taffy thought it a good idea, maybe he would broach Abra with the idea.

He watched the kids move around the yard as if searching for the outlaw.

Boy was that imaginary bad-man in a lot of trouble.

Abra stooped down, her legs dangling as if to slip from her perch on the metal slide. She held her hand out like an imaginary gun. "You hear me, you varmint? Get out here?" She pushed off and sped down the slope.

"I see him," Taffy squealed.

Shane's gaze had been on the beautiful woman, her face flushed with the bit of chill in the air and her play. Abra pounced to her feet and turned in his direction. If possible, he'd swear her blue eyes smiled along with those gorgeous lips.

"Daddy's Billy the Kid. Let's get him!" Taffy commanded the troops.

Shane opened the gate and ran forward, his imaginary guns lifted. He ducked and rolled between the fence and a hydrangea making shooting sounds.

"Gotcha," Taffy landed on his gut.

"Omph." He took the full weight of her, and then two little boys piled on top of him.

"We got you, Shane." Paulie giggled and bounced.

Shane laughed.

Abra stared down at him. Her gaze never seemed so vulnerable—and tender toward him.

For a fleeting second, desire crashed over him like a warm wave would a sandy Caribbean beach.

Maybe Taffy's relationship with the boys wasn't the only reason he couldn't pull away from the very sensual beauty Beau had married.

She embodied all he'd ever wanted in a woman.

But it was too soon.

He shook his head. He should feel shame for what he was thinking.

Abra was his cousin's wife, after all.

Abra's lips curled into a trembling smile before she turned away. "Okay, I supposed we should feed the mangy varmint." She took a couple of steps away, as if putting space between them. "Who wants cookies?" She squealed the question and ran toward the solarium's back door.

The kids climbed off of him and ran after her, leaving him to get up on his own.

Even if he could move past the fact that Beau had found her first, too much stood between them.

Like a murder investigation in which he possibly remained the chief suspect.

Chapter 8

Shane turned onto the road leading out of the holler and up the mountain to his home.

Only one light burned in Jeb's rented shack, and as he passed, Shane turned to see inside.

His new neighbor stood hunched over a table, apparently working on something with one hand. His other hand was pressed against the back of his neck. "Our new neighbor is the one decorating the store windows," he said to Taffy.

"Aunt Randa told me about him," she offered.

"Still a stranger, though. Got it?"

She gave him an exaggerated nod.

Shane continued on until the car lights glistened on the creek waters and illuminated the walking bridge leading to his porch steps. He passed them and parked under the overhang of the old barn. Soon, he'd have to pull the car into the spot he reserved for it inside the building that housed only his tractor and woodworking tools. He and Taffy would use the passageway Beau made

Shane dig out and reinforce. "For icy weather when you won't want to cross the bridge," Beau proclaimed.

That was the only reason he would use it. Small musty smelling passageways, no matter how well built, gave Shane the creeps.

Beau had always been fascinated by secret passages and underground tunnels. His enthusiasm obviously inherited from their grandfather, a man neither of his grandchildren ever met, except through the adoring eyes of their grandmother.

Shane opened his own door, and Taffy bounded out before he could get his seatbelt unbuckled.

She ran to the bridge over the creek and stood facing the waterwheel.

He came up behind her. "Brr. Aren't you cold?" The churning waters sent a chilly breeze in the air. In the summer, that was a nice place to stand.

"When will we turn it off?" she asked.

"Soon, I think." He placed a hand on her shoulder and directed her away from the cold breeze the wheel caused. She'd have pneumonia if she wasn't careful.

Shane dangled his keys, searching for the right one. He slipped it in the lock, pulled the key out, and ushered his daughter inside. The lift of the switch by the door illuminated the interior. He tossed his keys on the table by the door and turned the bolt lock. "Even sheriffs need baths before they go to bed, especially when they've been out hunting a mean hombre like Billy the Kid."

He trudged with her up the steps to what they called the west stairs that led to their bedroom suites and Taffy's play area. Taffy stopped at the top and looked toward the large window that allowed them to watch the wheel turn, dripping the creek's water as it moved.

"Something wrong?" he asked.

"Daddy, are Peter and Paulie okay?"

This wasn't going to be one of those five second

answers. Shane sat on the step, and she joined him. "Why do you ask?"

"A bad guy killed their daddy."

Shane stared out at the waterwheel. "Yes. A bad man killed him. Remember. I told you he was my cousin."

"I know. He's Aunt Randa's brother, so he'd be my uncle. That's what Aunt Randa told me."

Shane took a deep breath and let it out slowly. "He's Aunt Randa's brother. She's right about that."

"Well, Paulie told me ..." her voice lowered with each word "... Peter's scared, and when Peter's scared, Paulie's scared."

Shane listened to the lapping water, thankful for the peace, safety, and warmth of the home.

"Daddy?"

Shane forced his attention back to her. "So what makes Paulie sure Peter's afraid. Peter's a pretty brave kid."

"Paulie said Peter jumps at loud noises, and today he cried real bad." She pursed her lips and brought her closed fist down on her leg.

Shane smiled. "Did you let go of a secret?"

She nodded, lips still pressed together.

"Well, it's usually not good to tell anyone you're going to keep a secret, so you don't have to worry about making a slip, but in this case, I'm glad you told me. I need to talk to their mommy."

"Aunt Abra saw him cry. We all did."

"Honey, Abra's not your aunt. She's your ..." He clamped his mouth shut, needing to heed the advice he'd given to his daughter. This secret was his alone, and he'd almost blown it. "Just call her Abra, okay?"

Taffy stared up at him. "Peter said they wanted to call you Uncle Shane."

Shane shook his head. "I'm their cousin. They can just call me Shane. And let's make this clear: you don't have to call us Miss or Mister because we said it's okay. Everyone else gets that respect with their first names, if they let you. Otherwise, you use those titles with their last name."

"Yes, sir!" Taffy jumped to her feet and saluted.

"Go get your bath." He swatted her behind playfully. "Then come get me in the studio, and I'll tuck you in."

She hurried off, and he went downstairs. His agent had called him earlier in the day. An up-and-coming music star, Liz MacKenzie, liked a couple of the scores he'd written for other musicians. The fact that he was consistently nominated as Songwriter of the Year didn't hurt, and she'd specifically requested he write two songs for her next release.

Shane moved downstairs and through the living room and kitchen to the east stairs leading to his studio. He passed the gold records and award recognitions Randa insisted on hanging in a misshapen order that worked well for the curving stairwell. He couldn't look at them anymore. Not since Beau's death.

For Shane, they represented the reason his cousin left them behind.

Still, songwriting had given him a lucrative career. Before Beau had gotten Shane sober and off the drugs, Shane dreamed of joining his friend on tour with their once rocking garage band. Sobering up had cleared his head of the ungodly lyrics he had penned—some that his old friends still performed, words that had given him awards in the rock arena as well. Those he didn't celebrate, didn't mention, and he certainly wouldn't let Randa hang them on the wall—not that she would want to. He had pulled her into trouble with him, and by God's grace they had survived.

He'd donated those royalties to a local preacher who worked one-on-one with addicts. Shane gave his guilt over to God and attempted to allow God to do something good with what Shane had created in ungodliness. The awards for those songs were stashed away in the old barn behind his property where he hoped the rust and vermin would get to them. He hadn't earned any treasures in heaven for those lyrics penned from the depths of his own hell, but Shane prayed daily that the monies they received would earn the pastor and his sweet wife treasures that would never rust.

Shane sat down on the old stool, guitar in hand, and closed his eyes. "Heavenly Father, let the words I write be before You. Watch over my desires and match mine to Yours. Watch over Peter and Paulie. I'm so sorry Beau will never get the chance ..." Shane choked on the words. He shook his head and cleared his throat. "Father, I know I'm to blame for Beau's leaving, but even if he returned today, I'd never give up the precious gift You placed into my hands. Forgive me, though, for my anger and resentment. Beau will never know what his leaving took from me and what it gave me."

Thankfully, the Lord didn't mind hearing the same old prayers every day so long as the words came from Shane's heart. He loved his cousin, hated that he'd let Beau down, but at the same time, the anger at Beau persisted. If Shane had only been given one chance, one time to see Beau and show him that he'd remained sober ... a godly person who took his sobriety seriously. But that hadn't happened.

He strummed a few chords.

Anger. Pain. Heartache. Loss.

The emotions pierced him. All four belonged to him.

Happiness, contentment, soberness, joy.

How could he reconcile the war being fought deep in his soul?

He closed his eyes, continuing to strum. From somewhere deep inside, the words poured through his thoughts. His fingers moved on the strings.

He ran through the chorus a few times, making the words match the rhythm and writing them down. Then he moved to his computer. The lyrics outside the chorus were easy to make flow into the heart of the song. The words he would write were for Beau, but the world would hear it as a love song if Liz MacKenzie or another artist picked it up.

Time would tell, but Shane could only write the music that poured from his heart. Then he'd let it sit a couple of days before returning to it. He'd ask Randa to come over then, and together they'd play the notes, and he'd sing the tune. Randa had sharp insight as to whether one of his compositions would strike the right chord with an artist or an artist's fan base. She'd help him tweak it before he sent a demo off for his agent's approval.

He played the notes on the MIDI keyboard, going over portions of the song until he had the notations correct. Then he fit the words to the score, singing softly as he played. This creative world is where he found peace. Music and lyrics had been his playground for as long as he could remember.

Beau had recognized that in him after Shane had taught himself music and often played Grandmere's grand piano. Beau had purchased Shane his first guitar.

And Shane had used it to bring nothing put pain to Beau. Yet when Shane wanted to put it down, Beau had been his encourager. "Don't give it up. Turn it around. Use it for something positive." Beau had slapped him on the shoulder. "Anything can be bad if you do it too much or for the wrong reasons or with evil intent." He'd lost his smile for a moment. "Alcohol, though, is never good. Shane, don't fool yourself. Now that you've stepped over the line and found out that you're not immune to addiction, you need to give it up. Give it up completely."

He'd promised Beau he would, and Beau had made him take the promise back, saying Shane needed to stay sober for himself and not for anyone else.

Shane's cell phone rang, and he dug it out of his pocket. The time on the phone said midnight, and he didn't recognize the number.

"Shane Browne," he answered.

No one responded.

"Hello, are you there?"

"Where's my little girl, Shane?" the muffled voice asked.

Shane jumped from his seat. "Who is this?" He ran down the stairs, stumbled into his living room, and hurried up the other set of stairs.

The hall seemed longer than it ever had. He could no longer hear the water trickling on the wheel outside. The rush of blood to his ears covered every sound.

He rushed to Taffy's dark bedroom. Even her bathroom light was off. He turned in the darkness and moved to her bed.

Taffy was fast asleep, in her night gown. She lay curled up on her side, her curly hair combed but damp.

Shane sighed with relief, walking from Taffy's room. Then he pulled the phone from his ear and stared at it before placing it back. "Who is this?"

"She's not yours. She belongs to me."

Shane stopped moving.

"She took the baby away from me, and she gave it to you. Hid it from me, and I want her."

Shane moved his thumb over "end call" without pushing it. He sank down onto the top stair.

"Do you hear me?"

"Beau?" he whispered. "Is that you?"

The caller hung up.

Shane let the phone fall. It took two bounces down the steps. Bending forward, he wrapped his arms around his head, rocking back and forth. Beau would never threaten anyone, but he hadn't seen his cousin in six years. Something had to have changed within him to make him leave Amazing Grace as he'd done and to fake his death.

None of that mattered. Even if the Lord resurrected Beau and brought him back to life, Shane would never let him have the child Beau had abandoned when he'd left Jasmine far behind without one word of good-bye.

He looked up.

Or had Jasmine lied about not knowing the reason Beau left? Had Beau known about the baby his ex-girlfriend delivered?

Shane had never bought Jasmine's lie that Beau wasn't at fault. Now, Shane knew she'd kept secrets from him, too.

And the secrets he kept for Taffy's sake prevented him from reporting the call, which would definitely get his face off the Bodacious Cove Police Department's list of top suspects.

He allowed the smile to slither across his face as he pushed "end" on his phone and slipped it into his pocket.

They were going to get theirs, and he'd get everything he'd ever wanted.

He'd returned to Amazing Grace right after the murder, announcing his displeasure at the way things went down.

He hadn't been able to find out what brought Abra to North Carolina, and to The Gray Lady—the last place he wanted her—but he would get to the bottom of it soon enough. Although his original plan had fallen through, he had been sure the home would remain vacant, and he'd be free to search as long as he wanted for what he'd been trying to unearth. Somewhere hidden away inside The

Everybody's Broken

Gray Lady was wealth beyond imagination.

The arrival of Abra and the boys was keeping him from that treasure

Patience was never a part of his makeup.

He pulled the old musty chair away from the grime-layered desk. When he sat, a plume of dust mushroomed around him and settled on his jeans, already dirty from his last two nights' excursions.

The stabbing pain in his temples started. The torture spread, encompassing his entire head. He grasped his hair and pulled at it with shaking fingers, and bent forward, biting hard on his lip.

These throttled him when he tried to block out the phantoms' voices. Always with him, lately, they were trying to force him to do things he didn't want to do.

He'd given into them twice before, but the peace he thought they'd give him after seeking their vengeance and his desire had only been a dream.

Those who stood unseen in a corner of the darkness conversed among themselves.

"Shut up," his harsh whisper came forth with the frost of his breath.

So, tell us. Why is she here?

She's in the way.

She hears you, fool.

"She doesn't know," he whispered and winced as the pain rode across his forehead like a crashing wave, ending on his left side. "She never asked questions. Never knew because she didn't want to know. At least that's what I heard."

She's smarter than you.

Smarter. Smarter. Yes, much smarter.

She'll figure you out, and she'll be our undoing. Fool.

Three voices, taunting him—forever making him feel as if he couldn't handle things on his own.

"Leave. Me. Alone." He moaned. All he needed was the treasure. Wherever the grand dame had hidden it. He could still hear her voice, teasing him about the value of what was hidden here. She'd taunted him with tales of riches too innumerable to count as she droned on about her long-gone husband's family and their aid to the Jews in Germany.

They must have given the family something worthy of their lives. Gold maybe.

He'd given up trying to imagine what it could be.

But whatever it was, he had to claim the treasure. "I want it." He looked up and stared into the corner.

If you discover what we seek, she will take it from you.

Take.

Take.

"Leave me alone." His voice low, he stared once again into the corner. "I'm not killing her. I only kill when needed."

Jasmine ...

"Jasmine betrayed me. She gave my child to him."

Elizabeth St. John ...

"She laughed at me. Wouldn't tell me what I wanted to know."

Shane ...

They had almost gotten their wish with Shane. The interloper had been inches from his car, stepping back at the last second. Maybe Shane heard voices, too. Who knew?

If he'd killed Shane today, like the voices had wanted him to do, instead of waiting, things would have gotten very complicated, his anonymity uncovered.

But if Shane continued to move closer to Abra, all of his plans would be ruined. Abra needed to leave North Carolina. If he could get her to do things his way, there would be no need to kill her ... or the boys. If he couldn't find the treasure in the next few days, Abra could save most of their lives if she'd do what he wanted. Then the only one who'd have to die would be Shane—for taking what belonged to him—as Jasmine had done.

He half-expected the phantoms to pounce, but their voices fell silent. The pain in his head subsided.

He listened.

The phantoms would tell him to stay where he was, but the coldness had returned to wrap around him. If he could just get warm.

Abra would never know, and if she did, plan nullified. She'd never live to tell anyone about it. And he'd set it up as a murder-suicide, with Shane as the killer. He'd let the investigation settle down, and he'd negotiate with Dalton. Who wouldn't want to get rid of a home where a woman and her two children were murdered by another family member whose so-called daughter had also vanished?

He crept to the side of the room, waited a minute to make sure the voices didn't follow him, and slipped from his hiding place and into the house.

Abra sat on the floor between the twin beds. The boys' questions about the story she'd been reading stopped sometime ago. She continued to sit and listen to their rhythmic breathing. One would exhale, and the other would inhale. The cycle continued for … she peeked at the lighted clock on their dresser. How had it gotten so late? Peter and Paulie had been asleep for several hours.

She'd never forget those two very long weeks when she had longed to hear the little sounds of boys: their horseplay through dinner and bath time, the questions they asked as she tucked them in and then read to them.

The fact that the time had slipped by was evidence that she never planned to take her sons for granted again.

She used Paulie's bed to push up on and laid the book on the corner of the bookshelf separating their beds. Then she kissed each of their faces and snuggled the covers around them.

The house had turned cool, even cooler than it had been in the early morning hours.

Abra closed their door and crept downstairs. She stopped at the thermostat and set it at a comfortable temp, one where she would be warm under the down comforter but not too stifling that she couldn't breathe.

She climbed the stairs again, gathered her nightgown and her robe, and slipped into her bathroom, closing the door to keep the heat generated by the warm water inside. A long, hot shower was in order. The climb in and out and around the jungle gym and the running through the yard had worn her out just as it had the day before. Yet anything beat the loneliness of the time without her children.

She started the water, undressed, and climbed into the old claw-foot tub, pulling the curtain around the inside on the circular runner. The hot water ran over her tired body, and she washed away the sweat.

The image of Shane lying prone on the ground, that smile he offered the children, and the way his blue eyes settled upon her, stole her breath away and danced inside her memory.

With the soaped rag resting on her shoulder, she stopped and lowered her head.

Beau died only six months before, and when she looked at Shane, she no longer thought of Beau. She saw only Shane.

What woman wouldn't fall for a man who fell so readily into the role of Billy the Kid for the sole reason of bringing happiness to two little boys who missed their father so terribly? He seemed not to hear the whispered desires women shared about him or notice the glances cast his way. He seemed clueless to his appeal to every single woman in town with his dark hair and blue eyes surrounded by thick black lashes. Those lips with his crooked smile that always hinted at mischief she longed to delight in.

She jerked from the errant thought. She had to stop this. She was a married woman.

No. She was a widow who'd only loved one man in her life, and he'd been taken from her.

A tear mixed with the shower water, waking her from her remorse.

She missed Beau and their fun times. Today's play had lightened some of the longing she had for the times she had shared with Beau and their boys and had reawakened desire in her. Shane was just the poor unfortunate soul who stood nearby. She could not be drawn to him.

The creak of the old wooden door startled her from her thoughts. She stood motionless for a long minute, listening. When no other sound met her ears, she laughed at her fear. The house was locked. One of the boys needed a glass of water. That was all. She pulled the shower curtain back shielding her body with it.

The door stood slightly ajar. She peered toward the mirror that would give her a reflection into her bedroom.

Nothing.

"Mommy will be out in a minute," she called.

She rinsed and turned the water off then pulled the curtain back a bit to grab her towel on the old bronze bar. She leaned back into the tub and closed the curtain to stay warm against the air pushing in from the opened door.

Thinking better of it, she gave a little tug and set the opening where she could still see the reflection of her room.

A movement in her bedroom, seen through the mirror's glass, stopped her breath in between inhale and exhale. Something or someone too large to be one of her boys was in her room. She held back her gasp and sank back behind the curtain, listening.

No other movement.

She'd probably seen a shadow cast by the lights of a passing car. She lowered her head, shaking it a bit, but stopped.

Car lights couldn't open a heavy door.

Maybe the door latch hadn't caught, and the start of the heat, the air pushing out, had created enough force …

She bit the nail on her index finger. If she tried hard enough, she would find reason rather than stark-raving fear.

Finn was a good one to tell a ghost story. Any wonder she always had nightmares? His tales would stoke her imagination, and she'd imagine monsters in every corner. Especially in this beautiful old home with the noises she'd already heard.

She draped the towel around her and stepped out of the tub. Picking up her brush, she started at the damp ends of her long hair, loosening any tangles as she worked her way up to the crown of her head.

Something rustled in the upstairs hall.

"Come on, Abra," she whispered to herself. "Get yourself—"

The step creaked. The fifth one from the top. She and the boys had noted it as soon as they moved in. She planned to get it fixed but decided if the boys woke at night and wanted something, the noise would awaken her.

"Peter? Paulie? Do you need something?"

She waited, but only for a second.

Abra allowed the towel to drop, grabbed her robe, and slipped it on. She stopped at her bedroom door and listened a moment. Then she peeked down the darkened stairs and around to the other side of the landing toward the boys' room. Their door was opened. She remembered closing it.

"No," the whispered word fell from her mouth.

She hurried, her bare feet padding against the plush carpet.

She stepped inside the room and breathed relief.

Both boys were sound asleep.

But if it wasn't one of them—?

Downstairs, furniture scraped across the wooden floor.

Abra stood motionless for several minutes. Someone was in the house.

Her chest hurt, and she pressed her hand there as if to stop its thumping. She crept to the edge of the stairs, stopping to listen, then stepped down, skirting the stair with the squeak. On the first floor, she held to the banister.

Another creak sounded, and a door closed with a slight click.

But it hadn't been the front door. She was looking right at it. Or the French doors to the solarium, which she had decided to keep locked during the night. Beyond the French doors, the solarium was locked up tight, the windows shaded against an earlier feeling that her family was being watched.

The sound came from much closer.

The door had to be on the inside of the house.

If she had to guess, the noise came from the library, the room on this side of the locked solarium, across from the kitchen and kitchen nook. In between the stairs and the library, only a half bath, nestled under the stairs, separated the rooms.

She took a hesitant turn to the right and then stepped with caution along the wooden floors.

With a deep breath, she slipped her hand against the

wall, feeling for the light switch. She lifted it. The old chandelier in the center of the room illuminated the grand piano and the bench. Beyond that, the fireplace of gray rock and its wooden mantel sat beneath a large portrait of a beautiful young woman with raven black hair and a twinkle in her green eyes. Randa, Beau, the boys, and Taffy had gotten their green eyes from Elizabeth St. John.

The woman wore an elegant full-length emerald gown that either enhanced her true eye color or the artist had tried to embellish it. Elizabeth leaned forward over the very piano in this room as if looking on as a musician played. She wore a mischievous smile on her face. Randa had said Grandpere St. John had commissioned the portrait of Grandmere early in their marriage.

Abra wrenched her attention away from the smiling woman in the painting, but for a moment, seeing Grandmere's smile, so like both her grandsons', had eased her fears.

Now, without provocation, the fright came raging back at her. Something wasn't right. She'd been in the house for half a year, and she couldn't bring herself to think of it as hers, but she sensed that someone had been inside this room recently. As in moments before.

She stayed in the center, staring at the shelves and shelves of books that lined the right wall. A chill fell across her, despite the rush of heat from the vent above and the heavy robe she wore.

At no time had the library's ladder ever been moved toward the window. She had rearranged the lovely wheelback settee with its rich mahogany frame and plush white velvet. She'd placed the matching side tables and the Victorian globed lamps that sat on each toward the center of the room, leaving space for anyone browsing the collectible volumes to skirt around the ladder centered behind the furniture.

The wooden floor bore the scratches of a careless

shove, and the lamp on the table closest to her was askew—possibly the result of a careless push or perhaps a fall in the dark by someone who didn't notice that the room had been rearranged.

She gently lifted the furniture back in place, replaced the lamp, and pulled the ladder to where it had been. Then she ran her hand along the priceless volumes of classic works.

"Randa is right, Grandmere," she whispered and turned to face the painting. "You truly treasured your books. Beau loved to read. Never would go to the library in town. He had to buy them. I wanted to renovate Pap's game room and make it a library."

She smiled at the memory. "He wanted to make it a solarium. I always loved them, but that was because they were out of reach. A glass room on the beach ... salt water would do a number on the glass. So, I won." She wiped at a runaway tear. "We were making plans to start his library to have a place for all those books I never understood the reason he kept. He was so excited."

A sob broke from her. "He asked me to decorate it, but he had this idea ..." she twirled around her, taking in the very design Beau had given her "... this grand idea." She covered her face with her hands. "His heart never left you or this place. I see that now. I don't know why he left." She stared up into the smiling face. "I wish I knew why he kept this all a secret. I love his family. I love this home." Abra moved to the mantel and stared upward. "I've even come to love you through the memories of the rest of your family. We could have visited here, made it a summer place. Now I'm stuck here without him. Why?"

She sank to the floor where she stayed for some time, staring at the pattern on the polished wood beneath her. She should be talking to God and not to a woman in a painting.

She had become insignificant to God, and she was

lost in a world so unlike the one she had left behind.

Of course, she wasn't stupid. She'd moved away from God. Deep down, she wondered why God would want to be bothered by a little nobody. He was God. She had been arrogant to believe He would find time to listen to her furtive pleas when so much more was going on in the world. His world. His prerogative.

She gazed toward the bookshelves and the ladder and furniture that had been moved.

Her talk with Grandmere had done some good. With the scare behind her, she could understand how a little settling could cause her imagination to leap into warp speed, cause her to imagine a movement outside her bathroom door, and to jump to all kinds of conclusions. The boys had probably slipped in here to play. She had not prohibited them from any rooms in the house. At five years old, they were curious, but they had lived with a mother and an uncle who decorated fine oceanfront homes. Instinctively, they knew what not to touch. But a run around the settee could have moved it, pushed it against the table. The ladder would have been moved to allow more room for play. And like their father, they were good at keeping secrets.

If she kept finding reasonable conclusions, she might talk herself out of the thought that Beau's murder had driven her mad, made her imagine things that were impossible.

She pushed to her feet and stared at the woman. "Thank you, Grandmere."

Outside the library, the chandelier's light illuminated the hall and the kitchen nook across from her. The box delivered the afternoon before sat unopened along with the other package Mazzie had sent. She'd plain forgotten about them. After Shane and Taffy's departure, she and the boys had eaten, looked over some school papers, and went through their nightly routine. Abra had conveniently put the mail out of her mind.

Funny how the past molded eccentric behavior.

Letters she longed for in childhood that never arrived made her avoid opening mail in adulthood.

She yawned. Despite the desire to hear from her friend, Abra didn't have the energy to look at her bills or anything else Mazzie might have sent. Instead, she trudged up the steps. She peeked in at the boys once again then went into her bathroom to put on the gown and take off the damp robe.

As she slipped her gown over her head, the nightly rustling began.

The sound was distant from the bathroom. In her room, the noise, like the movement of papers was muffled but louder.

Abra grabbed her pillow and her blanket from her bed and hurried to the boys' room where she closed and locked the door and laid down between her sleeping sons.

At one point, a man's muffled voice rang out—an angry tone one moment and then calmer, apologetic the next. Just like the night before.

Chapter 9

The kids were wound up and ready to spring before school, but Abra hugged her coffee cup as she stood by the car and waited for them to exit the backseat. A long morning nap was on the agenda for another endless day.

The lingering notion of opening a decor shop and using her expertise to help cabin buyers and typical homeowners bring together a custom look appealed to her. Licensing, renting a shop, and a long-term obligation did not.

What if Beau's killer was found? What if Finn found his way home? She would want to return to Florida. After all, she missed Mazzie. Yet she found herself more attached to Beau's family—her family—the boys' only true kin now that Finn wasn't around.

Listen to her. *Kin.* The mountain language was even beginning to slip into her vocabulary.

She'd be glad when she could make the decision, when both places would feel completely safe.

The more she tried to shake the fear that someone

had free rein in her home, the harder it became to dismiss the possibility. She'd explored the library in the morning light, saying hello to Grandmere before checking the windows and looking for a doorway that maybe she hadn't noticed before. The conclusion: no one could have escaped from there.

Yet noises continued on through the long night, as if someone plundered a room somewhere beneath where they slept.

Elsewhere inside the old house nothing had changed from night to morning, begging the question of whether the only disturbance in the place was her fear-tainted brain.

"Mommy!" Paulie's excited squeal nearly made her spill her coffee. "There's Taffy." He tugged his backpack out of the car, and Peter scooted across the seat, dragging his pack with him. Up until this point, they had dawdled time away.

Shane pulled in behind Abra's car. Taffy exited and ran to Abra. Abra held up her cup and hugged her tightly with one hand.

Shane tugged at the bill of his brown tweed newsboy cap in what she considered a "good morning" salute. The day before, she'd noticed he hadn't shaved, and the growth seemed unintentionally rugged, the dark beard drawing attention to those so-blue eyes.

She took a deep breath and looked the other way, releasing the rope of attraction that threatened to pull her toward him, this desire to see both Beau's strong and Finn's carefree nature. Shane was a cross between the two men she mourned.

Add to that, Shane, most probably without realizing it, filled the void that both her husband and her brother had left in her and in the boys.

She and Shane walked in step to the school's playground. The school's doors would remain closed until the bell rang.

She'd never seen Shane with a cup of coffee before today. He lifted it toward her and then toward his lips. "To long, restless nights," he toasted.

She clanked her cup with his. "And how."

They stood in comfortable silence as the kids romped.

Abra leaned against the play yard's fence and yawned.

Shane did the same.

"So, what kept you awake?" she asked.

Shane stared into the playground, and Abra turned to watch Taffy and the twins on the monkey bars.

"You'd think they'd get tired of dangling there, but it's their favorite pastime," he said.

"Well," Abra turned and leaned her arms on the chain link, "below them could be anything their imaginations bring to life: a moat, a fiery pit, a vast ocean ..."

"A tankful of piranhas, sharks, or moray eels." Shane laughed and then sobered. "They're a lot alike. Have you noticed?"

Abra nodded. "They're cousins." She raised her eyes to the heavens, trying to reason their relationship. "You and Beau were cousins so they would be second cousins, right? I suppose you, Beau, and Randa shared some similarities."

Shane didn't speak for a moment. He cleared his throat. "I'm discovering that we're more alike than I ever thought possible." He stared down into his nearly empty cup of coffee before tipping it and allowing it to spill on the ground. "I've heard people say I look and act a lot like Beau, but I don't see it. Beau was straight as a board. Randa and I used to be bent on trouble."

"What?" Abra poured her cold coffee out as well.

"Randa and I have always been close—like sister and brother. Live here long enough and someone will tell you how miraculous it is that we turned out as good as we have—their words, not mine." He kept his eyes on the kids. "People think I followed Randa into trouble. Actually, she followed me, but I suppose it had something to do with the fact that everyone knew Randa struggled with the female authority figures in our lives."

They might have played together with the kids the afternoon before, but generally they danced around their personal lives. "What was your mom like?" Abra relaxed into the conversation.

"Hippy-dippy." He smiled so big she got the first hint of his dimples. "Imagine a flower child with the crown of clover woven through her long braided hair, tie-dye clothing, frayed jeans, sandal-clad only when going barefoot wasn't allowed. Homemade soaps, organic foods, and Jesus ..." He shook his head. "She really loved the Lord. She passed on that love to us. Beau actually had to help make God's love for me a lot clearer, but Mom was the one who made sure we weren't just involved with church. We were involved with Him." Shane pointed upward and then patted his heart. "See, sometimes I forget how close He always is."

Shane might find God close, but Abra wouldn't bother Him again. Worship Him, yes. Petition Him, no.

"Your mother sounds so different from you grandmother. The hippy-dippy part, I mean."

Shane leaned forward on the fence. "You'd probably expect me to tell you they had issues. Not so. Grandmere demanded respect, but she respected individuality. Randa was the problem child for both. Beau was his own man. Comfortable with Mom ..." he turned to face her "... who was his aunt, of course, and Grandmere. I loved my grandmother, but Mom was the apple of my eye. Randa thought Mom too loony and Grandmere too structured. Mom and Dad loved her and Beau as if they gave birth to them, but grief places layers over hearts. Dad's depression

Everybody's Broken

didn't help. He tried. I know, but ..." Shane pointed to his head. "Dad had his own problems, and even if he'd been perfect, I suspect Randa's broken heart over her father's death still wouldn't have mended."

"Do you sometimes worry about inheriting your dad's depression?"

Shane shook his head. "I resolved that with the Lord. When I drank, I had an idea of the demons Dad faced. If he'd stopped drinking and placed his trust in the Lord, he'd have fared much better. Dad's depression was something he clung to, as if the murkiness of sadness comforted him. He never realized that the rest of us suffered when he hid away."

A half-laugh lifted his chest a bit and then he settled with a resigned sigh. "He and Mom were complete opposites. Dad had to have been drawn to her light like Mothman to the Silver Bridge."

Abra laughed. "What?"

"Mothman ..." He shook his head. "Look it up on the Internet. It's one of the scary tales of the Appalachians, a myth blamed for a horrible tragedy. Mom made Dad happy. Dad's problems kept him from really earning much, but when he was up, he was high and mighty, and it seemed he and Mom were perfect for each other. But Dad's balloon would leak air every time he drank, and Mom would still be climbing high into the atmosphere. I know his distress had to bother her, but she never let on."

Sometimes Abra would find Beau staring out the window of their home especially after Pap's death. He seemed far away in a world of gloom, and Abra had worried over him each time. "How do you think your mom remained happy?"

Shane turned and leaned his back against the fence.

Abra remained facing the playground.

"I think she let Jesus carry all her burdens." He stared beyond her to the street. "I understand that we're to have joy in our hearts as Christians, but I think sometimes that joy, when looked at by someone who simply needs understanding, can hurt." He cleared his throat. "Your friend, Mazzie, now, I think she would understand what I'm trying to say. She was there for you—for all of us really. She cried when you weren't looking, but she took great pains to say things to bring a smile to your face, but then when you needed to cry, she gave you that shoulder."

Boy, he'd sure had his eyes on Mazzie for the few days he'd met her. Finn wouldn't like that. Her always friendly brother was fiercely protective when it came to his lady love.

"Perhaps if Mom had cried with Dad a bit, he might still be here." He pushed off the fence.

The bell rang before Abra could respond. Randa's sad face flashed across Abra's memory.

Did Randa need someone to cry with? Dalton never seemed at a loss for a joke, but the couple tiptoed around something—an invisible wall that separated them as surely as Beau's death separated them from him.

Taffy ran to her father. Shane bent down and kissed her cheek, but he grasped Taffy's hand. "Give me a sec. I need to speak to Taffy's teacher." He reached out his coffee cup to her, and Abra held it.

Peter and Paulie beelined directly toward their classroom.

Abra shrugged. "So much for that."

She waited while Shane pulled the teacher aside. The two entered into what appeared to be a serious conversation. When Shane nodded, he returned to Abra, slipping his arm around her shoulder. With his free hand, he took back his cup.

"The boys hightailed it to class. Didn't even look back." She stared at her tennis shoes.

"Ah, that's why you're pouting." He tweaked her chin. "That's the nature of the little beasties. You still

Everybody's Broken

look tired. How about a coffee at Manna from Heaven?" He looked at his watch. "I suspect the owner, Agatha, hasn't made it in yet, so the help might be in good moods when we arrive."

"I like Agatha." Abra pulled back from him. "She's different."

Shane made a noise with his lips then he nodded. "She's mellowed, I'll admit. You had to know her back when. Meaner than a rattlesnake that's made its bed with a party of fire ants."

"Well, that would be very mean, I suppose."

"Mouthier than a moccasin."

"The shoe or the snake?"

"Cottonmouth ... get it? Rattlesnake ... moccasin?"

"Yeah, I got it before you asked." She smirked.

They arrived at their cars. When Shane stepped away, the warmth he'd brought to the cool autumn morning slithered away with him. "Meet you at Manna?" He opened her door.

"Sure." She slipped into her car. "Sounds good."

Much better than the nap she'd planned to take.

Shane stared into the display case of goodies the coffee shop and bakery had to offer. Beside him in line, Abra seemed not to notice the looks being cast their way.

From the moment Abra arrived in Amazing Grace, the town buzzed with the news, and the town he loved had embraced Beau's widow with open arms.

They might whisper behind the family's back, speculating about the amount of time Abra spent with him, but that was life in the little burg. At some point, everyone became a topic of gossip.

Abra rocked from side to side, her fingers pressed

against her lips as she stared at the pastries. Randa had mentioned Beau had given Abra the habit, asking her to watch what she said by touching her lips first.

Perhaps if he'd done as Beau suggested, Shane might have avoided nearly spilling all of his secrets. He couldn't continue to make those mistakes, but the more he tried to stay away, the more he was drawn to her, and Taffy sure loved Peter and Paulie.

He loved them, too.

Abra inched closer to him. "Do I have something on my face?"

So, she had noticed the piercing stares, and that explained the fingers to her mouth.

"It's much worse than that." He tilted his head and looked about them then leaned back to her. "You're standing beside me."

"And that's a problem for these people, how?"

"They have questions they're afraid to ask."

"Or anticipating answers so their speculation can spin off in all kinds of directions."

"Yep." He straightened.

"We need to invite Mazzie for a visit."

He laughed at the thought of Abra's audacious friend coming to town.

Abra stepped back, staring at him. "You like her, don't you?"

"What?" He raised his brows. "What's not to like? She's beautiful, funny, and she could put anyone in their place with Southern class that would leave them thinking they'd been blessed when they were cursed."

Mazzie also loved Abra and wanted to protect her.

And so did he—protect Abra, that is.

"I've never heard you laugh that freely." She smiled. "The smile that comes with it is pretty nice, too."

He fought to get a handle on his emotions. "If Mazzie came to town, wives would lock their husbands away until she left."

"So, do I detect a little interest?" Abra stepped closer to the counter. "If so, I have to warn you that Mazzie and ..."

"I'm not interested in her," Shane said maybe a little too abruptly, but he had to stop Abra's vivid imagination. He couldn't have her thinking he was interested in her friend when he was in ...

No. He couldn't have her thinking that. "Mazzie intrigues me because I've never met a woman who seems to have stepped right out of the 1950's South. She wears it with all the coolness of a Hollywood star."

"I wish you'd met Finn." Abra said as they made their way in line to the display case.

"I hope I have the chance to meet him." Shane pointed to the case. "This one's on me. Whatever you want."

"I'll have an eclair and a cup of coffee." She looked around at the tables filling quickly and turned to face him, mischief in her eyes. "I'll get us a seat, sweetheart."

Murmurs wound through the line behind them, and Shane smiled.

Yeah, he liked this woman much more than the one Abra thought interested him.

His order complete, he took their tray, complete with several creamers and sugar for Abra, who sat in a booth by the window, her gaze trained in the direction of the empty storefront across the street. "Do you have to open the store?" she asked as he sat.

"That's Randa's job today. I have a few projects to finish."

"Have I thanked you for letting the boys help with some of your projects? Traipsing through the woods with you and Taffy has been good for them."

"For us, too." He took a bite of his frosted donut and wiped his mouth. "At first, I had to be stern with them.

They had no idea what we were doing. Taffy and I see wildlife all the time, but watching their awe allowed me to get the excitement back when spotting deer or elk. The first time they saw Bumblebee, I thought Peter would try to give her a hug."

"They're pretty secretive about Bumblebee. What is this creature, a rabbit or something?" She took a drink.

"Bumblebee's a bear."

Abra coughed out her coffee.

Shane used his napkin to wipe his face.

"You're out there finding bears?"

"Filming them." Shane swiped the napkin down the front of his cream-colored sweater dotted with darker brown spots.

"But they could hurt one of the children …"

"Yes, they could, but I'm not stupid, Abra." He wiped a little coffee from his sleeve. "We never get so close that I don't have two maybe three shots to stop a charge. I have a great telephoto lens. And Bumblebee's used to seeing us. She takes great pride in pretending we're not around. If I didn't know better, I'd think she performs on cue and might really like the boys."

"What about cubs? Won't she attack to protect them?"

He was at risk of losing Taffy's new partners in adventure, or he'd tease her about teaching them to drop down and lay motionless. "Do you think I'd risk Taffy's life? Bumblebee's a gentle soul, not that I'd ever forget she's a dangerous animal. I haven't seen her with cubs for a long while. Might be why she's taken with the boys."

She raised her fingers to her lips and didn't speak for a long time. Then she shook her head and lowered her hand. "But neither would Beau and look what happened."

He chose to ignore her. He could blame his cousin for a lot of things, and no matter the threat he received, Shane could never see Beau intentionally putting Abra, their boys, or Abra's brother in harm's way. "You don't have to do that with us, you know?" He stared out the window as he spoke. "Beau could be an idiot sometimes."

"What don't I have to do?"

"Hesitate before you speak." He turned back to her.

Her cheeks reddened, and she turned her focus to the world outside the bakery. Her eyes glistened, but no tears fell.

He pretended that his dark coffee held more interest than her discomfort. "I'm sorry, Abra. I mentioned your hesitation and your habit to Randa. She didn't mean to gossip. She only meant to explain it to me. I don't think she thought of it as giving away a confidence."

"And I never meant to make Beau sound like an ogre." She took another drink and kept her gaze on the world beyond them. "He wasn't, you know."

"I know. He could be tough but never without a touch of love. My house—"

"I love your house."

"He was tough on me, and I had no idea at the time that he was praying I'd wise up because he had plans for the place." Shane swiped at his eyes. "I'll never forget the day he handed me the deed to the land his father left him—acres and acres of prime wilderness—and the keys to the watermill, he'd helped me shape into a home. Beau said I'd turned a rough patch into a legacy, and he loved me."

Abra closed her eyes and a single tear slid from beneath her long lashes.

"Don't cry for me, Abra. I love Beau, but sometimes I'm as angry at him as I had been while I slammed the hammer against every nail that went into those renovations."

She nodded and more tears fell.

"I cry for you." He reached across and touched her hand. "He loved you. I never saw you together, but I know that much."

She wiped the sleeve of her sweater across her face. "How?"

"He stayed with you, and he was raising those boys. He wouldn't have done it short of loving each of you more than anything in the world."

"Shane, why did he leave here? It's lovely. The only person he knew in Bodacious Cove before he arrived was Finn."

Shane shrugged. He should tell her what he thought, but shame stopped him.

"I can't believe the accusation by the prostitute would make him leave. Beau was proud, but the need to clear his reputation would have made him stay. Don't you think?"

"I didn't learn about the accusation until after he left. As I understand it, Sheriff Dixon placed him on administrative leave. I left town for an event, and when I returned, Beau was gone. No one knew where. Randa was devastated. I was, too."

And with the call last night, Beau was back to haunt him.

"Can I ask you something?"

"Anything," he assured.

"Did you ever stay overnight in your Grandmere's house?"

"Often. When Mom and Dad would go on little getaways when I was younger, and I stayed with her when she wasn't able to get around as well." Heat rose from his neck into his face. Half the time, he might have been high or drunk—or both—but he took care of his grandmother.

"While you were there, did you hear someone moving around as if they're in the house, but they can't be?"

He shook his head. "Why?"

Abra looked down at her untouched eclair. "Last

night while I was in the shower, the bathroom door opened. I thought one of the boys needed me. I called, but they didn't answer."

He smiled. "Did you turn on the heat before your shower?"

"Yes." She leaned back.

"When the air kicks on, the doors open if they aren't tightly closed. Grandmere used to laugh about the shower door and say Grandpere was taking a peek at her the way he used to do." He smiled at the memory and his "Too much information, Grandmere," that caused his grandmother to laugh.

"That might explain the bathroom ..."

"But ...?" A pit of fear began to open up, shattering the little bit of peace he'd began to recover by simply being with her.

She inhaled and seemed to hold her breath for a moment. "When I was getting out of the shower, I could see into the bedroom." The words rushed from her with her breath. "You're going to tell me I'm crazy."

"No," he said.

Abra peered out the window once again. "In the mirror's reflection, I saw a shadow move in my room."

"A shadow?"

"Fleeting but there. I thought at first it could be my imagination. Then I heard the fifth stair creak. I was terrified. Couldn't check on the boys fast enough. Their door wasn't ajar. It was wide open, and I know I closed it when I left their room." She glanced at him and swallowed hard before she spoke. "It scares me to death to think that someone could have been in their room, standing over them while I was so close."

He touched her hand but waited for her to continue.

"Then it sounded as if someone bumped furniture downstairs. I hurried after them. That's when I heard a door close."

Shane envisioned the home's three entryways. "Front door, solarium, or kitchen?"

"Neither. I could see the front door, and ..." She graced her perfect lips with trembling fingertips then lowered them "... sometimes, I've thought I could see someone on the other side of the fence and hedges by the garage. When I looked again, though, they were gone. I can't get rid of the feeling we're being watched. I lowered the solarium's electronic shades, and when we headed upstairs for their story, I locked the French doors. They were closed and still locked, and I was closer to them."

"The kitchen door. Did you remember to lock it?"

Her eyes widened then narrowed. "I didn't check, but I'm sure I did. Besides, the sound I heard came from the library. I went in. I turned on the lights ..." She sighed, and the wariness he'd fail to recognize earlier became all too obvious.

"I can see you're uneasy."

"There's more," she whispered. Then she straightened, as if summoning strength from deep within. Maybe because of fear or because she needed courage to face what she thought would be his lack of belief.

"Abra, I'm listening. I believe you." In fact, he had a ghost story himself. But he couldn't tell her.

"I haven't gone into the library much, but I did rearrange the furniture recently. I usually stand in the doorway and look inside, but ..." she cast her gaze downward "... the library, until last night, was a painful place for me."

"Beau." The word was a statement and not a question.

Abra nodded. "Last night, after I heard the noise, I turned on the light and went inside. The ladder was moved."

"I noticed you'd moved the sofa ..."

A smile tweaked her lips. "Settee, Shane. A

wheelback. A valuable antique, but yes, it had been bumped. The floor is scratched, lamps not in place, and the ladder was not where I'd centered it."

"And the boys couldn't have played in there?"

Her shoulders lowered a little. "I thought of that, but I don't know when they'd have had time to get in there. We were together all afternoon."

"Maybe they played inside the day before or a couple of days ago. I hope you haven't forbidden them to go into that room. Grandmere wouldn't have that when we were children. Her library was our playground. Beau and I spent a lot of time there. He read. I played the piano."

Abra nodded. "Beau loved to read." Again, the fingers went to her lips, and she seemed hesitant to speak.

"What is it?"

She lowered her hand. "I'd consider the kitchen door and even the kids in the library, but when I returned upstairs to my room, trying to convince myself that my imagination had gotten the best of me, the noises started."

"Like what?"

"Movement. Someone is moving around inside that house at night. And I've heard a man talking."

"One man?"

"One voice. Angry one minute, the next not so mad, as if he's carrying on a conversation with someone who might be speaking too low for me to hear."

"From the first floor?"

She picked at the eclair then took a bite. "That's what's so crazy. There's no way anyone is downstairs, but the noises are from inside the house."

Shane remained quiet as she finished her pastry, wiped her mouth with her napkin, and sat back in her chair, hands folded in her lap.

He stood and tossed their garbage in the nearby receptacle while Abra rambled through her purse. When Shane returned to the table, she was still plundering.

Shane stared out the window.

Across the street, Jeb rolled a cart behind him. He paused a moment and looked into the empty storefront and then proceeded into the artist's shop next door. In less than a moment, the man began to tape grocers' paper to the window. His gaze drifted Shane's way, and Shane raised his hand.

Jeb nodded.

Abra looked up, triumphantly holding a tube of lip balm. She caught Shane's gesture and looked through the window and across the street.

Jeb ducked back down, and another layer of brown paper hid him from view.

"The window dresser?" Abra asked.

"Yep. He's got a lot of work ahead of him. Don't you go bothering him."

"Aw, I'd love to meet him. I worked as a window dresser for some mall stores when I was in school in New Orleans."

"That's right. You didn't go to Georgia. You'd have met Dalton there most likely since he and Beau were friends."

"Tulane. Majored in art studies, got sidetracked by interior design because Finn had such a love for it."

"You two were pretty close, huh?"

"Born almost exactly a year apart. Always together, except for college. I'm feeling lost without him." She opened the lip balm and ran it across her perfect lips. "I'm not used to the cold. My lips are chapping."

"Drink lots of water and use lots of balm," he advised. "Are you ready?"

"Sure." She stood. "Thank you for the reprieve."

"You're not done with me yet." He motioned her to move in front of him. "Let's go ghost hunting."

Everybody's Broken

Shane stared out Randa's dining room window at the kids clamoring around the swing set on the other side of the gate. Taffy's friend from across the street had joined the trio. They'd been playing since Shane had picked them up from school, and Shane hadn't taken his eyes off them unless they ran inside Abra's home.

Dalton left shortly after dinner to work on research for an important upcoming hearing.

Randa moved to the window beside Shane, handing him a cup of warm tea. "Something's bothering you."

"Something's been bothering you for a lot longer," he countered.

She didn't have a comeback.

He let it rest. "I went through Grandmere's house today with Abra. We turned it upside down."

"Looking for the sounds she's hearing, I reckon."

The sky outside was darkening much like the mood in this room. Shane wanted Abra and the boys locked inside before the black night settled over Amazing Grace.

"Did you solve Abra's mystery?"

He put his tea on the table and faced her. "Noises at night aren't Abra's only fear. She's seen a person lurking around the garage, and she has me convinced someone was inside the house last night."

Randa stared up at him. "I humored her when we talked about the noises, but that old house creaks and moans. That's why I was glad Beau inherited the thing. If I believed in ghosts, I'd say Grandmere's roaming."

"But we don't believe in ghosts. Abra says the noises are consistent. And I can't explain away a shadow in her bedroom."

Randa shrugged. "An overactive imagination. She's the creative type. If the two of you got together, you'd

141

have the place haunted by everyone from Grandmere, Grandpere, Mom, Dad, your parents, even Beau and Jasmine."

He jerked his gaze to her.

"Don't get all wide-eyed on me. I figured it out that night Abra mentioned Taffy's mother committed suicide."

Shane peered outside. He'd have to call the kids inside soon and make sure her friend got home. "What did you figure out?"

"Shane, he left her. I don't condone what you did, but Beau had no right to complain if you dated his girlfriend. Even if you did the wrong thing by sleeping with her, at least she could count on you to take care of her child."

"My child," he corrected. "Taffy is my daughter, not just Jasmine's." He'd rather hurt her with lies than to tell her the truth: Beau had left Jasmine in his wake, too. He'd never looked back, and Jasmine had blamed herself.

Shane took a deep and steadying breath. If Beau could leave Jasmine without thought, the fact that he hid in the shadows making threats couldn't be too far beyond reality. This had to be a side he'd kept hidden from them. Could the claims made against him by the town's prostitute be true? Perhaps he'd been the one to kill Abra's father. Life may have been about to unravel for him in Florida, so he staged his death, perhaps Finn was the one laying dead in the uniform. Maybe someone had helped Beau stage the picture Abra claimed to have seen.

That would also explain the boys' silence. How fearful would it be to know your father was a liar and a murderer?

"Well, there's no wonder Abra's imagination is working overtime," Randa's continued conversation broke into Shane's fears. "Beau didn't die peacefully." She stood, turned away from him, and wiped her eyes. "He was an honorable man. I should have realized that, even with the accusations. He didn't do what Magda said.

We all grew up with her in this town, for goodness' sake."

Shane closed his eyes and took a deep breath, glad he'd kept his wandering thoughts to himself. He'd let Beau destroy Randa's heart. He wouldn't take Randa's misguided truth and mold them into the lies that they were. He'd let her mourn the brother she'd thought she lost. Randa would learn the truth if and when Beau decided to let them all in on his twisted game.

Shane moved to the back door and opened it. "Boys, time to go in. Taffy, you and Melissa come on over. We need to walk her home."

He shut the door against the complaining and watched as the kids said good-bye to one another. "Why don't you tell me what's going on between you and Dalton?"

"Nothing's going on." She turned back to him. Her face was strained, and she fought back tears. "We'll be fine." She cut her gaze to the opening door.

"Aunt Randa, can Melissa and me spend the night with you and Uncle Dalton this weekend so we can play with Peter and Paulie?" Taffy jumped up and down.

Randa fell back as if Taffy had punched her. "No, honey, not this weekend. Maybe some other time. I—I have to get up and go to work. This Saturday morning, we reveal the windows, and your daddy will need help getting ready to perform. Abra mentioned decorating on Saturday. I'm sure you'll be a part of that."

Randa only rambled when she wanted to avoid the truth.

Taffy leaned against Shane's leg.

Randa bent down, cup still in hand, and stared into Taffy's face, where the pain was so evident Shane winced. "I'm sure Melissa can help us, too."

Taffy's smile returned, and the girls squealed.

"Let's walk Melissa across the street." He started out the front door, the girls in front of him. When the younger ones were out of earshot, he turned, pointing a finger at Randa. "You and Dalton are entitled to your secrets, and you can distance yourself from us and hurt her feelings—Taffy will get over it—but if her being Jasmine's daughter is the reason, I won't stand for it."

Tears pooled in Randa's eyes. "That's not the reason, Shane."

The kids reached the edge of the sidewalk. "You all wait right there," he warned before giving Randa his attention. "Then what?" he asked.

The tears ran down her face. "You made mistakes, too, Shane. Why is God punishing me?"

"Why do you think God's punishing you?"

"My mistakes. The ones I made in high school ... before Dalton ... God is making me pay. You slept with a woman; she had your child, and you have that child ..." Randa trembled now. "Jasmine had you, and she did the right thing. I—"

Shane reached to hug her.

She held up her hand. "No!"

"Randa, tell me. What's going on?"

"The doctor isn't sure I can have children, Shane. Dalton and I aren't going to have the family we wanted, and it's my fault. God's punishing Dalton for what I did."

"Oh, honey—" He's started to break down her invisible barricade and wrap his arms around her, but Randa slammed the door. The lock turned.

He'd been shut out.

"Daddy!" Taffy called.

At least she hadn't noticed. He made his way to the curb, led the girls across the street, and knocked on Melissa's door.

"Well, you're finally home," Melissa's mother teased.

"'Night, Taffy." Melissa squeezed through the door.

"Thank you for letting her join them. She's been

Everybody's Broken

hearing them play almost every evening. I've been meaning to introduce myself to Mr. and Mrs. Carmichael, but time gets away from me."

Shane wrinkled his brow and tugged his hat. Surely, with the gossip in this town, everyone knew Abra was Beau's widow. Tammy Colbert and her husband, Fred, had lived here for a couple of years. They weren't nosy neighbors, or so Dalton and Randa indicated. Fred worked himself to death as a real estate broker, and Tammy was a stay-at-home mom. Maybe they chose not to listen to rumors. "Abra was married to my cousin, Beau. He died in Florida several months back."

Tammy's gaze roamed across the street. "But he said …"

"Who?" Shane turned to look.

"I met him once about a year ago. Nice guy. I'm talking about the man I see leaving the house—well, the garage. I introduced myself to him way back. He said he was Beau Carmichael, and he owned the house. I didn't think much about it. I knew the house had been empty since we moved here. Fred had a client interested in the place, and when I told him Mr. Carmichael was home, he tried to catch him to see if he was interested in selling because he had someone interested in buying the place. We didn't see him again. Then when the little boys arrived, I assumed they were his sons."

Had Beau returned to Amazing Grace to check on the house without telling anyone? Maybe he hadn't been able to slip away as smoothly as he thought he could. He'd met Tammy, who was a new neighbor since Beau's departure. "That might have been Beau. Maybe he returned to town, and we missed him."

Tammy shook her head. "The Mr. Carmichael I met isn't dead. I saw him again two weeks ago."

Shane tensed and squeezed his daughter's hand. She wiggled free then slipped her touch back into his. He cast a wary glance toward Taffy.

Tammy gave him a nod of understanding. "I need to get Melissa ready for bed. Maybe we can talk some other time."

Shane took a deep breath. "Definitely. You have a good evening."

Taffy clung to his hand as they walked to the car. Frightened green eyes stared up at him. "Daddy, aren't we going to tell Abra about the man?"

"Not right now, and we don't have anything to worry about." He wanted his daughter to have peaceful dreams tonight, no fear of a stranger. He also didn't want to alarm Abra to the fact that her husband might be planning to pull them both into a nightmare.

If he could talk to Beau, maybe he could convince him to turn himself in. Abra would probably stand by her man, see him through the legal process, hospitalization, imprisonment, or whatever would come Beau's way.

Shane never thought he'd fear the man who'd saved his life, but right now, talking to a seemingly psychotic Beau scared him witless.

"Peter says there's someone watching them."

Again, Shane wrapped his hand a little too tightly around his daughter's.

"Ouch," she wiggled her fingers. "He said someone handed him a note through the bushes."

"Who? What did the note say? Did Peter tell you?"

Taffy shook her head. "Not even when Paulie and me called him a liar."

Shane started around the front of his car but stopped. He bent down on his knees and looked her square in the eyes. "You never say that about anyone again. Do you know how ugly that word is?"

She shook her head. Tears sprang to her eyes.

Great. Now, all he needed was Abra in tears, and he'd have every woman in his life hysterical. And all

Everybody's Broken

because the weight of his deceits was pressing down hard upon him.

"Honey, lying is so bad that the Bible says God hates it. So, when you accuse Peter of being one, you're saying he's doing something God hates. What if he's telling the truth? How would you feel?"

She sniffed. "Like I do now." She wrapped her arms around his neck. "I'm sorry, Daddy. I'll tell Peter I believe him."

Shane closed his eyes and buried his face in her thick sandy blond locks. What a hypocrite he was. Shaming her for wanting the truth while failing to give it to her and to everyone else he cared about while their lives crumbled in around them. "I love you, Taffeta, with all my heart."

"I love you, Daddy."

He stood to help her into the car. A movement in the upstairs window of The Gray Lady caught his attention. Abra stood in her bedroom. She lifted her left hand in good-bye. Her right hand she wiped across her eyes.

Great.

The gals in his life were all hurting—and he had no courage for the truth.

The coward's life was no way to live. He needed to pray and ask God to forgive him and to help him tell his family everything including the fact that Beau, the man they once knew and loved, was dead, but a new and very ugly and scary man had been resurrected.

Not that they would believe him.

Abra straightened and leaned back with her hands pressed to the small of her back. She looked at the clock and widened her eyes.

She'd been so engrossed in painting her surprises for

Saturday's decorating, that she'd lost all track of time.

And upstairs was entirely too quiet. She left the nook and headed that way.

Peter and Paulie had taken their baths as she'd asked and were dressed in their PJs, both sleeping soundly on top of their covers. She pulled the blankets from underneath and tucked them each in, kissing one then the other on their foreheads. "'Night, precious boys," she whispered as she walked out of their room.

On the upstairs landing she halted, listening.

Nothing. All was quiet. No voices. No movement.

Downstairs, she stared at her work. This was what she was born to do, even if only for her sons to have autumn decorations in a real autumn setting or for a church harvest festival. She capped her paints and carefully took each of the four cloths she'd used for her surprise into the laundry room—a place the boys avoided like the plague.

With the brushes cleaned and everything put away, she settled at the table where she'd been working. She looked longingly through the locked French doors to the closed up and shaded solarium.

Things had been quiet, but she'd been sure someone watched her and the boys as they ate. With darkness falling, she took no chances that anyone could see or get inside.

Unearthing a good read from Grandmere's library tempted her, but fear held her in place. Earlier, she'd followed Shane through the house as he searched every corner, checked each window, and even examined the library. They located no seams in the wall, and no drafts lilted through the bookshelves. Shane suggested clearing the shelves, but by that time, he had to leave to pick up the kids from school while she prepared some snacks.

Abra looked around her for something of interest. Three packages sat on the nook's desk: the two she'd received days before and one Shane said he'd found sticking out from under her doormat when he returned with the kids. Mazzie had been busy, but Abra had no real compunction to open them. Bodacious Cove was a life she yearned to reclaim. Opening up the packages would make that longing harder to push away.

The people of Bodacious Cove were her family. She'd grown up in their midst. How could she stay away? Besides she was bored here.

Abra had hinted at helping Randa in the store. That had not happened. Even though they'd fallen into a comfortable friendship, over the last few days, Randa grew more aloof. Abra hesitated to breach any imaginary lines Randa had drawn to keep her at a distance.

Abra lowered her head and rested it on her arms, staring at the boxes. In a way, she'd built a wall to keep Mazzie out of this new life. All because she hated the longing that settled deep inside her—like the constant ache she pushed away when she thought of Beau and Finn. At least Mazzie was alive and somewhere reachable.

"Enough, Abra. Grow up. Mazzie's still here." She picked up her cell phone and let it slip down her fingers to the table, holding it there.

The phone vibrated before it rang, and she jumped.

Her nerves were about as frayed as they could be without completely coming undone. She pressed answer without looking at the ID. "Hello?"

"Hey," the voice said. "How is everything?"

Shane? She smiled. "I'm locked in tight. Thank you."

Silence greeted her.

"Are you okay?" she asked.

"I'm fine, Abra. Take care of those boys. You're not as secure as you think."

Beep. Beep. Beep.

Abra stared at her phone. She checked her call list.

Unknown Caller. The number was blocked. Beau had made sure his work phone read that way. As a police officer, he had to be careful.

She sat for a long moment, replaying the familiar cadence in the man's tone. Maybe it hadn't been Shane. Trace Bastion usually called her with updates from the police station. Perhaps he used his work mobile to check up on her. That would explain the familiarity.

Her phone might have dropped the call. That happened in the mountains. Not so much in the wide-open expanse of the beach.

But why would he call her this late?

She stared at the phone, trying to strengthen her lagging desire to remain strong. She missed her home, her husband, her brother, her best friend. And she was very, very afraid.

She perused her contacts and tapped the number.

"Abracadabra!" Mazzie answered. "I was afraid you'd left me behind."

This had been a bad idea. Tears flowed down Abra's cheeks, and she couldn't speak. Mazzie was the only one left who truly knew Abra from the inside out.

"Too cold for you up there?" Mazzie's teasing voice reached deeper into Abra's heart and wrenched more grief and sorrow.

"I want to come home." Abra managed to get the words out without sobbing. She cringed at the little-girl whine in her voice. "Has it been quiet there? No new problems."

Mazzie didn't answer.

"No new problems?" Abra pressed.

"If I tell you there hasn't been, you'll pack up and move back here." Mazzie's Southern sass lightened Abra's heart.

"Actually, no, smarty pants." Abra wiped her tears. "The boys enjoy school, and unlike their mother, they love the cold weather. We're staying at least until the end of the school year."

"That a girl," Mazzie uttered a half-hearted cheer.

Abra wiped her tears. "You didn't answer my question. Any problems?"

"Someone broke into Finn's place a couple days ago. We didn't find anything missing. Trace says you shouldn't let your guard down."

"Trace, is it?" Abra's ears perked at the almost congenial sound of the once-hated detective's first name.

"I've decided he's not that bad. He didn't claim Finn had burglarized his own home and seemed genuinely sad to think we may never see Finn again."

Mazzie was giving up on Finn, and deep down Abra wished she could do the same. "He's a good guy. Beau always told me he was a topnotch cop. Are you thinking of moving on?" Abra clenched her hand so hard around the phone that she thought it would crumble.

"I'm moving on as much as I can."

Abra blinked at the curtness in Mazzie's tone.

"Just like you've done. Have you looked at another man since Beau's death?"

"I—"

"I don't think so," Mazzie snapped. "Heaven is the only place Finn will be shed of me. For a while, at least."

Abra half-laughed, half-cried. "I wish you could be here."

"Well, invite me." The tease was back in Mazzie's sass. "I haven't missed one of your birthday parties since we were born. Tell me when and where, and I'll be there, costume ready."

"No." The single word fell from Abra's lips. "This is the first year without Pap, and he's the only one who could pull out a costume party and say, 'But you know, this isn't a celebration of that pagan holiday.'" It's a—"

"Celebration of my daughter, Abracadabra's

birthday." Mazzie's laughter rang across the miles. "How I miss that dear enigma."

"You could leave the costume behind and be here."

"Oh, I don't know. What's your birthday without a party? It'd be me and you sitting around crying over everything we've lost."

"But the boys would love to see you. Shane said he'd love to see your style turn this little town upside down."

"Did he now?"

"It is pretty up here despite the cold."

"Well, you've given me some time to make plans. I'll let you know next week. What have you decided to do with the business or the building?"

Abra shrugged as if Mazzie could see her. "There's an empty storefront here."

"Seriously. You're going to open a firm there?" The decibels in Mazzie's voice climbed as she spoke.

"You do love me," Abra teased. "I wasn't thinking of a firm. I want to sell furniture and accessories and offer decorating ideas to customers who have trouble imagining the magic they can bring to a home."

Silence reigned between them for a long moment before Mazzie cleared her throat. "Then do it. Is the space a lease or a purchase?"

Abra laughed. "I don't remember. Whatever it is, I think the real estate agent with the listing lives across the street from me."

"You'll want to lease. See how you do. If the startup makes it, you might want to buy later or relocate."

"I must have learned something from you. The place has three floors, and I thought if I could eventually purchase, I would check on zoning. Someone would pay a pretty penny to lease a loft apartment, or I could keep it commercial space."

"Good. If you get this started, train up your employees, and the business can remain open whether you're here or there, be an extension of the firm. Mountain to beach."

That was Mazzie. She always came up with the good ideas. "You think it would work?"

"What I think, darlin', is that you and Finn have enough expendable cash. You can afford to fail, and if you don't fail, there's no crime in adding to your holdings. By the way, your accounts are all reconciled. You can thank me with a nice big dinner at some fancy mountain restaurant, Ms. Thrifty."

"We learned from Pap," Abra shot back. "And what's in the envelopes and box you sent?"

"Envelopes? I sent one, and it has some correspondence I thought you'd want to see. Customers wishing you well. Some nice notes from the good town folks."

Abra picked up the envelope Shane had brought her. She opened it. Without looking inside, she placed it on the table. "And what did you slip into the box?"

"I didn't send you a box."

"Then who?"

"If you'd open your stuff, you might find out. What is it with you and mail?"

The fact that Mazzie never figured out the reason for her aversion surprised Abra.

She walked into the kitchen for the scissors she kept in her catch-all drawer.

"Open it up, already. I'm dying to see who sent you what?"

"That's the problem." She slipped the scissors along the clear shipping tape. "No one has my address but you."

"And Shane and Randa and Dalton and probably several others. You've been hold up there for a gazillion years."

Abra laughed aloud. "Six months doth not a gazillion make."

"In Mazzie and Abra time it does. We've never been apart. Why do you think I turned down Harvard and went to old Tulane?"

"You did not do that because you wanted to be with me," Abra countered. "You said you didn't want to go to some highflautin' school where they couldn't say their r's. I remember because Pap reminded you that you've never ended a word with 'ing' in your life because you don't use the 'g,' and he thought Harvard could teach you to do that."

"That crazy old coot." Mazzie's voice filled with love. "He would have paid Harvard tuition for me, but I couldn't bear being separated from you and that far away from Finn. At least, we could see each other sometimes."

"I've abandoned you," Abra's whispered words sprang from the depth of her being. "I need to be home with you. We need to go through this together."

Mazzie sniffed. "You need to be there and safe. I'll be there for your birthday. I promise. We've never missed being together on our special days, and I'm not starting that now, but it's too dangerous for you here."

Abra pinched her lips together. Mazzie thought Pap's death wasn't an accident. The conspiracy theory sickened Abra.

"So what's in the box and the envelope?" Mazzie asked.

Whatever the gift, the sender had wrapped it in clear bubble wrap. Using the scissors, she pushed the edge against more wrapping tape and slid into the popping plastic.

Three Georgia Bulldog keychains fell upon the table. Abra picked up the first. *Hi-Jinx* was etched into the gold on the back of the first, *Helium* on the second. She picked up the last with trembling fingers and dropped it. "Hillbilly. It says *Hillbilly*." She paced away from the table and back. "One is Beau's. The other belongs to

Finn."

"What are you talking about?"

Abra reached for the opened envelope and shook it so that whatever was inside would fall out. A photo. She turned it over and pulled back as if burned. She didn't think anything could be as bad as the picture of Beau's murder. Her hands shook as she picked up the photograph: a young, auburn-haired woman dangled from a noose on a rope tied around a ceiling beam. Beautiful snow covered mountains visible through the large glass panes outside the room stood in stark contrast to the grayish color of the woman's skin and her hazel eyes opened wide. Eeriest of all was the contented smile on the woman's face.

This had to be a prank.

"Are you going to tell me what's going on, or do I hang up and call Dalton?"

Abra turned over the photograph. *Jasmine Roy also took away something I wanted badly. Don't think you can keep me from what I want.*

Abra gasped and dropped the phone.

Mazzie's muffled voice brought her out of her shock. She bent and picked up the phone. "Mazzie," she whispered. "What was the name of the woman Trace said was Shane's daughter's mother?"

"I don't remember. Why?"

Abra bent to her knees, folding herself over and clutching her hair. This couldn't be happening.

She straightened, stood, and faced the locked French doors and the solarium beyond. "I think the killer is here."

Chapter 10

Abra paced in the lobby of the sheriff's department, clutching the box. The back door opened and closed. The deputy at the front desk shot up from his seat. He followed a middle-aged man dressed in blue-jeans and a tan uniform shirt into a glass encased office. The deputy turned to look at her.

The man scooted around the deputy. "Mrs. Carmichael." He held out his hand. "I'm sorry I haven't gotten around to saying hello or giving you my heartfelt condolences."

Abra stared at the nametag on the man's shirt, looking for the right words to say.

"I'm Sheriff Daniel Dixon. Beau used to work for me. A very good deputy and an honorable man. I was sorry to hear about his death and even sorrier I got notice too late to attend his funeral."

The fog cleared, and she frowned. "You weren't called right away?"

The sheriff shook his head. "I barely had time to let

the family know. The chief apologized. He said he'd told Beau's partner to call."

Two weeks between Beau's death and his burial and the one man who may have known how to contact anyone out of state for Beau had failed to do so. One more indiscretion to add to her pile of anger toward Loyal Herman. Mazzie for Mayor.

She pushed the thoughts away. "I understand Beau left here due to an accusation against him."

Sheriff Dixon moved aside and motioned her into the office. "We took the appropriate steps to clear Beau and our department's reputation. The woman confessed she'd been paid to lie, but she refused to divulge her benefactor. Her retraction came too late. Beau had already left."

"You knew where Beau had gone?"

The sheriff nodded. "I believed in him, and assured him I'd give a good reference. He took me up on the offer."

Abra took a seat and waited for him to sit. The sheriff leaned forward, hands clasped on his desk. "My deputy says you asked to see me."

She placed the box on his desk, keeping her hand over the lid. "I thought this came from my friend since it arrived with another package. I opened it last night along with this." She dug into her overlarge purse and pulled out the envelope Shane had given to her. She kept her hands pressed down on both. "I have handled the items. I didn't realize what they were." She lifted her gaze. "Sheriff, who is Jasmine Roy?"

There. She saw what she expected from him.

Discomfort.

"Beau never told you about Jasmine?"

Abra shook her head. "But I've heard her name."

"What do you have for me?" He reached across the desk.

Abra pulled back. "I don't mean to be rude, but I

asked a question."

The man leaned back in his chair. "Mrs. Carmichael—"

"Call me Abra."

He took a deep breath. "If Beau wanted you to know, he'd have told you."

"The man I married kept a lot of secrets. I'm trying to deal with them. Please tell me who she was to him."

The sheriff drummed his fingers on the desk—once, twice. Then his unflinching gaze settled on her. "Many of us thought Beau and Jasmine would marry. When Jasmine left town, I assumed she met up with him."

Truth shredded Abra's fairytale love apart one new revelation at a time. What a love-lost creature she had been.

Her breath quivered as she fought to hold in the bitter emotions swirling around her. She lowered her head and gathered the strength she would need. "My husband, my brother, Dalton Rylander, and Jasmine gave each other nicknames. They called themselves the Four H Club or some such. Each member had a University of Georgia keychain with a nickname inscribed on the back. I received three of those keychains in this package. Yesterday, Shane Browne said he found this envelope on my porch. There's a photograph inside." She slid everything toward the sheriff.

He kept his gaze on her for a moment. Then he opened the box and peered inside. Again, his gaze shot to her. "You're the only one who's touched these?"

She nodded. "Yes."

As if not believing her, Dixon closed the flap with the tip of his index finger. "No return address?"

"Like I said, my friend sent me an entirely different envelope containing some of my mail received in Florida. I assumed she'd forgotten to place something inside the box and sent the envelope separately. This envelope arrived yesterday, and I opened all three last night."

The sheriff left her without a word. Before he turned the corner, he stopped to speak to the deputy tending the front desk. He angled and kept an eye on her. Abra turned away, hands on her lap. She'd been married to an officer. Dixon wanted the man to watch her.

A moment later, Dixon muttered something to someone. He re-entered his office wearing latex gloves.

Sitting, he pulled out each of the keychains, holding them one by one via the empty ring before placing them on his desk with the inscription upward. Then he picked up the envelope and allowed the photograph to slide out. He whispered a curse and then apologized to the Lord and to Abra.

"I'm sorry. I should have warned you."

He nodded and turned the photo over again to read the note on the back. "This is why you asked who she was?" He turned his piercing gaze upon her.

She placed her fingertips at her lips then moved them away. "I heard her name once—after Shane Browne was implicated in Beau's murder. Is that the woman Beau lo— was involved with before I met him?"

"Yes, it is." Sheriff Dixon didn't hesitate.

"That is not a crime scene photograph."

The man examined the photo. "I think not."

Abra stood. Everything within her told her to give the evidence to the authorities, so why did it feel like a betrayal? "That picture came to me here. Shane said he found it on my porch. He knew where Jasmine lived when no one else did. He says he lost contact with her after he brought their child home to raise."

"Do you believe Shane Browne murdered Jasmine Roy?" The man's voice was strong, yet gentle.

"I do not." She spoke each word with conviction. "But I came here for my boys to be safe. These were sent to me here. We're no longer safe."

"Will you give me a chance to get to the bottom of this?"

Abra sunk back into the chair. "I think you should know that the night before I arrived here with Beau's family, a similar type of picture was plastered to my kitchen window for me to see."

"Go on."

"The picture, from the scene of Beau's murder, was not a police photo." She reached across the desk and touched the photo. "Coincidence?"

"Describe the photo you saw that night."

"Beau was dead, on the ground. My brother, Finn, was slumped against the steering wheel. There was blood inside Finn's truck. The boys had his blood splattered on their skin."

"Your boys were mostly unharmed. I know."

"Yes, that's right."

"And Finn's truck was never found."

Abra nodded. "No sign of the truck or Finn. Before Beau's funeral my friend found the boys on her porch cleaned and dressed as if whoever had taken them expected them to attend the burial."

"Have they said by whom?"

Mazzie's sad face danced in Abra's memory. Her declaration that she'd never forgive Abra quieted Abra's angst, and she pulled a close truth out from the depths of her. "We've never gotten a clear indication from either of them. They don't talk to us."

Dixon picked up a pencil. With the eraser end, he moved the three keychains so that she could see them. The point of the eraser went to the first one. "Hillbilly. I know that was Beau." He moved the eraser to the middle keychain. "Helium was Jasmine." The eraser moved to the third.

Abra winced. Why did this one hurt her the most?

"Who is Hi-Jinx?"

"Finn. He and Jasmine must have had a lot in common."

Dixon leaned back in his seat. He gazed toward the outer office.

Abra didn't turn even when he gave a slight shake of his head and held up his hand as if commanding someone to wait.

"Let me ask you a couple more questions."

Abra shifted in her seat. "Anything."

"You said they called themselves the Four H something or other. That would indicate to me that one keychain might be missing. You mentioned Dalton. Is he the fourth?"

"Yes." Abra sat forward. "There were five of them, not four. Dalton and someone else. But I can't remember. The days after Beau's funeral—except having my boys back—are a little out of focus."

"So you don't recall if you've met this other individual?"

"I never knew of or met Dalton, Shane, or Randa before the funeral. I don't think it likely I met this other person."

"A male?"

"As I recall." She nodded toward the keychains. "Finn met Beau and Dalton at the university."

The sheriff leaned forward. "You said Beau kept secrets, but Finn had some, too. Am I right?"

Abra blinked. "There's a difference in Beau and Finn's silence."

"And that would be?"

"Beau purposely never told me about his life here. Finn's silence kept him from betraying a confidence."

"You, Mrs. Carmichael, are either very trusting or you didn't want to know the truth."

Bullseye. And the arrow stung.

"Who are you afraid of here in Amazing Grace?"

Everybody's Broken

Abra startled. Who had her so terrorized? She stood again and turned toward the door, fighting to get air into her lungs. She clutched at her chest. "Sheriff, I don't know."

"Abra, are you okay?"

Abra tensed at Shane's voice. Dixon must have asked the deputy to call him. She dared to look.

He angled into the door and stood behind the chair Abra had vacated. Dalton blocked her exit.

"I'm afraid." If only the fear had fled from her body in the same way her confession had.

"Why? Has something happened?" Shane begged for an answer.

Dalton leaned against the doorjamb without a word.

The sheriff stood. "I'd like the three of you to come with me, please." He pushed past Dalton and headed down the hall.

Abra remained next to Shane, unmoving.

Dalton didn't relinquish his space. "What's going on? Is Shane being taken into custody on a fugitive warrant?" Why did his wording make Abra feel as if she—and maybe Shane—were the victims of a prank?

"Gentleman, Abra, when someone asks you to follow and leads the way, the polite response is to do as asked." Sheriff Dixon stood in the hall. "Counselor …" He nodded to Dalton.

Dalton pushed off the door and led the way. Shane placed his hand at the small of her back, and some of the fear within her recoiled. "I'm sorry. I think I may have caused you more trouble, but …"

He squeezed her shoulder. "I trust you."

She walked into a room that seemed more like a conference room than the interrogation closet of Bodacious Cove. The one-way mirror measuring three times the size of the one in Florida was an indication to Abra that this might not be a leisurely conversation.

Otherwise, they could have talked in the sheriff's office.

Abra's hands trembled as she grasped the arms of the chair and lowered herself into them.

No matter where the evidence pointed, she meant what she'd said to the sheriff. Shane Browne couldn't have killed Jasmine Roy to gain the custody of the daughter he loved so much.

Shane took the chair beside Abra, who had lost all color in her face. Her fingers gripped the chair as if letting go would send her on a roller coaster ride of terror. He slipped his hand over hers. Their coldness seeped into him.

Shane shot a look at Dalton, whose attention rested squarely on the sheriff. The two men were locked in a game. Who would break the silence?

A deputy with gloved hands entered the conference room with a box and an envelope—the same box Shane saw at Abra's house after he secured the envelope from her porch.

With latex-gloved hands, Daniel reached into the box and, one by one, laid out the familiar looking keychain. *Hillbilly, Helium ... Hi-Jinx.*

Shane moved back as if each were a copperhead and threatened to lunge at him.

Beside him, Abra shifted to the far side of her chair.

"Something wrong, Shane?" Daniel cocked a brow.

The slight move of Dalton's hand kept Shane from spilling the questions he longed to ask.

Dalton stood and reached into his pocket. The deputy standing at the end of the table moved his hand toward his holstered gun.

"Stand down, Bill." Daniel chuckled. "You're here

for chain of custody with the evidence. Don't shoot the counselor."

Dalton didn't smile. He did hesitate briefly before pulling his keychain from his pocket and laying it, inscription side up, beside the others.

Handsome.

Daniel pressed his lips together. "Dalt, do you have a bone of humility in you?"

Dalton laughed, and the tension in the air toned down a notch. "Jasmine dubbed me with the name."

"So the nefarious H club has broadened by four known individuals?"

Abra's sharp movement caused Shane to look in her direction. Her head was tilted, and her mouth open to speak. Instead, those slender fingers did their trick. She remained silent.

"We were the Five H Society," Dalton offered.

"And the fifth member was …?"

"Russell Price."

"Never heard of him." Daniel said. "How'd you meet him?"

"An unfortunate set of circumstances. He barely made it through pre-law. I tried to help him, but shortcuts were his forte, and I didn't like doing double work for single credit. He was highly intelligent but dangerously close to flunking out. He didn't make it into law school."

"What made Mr. Price and Mr. …" The sheriff looked to Abra. "I'm sorry. I don't recall your brother's last name."

"Finn Osteen," Abra whispered the name as if saying it aloud cost her too much.

Daniel eyed Dalton. "Mr. Price and Mr. Osteen must've been close enough friends for you, Jasmine, and Beau to let them into your tight circle."

Abra lowered her head, and a single tear fell on her jeans. Shane squeezed her hand, but she didn't look up.

This was how the pain of rejection looked on the outside. Randa never seemed to have a problem with not being a part of their silly club. Shane would have never asked, but Beau and Dalton never offered him membership.

A silly thing for a teenager to worry over, and it didn't bother him now—not like the pain that learning about this caused Abra.

"I know I didn't phrase it as such, Counselor," Daniel broke into Shane's wondering, "but I meant that as a question."

Dalton blinked, his attention on the keychains on the table. He stared up at the sheriff. "I'm sorry, Daniel. Would you repeat the question?"

Daniel shook his head and smiled. "What was so special about Mr. Price and Mr. Osteen that they were deemed a part of the club?"

Dalton leaned to look at Abra. "Finn was one of us from the start. Not Russell. The idiot didn't give up easily. I made the mistake of introducing him to the others. You know those types of people who have no filter; they never know when to make an exit, never quite figure out that they aren't wanted around and always seem to have an agenda? That was Russell. Beau and I would've been long shed of him because, at first, his agenda had been Jasmine."

"What'd Beau have to say about that?"

"Nothing. The clown didn't have a chance to win her from Beau."

"So you put up with him?"

"Jasmine and Finn had bigger hearts. One day, Jasmine showed up with two keychains. One she gave to Finn, the other to Russell. She'd only wanted to include Finn, but she would never hurt anyone's feelings." Dalton ran his hand through his hair. "After that, we couldn't get rid of Price. He even followed us here without invites. That's when I sensed his agenda changed. He was drawn to Mrs. St. John."

Shane couldn't help the spurt that he sent between closed lips. "Everyone loved Grandmere. Price was totally useless, if you ask me."

"Finn was special, but what made him fit?" Abra asked. "He's nothing like you or Beau."

Dalton leaned around Shane. "You can ask that about your brother?"

Fingers slipped back around precious lips, and she shook her head as the tears fell.

"How did you meet Finn?" Daniel took back control of the meeting.

"Beau met Finn on campus and introduced him," Dalton said. "Later, we shared a two-room apartment. Before we moved in, the three of us, Beau, Finn, and me, we played a game of rummy, and I won. The prize was the single room. Beau and Finn had to share a room."

"Where did Jasmine stay?" Daniel cut a look to Abra who studied her lap.

"Sorority house. You knew her, Daniel: a smart extrovert who had no problem with that type of environment."

Daniel nodded. "And Price, did he seek to join you?"

"We rigged the card game. Jasmine sat between Finn and Beau, pretending disinterest, but she fed me what I needed to know about Finn's hand." Dalton smiled, seemingly lost in the memory. "If Finn had gotten the room, Russell would have weaseled his way into the setup. Despite her big heart, Jasmine didn't want him there either."

Abra's gaze remained on her hands, but her tears had dried.

Shane wrapped his arms around her and she leaned against him.

"I remember seeing Beau and Jasmine together at break," Daniel said. "I ran into them on occasion. As you know, we all thought she and Beau ran off ..."

"Sheriff." Shane tilted his head toward the woman he held.

"I know," Abra said without looking up.

Dalton heaved a very heavy sigh, one Shane felt to his core. He didn't want the truth coming out. Not in front of Abra. Not for the sheriff. This was a family matter.

"I knew she wasn't going to Beau," Dalton said. "He was the last person she wanted to see." He wiped at his eyes. "They'd had a terrible fight. First one ever that I could recall. She told me she'd dared to question his character after the accusations that got him suspended from the department, and she doubted he'd ever forgive her. She left town like Beau had: quietly and without telling anyone her plans. I only found out she'd gone to Colorado after her suicide. You told me after her father mentioned it to you."

Jasmine had never mentioned anything about her fight with Beau, never said anything untoward about him at all. Yet, Beau would have been hurt badly by her distrust of him, and coupled with Shane's departure for what Beau would have considered dangerous ground in light of his alcoholism and drug use ... *Dear God, did I help to drive him mad?*

"Beau ended up in Finn's hometown almost immediately. Abra indicates she heard mention of Jasmine on one occasion." Daniel tipped his head in Shane's direction.

Shane hugged Abra to him. "I knew where she was before the suicide. She called me about Taffy. She wanted me to raise the baby."

"Bill." The sheriff looked to his deputy. He held out his hand and took the envelope. "Did you log in the evidence?"

"Yes, sir," Bill answered.

"Make note of the current time, location, persons

present, and the reason I have the items. We'll log them into the evidence room when we're done. You can leave us."

Bill stepped out.

Daniel reached into the manila package and brought out what looked like a paper. He laid it on the table.

Shane leaned forward to read the writing, almost bumping heads with Dalton. *Jasmine Roy also took away something I wanted badly. Don't think you can keep me from what I want.*

"Abra said you brought this to her yesterday, Shane." Daniel said.

"I found an envelope on her porch and brought it inside."

"What's going on here?" Dalton asked.

Abra straightened beside Shane. "I'm trying to learn who killed my husband. The box was sent to me, and then Shane brought me the photograph. I had to bring them here to Sheriff Dixon."

"What photograph?" Shane reached for the paper.

Daniel slapped his latex-covered hand down over it, pulling it away before zeroing in on Dalton. "What else do you think's going on here? Care to enlighten me?"

"First of all, Jasmine gave me her keychain the day we learned Beau hightailed it out of town. I met her out at the ball field. We stood on the banks of the Jordan River, and I begged her not to toss it into the water. She dropped it into my hand and with tears in her eyes declared that she'd ruined everything, and she couldn't bear to keep anything that reminded her of Beau." Dalton ran the tip of his finger down the hardwood arm of the chair. He cleared his throat. "I knew that day we'd never be the same. None of us."

Shane straightened, Dalton's words cutting him deeply. That wasn't why Jasmine gave up Taffy. He'd seen the way she looked at her child. Jasmine cherished the baby. She'd sacrificed to know that her daughter was cared for and loved by Beau's family. Why she'd chosen him would remain a mystery, but he was glad she had.

"What about Finn's keychain?" Daniel asked. "Any idea how it got in with the two that you now claim you had in your possession?"

"I would suspect he had his on him when he ... wherever he is, I mean."

"And Beau?"

"I know where Beau's was. I placed it there myself with Jasmine's," Dalton said.

"And that was ...?"

"The garage at Abra's house. Under the car in one of those magnetic boxes where people hide their keys. I used to drive the Mustang from time to time so she doesn't feel neglected. For some stupid reason, I put the keychains together and kept them in that box."

Daniel nodded. "I wondered what happened to that beauty. Made me jealous to see you driving her around town."

"I haven't been in the garage since Abra arrived. I've been thinking about approaching her and letting her know the car needs to be driven. She won't go inside the building."

If possible, Shane could have sworn the sheriff's ears perked. "That true, Abra?"

She nodded. "It's too hard." She wrung her hands, and Shane reached to clasp them in his. "I—I've only started to explore the house recently."

"Any reason for that?"

She stared up at the ceiling for a moment. "Beau led a life without me. He never once told me about the people he had loved, the life he had led."

"And we find ourselves back to our earlier conversation about trust. You never asked?"

When she met the sheriff's gaze, tears streamed down

her beautiful face. "I was afraid."

"Afraid of Beau?" The question fell from Shane's mouth.

Again, she looked down, her hair hiding her face from him. "Afraid he would leave ... like my mother."

Daniel leaned back in his chair, arms folded across his chest.

"I was a little girl. Momma was angry at Pap for something. I kept asking her questions while she threw her clothes into a suitcase. Finally, she looked directly at me and said, 'I never bargained for this.' Then she slammed the suitcase, zipped it up, and ran downstairs. Finn pulled me into his arms as I kept screaming out her name. My mother never came home again."

Abra broke down into sobs, placing her hands over her face. "Oh God, why did you take Finn? He was all I ever truly had."

Shane held her closer. "You had your father."

She pulled back from him and accepted a Kleenex when a deputy entered with a box.

Shane cut his gaze to the camera lens in the corner. Of course, ... they were being monitored. That's how the deputy knew to enter as if on cue.

"Pap?" Abra laughed through her tears. "He was larger than life, and before he met Jesus, he bought into his own godhood. The Lord conquered his pride after Momma ran out on him. Pap's empire had been in full swing. The town he built up was thriving, and apparently, his wife hadn't been enough for him. I grew up thinking, with a little girl's heart, that I hadn't been what my mother had bargained for. Even though I know Pap and all that came with Pap was a problem for her, something still tells me I was the problem. Pap always said Momma loved us, and her leaving was his fault, but the pain still digs into my gut when I think of that day. So, when I fell in love with Beau, and he begged me to let him start over, after Finn confirmed that Beau was a good man, I didn't dare ask questions that might make him leave."

Shane clenched his jaw, but before the glue of emotion fixed his anger at his cousin too firmly, Daniel pulled the paper back. "Abra, you didn't know there was a car or a keychain or keychains with the car?"

Abra's eyes widened. "No."

"You didn't plunder around in the garage and find them? You didn't have Finn's keychain all along?"

"No!" Abra spoke with such force that Shane pulled from her.

"I talked to my friend last night. She said Finn's house had been broken into recently. Nothing seemed stolen, but—"

"Dalton, do you have any idea if your Five H club did anything to make someone want to take revenge upon each of you?"

"Daniel, four of us worked hard to graduate," Dalton countered. "The fifth one used me to get him through."

"Think hard. You're not the only one I'm concerned with," Daniel said.

"No. I promise you," Dalton said. "We were just four good friends and a tag along who preferred spending time together studying or going to a movie or attending games. We were always together, except on breaks. Finn went home to Florida. Russell sometimes ended up with us. Grandmere always took him in. He genuinely loved the dear old broad." He smiled at Shane. "Beau hadn't cared, but it made Shane jealous. He won't admit it, but he was a Grandmere boy."

Not funny. Shane told him so with a scrunched-up face. Besides, no one could confuse Grandmere's love for Beau with her love for the other two children of her offspring.

"No idea who would do this to one of you?" Daniel turned over the photograph.

Shane gasped and stood, pushing his chair back. He hugged his hands to his waist and bent forward. He'd known about the suicide, but why had she done this to herself? Why the macabre smile? He turned toward the wall, thinking he'd be sick. That was Taffy's mother. He never wanted to see her that way.

Dalton cleared his throat. "Sheriff?" The fear lacing that one word brought Shane around.

"You see the problem with this, don't you?" Daniel tapped the photo. "Abra does, too."

Shane blinked. "This isn't a police picture?"

"I doubt it, son. Dalt, care to enlighten us all with your *lawyer-esqueness*?"

"A crime photographer would have photographed the scene as it had been found."

"And ...?" Shane pushed.

"There's nothing anywhere near Jasmine that indicates she stood on it—a chair, a stool, something she could have tipped away from her." Dalton pointed. "There's a chair there, a heavy one.

"She couldn't have kicked it nor would it have slid that far," Abra added.

"Anything she used most likely would have fallen over, leaving her hanging there." Dalton rubbed his red eyes. "I suspect her neck didn't break. She suffocated. And the photographer, most likely the killer, watched her slowly die."

Shane faced the wall again. His shoulders shook with his sobs. "I never knew, Daniel. Dalton told me you said it had been a suicide. I believed—"

"We all believed," Daniel said. "This picture says differently."

"You can check the coroner's date of death against our whereabouts," Dalton offered.

"I'll have to know where to find that coroner, if only to make sure that young girl's murder isn't going uninvestigated."

"Taffy was born in Denver," Shane offered.

"As Shane said, he saw Jasmine one time after she left town, nearly six or seven months later and a couple of months before her sui—murder," Dalton added.

"She called you about the baby, and that's the only time you heard from her?" Daniel directed the question at Shane.

"I didn't know anything before that—the pregnancy, where she'd gone. Nothing." Shane glanced at Abra. "She called me and told me she had a child. She couldn't keep her, and I should come and get her. I left immediately. I flew to Denver. Jasmine named me the father on the birth certificate. Arrangements were made. I had everything I needed, including full custody. Daniel, you told us what Jasmine's father told you. He, by the way, does not know Taffy is Jasmine's child. She wanted it that way."

"So you and Jasmine did get together at least once before she left town?" Dalton asked.

Shane bit his lip before speaking, and for the first time, understood Beau's gift to Abra of teaching her to hold her tongue. He took a deep breath. "I saw her a time or two, yes." The words were true enough, but Shane was sure Dalton was digging for something Shane would never betray. "She never told me about her fight with Beau. And I have always thought he left town because he'd given up on me. I still do. He left when I attended the CMAs the first time one of my songs was nominated for Song of the Year. Beau probably thought I'd yield to temptation and fall back into that lifestyle I left behind."

Dalton stood and motioned for Shane to sit. "I only know what she told me. We can't know for sure. Beau's leaving Amazing Grace has left as many questions as his death."

Daniel took the picture away.

"Three out of five keychains are in evidence," the

sheriff said. "Three out of five of you are dead."

"No ..." Abra's harsh whisper cut the air. "Finn can't be dead."

Dalton leaned over Shane once again and reached for Abra's hand.

She grasped it, giving him a squeeze then dropping her hold.

"You keep up hope, darlin'. He's out there. I know it."

"If he is," Daniel picked up the keychains with his gloved hand and dropped them one by one into the box, "he might be playing it smart. Perhaps he saw Beau's killer. Maybe Beau wasn't his first victim, and the killer has unfinished business to resolve." He looked to each of them, fixing his stare on Abra. "I understand from the Bodacious Cove Police Department that Beau suspected your father's death was a homicide."

She straightened. "He never told me that."

"Abra, Detective Bastion called me. I knew about the recent break-in at your brother's place because the incident caused Bastion to be worried for you. He told me he and Beau had been investigating the likelihood your father was accidentally poisoned by someone looking to kill Beau."

Abra's face paled. "Beau never said that to me. Mazzie tried to tell me after Beau died, but I thought she was doing some crazy speculation." She closed her eyes and swallowed hard. "Beau kept so many secrets."

"Was Finn with them at the golf course the day your father died?" Daniel asked.

Abra shook her head. "Finn hates golf."

"We can't rule out Finn's involvement in the deaths."

Abra opened her mouth to speak.

Daniel held up his hand. "Being missing and presumed dead is a very good alibi."

"But the picture I saw of him in his truck with the

boys?"

Daniel shrugged. "I'd like to see that picture."

"No one saw it but me. We didn't find it," Abra admitted.

Shane swallowed hard. His speculation that Beau might have staged his death seemed more likely. Maybe the allegations against Beau had started his descent into madness. What if Jasmine had known Beau was coming unhinged? Why else would she believe a prostitute over her boyfriend? She fled Amazing Grace before anyone knew of her pregnancy. Perhaps Beau had tracked her down and killed her without knowing about Taffy. Beau was a born investigator. He could have recently located the birth records, realized the truth ... though Jasmine had placed Shane on the certificate.

Or Beau might think Shane had slept with Jasmine.

All of the above could have set him off again after all this time.

Thank You, Lord, that Beau spared Abra and the boys.

"If it's real, whomever we're looking for likes what he's doing so much he's willing to create evidence, that if found on him, could implicate him in the murders."

Shane needed to tell Daniel his suspicions, but no one would believe him.

"Dalton, if you can contact any of your college buddies to see where Price might have lighted, I'd be interested in knowing his last known address and whether he's dead or alive."

"I hope he's dead," Dalton muttered. "Better than having him back in our life."

"Don't contact him. Bring me any information you get." Daniel pointed to Dalton. "I mean it. You're not stupid. If you contact him in any way and something happens to him, you and/or Shane could be dragged into this, and Shane doesn't need your help to hang—"

Abra's gasp cut off the sheriff's word.

He blanched. "Sorry. Poor choice of words. Anyway, you need to be vigilant and very aware of your surroundings. Understand?"

"Sheriff," Shane ventured. "Some things have happened, and I think you—and Abra—need to know about them. I spoke to Tammy Colbert last night." He glanced to Abra and back to Daniel. "She indicated that a year ago, she met a man leaving The Gray Lady. He told her he was Beau Carmichael."

Abra gave her head a fierce shake. "Beau never left Bodacious Cove without me or without me and the boys."

"Are you sure?" Shane implored.

"Absolutely. Why would you ask?"

"Because of the noises you're hearing. The Gray Lady is known to have secret entrances, and Grandmere left us to find the way in. Beau had a love for them, even built one at my place from the garage to the house."

"So?" Abra countered.

"Tammy told me she saw the same man two weeks ago."

"She's confused ..." Abra's fingers went to her lips. Then she lowered them. "She didn't meet Beau."

Daniel leaned forward, hands clasped, eyes narrowed in Shane's direction. "You said things happened. What else?"

"Two nights ago, I got a call. I'm sure it was Beau."

"I received a call last night telling me to be careful of the boys," Abra said.

"Beau?" Shane asked.

She shook her head. "No, but a familiar voice. I thought it was you at first. After the call dropped, I realized the voice was familiar, but not you. The call was blocked. Since law enforcement sometimes blocks numbers from department phones, I thought it might have been Trace."

Shane partially stood and dug in his back pocket, pulling out his phone. He scrolled through his recent contacts and rested on the one he'd received.

Abra pulled out her phone. She held it to his and showed the blocked message and not the local number he didn't recognize. Different callers, probably.

"Bill!" the sheriff bellowed. "Bring me two evidence bags." Then he re-situated himself, almost as if a weight on his shoulders needed shifting.

"Your caller sounded like Beau?" Daniel asked Shane.

Shane froze, thinking back on the call. "My caller's voice was familiar, too, but what he said made me aware of who he was. Can I see the back of that photograph?"

"Don't touch it." Daniel produced the paper again.

"Basically, the caller told me Taffy was his, and he wants her. He thinks he's going to take my little girl." Shane bounded from his chair. "Beau …"

Daniel beat him to the door. "Beau Carmichael is dead, Shane. And he was no more capable of murder than he was capable of compromising a prostitute."

Bill pushed inside the room.

"Bag these phones for evidence." Daniel held them out. "I'll get them back to you as soon as possible, kids, but we need to see what we can ascertain. Getting information from a carrier is as hard as working a Rubik's Cube, but we might get lucky. Abra's call could have been innocent, the detective, for instance. Shane, I don't know what to think about your call."

Abra gripped Shane's arm.

He turned to her.

"Beau wasn't who I thought he was, but one thing I know: he would never kill anyone without cause, and he'd never threaten a child."

Dalton stood. "Abra's right and, Shane, you said it yourself. Beau never learned about you and Jasmine."

Everybody's Broken

Shane winced again. "He could have found out." Part of lying was leaving out some of the facts, but he was trapped here between the devastation the truth would cause Abra and the pain it would inflict upon Dalton and Randa.

"Besides, why would Beau think Taffy was his? And Beau would never strike from behind. You'd see his scowl and his balled fist a mile away if he thought your relationship with Jasmine had been behind his back."

Shane ignored Dalton. "Was it Beau that died?" he pleaded with Abra.

"I thought so."

"I know so." The leather of Daniel's holster creaked. "Bastion told me Beau was forensically identified beyond a shadow of a doubt. I can assure you that he was a victim and is not a murderer."

Shane let the weight fall from his shoulders. Anger with Beau was enough to carry around. Fear of him was insurmountable—even though Beau had never done one thing to make Shane frightened of him.

Abra stood between Daniel and Shane. "Do you think this could all be about Jasmine and Beau and nothing to do with Pap or Finn or me or any of the rest of us?"

The lawman pressed his lips tightly together. Then he put his hand on Abra's shoulder. "I know you're frightened. It took a lot of guts to come in here today to give me evidence you thought would pin a murder on a man you believe is innocent. I wish I could tell you that you have no need to be afraid."

"But you can't. I understand," she said.

"Because your father is dead. Your brother is missing. An innocent woman was murdered in Colorado. Shane has been threatened, and you might not have thought I heard, but Shane said you're hearing noises inside your home. If I put Beau names in the middle of a piece of paper and wrote all that's happened around the

179

page, I could draw an arrow from each occurrence directly to his name. I want all of you to be afraid, because that means you'll be careful."

Dalton leaned forward and pecked Abra's cheek. "Would you do me a favor and stop by the store and look in on Randa?"

Abra nodded and scooted out of the room.

"You've always been a smooth one, Dalt. Give her someone else to worry about. Good ploy." Daniel winked. "Shane, Abra told me she didn't suspect you for a moment. I had my deputy call you here so she could see her faith in you confirmed."

"And you gave Shane and me the shock-and-awe treatment to do it?" Dalton shook his head as he headed out the door. "Not cool, Daniel. Not cool at all. I'll never forget seeing Jasmine like that."

"Sue me. I needed to see Shane's reaction. No one can fake the horror I saw on his face. Shane, you watch that little girl of yours, and both of you keep an eye on your family. The department will do the same. After all, Beau was our brother, too."

Shane closed his eyes and took a deep breath.

"Something wrong?" Daniel asked.

Shane shook his head. He bit his lip for a long moment, staying the emotions welling inside. Then he inhaled deeply again. "That's why you did that for me."

Daniel cocked his head. "I don't follow."

"When I got in trouble, you didn't file charges. You handed me off to a warden who gave me 'hard time' but kept the charges off my record. Did Beau have to ask?"

"If you're inquiring if Beau asked for special favors for you, the answer is no. He did the exact opposite. He asked me to accept his resignation so that he could see you through the judicial process. That's when I introduced him to the preacher and his wife. I thought he'd send you to their place, but he said he had a special

Everybody's Broken

project for you, and he asked for the leave to finish it. He told me, with all sincerity, that you would either clean up your act, or he would quit because he was sure you'd go to jail."

Shane lowered his head.

"But he also told me, again, that he believed in you, that you'd lost your way, and you needed someone who loved you to put you back on the straight and narrow. He thought he'd let you and Randa down when he left for college, which makes me wonder all the more why he let everyone down by moving away with nary a word."

"Sheriff, I appreciate your help. I never thought to tell you."

Daniel lifted his gaze to Dalton. "Would you excuse Shane and me for just a second?"

"He doesn't waive his right to counsel," Dalton cautioned.

"This has nothing to do with anything about the case."

"I'll be outside." Dalton left them.

Daniel waited until Dalton went out the front door, following Abra. "Shane, Beau was proud of you, son. Don't think for one moment he left because of you."

"Then why?"

"Maybe his fight with Jasmine. I know he loved that gal, and when someone you love betrays you, the wound can be a deep one, especially with someone who took loyalty as seriously as your cousin. I'm afraid Beau probably took the answer to your question to his grave. But let's say he threw up his hands and walked away because you attended an award ceremony, that he couldn't face your downfall … that has nothing to do with you. Beau made the decision."

"I understand that in my head, Daniel, but my heart keeps telling me I let Beau down when he had so much faith in me."

"You didn't say so, and I get the idea that no one else has caught on, but Shane, you're raising your cousin's little girl as your own when, for whatever reason, he didn't want to come back here."

Shane wiped the back of his eyes with his hand. "How'd you figure it out?"

"Experience and a watchful eye. I saw the glow on Jasmine's face, and I knew you weren't dating her. I saw her only with one other guy before she left town, and that wasn't you or Beau. Could have been that Price fellow for all I know."

"Taffy is Beau's," he whispered the words he'd kept quiet for the rest of the world. "DNA proved it, not that I ever doubted Jasmine. She wanted to make sure I knew, as if she thought I'd ever doubt her."

"Taffy is yours," Daniel's eyes softened. "A father ..." he cleared his throat "... is the one who takes care of you. Trust me. I'm not a father, but I know that's the truth."

"I can't tell Randa and Dalton. And I don't want to hurt Abra any more than she's been hurt."

"Well, let's do our best to keep from it." Daniel clasped him on the shoulder. "And I'd like you to be at her house in about forty-five minutes. Make sure she's there."

"I don't understand."

"She's hearing noises. She's getting phone calls. A neighbor claims to have seen Beau last year and recently." He put his finger to his lips as if asking Shane to keep another secret. "I get the feeling The Gray Lady is also a part of this."

"Thank you, again, Daniel."

"Have Dalton and Randa there, too. Maybe they know something and haven't realized its importance."

Shane started out the door but stopped. He didn't care if he looked like a big kid. He threw his arms around

Everybody's Broken

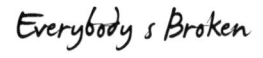

Daniel's neck for a quick hug then hurried out the door.

Chapter 11

Abra walked behind the others as they approached the detached garage. A well sat off in the far corner of the area surrounded on three sides by the ivy-covered fence. Shane had informed her of it once, and she now confirmed the round metal lid with an old hand pump could not be opened and had probably not been used for decades.

The two, large garage doors and a smaller regular entry faced the fence toward The Gray Lady, leaving enough room to back out a car, turn, and pull onto the street from the thick concrete slab. The back of the building fronted a smaller home, but the vine-clad fence did the job of hiding it from the sweet owner's view. Abra had met Ms. Frieda a few times since her arrival, but she hadn't seen her lately.

Abra never parked here. If up to her, she'd never enter, but Dalton said this is where he'd left Beau's and Jasmine's keychains along with the key to the car Beau had left behind.

Shane walked around the building as if seeking something. Maybe Jasmine had sought out Shane for comfort after Beau left. Emotions could have left them open to ...

A cool breeze fell across her warming cheeks. She didn't want to think of Shane falling to such temptation.

If their indiscretion led to Taffy's birth, well, God often turned mistakes into blessings, and that little girl was definitely that. God's attention to detail was breathtaking.

From her spot at the edge of the drive, Abra spied a man-size shadow at Frieda's screened door, surprisingly open on a chilly day. Ms. Frieda said she had a son who lived out of state. He'd probably come for a visit.

Since the keychains were a connection, Sheriff Dixon wanted to start his search with the garage and finish in the house.

The jingle of Dalton's keys brought Abra forward to stand beside Randa, who stood behind Dalton and the sheriff. Shane wandered over without a word.

Dalton pulled out a key to the smaller door on the far left of the building. Sheriff Dixon held up his hand. The lawmen reached in his back pocket and pulled out latex gloves and an evidence bag. He tucked back the bag and slipped on the gloves. Then he held out his hand for the key.

Dalton's face reddened. "Not used to being on this side of a crime." He dropped the key into Dixon's hands.

"I understand." The sheriff gripped Dalton's shoulder then slid the key into the door's lock and pulled it open. He went inside and within seconds, one garage door and then the other slid upward.

Abra's eyes widened and then narrowed at the vintage dark blue Mustang. She'd seen that car before. In a magazine that Beau never allowed her to throw out. She had guessed it only a dream of his to own that type of vehicle. Now, she knew why he simply smiled whenever she'd suggested they find him a car to fix up.

"He loved Blaze." Dalton smiled at her. "She was featured in a hot rod magazine."

Abra's vision blurred. Anger. Sadness. Bitterness. Even jealousy. All wrapped in a tidy little package of regret. She hated that car, despised what it stood for. Her emotions stopped just south of hatred for Beau.

"Are you okay?" Shane slipped his arm around her shoulder.

She swiped at the tears on her face. "Didn't he realize that not telling me, not letting me in on his life, was a lie? He could have kept his car. We could have shared this house. He should have told me about Jasmine. The boys and I would have known all of you." She turned into him, releasing a rolling tide of emotion.

Her anger at Beau had marched forward.

Hated for dying.

For lying.

For not being the person she thought he had been.

For being so foolish that her brother had been taken away from her, her children had almost been killed. And she was beginning to believe Beau responsible for her father's death.

Shane's hold tightened around her, and she clung to him, fighting back a scream of frustration.

"I'm here," Shane whispered into her hair. "I'm here. I'm not going anywhere."

She laid her head upon his shoulder. "Please, please don't lie to me. I can't take one more breach of my trust in anyone."

His hand brushed her hair. "I'm sorry. I know the truth has to hurt."

An understatement. Her sobs intensified.

"Abra." The emotion Randa placed in Abra's name brought reality flooding back.

Abra pulled from Shane's embrace. "I'm sorry." She wiped the arm of her sweater over her face.

Randa waved a kitchen towel in front of her. "This time my habit of carrying these around paid off but too late to save that sleeve and Shane's shirt from all that snot."

Abra couldn't help but smile at Randa's light-hearted demeanor. She took the offered towel and wiped her face. "I'm sorry," she said again.

Shane used his thumb to wipe the moisture remaining on her cheek. "We know this is hard on you."

Abra nodded. Somehow, Shane understood her pain.

She stepped inside the garage, determined not to look at *Blaze*.

Dalton bent down, pointing underneath the car wheel. Dixon stooped and when he stood, he held a small box. Something rattled within.

"That's where I kept the key."

Dixon opened the container and lifted a solitary metal object.

"The last time I drove this car, Beau's keychain had the key on it, and Jasmine's was inside," Dalton said.

"And you're the only one with a key into here?" Daniel reached in his back pocket and pulled out the evidence bag. He placed the key inside the box and dropped it into the bag. "And as far as you know, you and Beau are the only ones to handle this box, the key, or the car?"

"Beau kept a key to the garage, I'm sure." Dalton nodded.

Randa shook her head. "No, baby. He left them all here—his keys to the house, which I gave Abra. The keys to the car and the garage, which you have."

Daniel opened the car door and began to look inside.

Abra stood back, hands over her lips. She never thought she could feel more pain than she'd felt at Beau's

Everybody's Broken

death and Finn's disappearance. Yet, the love she'd had for Beau bled from her heart, leaving her totally undone.

Shane moved around the fairly clean garage. He stared at the overly large work table and the tools dangling on the peg board above it.

The smooth concrete floor was laid in sheets with six distinctive larger slabs, their seams from front to back and from left to right. Three very narrow slabs lined the back of the building.

Shane walked along each line, bending down occasionally before moving forward. He stooped and studied the legs of a workbench at the left back corner then slid his body under the high table, almost flat on his stomach. He ran his finger along the seam that met up with the smaller section. Touching the sturdy wooden leg, he peered back at the front legs.

As he stood, he caught her gaze. Something garnered his attention, and she had an idea that the back legs on the smaller slab and the front legs sitting not on the slab next to it, but the one beyond, had something to do with his curiousity.

He winked then began studying the walls. His attention focused on a few spots here and there. Then he would move on. He pushed or pulled on anything that seemed to be a handle.

Dixon stepped out of the car, arms folded, his attention riveted on Shane's every move.

Only when Shane moved his hand down a seam in the wooden wall and slid his finger into a hole did Dixon move forward. Shane pushed.

The wall gave a bit.

Shane glanced back at Dalton and raised a brow. Then he turned his shoulder to the wall and slammed into it. The partition swung out, and Shane fell through. Sunlight from the back of the garage spilled inside.

Abra stared, her eyes wide, but Randa outright

guffawed.

Not Dalton. "I never knew there was a back entrance."

"Neither did I." Shane stood and wiped his hands on his jeans, "But with the noises ..." Shane turned to Dalton who remained stoic. "Beau has ..." he cut his gaze to Abra "... had always loved secret doors and passages. Grandmere's tales of Grandpere's heroic family hiding Jewish refugees on their farm in France fascinated him."

Dixon examined the door. "This is well done. I don't remember your grandfather as a craftsman."

Shane shrugged. "Grandmere claimed he kept it quiet. He always feared that the day might come when others would need refuge, and he wanted to be above suspicion."

"I can imagine that living in that time, being a part of the history of hiding innocents, fear of being caught could do that to a man." Dixon's jaw clenched. "That's a legacy." He looked Shane in the eyes. "Passed on to each of his grandchildren, as far as I can see."

Shane nodded, but he didn't smile at the compliment. Maybe the truth had slammed into him as well. His cousin had no such legacy. He had been a cowardly liar.

"This could be how our Beau impersonator found his way inside," Dixon said.

"Beau? Impersonator?" Randa gasped.

"I'll explain later." Dalton told her.

Dixon stepped outside, pushed the door shut, and after a few moments, tugged it open. "There's the same, almost indiscernible notch on this side. When you push it in, a small latch above it moves up and allows the door to open. Pretty ingenious."

Dalton stepped to Dixon's side and examined the find. He started to speak but stepped back, remaining silent, watching Shane for so short of a moment, Abra could have imagined it. The lawyer in him must have realized Shane had implicated himself.

Abra went to Shane's side and slipped her hand into his.

His warm fingers wrapped around hers.

She closed her eyes and caught her breath. Coarse emotion flowed through her. Raw. Unbridled.

Beau had lied to her. Had lied to them all.

Shane wasn't a liar. He cared.

"Who else would have incentive to search for one of your grandfather's passages?" His gaze fell on Randa and not Shane.

Randa shook her head. "I wasn't one to listen to Grandmere's rambling." Her face hardened. "And Beau obviously wasn't one to share a lot."

Randa's words mirrored the screams of Abra's heart.

"That was just his way." Shane's touch left Abra. He placed a hand on Randa's shoulder.

Dixon snapped his fingers twice. "Back to the question, folks. Any idea who would look so hard that they would be able to find the entrance, find a hidden key to a car, and take only those keychains when this sweet ride is sitting right here?"

A blush rose on Dalton's cheeks, but he said nothing.

"Any ideas?" Dixon pressed.

The others shook their head.

"Randa doesn't come in here. She's never had a reason," Dalton said. "Shane or I mow the lawn with my equipment. I don't think he's been in here since—"

"Since Beau left, and we thought maybe he'd taken the car," Shane answered. "We came in to check."

"Abra hasn't been in here. You saw her reaction. For a place she's never lived, Beau's memory must haunt her terribly." Dalton sent a warm smile in her direction. "And then she has to put up with us. I'm the only would-be culprit."

Dixon played with the once-hidden door for a

moment longer. He stepped outside and looked around a bit before returning. "There's another possibility."

No one spoke.

"I'd say finding a secret opening like that would take some time. Perhaps, someone who was around here a year ago had a reason for pretending to be Beau."

"What?" Randa asked.

"Honey, I'll explain later."

"Let's go explore the house, shall we?" Dixon lowered the garage doors and led them out through the smaller entrance. "Shane, you all did some exploration inside to try to turn up a place someone might hide?"

Shane nodded.

"We didn't find anything. I actually thought I heard a door close in the library a night or so ago." Abra massaged her fingers into her temples as she poured out her story. She finished with a deep exhale. "But we couldn't find anything."

"Let me have a look." Dixon headed out.

"Daniel, any idea how long it will be before I can get the key back to the car?"

Randa winked at Dalton. "His mistress needs some attention."

"When the killer is caught," Daniel said. "And keep out of it. Depending upon what I find in the evidence I have now, I might need to have her hauled in."

Dalton turned to Abra. "When we get her back, I'll take her for a spin. This baby has horses under the engine, and they need to run."

"Drive it for yourself." Abra followed after the sheriff. "Do whatever's necessary to put the car in your name." She took a very deep breath. "I hate that thing."

And the man who used to own it.

He shivered as he moved to shut the front door. Frieda was a forgetful woman.

Voices brought him to a halt. Not the phantoms this time. People stood outside the side of The Gray Lady's garage. He spied their movement through the withering ivy.

Abra looked his way, and he stood motionless. He couldn't let them see him, and the best way to go unnoticed was to appear unnoticeable.

Something else seemed to grab Abra's attention, and he scurried out of sight and stood, parting the musty curtains covering the front window.

The voices didn't carry far enough for him to hear, so he slipped into the kitchen and onto the side porch just out of view.

Sobs cut through the chill. He'd heard the sound of it enough lately to know that Abra was playing crybaby again, mourning her first love.

He crept out of his hiding place and into Frieda's yard to the left, behind the garage, on the other side of the covered fence, turning to make sure the old hag he'd moved in with was still asleep upstairs. He'd slipped her the pill, and he expected she wouldn't wake up for a good long while. If anything, the old biddy was getting her rest.

He was doing his best to keep her alive. If she stayed out of the way, the phantoms might decide she wasn't a worthy victim.

He'd hate for the voices to start chanting their mantra *kill, kill, kill.*

When Frieda was awake, he pretended they were friends. Let her believe what she wanted. He'd stayed vague about where he had lived and even who he was. Not hard when someone had a bit of dementia. You just repeat, "I told you that. Don't you remember?"

"Oh, yes, yes. I remember now."

Of course, she couldn't remember something he'd never divulged, but either pride or fear for what she was losing kept her from admitting it.

She didn't snoop too much, and that kept her safe.

To Frieda, they were two poor souls with loneliness in common. He'd let her play her lonely card, thinking she was worse off than him.

The old bat wasn't lonely. She had a brother who visited her once or twice a year, and a son called her dutifully every Tuesday night at 7:00 p.m. He had to keep that in mind, because if she was drugged and asleep and didn't answer, he might visit or send someone to find her, and the voices wouldn't like that at all.

He was the lonely one. Everyone he'd ever known betrayed him or stole from him.

The back of the garage rattled, and he stifled a laugh when Shane fell through the back door. Shane had discovered the secret entrance to the garage. He watched, a smile pushing his lips wider. The entrance into the tunnel that led inside the house would be near impossible to locate, especially since he'd found it entirely by happenstance. That old granddad had been a crafty guy.

Not likely that these interlopers Abra allowed into the yard would ever find their way into the house from the garage.

The local sheriff—very recognizable in the small town—stepped out of the door Shane had crashed through. He played with the latch and studied the door before ducking inside and closing the door.

Slinking to the corner of the old woman's yard, deeper into the hedges, he waited to see if they would exit the front. Maybe then their voices would carry to him.

For a long few moments, all went silent.

Then the sheriff stepped through the garage door again and looked upward. He followed the sheriff's line of sight and closed his eyes. The lawman stared at the top of the concrete light pole, the one he'd already broken once—the one the old lady yammered on about how the city wouldn't fix it. Well, they had—once. Not that she could remember.

He'd broken it again.

The sheriff's attention on the light or the pole could prove to be a bad omen. A very bad thing.

Despite his worry, he licked his lips and smiled.

Then the pain in his temples hit him full force.

The phantoms had returned.

He's on to you.

All he needs to do is check with the city.

He'll find out that it's been broken before.

And there would be a heavy patrol around the neighborhood.

Get in there before you can get caught.

Right after they leave.

Stay hidden inside.

He shivered. The old man hadn't run ducts to cool or to heat his secret room. Inside, he always suffered the constant ache in the tips of his fingers and the cold that stung the tip of his nose. The blankets he stored inside needed washing. They stank of mold and mildew, and they were moist, like everything else inside there.

If only he had more time before they'd caught on.

Courage, you mean.

Maybe the gumption to do the work required.

Yeah, weak and lazy. That's what you are.

What was he doing letting them run their mouths? "Shut up!" His hoarse whisper cut the silence. "He'll hear you."

The sheriff stopped for a moment, standing still.

The phantom's laughter swirled around him. If they weren't careful, the sheriff would find him here.

Maybe they wanted him caught.

Then they'd have the treasure for themselves.

He closed his eyes, willing the pain away.

No, the phantoms needed him. He was the only one smart enough to figure out where this treasure had been placed. "The treasure of royalty and commoner's alike," the old grand dame had bragged. She always made the valuables sound better each time she talked of them. "Worth more money than could ever be gathered by all the kingdoms of the world. Right here at my fingertips."

He'd begged her to tell him what she meant, but she'd only smiled. "You'll figure it out someday."

He never had time for riddles, and her decision to keep her secrets had cost her life. No one ever figured it out. Old age they'd said.

Old pillow over the face, more like it.

Small town cops were the easiest to fool.

The sheriff shook his head and ducked inside the garage again.

How could he have been so careless? Thinking of the past with so much at stake here. This time the phantoms were right. He couldn't argue. He needed to get in, grab the blankets, and get out without being seen. And if he got out he might want to avoid the temptation of the search for a while. Not laziness. Diligence. A change in plans.

But why were they searching? He'd been so careful not to leave clues, to stay out of sight.

Once inside the hidden place you can slip into the warmth of the house.

She doesn't need to know until you want her to know.

But he's stupid.

He grabbed at his head to clear their ridicule. He wasn't stupid. He was smart. The phantoms didn't know about that first misadventure when he'd sneaked into the house, the water running in the shower pulling him up the stairs. He wanted to keep it that way. And he'd keep to his plan. Not theirs.

Everybody's Broken

The sheriff stepped back inside and closed the door.

He crept forward to the end of the fence near the street and peered around.

After a few moments, the sheriff led the others out of the garage: Dalton and Randa ... and Shane with his arm around Abra, and Abra leaning on him for support. Shane would never change. Already, he was taking something else that didn't belong to him.

Hang them.
Hang them together.
Dangling on the same beam.

"No," he spoke aloud and startled.

The group had entered the house. No one had heard.

"I'll handle it my way. Beau had been close to signing the contract for the sale of the place." He'd even driven to Florida to meet with Beau. "Too bad things happened like they did." He needed to put his old buddy, Fred Colbert, into action soon. Fred salivated over the commission before Beau's death. Manipulating him had been easy. He only had to make sure Fred's wife never saw him again, keep the meetings with Fred, as always, at a place where they weren't likely to run into her. She knew too much, and the voices wanted her dead.

Stupid boy.
Never listens.
He's going to get caught.

The phantoms were wrong. He'd get it all, or he'd die trying.

Assured that the group had gone inside, he slipped around the fence and into the little slice of acreage between the empty lot and the back of the garage, but he didn't go inside. Getting into the garage was only the second part of getting into the house. No. He wasn't stupid. He'd found the tunnel entrance when no one else had.

He kept low and made his way to the well, lifting the

pump handle. The slide of concrete met his ears, but he already knew they couldn't hear it from the house. He crept into the garage, and slipped with caution through the opening in the floor. Once at the bottom of the five steps, he reached up and with relative ease, compliments of dear old granddad, he closed the opening.

In and out with what he needed, and he'd stay away for a while. His new plan would work better.

Chapter 12

Three nights sleep without noises within the home had done Abra well. She smiled as Paulie woofed down a large piece of pancake. On the other side of the table, Peter dunked his bacon into the syrup, but instead of sticking it in his mouth, he stared into space. Something had to be weighing on his mind.

The house phone rang, and the three of them looked at each other.

Abra giggled. "That's a sound we don't hear too often."

Peter ran to pick up the line. "Caramichael residence," he said as he'd been taught. "Hi, Mr. Colbert. Yes, Mommy's here. Hold on."

"It's Melissa's daddy. I didn't do anything. I promise."

Abra scrunched her face and narrowed her eyes. "Then don't look so guilty. Please finish your breakfast if we're going to get things cleaned up and make it to town on time for the reveals."

Peter trudged back to his seat.

"Mr. Colbert," Abra said. "How may I help you?"

"I hope I can help you," the man said.

Abra hadn't met either of Melissa's parents, but Randa once told her Fred Colbert hit town selling real estate, and he never stopped. "You must have realtor radar?"

"Really, why is that?" The man had a gentle laugh, nothing abrupt. She half-expected him to come across like a used car salesman.

"I planned to call you this morning after the festivities downtown to see if I could take a look at the corner storefront on Main. I didn't know if you had office hours on Saturday."

"Well, that is a surprise. Yes. I do, and I'd welcome a chance to show you the property and to meet you. Melissa has told me all about your sons. How about we meet around eleven? I have another business proposition to talk over with you?"

"I can't imagine." Abra looked to her boys and pointed at their plates and to the sink. "I'll see you then. Thank you." She hung up. "I'll get the dishes in the dishwasher. Go grab your coats."

Paulie hurried away, and Peter followed slowly after. By the time Abra had the dishes rinsed and in the dishwasher, they both stood dutifully waiting for her. She grabbed her own coat and herded them outside.

Abra locked the door, zipped Paulie's coat, and turned to help Peter. He already had his in place.

She slipped her hands into theirs and headed out the walkway and toward the historical downtown district. Shane said the reveals would start across from Count It All Joy, work down one side and then the other, ending at the toy store.

Crowds gathered in front of the first shop, making it

Everybody's Broken

hard to see. "We're going to miss it if you don't hurry," Peter complained.

Abra peered down at him. "Any more words spoken in that tone will find you back home and in your room."

Peter pressed his lips together.

"We don't have to be the first to see it, honey. The window won't change as the people move away. It'll give us more time to enjoy it, right?"

"No, Mommy. Shane's playing his songs after they take off the paper from the windows at his and Aunt Randa's store, and then he said they would help us decorate our yard, and tonight we can go to his house, and we're going to have a bonfire." Paulie jumped up and down, moving her arm with him.

"Uh-huh." Abra smiled. "I believe that you two and Taffy have reminded me of our plans quite a few times. We'll get to the store before Shane's performance."

"I don't care about Shane's singing," Peter said. "I want to see all the windows."

Her five-year-old scoundrel wanted to watch the unveiling of store windows. What was up with that? He wasn't the creative one. He took after Beau—living in a real world and not one to have an interest in the creative side.

"Well, okay." She scooted through the crowd.

A taller man moved aside and motioned that she and the boys could step to the front. Abra thanked him and stood to await the first reveal by the proprietor of Heaven's Stage Photography.

Finally, the elderly photographer made a big show of peeling back the covering on the shop's large window. A farmer's fence, the type that zigzagged its way along a property line and yellowing grass had already been painted onto the window, and with the window revealed, Abra widened her eyes. The window's floor area had been covered with real autumn leaves. A cutout of a man bending and looking through an old box camera on a tripod focused on the crowning achievement of the window. A very large framed photograph of a field with the same fading grass and autumn leaves depicted by the window dresser also showcased a single large tree, the window and photograph's imagery flowing together beautifully.

Abra took a deep breath and leaned forward. A large knot hole painted on paper and attached to the photograph contained a heart with what was supposed to be carved letters: F.O. + M.H.

Around her, the conversation was one of awe and excitement. "He did this all up and down the street. I drove through here late a couple of nights and watched him paint the outsides of the windows. The guy's amazing."

"All of this was done in less than a week. I don't know if the man got any sleep at all."

"Can you imagine? If he did this at each store, the Asheville paper's coverage will bring a lot of traffic this season."

"A good thing, don't you think?"

Peter pulled her closer to the window and studied it with awe. As the crowd moved to the clothing consignment shop next door, Abra peered down at him. His face was lit with a smile as he beamed up at her. Then he stared back at the painting.

"Are you thinking of becoming an artist now, Peter? I thought you wanted to become an astronaut."

"No. I'm going to be a policeman, and I'm going to catch people that kill people."

Paulie tugged her forward, but she stood her ground and frowned down at the usually patient twin. "Hold on. Peter and I are talking."

Peter stepped even closer to the window. "Mommy, don't you see it?"

Everybody's Broken

"It's beautiful, isn't it? Did you know Mommy used to do this type of work?" She gazed back up to the beautiful exhibit.

He lowered his head. "I know."

"Peter, what is it?" She bent in front of him.

He shook his head and walked forward with his attention still on the ground.

They followed the crowds to each grand reveal. At the end of the first side of the street, she moved past the horde waiting for the light to change to walk to the other side. The empty storefront called her name. The boys tugged at her, but she pulled them back. "Mommy wants to see something." She maneuvered through the crowd and stared into the shadowy store.

Now that she'd talked to Mr. Colbert, she couldn't wait to get inside. She led the boys into the store's alcove and peered into the glass. The place was huge. She'd definitely be able to set up some furnishings and accessories. She could almost see a nice counter in the middle of the store with stools where she could casually talk to her customers and share catalog information, make appointments to view the homes, the offices, whatever they planned to decorate—and more importantly, find a purpose to her life once again.

Peter stood looking out at the road as the window-watchers crossed the street. Abra hurried after them before the jay-walk bird squawked.

Each window was a creation of art, using the store or something from within the store as the theme. Walking with the crowd, she kept looking back. Peter did the same. Something niggled at her. Whatever it was hung at the edge of her reasoning, just far enough to keep her from snatching it.

Saved by Grace Antiques and Ice Cream's window ran across the front of the entire store, but the window dresser had succeeded in using the antiques to set up a cozy old-timey kitchen, complete with an antique wood burning stove. A table beside the stove held a recipe, and the boxed and bottled ingredients lay about it. Abra didn't need to think hard to know what the recipe was: peanut butter and chocolate pie. Her mouth watered and then her eyes. She pushed the tears away. Pap loved that pie. She'd even tweaked the recipe to add a thin layer of chocolate mixed with coffee that when placed in the refrigerator hardened and added to the flavor. Antique coffee and chocolate tins were included in the display.

"Let's go to the next one." Anything to keep the memories at bay.

The bookstore and small eatery called The Tree of Knowledge had rows of books facing the windows, but the designer had used a small spot in the middle of the store to create another tree scene. A large cardboard cutout sported the red, orange, and gold leaves of fall with leaves hanging down, giving the illusion that they were falling from the tree. The clear filament could probably be seen when inside, but from the outside, the scene was magical, especially with the cutout of a young girl. The teen was dressed in a coat, her arms hugging her legs as she sat on a blanket. Above her, a dialogue box gave the audience her thoughts. *Stay gold, Ponyboy. Stay gold.* A book, *The Outsiders* was opened on the blanket beside her. Even without the prop, Abra would have known the title.

"What does that mean?" a woman asked a man beside her.

"Got no idea," he answered. "But it sure is nice otherwise."

Abra smiled at the couple. "I've met the people who own the store. The woman is a retired English teacher. The quote is from the book the girl's reading. The scene is such a tender one, that the girl would have placed it beside her to soak in what had happened. The story was written by a seventeen-year-old, and for years, and maybe even now, the story was required reading for high schools."

"That must have been some story for you to recognize that line."

Warmth climbed up Abra's face. "My father and my brother teased me because I woke up screaming those words." She pointed to the dialogue box. "The moment those words are spoken in that story is very powerful—a sad moment. I think I cried myself to sleep that night."

"Wow!" The man smiled. "I suppose it must have done the same thing for the artist. Who is he or she, by the way? Do you know?"

Abra narrowed her eyes. "No. I never thought to ask. But my friends own the toy store. They might be able to tell you."

"I wonder why he didn't do the unveiling. Would have been a nice touch."

Abra shrugged. The thought had not occurred to her. "Someone said he'd put all of this together in a week. Maybe he's exhausted."

The woman laughed. "I can imagine. Not only the physical labor but the mental task that come with such creativity."

Abra smiled. The woman obviously wasn't the creative type—at least not in design. The creativity always rejuvenated Abra, made her feel more alive.

She turned and stared back at the empty storefront. Maybe that feeling of being alive would settle over her again.

"Mommy!" Paulie tugged. "Taffy's getting ready to take the paper off the window."

Abra didn't admonish him. Of course, he would be excited.

She allowed him to tug her forward, but Peter held her back.

She looked down at him once again.

His solemn face had a tear tracking down his cheek.

"Peter, come on!" Paulie urged but stopped. He came back to stand beside her. "What's wrong?"

Peter swiped at the tear. "Nothing!" He released Abra's hand and stomped past her. "Bunch of stupid people."

"Whoa-ho!" Abra snatched his jacket and pulled him back. "Young man, that "s" word isn't allowed in our house, and you know it."

"I'm not in a house." He stared back, arms crossed, as if daring her to deny his truths.

"Our home is with us wherever we go. It's us. Do you understand? We're family, and the home isn't just a place with rooms where we live. It's us."

"Like church isn't just a building," Paulie added.

"But our whole house isn't here, Mommy. Then how can we be one."

Abra swallowed hard. How could she not have noticed?

Because Peter wasn't usually the sensitive one. That was Paulie's M.O. If Paulie had been the one acting like this, she'd have caught on quickly. But Peter was so much like his father. So driven by common sense and fair play. So stoic in his emotions.

The artistry, the designs, they reminded him of his uncle and most likely to times that they'd all spent with their father. Finn had easily put together designs for school and church plays—every church event, really. He'd even helped Pap decorate for her parties. Pressed cardboard and canned paint were Finn's best friends, and he could work wonders with them.

And … he always added in little secrets for his family that no one else would know.

Abra turned and looked around her.

Had Peter seen it from the start? She stared across the

road. What was it about that window? She couldn't remember. But the peanut butter pie's special ingredients ... the girl reading Abra's favorite young adult novel, having the same thoughts about the words that had grabbed her heart and stayed with her for years ... what else had she missed?

Shane stepped into the doorway of the toy store, an acoustic guitar in his hand. He smiled at Abra and turned his attention to the crowd. "Give us just a minute folks. We have two special guests who are going to help unveil our windows today. "Peter and Paulie, will you help Taffy with the honors?"

Peter threw his arms around her legs. "I'm sorry, Mommy."

And off the boys ran, leaving Abra to stand outside in the crowd.

Inside the store, Randa bent over the children giving them instructions. Taffy climbed up in the window to Abra's right, and the boys shared the window on the left.

Taffy carefully pulled down the brown paper that had been used all over town. The folks around her gave a collective awe.

Abra stepped closer to look at the brick sidewalk created at the front of the window. Cardboard children in costume walked along a leaf strewn path. Miniature fences and cardboard trees, without leaves, fronted the silhouettes of three homes, all with autumn decorations in their yards and porch lights aglow. In the last house, though, a large man stood in the doorway, a bowl of candy in his hands. A man and woman each held the hand of two look-alike boys. Though Pap never allowed Abra and Finn to do the trick-or-treat thing as a family, he always handed out candy because he couldn't bear to let a child down. "Some folks just plain don't get that you can make of things what you want. God would rather them come to a home that's safe. My conscience is clear." Not that many kids who lived on the beach went door-to-door anyway. They usually went party-to-party, and often Pap's birthday parties for Abra were the best and the safest place. No alcohol. No scary stuff. Just a place to have fun.

Abra tensed. Again, she'd lost herself in memories evoked by the scene in front of her.

The crowd moved away from her, and she went to stand beside Shane. "Who's the artist?" She fought to keep the tremor from her voice. "Is he around?"

Shane looked through the crowd. "He collected his pay early this morning. I haven't seen him since. He looked worn out, and he's not well anyway. Great work though, huh?"

"Amazing. Every window is a showcase. This town—"

"Will definitely be hiring him for Christmas decorations," Shane interrupted.

"Maybe I'll be his first customer," Abra worked at keeping the conversation light. "I'm thinking of opening that store I mentioned."

Shane smiled. "Decided to stay with us? Good."

"Someone's gotta make sure you stay safe. Might as well be me. I meet with Fred Colbert …" she reached for her absent phone and almost said the sheriff's name in vain "… in about an hour. Any word on our phones?"

"Nope." Shane turned his attention to inside the store for a moment then back to her. "Glad you have enough time to stay and watch me play the fool."

"I don't think you could ever be mistaken for a fool." Abra leaned against him.

"You didn't know me when." He smiled and pointed. "There go the boys."

Peter and Paulie snatched at the paper, pulling it down and causing Randa to reach in and take it from them.

Everybody's Broken

"Boys ..." Abra sighed.

"You don't think Randa knew what they'd do? She had Beau for a brother and me for a cousin."

Abra giggled. "Yeah. Okay. You're right."

Abra stepped up to the window. This one was a cute understated Thanksgiving scene. A table took center stage. A family of mannequins, probably borrowed from the consignment shop and dressed for dinner in consignment clothes, sat around a rustic table and four chairs that Abra remembered seeing in the antique shop. The dark-haired girl mannequin looked over her shoulder and into the corner, closest to the window at a smaller kid's table; around it sat a stuffed otter, a cat, even a hedgehog. The table was filled with a child's tea set. Real plates and bowls, all mismatched, adorned the family's table as if showing that the family was not rich, but thankful. More borrowed wares from Grace's Antiques, most likely. Cardboard was used to represent the turkey and other food on the serving plate and in the bowls. A red brick wall made from wallpaper covered cardboard hosted an overlarge framed charcoal sketch of a real-life family—a man, a woman, and two small children—a boy and a girl.

Abra took it all in. As a decorator, she realized the focal piece of this design was the picture on the wall. She took a step back to study it all together. The purposefully understated simplicity was not lost on her. This family loved one another. A mother and father who cared that their daughter had set up a table for her stuffed pets.

She'd done that once when she'd been very young. Her mother had helped her set the table for her little friends. And they had used Abra's tea set. That may have been her last holiday with her mom.

She lifted her gaze to the portrait. And blinked. And blinked again. The picture's image did not change.

She swirled toward Shane. "Who's the artist?" Her

voice cut through the hushed tones of the crowd.

"Jeb Castor," he answered.

Abra swayed but caught herself before she fell against Shane.

"Are you okay?" he asked.

Abra looked back at the picture on the wall. She took a shuddering breath and brought her emotions under control. Then she forced a smile into place, afraid to let hope take root in her heart. "So, when do you start playing? The boys have been looking forward to hearing you."

"What about their mother?"

"Oh, I've been dying to find out what you really do for a living," she teased, "besides hiking and working in a toy store, helping out defenseless widows, and playing Billy the Kid."

He tilted his head but remained silent for a long moment. "Are you sure you're okay? Nothing happened at the house last night?"

The noises had disappeared, but she still locked herself and the boys in their room each night.

"Nope. I'm fine. Never better. Excited to meet the realtor so I can see the storefront. And the boys are excited for the rest of today's plans."

"Tell me about it. Taffy was looking around for firewood early this morning so we could get the fire started 'more easy,' she said." He leaned back and watched Abra for a moment.

She focused her attention on the portrait in the window. If he didn't leave, she was going to have a meltdown in front of him.

"Well, I better get ready to perform." Shane touched her arm.

Abra nodded, but she didn't follow. She moved closer to the window, her eyes on the portrait. The image of a much younger Pap with his hand firmly on Finn's shoulder and his other arm around long-gone Mom and Mom's hand resting on Abra couldn't be mistaken, even in the sketchiness of the drawing.

In the reflection of the glass, Abra could see the photography studio across the street. She spun around. That was it. The initials on the tree.

F.O. and ...

F.O. + M. H.

Abra rested her hand against her chest and forced herself to breathe slowly. She did a slow pivot on her heel, looking about her for anyone who looked familiar.

A man at the corner of the store, standing by the alleyway nodded to her. The smile he offered didn't quite reach his eyes.

Abra looked away.

She'd seen that man before. Once, maybe twice.

But she couldn't remember where.

She forced herself to walk into the store with an easy gait.

Either Finn Osteen was in Amazing Grace or someone was making it look like he was.

Jeb woke with a pounding headache and an incessant ringing coming from somewhere in the small cabin. He turned his head and stared at the clock until the numbers cleared.

Ten o'clock. The first reveal had started an hour earlier, at nine o'clock to afford the last store—the toy store—not to delay opening by an hour.

He'd come home after collecting his pay—which came with generous tips, and he'd fallen asleep. He started to raise his head. The ache from earlier had blossomed. He probably needed to drive to the emergency room. He couldn't be too careful after ...

He moaned and dropped back against the pillow. He wasn't going anywhere. Not right now.

The ringing stopped for a moment and then picked up again.

This time, the vibration caught his ear. His cell phone. He covered his eyes with his left arm and reached to the table to his left.

He stared until the name on the I.D. became clear and slid his fingers across the screen. "Yep," he answered.

"Man, I wish you could be here. You're a success." Dalton's raised voice made Jeb wince.

But Jeb also smiled. "I'm glad."

"Glad. This is amazing. You wouldn't believe the crowds. This thing you've done, it has feet."

He'd have more income coming in soon. That made him happy.

"I'll be right there, babe. Give me a second to finish up this call." Dalton had pulled the phone away then back. "Give me a sec, Jeb. I need to get outside."

Jeb waited.

"We've got a problem. I don't know if you're going to be able to keep yourself hidden for much longer. We've had several customers ask who you are and where you are, and I overheard Abra ask Shane the same question. And she's thinking of opening a store here." Dalton coughed. "At least she was. Right now, she looks a little south of terror-ridden."

Despite the headache, Jeb sat up. He rubbed his eyes and leaned over to stare at the floor until the queasiness went away. "What do you mean?"

"Shane mentioned it. Asked me to keep an eye on her. Said she looked like she'd seen a ghost when the boys revealed our second window."

Jeb fell backward onto the bed again.

Muted voices sounded from the other end of the call.

Everybody's Broken

Then they cleared, and Jeb could imagine the milling crowd.

"Sorry about that. All kind of people asking questions about you. Did you say something?"

"I don't know what to say except maybe that's a good thing."

"What?"

"Our plan's not going as expected, Dalt. It's stalled. We're no closer to getting what we want. Maybe getting her out of town is a good thing."

"That can't happen. We've got things in motion. We're close. With just a bit more tweaking, we can get this business over with."

"How's Randa doing?" Jeb asked.

Silence filled the distance between Jeb and Dalton.

"How's she doing?" Jeb pushed.

"Low blow, man. Low blow."

"You're going to lose her." Jeb again covered his eyes with his arm. "Take it from me. Life gets pretty lonely when you can't be with the woman you love."

"I hear what you're saying, but isn't this more important?"

Jeb shook his head though Dalton couldn't see him. Nor could Dalton see the single tear that trickled down the side of Jeb's face and into his hair—badly in need of a trim. Whether his emotions were amped because of his pain or his heartache, he couldn't tell. He'd never been one to cry.

But he'd never been a hermit, either. This life wasn't good for him.

"You there?" Dalton asked.

"Yeah. Listen. I know you're busy right now with Shane's performance, but when you get a free moment I need a favor from you."

"Might be a bit tough to scoot out of here until the crowd dies down."

213

"I understand. But sometime ... I'd appreciate it."

"We're having dinner at Shane's. I'll have to get by before I bring Randa up. They wanted to ask you to join us, but under the circumstances, you understand."

Jeb closed his eyes tightly against the emotions. He cleared his throat. "If you could give me at least an hour before the dinner, I really need your help with something."

"I'll be there. Can I bring anything?"

"No. I'll see you then."

Jeb let his arm holding the cell phone fall beside him. Then he picked it up and peered at the device. He scrolled through his contacts to her name. New life. New phone. One number he'd never forget. He'd added her information if only for comfort's sake. The agreement had been no contact. With a grimace, he hit dial to break that pact.

"Hello." Her voice ran over him like the sun pouring out from under rain-drenched skies. "Hello," she repeated.

He swallowed hard.

"Listen, if you're trying to scare me, it's not going to work."

Scare her?

"Either say something to me now or come after me. I'm tired of these games, you mangy old hound dog!"

"Please tell me you haven't said that to any other unknown callers," he managed to say.

Silence greeted him.

Jeb pressed his hand over his eyes again. "Say something," he whispered.

"Oh, baby, I thought I'd never talk to you again." Her voice melted into that smooth-as-chocolate resonance he loved. "You never called. I've been so worried."

"I need you. Can you come?" He sobbed the words.

Everybody's Broken

Chapter 13

With the boys and Taffy perched on stools at the back of the crowd of children and their parents, Abra made her way through the folks near the front and to Randa who busily rang up sales.

"Let me help," Abra started to step behind the counter to help Randa bag up the purchases for the customers.

"No," Randa's curt response cut through Abra. "Go watch the show. I know how to do this."

Abra stepped away and back to stand near the kids.

Two steps led up to where Shane stood on a stage, his guitar strapped over his shoulder as he plucked a string and tuned, strummed another, and tuned again.

Randa stayed close to the cash register and to the apple cider and cookies she'd brought in. Abra fought to keep from looking in her sister-in-law's direction. After her enthusiastic welcome to the boys, Randa's curt dismissal stung like the tentacles of a jelly fish that once wrapped around her leg—only vinegar wouldn't help this sting.

Dalton stood to the side of Shane. He raised his hand and used a remote. The projector filled the screen with blue and then the title: *Bumblebee's World.* A large black bear sat on its hind legs and seemed to be waving at the crowd. On closer inspection, the big old fur ball batted at a limb on a tree. Abra gasped.

"Look, Peter. It's Bumblebee." Paulie pointed.

"Shu—ut up. You want Mom to hear?" Peter groused.

Abra moved to stand between them. She bent down so only the three children could hear her. "Mom already heard, Peter Carmichael. Shane told me. Since when do we keep secrets from each other?"

Peter sat back in his seat. "You caught that, but you didn't catch—"

Abra leaned close to his ear. "I got that, too." She straightened.

He stared at her with wide eyes. "But ..."

She shook her head and put her finger to her lips before looking to Paulie. What a fine example she was setting for them. They would have to talk about this tonight, after the decoration of the yard, after the cookout at Shane's place, and maybe if they were too tired, she could put it off until after church tomorrow, find some time to mull it over in her mind.

But she'd already reasoned that the window dresser's hints could only come from Finn.

"We're about ready to start." Dalton patted Shane's shoulder.

Shane moved to the side away from the microphone, and Dalton leaned forward. "Most of you need no introduction to Amazing Grace's own award-winning songwriter. Shane has written many tracks for a variety of country music and Christian artists. You've won how many CMA awards?" He turned to eye Shane who shook his head. "Well, I've lost count, but I know two of them were for Song of the Year, two years running, and he's still collecting Dove Awards, and a little birdie tells me he may be up for a Grammy this year as well."

Shane straightened, eyes wide. Then he settled, rolling his shoulders almost as if the news carried a heavy burden for him. He was humble about the awards on his wall, downplaying them, saying Randa arranged them there.

"Okay, I'll quit bragging about our family phenom. Here's Shane Browne performing music from his latest and soon-to-be released homegrown CD and DVD, *Bumblebee's World.*" Dalton left the stage to much applause.

"Welcome to *Count It All Joy.*" Shane moved in front of the microphone. "We're glad you're here with us. If you haven't gotten some of Randa Rylander's famous apple cider and snickerdoodle cookies, you're missing out on a treat." He smiled at his cousin and strummed the guitar again. "For those of you visiting Amazing Grace today, I've already been introduced, but I'd like you to meet my co-writer, co-producer, and my wonderful daughter, Taffeta."

The crowd turned and cheered, and Taffy smiled and waved, her little cheeks red.

"Taffy and I love to hang out in the woods with Bumblebee Bear and his friends. Recently, we took two of Taffy's …" He stopped and strummed his guitar, as if at a loss for words. "Sorry. Two of Taffy's friends have joined us as part of the team, and …" Shane turned to the screen. "… let's just say Bumblebee took to them like an otter to play … like a beaver to a stick … like a raccoon to a heist … oh, and like a bear to a picnic basket."

The kids giggled.

Abra blanched. Friends? The boys and Taffy were cousins—second cousins—but the relationship was a definite.

"Taffy and I are going to share our latest songs to go along with the adventures we've had with Bumblebee Bear, Oscar Otter, Roscoe Raccoon, and a few of their very best friends. This CD and the DVD aren't available today for purchase, but you can pre-order at the register, and our shelves are stocked with our first two offerings."

Shane tapped his foot and started into a song. The video behind him played as his lyrics and that voice—who knew he had that talent—entertained children and adults alike.

Abra's attention moved from the exceptional video of the mountain creatures to Shane's animated, playful face.

He talked to the children, even sat on the edge of the stage. He invited kids forward to sing with him. When they finished, he gave each co-performer a copy of one of the earlier DVDs.

Abra got lost in his performance and only the thunderous clapping, whistles, and children's glee shook her from her reverie.

She blinked, and her gaze tangled with Shane's. He smiled. Then he winked and gave a slight nod toward the boys. He wanted to introduce them. Despite his earlier slight at them, what could she say?

She answered with a forced smile.

"Taffeta, would you join me, please."

Taffy made her way through the pile of children seated on the floor and climbed on stage with her father.

Abra couldn't imagine how a mother could give up her child, why Jasmine had made the choice to give away that precious gift from heaven, leaving Shane to raise their little girl alone.

Pap had been both mother and father to Abra, but still, with her mother's departure, Abra's heart held an often-visited ache that only her mother's arms around her could soothe. The pastor often told her that God could fill any void, but when she'd asked him if his mother had ever walked out the door on him, he shook his head.

Abra suspected that God could take away the pain, the anguish over losing her husband, her father, her brother's disappearance, and her mother's abandonment and replace it with joy. Her mind knew He would hold her close. Her heart told her not to bother Him.

Taffy stood beside her father as the crowd applauded her talents as a songwriter. She smiled, and her green-eyed gaze twinkled.

"Peter and Paul Carmichael, come on up here, buddies."

The twins looked in Abra's direction. She smiled and motioned for them to do as Shane had asked.

They rushed forward, both turning to smile at the crowd.

"These two fellas are great with bears." Shane smiled at her. "But don't tell their mother. She might not let them go into the woods with Taffy and me again. But honestly, Bumblebee acts differently when they're around. She has always kept her distance, but she frolics for the boys. The videos we took would not be half as good if they hadn't been around, and I just want to tell them both how much Taffy and I appreciate them and look forward to many more hikes in the woods, Mom permitting."

That was a nice thing for Shane to do. She'd forgive him for the earlier slight.

"Folks, thank you for spending time with us today." Shane waved.

He approached her with all three kids flanking him, and somehow, he managed to slip his arm around her. "Thanks for staying."

"Thanks for being so wonderful." She turned in his arms, planning a thank you kiss on his cheek.

Their lips met.

Abra leaned closer, her arm slipping around his

waist, his kiss deepening.

The noise in the store faded first, and then it seemed to dissolve. No one else was there. The world consisted of only her and Shane.

Then the children giggled.

And the store returned.

Abra crossed her arms over her chest and watched the boys and Taffy cutting up behind the cash register where Randa talked and rang up purchases in the packed toy store.

"Are you sure about watching the boys while I'm gone?" Abra brought her attention back to Shane, which added another layer of warmth to her already burning cheeks.

"Go meet with Fred. Yes, they'll be fine." Shane smiled. "They won't want to cross their Aunt Randa."

Abra took a deep breath. "If you're sure."

"I'm positive. Dalton's around here somewhere."

"No." The ding of the cash register followed Randa's words. "He had an errand to run. Once he's done with that, he'll get the mower out and mow our lawns so that we can do that decorating." Gone was the brisk woman who'd dismissed Abra earlier. "Go ahead, Abra. They'll be fine."

Abra moved around the counter and leaned in to kiss Randa's cheek.

Randa held up her hand.

Abra stepped back, the pain of rejection stinging her again.

"You're not going to kiss me like you kissed Shane, are you?" Randa teased. "I'm glad most of the kids weren't still around you. That was a PG-rated kiss, if ever

Everybody's Broken

I saw one."

Abra waved her off. "See if I ever try to show my sisterly affection again."

Shane had lowered his head and was shaking it. He raised his gaze to Abra's. "Don't worry. Go."

"Give me thirty minutes." She hurried out the door and down Main Street.

Colbert's office was located on Market Street. Close enough to walk but Abra jogged, anxious to see the space where her newest brainchild might be birthed.

She stood on the porch of the old Victorian turned realtor's office and caught her breath.

Inside, the bang and rattle of someone closing and opening drawers and moving furniture announced that Fred Colbert was inside. She hesitated and tried the door.

Locked.

She waited without knocking. Getting ready for a potential customer was something Abra understood. Maybe time had gotten away from him. Perhaps he'd been in town with his family earlier this morning.

The glass in the door revealed a man backing out of a room. He closed the office and looked toward the front entrance. Abra and the man startled at the same time.

Fred Colbert had been the person standing outside the toy store. She had most likely seen him around town and didn't recognize the neighbor-realtor connection. What a relief.

Fred flipped the lock and pulled open the door.

"Mr. Colbert? We had an eleven o'clock appointment. I'm Abra Carmichael."

A wide smile lit the realtor's face. "Yes. Abra. How are you? Sorry about the locked door. I parked in the back and didn't think to unlock the darn thing." The man brushed his hands over his lime green shirt and his tan Khakis as if he might have lint.

"Nice to finally meet you." Abra held out her hand.

"Fred." His eyes crinkled with his smile. "We're neighbors, after all. Not that I'm home much."

A dark blue jacket hung on a coat rack in the corner, and Abra's eye for color tried hard to make it match what the man wore. Maybe he kept a coat here in case he wore a suit and left his jacket at home. "I didn't recognize you when I saw you outside the toy store earlier. I'm sorry."

The smile deepened. "When I saw the two lookalikes, I wondered if it was you. I should have said hello, but with the crowd, I imagined embarrassing myself and trying to explain to someone who wasn't you why I made the mistake."

Abra nodded. That explained the intense scrutiny on his face. "I'm anxious to see inside the building. I noted three stories. Do you know the square footage, and are all three stories included in a single lease?"

He scrunched his face. "I'm sorry to say that someone left a deposit with me earlier. They're coming in Monday after I've had time to draw up the lease."

"Earlier?" Abra's disappointment got the better of her. "But you were in town."

He motioned for her to take a seat. "Let's sit out here in the outer office. Without my secretary, here, I think it would be better, don't you? The wife tends to get a little jealous."

Abra pointed toward the front door. "We can sit on the porch if you would feel more comfortable." Something deep within jangled her nerves. She didn't like this double-dealing man.

"Here's fine. May I offer you something to drink?"

Abra shook her head and remained standing. "Actually, if the storefront is taken, I suppose our business is done. It's a lovely location, and I'm surprised that it lasted this long."

"True," he agreed. "The owner did want a higher lease due to the prime location and the other two stories. I think it takes a shrewd businessman—or woman—to realize what that would be worth. But I did mention on the phone that I have something to talk over with you."

Yes, he had. Abra took the chair he had indicated, and Fred sat behind the only desk in the front room, possibly his secretary's. "I have a buyer who loves The Gray Lady. The man said he visited town last year, and the place caught his eye. He's one who believes he can buy whatever he wants. Cash offer."

Abra leaned back in her chair. She brought her fingers to her lips and let the correct words tumble into place. Could this buyer be the man inside her home, the one who claimed to be Beau?

"The Gray Lady is my husband's inheritance to our boys. I didn't realize that until recently, but she's all the boys have that belonged solely to Beau."

"You're from out of state, aren't you? Have you decided to stay on?"

"I haven't made that decision, and I suppose if I had been able to lease the storefront, I might find myself staying here. But Beau's family would help make that decision. The Browne/Carmichael clan have heritage there. If I decide to sell, I would offer it to them first. Despite what they say, I think they'd hate for it to slip away from them because Beau's widow up and decides to cash in. I don't work like that, Mr. Colbert. Lives are more important, and ours have been shattered by the heinous act of some murderous individual. If I can, I'd like to try to help put some pieces back in place for our family."

The words came out, flowed like a river, and Abra's heart warmed with each revelation. "I love them like I once loved Beau." She stood. "I won't waste any more of your time, but if the lease falls through, please let me know."

Fred got to his feet. He looked beyond her as he

pushed in his chair. "Well, if you're not willing to sell The Gray Lady, perhaps if you plan to return home, you'll think of renting it. Perhaps that would be a compromise for this gentleman."

Abra nodded. "I might just do that, with an adequate security deposit, of course. The house has things in it that can never be replaced. And Beau's family would have to agree."

Fred shook her hand and looked at his watch. "Oh, look at the time. I have another appointment out of the office. I hope you'll excuse me."

He rushed down the hall and out the back. Abra turned toward the door and started to call after him. If she left, the place would remain unlocked.

The door opened and a woman entered. "Oh, hello," she startled. "Abra, right?"

"Yes."

"Tammy Colbert. Fred's wife."

Abra pointed down the hall. "If you're looking for your husband, he just left. Said he had an appointment away from the office."

Tammy smiled. "Yes, with me. I thought I'd come here first instead of meeting him at the restaurant. He usually does run late."

"I'm the culprit. I'm sorry. I set an appointment with him this morning. He might not have realized the conflict."

"No need to apologize. Fred does get caught up in his work." Tammy grinned.

"And it was all for nothing. The place I wanted to lease has been taken, but I'm glad to meet you. I enjoy Melissa when she comes over to play with Taffy and the boys."

"I should have said hello earlier." Tammy looked toward the road. "Well, Fred and I get so little alone time that I'm looking forward to lunch today. I better get back to the restaurant before he thinks I'm the one who's forgotten."

"I'm glad you came. He's apparently excited about the date, too. He left so hurriedly, he didn't lock the door."

Tammy dug in her purse and pulled out her keys. "I'll do that."

Abra nodded and stepped out the door with the woman. "If you're not busy, please feel free to stop over for coffee one morning. Maybe Randa will join us. I'd love to get to know you."

Tammy turned the lock and pocketed her keys. "I will. I have so much time on my hands, and Fred doesn't want me to work. I keep my license just in case, but he wants to take care of us, he says. Then he spends all of his waking hours doing that."

Abra laughed. "Yes, I saw that in the few minutes we talked." She started away. "I'll see you soon."

Halfway down the walkway to the sidewalk, Tammy passed her. "I'll be sure to stop by. See you, Abra."

Abra waved, but Tammy didn't see her. She was dressed up, her makeup beautifully applied, and she ran in high heels.

Tammy had a right to feel jealous, but she wasn't competing with other women. Her husband's lover was his business.

Maybe that explained Abra's dislike of the man. He left his family alone for the sake of making money.

Death had separated Abra from her husband, and the lies she'd learned after his death numbed her to the love she once had for him.

Life was separating Tammy and Fred, and Abra mourned for the couple she barely knew.

Everybody's Broken

Chapter 14

Decorating accomplished, Abra came inside from the cold. She pulled back the living room curtains. Outside, orange and purple crisscrossed the darkening Carolina blue sky. The boys and Taffy played in the front yard, frolicking in front of her surprise: a large antique farm wagon filled with haybales, which Shane had retrieved without the help of the absent Dalton.

All afternoon, they'd stuffed the scarecrows with hay and adorned them with thrift shop flannel shirts of red, green, and blue and faded and worn blue jeans. Thin ropes Abra purchased and cut into pieces circled their wrists and ankles, holding their gloved hands and booted feet to the hay. Abra had painted each scarecrow's face, giving them distinctive personalities. One even had a friendly gapped-tooth smile.

While the hay-stuffed country boys might frighten a few crows, they wouldn't scare the neighborhood children, and Shane's ingenuity had added to the design. A washtub with a pole and string attached, an old washboard he'd found in The Gray Lady's basement, and a pair of spoons pressed against one scarecrow's straw leg, had turned the four wagon mates into a band. Shane had laughingly dubbed the instrumentless fellow on stage with the band, Uncle Dalton.

Pumpkins enhanced the autumn look, both on the wagon and the porch, which were both adorned with pumpkin lights.

The work done, Shane promised he'd keep the kids busy while they waited for Dalton to return from the apparently complicated errand.

"They're having fun."

Abra shuddered at Randa's sudden arrival.

"I'm sorry I scared you. I decided to come back in through the solarium. I didn't knock."

"No need to knock. The door's always open to family." Except at night. Then the doors remained locked tight.

Randa touched Abra's shoulder. "Thank you for saying that after my behavior at the store."

Abra let the drape fall. "I can't imagine all you had on your mind: sales, Shane's performance—"

Randa raised her hand. "Friends don't make excuses for those who hurt them. I know I made you feel unwelcome. You didn't have to say a word. The truth was written all over your face."

"Any word from Dalton?" Abra asked. "The boys will be getting restless soon. They're looking forward to going to Shane's place."

Randa lowered her gaze and shook her head. "He might not come home for a while. I was going to suggest that you and Shane head up with the kids. We'll join you if he gets back in time."

The darkening living room was not Abra's favorite location. She led Randa to the foyer. "Is something wrong? I know I shouldn't pry, but like you said, we're friends, and your pain is also written on your face."

Everybody's Broken

Randa brushed her hair back. "Dalt and I had an argument this morning and then again when he wouldn't divulge his errand." She took a stuttering breath then released it. "I trust him. I do, but there's so much between us these days."

"I've been so worried."

Randa straightened and breathed deeply again, the rush of air emitting a little whistle. She'd hidden it well, but she'd been crying. Her nose was plugged. Her lips trembled, and she didn't speak for a moment.

Then she stepped away from Abra as if putting space between them. "The truth is, there's nothing between us. We thought that by now we'd have children." Randa lifted the hem of her t-shirt and played with the tightly stitched seam. "The emptiness in my heart has created this void in our feelings for each other. I'm angry most of the time. Of course, I try to hide it from everyone. Shane got a taste of it recently, and he's shied away from the subject. He doesn't realize it, I'm sure, but he's sheltering Taffy from any vindictive words I might throw her way. And Dalton ... I love him more than anyone on earth, and how do I show him? I make the old adage true. I hurt him the most."

Abra led Randa to the pew-like seat that ran the length of the foyer. "I'm sorry. Have you been told you can't have children?"

Randa nodded and swiped angrily at her tears. "The tests are inconclusive. The doctor feels it will be difficult for me to conceive." She bounced her leg up and down. Her stare fixed across the space to the face of the old grandfather clock. "Can I trust you not to tell Shane something if I share it with you?"

Abra's fingers found her mouth again. She hated secrets and lies. Look where they'd gotten them so far. Still, Randa needed freedom to unburden. As Shane had said, his cousin needed someone to listen. "Sure."

"I'm the reason. What I did ..."

Abra dropped her hand and tucked her fingers in between Randa's curled fist.

"Shane and me ... we got in a lot of trouble in high school. We ran with these kids that grew up on the wrong side of town. I got involved with the brother of Shane's best friend at the time. He was a couple of years older than us. I should've known better. I was sixteen." She faced Abra. "I got pregnant."

Abra fought to hide her surprise. She tightened her hold on Randa's hand, her attempt to reinforce the fact that she would never judge.

"I knew I had a little person inside of me. I thought for a while that I loved the baby, but then the baby's father got drunk. He'd been strangely silent from the time I told him. I pressed him for an answer, but I suspect I knew all along. The baby would be my responsibility. One night he told me how he didn't love me. He could never love me." Randa jumped to her feet, pulling her hand from Abra's grasp. She paced back and forth. "His words struck me so deeply that I took my spite out on that innocent baby. Fueled by anger, I forgot any love I might have had, and I killed my child." She stared at Abra, her eyes narrowed, her breathing labored.

Abra held her gaze. "I won't tell you that what you did wasn't an awful mistake."

"I don't have the excuse of a mistake, Abra. I knew what I was doing. When I left that clinic, I hated myself for it."

"Does Dalton know about the baby, about the decision you made?"

Randa looked toward the ceiling then back to Abra. "Dalton is the reason I know God accepted my cry for forgiveness."

"How so?"

"The clinic I went to was in a little place on the

Everybody's Broken

outskirts of Asheville." She stared straight into Abra's eyes, but her gaze was somewhere else, perhaps on a long-ago street in front of a clinic. "I stepped out the door I should have never entered at all let alone by myself. They told me to have someone bring me, but they didn't care. I was a number to them. I was a woman with another child they'd saved the world from." She didn't blink. "I walked out the door, and the sun burned down on me, and I thought of the sounds ..." Randa's body trembled. "The awful sounds ..." She covered her mouth with her hand and stood that way for a long moment before she shook her head as if not willing to visit the inside of the clinic in her imagination. "The sun was hot, and I was dizzy and confused. I stood there for a moment looking around the parking lot. The spaces were mostly empty, but I couldn't seem to focus on which car was mine." Randa wrapped her arms around her waist. "Then someone says to me, 'Are you okay, babe?'"

Abra wiped a tear from her own face and stood, waiting for the rest of Randa's heart-wrenching story.

"Dalton wrapped me in his arms, and he held me to him while I cried and cried in the middle of that parking lot near the clinic doors." A smile peeked through for a brief second. "More than one parent pulling a daughter into the clinic that day turned and walked away before they caused their child to make the same mistake I'd made all on my own. Momma, always a loving, free-spirit, and even Grandmere, who wasn't as judgmental as I always thought, would have rejoiced and helped me to care for the baby."

"You were hurting, Randa."

"Dalton never said where he'd heard the news. I don't remember telling anyone. I'd walked away from those Jordan River kids when I was treated so badly. I didn't talk to Shane or call Beau, but yet, there stood Dalton, a long way from Athens, Georgia, cutting classes." The tears poured down her face. "'Babe,' he said. 'I wanted to tell you in person that I would help with the baby. Am I too late?'" Randa lowered her head and a tear hit the foyer's marble floor. "That was when I noticed."

"What?" Abra waited, barely able to breathe.

"Dalton was crying, too."

Abra sat hard on the bench. "Randa, that man is wonderful."

Randa laughed aloud through her tears. "Don't I know it, but I've hurt him. I've subjected him to a life without children. If I'd waited, if I'd loved that baby more, Dalton would have had that child to love and another one, I'm sure of it.

"I'm so ashamed of what I did to that poor baby growing inside me. That baby should have been able to trust its mother for protection."

Abra stood and reached for Randa's hands. In the darkening shadow of evening, the children's laughter drifted in from the outside.

Tears ran down Randa's face, but otherwise she didn't move.

"David had a son." The words flowing from Abra's mouth surprised her. When was the last time she used scripture to make a point?

Since she'd thought herself too unworthy to pester God.

Randa stared at Abra during her long pause.

Abra had her full attention. No use not to go on now. "That son died as a result of something David did. Do you know the story?"

Randa nodded.

"Then you remember what David said."

"No." The word came out as a low moan.

"He prayed and fasted and wept for that child's life, but he'd already done the misdeed, and God had

Everybody's Broken

proclaimed the child would be taken from him."

Randa's eyes widened. "Please don't—"

Abra held up her hand. "When the baby died, David ate. His servants questioned why he had wept so terribly before the child died, and not after. David told them that while the baby was alive, God might have changed His mind, but with the baby gone, David would one day see the child, but the baby would not return to him."

"I don't understand."

Abra pushed Randa's hair behind her ear and placed her hand against her sister-in-law's moist cheek. "You will see your child again, Randa. You know the Lord. Bless your heart, you've been taking me to church with you all these weeks. Even on the day this happened, you saw some good come out of what you'd done. No, God didn't want you to do what you did, but your baby's death possibly meant that those girls who left before they entered that clinic may have kept their children. Your heart has been so burdened. I'd like to say I understand what you're feeling, but I don't. Yours is so much heavier than mine."

"No," she whispered. "I haven't been alone without my husband." Fresh tears fell down Randa's face. "Oh, Abra, I've been so awful."

"You've been weighed down with grief over the baby you lost and the baby the Lord hasn't given you yet. We can all see it. No one talks about it, but Shane and Dalton are worried. I see it in their faces, too. I guess we're all walking mirrors, huh?"

"I've been so centered on my pain, so completely oblivious to what everyone around me has been suffering. Dalton …" She turned one way and then the other. "I need to talk to Dalton."

"He'll be here soon," Abra reached and engulfed her sister-in-law in a tight hug. "Thank you for sharing your painful story. That's the privilege of friendship. Mazzie and I spent many a night sharing our troubles with each other. Other than Finn and Beau, I had no one else."

Randa pulled back. "We have that in common. I had Beau once upon a time, but then it was only Dalton and Shane. I suspect the callousness of the baby's father was the curtain pulled back on the world Shane and I had fallen into. I'd gotten pregnant before Shane's arrest and Beau's imprisonment of him," she sniffled, "and after the cold indifference, I shut myself off from that world. Then Beau dealt with Shane, and Dalton stood by me."

"Well, out of the ruins ..."

Randa turned sharply. "Did you hear that?" She hurried down the hall leading to the back of the house.

"What?"

"A click. A door. I heard it." Randa looked around. She stepped into the kitchen, stared at the door, and then back at Abra. "Are they all out front?"

Abra was torn between leaving Randa alone and running to peek.

Feet stomped on the porch and the front door swung open.

Randa pushed past Abra and ran into Dalton's unsuspecting arms, any strange sounds seemingly forgotten.

"Whoa." Dalton fell back and fought to steady himself.

"I love you so much, Dalt."

Dalton peered over his wife's shoulder and raised his brows.

Abra smiled.

For once, since her long journey alone without her husband, taking God's side of things filled Abra with a sense of well-being. *All things work together for good to them who love God ...*

For so long, she'd been fighting those words. Now the deep and abiding truth of them sank deep inside, yet

Everybody's Broken

something within her pushed back against the thought.

As Dalton clung tightly to his bride, whispering words of love into Randa's ear, Abra stilled.

What's the good in all that the boys and I have lost, Lord?

"Well," Shane entered, followed by three little ragamuffins with leaves in their hair and on their clothes, "how does pizza sound? We'll have a cookout at my place another time."

Abra looked upward, the memory of Shane's wonderful, deep kiss filling her with warmth against the chill coming through her front door. No. Shane could not be God's answer.

Dalton kissed Randa and turned with her in his arms. "Sounds good, buddy. I might have to go out again. A friend is at the hospital. They might release him. If so, he'll need a ride home."

"Who?" Three adult voices chorused.

Dalton hesitated. "Jeb ... the town window dresser." For some reason, his gaze remained fixed on Abra for maybe a beat too long.

Abra couldn't breathe. This man that had loved Randa so well—he couldn't have kept her from her brother all of this time?

He stood with his ear against the partial crack he'd allowed to remain so that he could hear. He'd been staying away, but the phantoms pushed him through the passageway, eager to see if his scheme was unfolding as planned.

Some of what he eavesdropped on—Randa's confession to Abra—was known to him. The baby Dalton wanted to keep. The sad man who hadn't made it in time.

Dalton had been willing to throw his whole life away because his darling Randa had crawled into bed with someone else.

Randa was an idiot. Anyone could have seen that Dalton had it for her bad.

Dalton as a father intrigued him.

He'd never be able to love a kid.

No. Loves himself too much.

A kid would tie Dalton down.

The voices had their facts straight this time, but their screeching caused the ache in his head to intensify. He shut the opening and winced.

"Did you hear that?" Randa said. Then footsteps pounded on the floor.

Stupid!

Imbecile!

Mo—ron!

He held his breath as Randa apparently turned in the opposite direction.

A clamor from the front of the house gave him room to exhale.

Happy chatter greeted him. Good. They were all inside. Dare he peek out once again? He opened it wide enough to feel the warmth of the heat brush his cheek.

"Sounds good, buddy," Dalton said. "I might have to go out again. A friend is at the hospital. They might release him. If so, he'll need a ride home."

"Who?" voices asked, curiosity evident.

"Jeb ... the town window dresser."

Jeb?

He tipped his head looking at the beams above him. No one he knew.

"What do you know about him?" Abra asked. "I mean, has he lived here long?"

"Ah, no. He hasn't. He came to town recently. I suggested he ask around about some work."

"Did you know he was that talented?" Shane quizzed. "I mean, the man pulled rabbits out of his trick hat all over town this week. I saw him for a brief second this morning, and he disappeared."

"Why the third degree?" Dalton's voice held an edge. "He left because he'd been up all night working, and he felt terrible."

"He did look bad," Shane agreed. "But how did you know he could pull this together for the town—who wants to thank him, by the way?"

"Jeb's a friend."

"No," Shane countered. "You said he just came to town."

"So did Abra. I consider her a friend."

"No ..." Randa laughed. "Abra arrived half a year ago, and she's your sister-in-law. Jeb arrived last week. Come on, Dalt, spill."

"He's a good guy. What can I say?"

"Does he know me?"

Abra's question nearly made him tumble away from the opening.

"Why would you ask that?" Shane turned his curiosity on her. "Something wrong?"

"Where does he live? Does he have a place to stay or could he be hiding in this house. Randa just ..."

"Hold on." Dalton stopped her.

"Jeb lives up by me," Shane answered. "It's a rundown old place, but I've seen him there in the evenings."

"Why are you asking?" Dalton repeated Shane's earlier question.

"Because he's Uncle Finn!" One of the boys announced. "You said you saw Uncle Finn's hints in the windows, Mommy. He told us not to tell you anything. Uncle Finn was afraid if the killer knew he was alive, the killer would shoot all of us. Finn told us to stay quiet. We did, Mommy, but Uncle Finn is here."

He almost laughed aloud at the little boy's useless hopes and dreams. Finn was good and gone.

As gone as gone can be.

Dead to the world.

A cold cadaver.

Just like the man he'd killed earlier today.

At least that's what he'd been told. Finn was shot right after Beau. He'd seen Beau go down. He'd heard the second shot as he'd scurried away from the scene.

He hadn't been happy about Beau's death, not when he'd been so close to getting what he'd wanted, but whether Finn lived or died meant nothing to him.

You sure about that? Why is Abra here?

What hints did he leave in those windows?

The kid did say Finn knew who killed Beau. If they find out the truth from that guy, they're gonna be looking for you.

He fell against the wall, grasping his hair in his hands. His body slid down the concrete.

Their taunts wouldn't make him kill again. One killing in a day was enough.

Everybody's Broken

Chapter 15

Jeb opened his eyes to a dark room. The drugs running into his IV were good. The doctor was right. He hadn't eaten or drank much over the last week, making him dehydrated and malnourished. Along with the muscles that had been working overtime when they should be resting, Jeb Castor had been a hospital stay waiting to happen.

Beyond the room's window, all was dark except for the lights of homes on the nearby mountains.

The cold air hit him like a wintry blast. He fisted his hands around the no-frills white cover and tugged it up around him.

Something rustled beside him. He startled and turned.

A woman, by the shape of her, stood next to the chair Dalton had parked into the corner after his earlier visit.

He swallowed hard and fought the unmanly sob welling in him. He'd wanted to hold her for so long, to run his hands through that short, dark mane of mahogany, to inhale her perfume, the one only he was allowed to purchase for her—Opium. She'd drugged him with it and with the soft lilt of her Southern twang, making him fall so in love with her he thought he'd die if he had to go one more minute without her. Her voice always sent his desire into overdrive.

She bent forward, her hair falling against his face. Moisture, possibly a tear falling from her beautiful high cheeks to grace him with a hint of her emotion against his scraggly face. If only he could see her.

"I've missed you so much," the woman whispered, breaking the spell he'd cast over himself. The wrong woman but one he also loved more than his own life—in a very different way.

"Abracadabra?" His voice flowed rough with disappointment, but in the same moment, he threw his arms around her and held her to him. "Abra," he cried into her long dark hair. "I missed you, too."

"She's coming," Abra pulled away. "When I knew it was you, I called her. She said she'd talked to you." With each word, the edge in her voice sharpened like a knife.

His eyes grew accustomed to the darkness.

She wiped tears away with both hands and stepped from his side.

The cold air brushed over him.

"Oh, Finn. Why?"

Finn pushed up and winced. He fidgeted for the button on the side of the bed. The soft whine irritated him as his feet rose. He pushed another button, and somehow ended up with his head lower than his body and his feet in the air.

Abra stood silent. He lifted his head to see her.

Her lips were pressed tight, and she'd covered her mouth with her hands.

"Are you going to stand there and hide your smile, or are you going to help me?" he snapped.

She shook her head and soft giggles flowed from between her fingers. His own body quaked with laughter.

Abra finally moved toward him. She pushed the button, and his feet went higher. "I know you didn't kill Beau, if that's what you think I'm asking. I want to know why you kept so much from me."

"All you need to know is I didn't do it."

She pressed the button again.

"Okay," he said, all humor pressed away from him by the burden he carried. "I loved him like a brother," he whispered.

Abra deftly lowered his feet and raised the head of the bed.

Too late. The hooves of the thundering headache returned. He closed his eyes tightly and opened them. "How did you know I was hospitalized? Did Dalton tell you?"

"Dalton is as good a liar as you and Beau put together." Her words carried dark emotion. "Peter saw your hints. When Dalton came home tonight, he mentioned the window dresser had been hospitalized. I started questioning, and Peter's insistence that you were the mysterious fellow making magic all over town, caused Dalton to confess."

"Where are the *phews*?"

Abra smiled. She'd always been amused by his nickname for the twins. "Shane took them home. Randa sat with me until Dalton came back after they admitted you. They asked me not to go out tonight, but when Dalton went home with Randa, I waited until I thought they'd be asleep."

He leaned his head back against the pillow.

"Finn, I didn't put the boys in danger by leaving them with Shane Browne or trusting Dalton Rylander, did I?"

"No. They're in very safe hands with both of them. And it's Jeb ... Finn Jebediah Osteen, but here it's Jeb Castor."

"Castor? Like the oil?"

"I made it up. Sue me."

In the hallway, something squeaked by.

Abra turned her attention there. A tear slither down her face. "I don't know who to trust anymore."

"I'm here. You have me."

Her silence scraped his nerves like a fillet knife against the scales of a dead fish.

His sister had always been too trusting, but he never wanted her to have to face a reality like the one she was living now.

"Why are you here?" She took a long time turning to him.

"In Amazing Grace?" he asked.

"I'd like to think you came looking for me, but I meant here in the hospital."

"I came to town seeking refuge and a place to lick my wounds, but I was glad when Dalton told me you'd been here awhile."

"Why are you in the hospital?"

"Exhaustion, lack of nourishment, dehydration, pain."

"I can imagine, but there's more. I know it." She moved close to him once again and reached for his hand.

He slipped his fingers around hers. They'd never been ones to fight. He'd like to think he'd loved his sister from the moment their parents brought her home from the hospital, but Pap once told him he'd tried to hide Baby Abra in a closet and pretend she hadn't come home to take his parents' attention.

All he could remember was the desire to always protect her. That's why this horrible mess he'd gotten them into hurt so deeply.

He'd failed to guard Beau, Abra, and their boys. And he'd lost so much in the trying.

"Finn …"

He shot her a warning glance.

Everybody's Broken

"Jeb?" She squeezed his hand. "Tell me what's wrong with you?"

No way would he be able to brace her for this. Like a Band-Aid on a scab, he'd have to pull the truth out quickly. "I was shot in the back of the head. The bullet came from the side, grazed some nerves. God protected me."

Her fingers tightened around his. "Who shot you?"

"Abra, you're going to have to trust me and Dalt. We have to play this out. You're smack dab in the middle of a heap load of trouble. If you're not careful and don't pay attention to us, you and the boys could get hurt."

"Dalton must have told you that Shane and his little girl might be in trouble, too. I don't want him ending up like—"

"We're trying to prevent that from happening ... to all of you."

"I've been in the middle since Beau Carmichael walked into my life, haven't I?" She stomped her foot, yanked her hand from his hold, and turned away from him, whirling back, hands on her hips. "You've known even before Beau was murdered."

"Stop!" He raised his voice. "You need to think of the kiddos. They're in danger."

"Who did this to us, Finn?"

"Jeb," he ground out the name. "I'm a wanted man, and if you can't, for once, open up that pretty little mind of yours and see that we're not living in a bubble, you're going to let the killer get away with what he's already done and what he'll do if he feels his plans unraveling."

"Peter and Paulie were with Mazzie the whole time, weren't they?" She paced away from him and back.

The question, coming out of left field, had him floundering for a pop fly that was sure to fall on the head of the woman he loved. And Mazzie didn't like being conked on the noggin. He'd known that before the day

243

she'd taken down Beau during a church volleyball game. Trouble was, Mazzie had been fighting for Abra, for the truth Beau continued to hold back.

"I want to know if my best friend watched my soul nearly die every day my children were out of my arms, every day I wondered if they were thrown into the ocean or the river, every day I watched the waves crash on the other side of the windows to my house, wondering if the sharks had eaten them or if their little bodies would wash up on shore. I want to know, *Jebediah*, if Mazzie could betray me like that, and if she could watch me hurt, how can I ever trust either of you again?"

Finn swallowed hard. He'd never seen Abra this angry. "She did it to keep us all safe, to give me time to get away, to find treatment."

"A bullet wound is going to draw a report from the hospital," she pressed.

Perhaps his sister had lost all faith in him after all. He'd like to play it up big, tell her Mazzie dug the bullet out and that she'd saved his life, but nothing so dramatic happened. Oh, he'd been hurt. He still didn't know how Mazzie managed to get him out of the truck and into one of her empty rentals. He didn't know why the boys stayed in the truck until he could get his faculties about him or how Mazzie had gotten him cleaned up and lucid enough to allow him to slip out of town to medical treatment hundreds of miles away, with the story of an accident.

During those days in the rental, he'd dreamed Beau was there. He'd even thought he'd heard Beau talking to the boys. But it had been a dream. All of it.

He'd never tell Abra the truth. Not now anyway. He and the boys had watched Beau die that day.

"I have some nerve damage and a chipped bone, and you're causing the headache that brought me in here to come back."

Abra folded her arms across her chest and stared at

Everybody's Broken

him for a long moment. "So, I'm supposed to walk out of here, pretend you don't need me, that you didn't lie to me, that my best friend never betrayed me, and that I know nothing of yours and Dalton's plans."

"That's what I'm hoping." He rolled his neck, pushing away the galloping horse of apocalyptic pain. "After you stop by the nurse's station and hint to them that I might need more painkillers."

She glared at him for a long moment. Then she leaned close. "You know that beating Mazzie gave Beau?"

He stopped his rubbing and jerked his gaze to her. "Yeah?"

"If you didn't look so bad right now, I'd start on you and finish up on her." Abra stormed toward the door.

"Wait!"

"Sorry, sir. Wrong room, but I'll let one of the nurses know you need help."

Jeb stared after her.

Mazzie was leaving from Florida to arrive in North Carolina to meet the anger he'd apparently unleashed in his sister. When they collided, things could get pretty ugly, unless Abra's great propensity for forgiveness returned.

Although, he'd like to see how Mazzie would get herself out of this one. She could be pretty creative when necessary.

Chapter 16

Abra sat alone on the left side of the beautiful old Baptist church. Since she'd arrived in Amazing Grace, she'd been to every Sunday morning service with her new family, sitting in the same pew that seemed set aside for the Brownes and the Rylanders, and now the Carmichaels, who crammed into the row until the kids were led out by a Children's Church volunteer after the song worship. The third week of the month, though, the kids in Children's Church sang a special song, and the four adults didn't have to motion for squirming kids to stand up and sing or to hush up during the prayer.

Where were Shane, Randa, and Dalton? She'd seen Dalt wolfing down a strawberry donut before rushing to the teen class he and Randa taught together. Everything within her wanted to challenge him about his lies of omission, but she'd stayed quiet. Finn could tell his friend that she knew, and he could approach her or pretend everything between them was fine. Right now, she was too angry to speak, and she had no desire to cover her mouth with her hands.

Taffy and the boys, dressed nicely after a sleep-over at Shane's, had waved at her before running off to class, but Randa and Shane had been noticeably absent. Shane had not attended the class they enjoyed together.

Abra stared out the floor-to-ceiling glass. A cross separated the panes, the beams of the cross giving way to thinner golden bars that braced the beams and glass into the structure. She found it difficult to pay attention to the pastor with the creek rushing by outside the windows, and the golden and red leaves, more and more drifting to the ground.

Abra was torn between wanting to see the pristine white snow Randa described and heading back to Florida where she could snuggle inside her home on cold days and stare out at the ocean and the beach always empty of tourists when the cold crept that far south.

Pastor Quinn Moxley stopped beside the pew and held out his hand. "Good to see you."

"And you," Abra said. Seemed to her that someone as nice and friendly as Quinn would have settled down with a wife and kids by now, but the pastor remained single.

"Randa." Pastor Moxley nodded as Randa entered the pew from the opposite direction. "How are the plans for the Harvest Festival? Do you need anything?"

Randa sat beside her, the smile she wore brighter than any she'd shared since Abra had come to know her. "No need to worry, Quinn."

"You're terrific, and thank you for volunteering, Abra. Randa told me you've been working on decorations." He smiled and left.

Abra bumped her shoulder. "I'm bored to tears, and since I didn't get the storefront I wanted, I'm desperate. Please keep me busy."

"I promise." Randa nodded.

"You're happy today."

Randa raised her brows and leaned away from her. "I am very happy."

"Did Dalton leave after Sunday school to tend to his wounded window dresser?"

Randa shook her head, clearly oblivious to the sarcasm Abra had laced into her question. "Nope. You'll see him in a minute." She chuckled. "Shane remembered something his mom made years ago for his dad to wear when we sang the song similar to the ones the kids are going to sing today. Took a little convincing, but Dalton's helping out. He's in a good mood as well, so it wasn't too difficult." She winked.

Randa peaked Abra's interest. Shane usually played his guitar for the children's choir, but Dalton always sat in the pew. She couldn't imagine. Her anticipation grew as Randa squirmed and fought to keep from giggling. Abra had to cover her mouth and bite her lip to keep from joining in. If she lost it, they'd go into a fit of laughter, and Abra had no idea what could be so funny in the Lord's house on a Sunday morning.

After the opening song and the prayer, the door to the left side of the church, leading from the Sunday school rooms, opened, and the kids filed in.

Shane stood at the door as one of the volunteers made sure the kids took their places in front of the pulpit. He continued to motion for several long seconds before a large white, anorexic rooster with scrawny yellow legs and a red floppy crown stepped through the door.

With her hand over her mouth, Abra widened her eyes and turned to face her sister-in-law.

Randa bobbed her head up and down. "Hilarious, right?" She snickered. "Well, God has a sense of humor, and no one can ham it up—I mean cluck it up—more than Dalton."

Dalton stopped, stared at the congregation, folded his white wings, and moved his head back and forth as he made his way to stand behind the kids who struggled with their composure.

Shane settled on a stool to the side of the kids and stared down at his guitar, his shoulders rising and falling. Then he took a deep breath, raising his shoulders one more time before letting out a breath.

Dalton flapped his wings, "Cluckety cluck, cluck, brawk, brawk, brawk."

Shane fell forward in laughter, and the stool slid out from under him. He caught himself and sat.

"Boys, the Methodists are going to beat us to the Chinese restaurant if you keep this up." Pastor Moxley, standing at the back of the room laughed into his mic.

Shane nodded, took another deep breath, and strummed. Dalton repeated his *cluckety, cluck, cluck, brawk, brawk, brawk* and the kids broke into a fun version of *Don't Be a Chicken*, a song about standing strong for your faith.

Peter and Paulie sang out, Peter a little off key. Taffy faced him for a second. Catching a look at Dalton, she beamed as he winked down on her. Otherwise, he stood still until the chorus when he sang with the children and offered his "cluckety cluck, cluck, brawk, brawk, brawk."

The song ended and the church broke out in laughter and applause.

The kids filed out for Children's Church with Dalton and Shane following.

Pastor Moxley stepped to the pulpit. "I don't think that gangly old rooster had enough meat to fry him for Sunday dinner. Good thing most of us do meet at the Chinese place."

Randa guffawed and fell against Abra.

Abra's eyes filled with happy tears. She would start praying for her friends, and maybe God would open His ears to her because her prayers were for someone she loved, a couple who would be wonderful parents.

Everybody's Broken

Maybe then she could believe that God cared about her and the boys.

Abra stared at the cross, and the one on the wall behind the baptismal at Bodacious Cove Baptist Church came to mind.

She closed her eyes and bowed her head. More tears fell. *I'm so sorry, Lord. You brought Finn to me, and I didn't thank You for keeping him safe. All I did was stir up anger for those You have given to and kept with me.*

Randa slipped a Kleenex into Abra's hands and an arm around her shoulders. "You okay?"

Abra looked up to her sister-in-law. The pastor had not spoken one word of his sermon, but a scrawny chicken and a cross brought the truth home to her. "God loves me," she whispered.

Randa smiled and hugged her tight. "Of course He does, and we love you, too."

Abra leaned her head on Randa's shoulder and stared at the cross on the window and for once focused on it and not the scenery outside.

The sheriff's car came into view as soon as Abra turned onto Sycamore Street, but not at her house. She breathed a momentary sigh of relief then gasped. The car was parked in front of the Colbert home.

She pulled into her drive and hurried up the steps of their house, her boys in front of her.

Peter turned to peer over his shoulder. "Is Melissa okay?"

"I'm sure she is." Abra unlocked the door and ushered them inside. A heavy cloak of dread clung to her.

"What if she's not?" Paulie tugged on her dress. "I'm scared."

Abra bent down and stared into their large green eyes. Time had come for them to get past their fears—all of them. Yet, even now she listened carefully for movement in her home, sensing that someone was watching. "I can't go over there right now. The sheriff would think I'm intruding. Remember how Daddy always said that when he was on a call and the neighbors show up, he couldn't get his job done?"

Peter nodded. "He said they think they're helping, but they're—they're—"

"Objecting!" Paulie said loudly.

"Obstructing." Abra touched his nose. "Yes, the sheriff is either checking on something or someone called him to the house. No matter how worried we are, we need to wait."

A knock on the door startled her.

Peter started to open it, but Abra jumped to her feet, pulling him back.

She tugged the kids behind her and peered through the peephole. Then she opened it. "Hello, Sheriff."

"Abra, can we come in?" he asked.

Tammy stepped from behind him. Abra hadn't seen her there.

"Please." She pulled the door back to let them inside.

"Boys, would you mind letting me talk with your mother and Mrs. Colbert?" Dixon asked.

Peter looked to her, and she nodded, but when they started upstairs she moved after them. "Have a seat in the living room. I want to see them safely upstairs."

Dixon nodded. "Please hurry."

Abra raced the boys upstairs. She pulled play clothes out of their drawers and gave them the hangars to place their good clothes on. Then she crept around hurriedly to make sure they were alone. "Stay here until I call you."

Downstairs, Tammy sat in the chair by the window, her left hand fisted around something. In her right hand, she held what looked like a photograph. She shook her head and sobbed into her fisted hand.

Not so long ago, Abra had done this with Loyal Herman and Trace Bastion standing over her. Abra prayed that her neighbor had not received similar news, but if so, why would the sheriff bring her here? "Tammy, what is it?"

Tammy stood. "Fred. He's missing. He never showed up for our lunch. You said that he was going to meet me."

"Abra, you met with Fred yesterday?" Sheriff Dixon asked.

"Yes, at his office at eleven. Tammy saw me leaving. I had planned to make an appointment with Fred to look at the corner store on Main Street, but he called because someone had contacted him about buying this house."

"Your house phone, right? I still have your cell."

"Yes, our house phone."

"Do you mind if I look on your caller ID?"

Abra shrugged. "No, no. Go ahead."

"Did he call you from his office?" Tammy asked.

"I don't know."

Dixon walked back into the room. "Tammy, Fred did call here from the office. He turned to Abra. "Can you give me any details about the conversation? Did anything seem strange to you?"

"The phone call seemed normal enough."

"How did Fred seem during the call?"

"Friendly but conducting business." Abra shrugged. "I hadn't met him yet, so when he was in town a little earlier, I didn't realize who he was."

"Fred hanging out in town? I don't think so," Tammy's voice went shrill. She wiped a badly decomposing tissue against her eyes.

Abra left her and returned with a box of Kleenex. She longed to put her arms around the woman and tell her everything would be okay, but Mazzie hadn't done that, and Abra had appreciated her promise-less silence.

"What makes you so certain he couldn't have been downtown?" Dixon asked.

"He had lined up a couple of early morning showings. I called him around ten to remind him of our lunch, but he couldn't talk, said he had someone with him."

"Did he say who this person might be?"

Tammy shook her head and pulled several Kleenex from the box. "He's meticulous about his calendar. He didn't have anyone down at that time. I assumed someone walked in off the street. They do that sometimes." She blew her nose.

"I arrived for my appointment at eleven," Abra said.

"Anything seem strange to you?" Dixon faced Abra.

"The office door was locked. He took a minute to come out of what I assume was his office. I think the fact that we hadn't recognized each other in town startled both of us. He said, and I think he was joking, that we should sit in the outer office because Tammy was jealous when it came to other women. He informed me someone had beaten me to the lease on the storefront, and he asked about my willingness to sell this place. We both left without what we wanted."

Tammy shook her head. "Abra, Fred knows who you are. He's seen you come in and out of the house. And the storefront on the corner?" She looked from Dixon and back to Abra. "No one's leased it. We own it. He would have called me to tell me if anyone had taken it."

Abra straightened. "We talked about our seeing each other downtown, and he even commented that he'd seen the twins with me and wondered, but he didn't want to embarrass himself." The tug of Dixon's gaze drew her to him. "Sheriff, Fred never divulged ownership in that property. He even elaborated on the owner realizing a savvy businessperson would recognize the value."

"Fred would never hold back information on any of the properties we own. He would have given you the lease agreement to look over or take to an attorney."

"I can't think of any reason why he wouldn't be upfront with me." Underneath Abra's sweater top, goosebumps prickled.

Tammy put her hand to her head. "I can't imagine Fred ever telling anyone I was the jealous type. I trust my husband. He's a workaholic, but he doesn't look at other women."

"Has he been known to sit in an outer office when meeting with single females?" Dixon asked.

Tammy shook her head. "No," she wailed the word. "He has his desk organized. Everything he needs is right there."

"Tammy tells me she was supposed to meet her husband at eleven thirty, Abra."

"That's understandable if he knew he didn't need to show me the property, and he only wanted to see if I would be willing to sell The Gray Lady. He was very rushed when he left. Remember? He didn't lock the door. You had to do it."

Tammy sobbed. "None of this makes sense."

"Tammy, has Fred ever mentioned someone wanting this property?"

Tammy sat for a long moment. Then she pushed forward. "Back around April or May, he thought he was close to a deal. He told me he'd talked to Mr. Carmichael, and he was thinking it over, but every time he thought they would close, Mr. Carmichael delayed."

Dixon stood with his hands on his leather belt. He stared out the living room window, seemingly deep in thought.

"Did he ever tell you the name of this potential buyer?"

Tammy thought for a second. "If he did, I've

forgotten, but Fred keeps everything on file." She peered up at the sheriff. "He could have had an accident. His car could have gone over a mountain ... Where is his car?"

Dixon wiped a hand across his brow. "Let's not let our imaginations run away with us." He reached down and took the object out of Tammy's hand and held a photograph out to Abra.

She stared down at it and back to the sheriff. "I don't understand." Blood drummed in her ears, a warning signal. "Who is that?"

"Fred!" Tammy wailed. "You met him yesterday."

Abra put her fingers to her lips. Her entire hand trembled as she looked down at the picture in Dixon's hands. "Sheriff ..." Her stomach soured, and she cupped her fingers over her mouth, waiting for the queasiness to pass.

"Abra ...?" He waited.

"I met with someone in Fred Colbert's office yesterday, but it was not the man in that picture."

Chapter 17

Abra walked with the sheriff and Tammy out onto her porch. Tammy could barely stand. Abra was well-acquainted with the rubbery legs, the fight to hold it all together, and the sense that nothing would ever be the same.

She touched Tammy's shoulder.

The woman turned and Abra wrapped her in an embrace. "I'll be praying," she whispered.

Tammy nodded against her.

"I mean it. I'm not just saying it." Abra captured her attention by holding her stare. "Let me get the boys situated with Shane or Randa, and I'll be over to sit with you."

Tammy shook her head. "I've called my mother. She should be here soon. I appreciate it, but Mom's a little shy with strangers."

Abra pushed a smile into place. "Then I'll send you both over some dinner, and I'll help Sheriff Dixon in any way I can."

Tammy hugged Abra once again. "Thank you. I don't think I could pull anything together for Melissa right now."

Abra nodded as Sheriff Dixon led Tammy down the steps and across the road.

Tires screeched to a stop in front of The Gray Lady. Shane jumped out and Taffy followed him. Another car raced past and pulled into Dalton's drive. Randa and Dalton nearly beat Shane and Taffy to the porch.

Before they could ask questions, she held up her hand. "Taffy, let's let you go upstairs with the boys." She took Taffy's hand and saw her safely to the boys' room.

Peter and Paulie were playing with Legos in the spot between their beds. "Mommy, is Melissa okay?" Peter asked.

"She's fine, baby. I want you three to stay up here for a bit more."

She backed out, blowing each of them a kiss. Then she hurried downstairs to the porch.

Sheriff Dixon had returned.

Shane moved to stand beside Abra. He pulled her toward him, his arm around her waist. Abra closed her eyes, feeling the protection he offered.

"Tammy needs to rest. I don't think she slept a wink overnight."

"What's going on?" Dalton asked.

"That appointment I had with Fred Colbert yesterday … apparently, someone masqueraded as the realtor." Abra trembled.

Shane tightened his hold.

"I probably met with Beau's killer instead."

Dalton straightened. "What'd he look like?"

Sheriff Dixon lifted a brow. "Dalt, you think you know who it is?"

Dalton looked at Randa and back to Abra. Then he tipped his head twice for Daniel to follow him to the edge of the porch. Shane started to follow, his warmth leaving Abra. Dalton held up his hand, and Shane moved back to her. "Are you okay?"

Abra shook her head but then nodded. "He's dead."

Randa blinked. "What is going on and why is everyone hiding things from me?"

Abra reached for her hand, and Randa's warm fingers slipped around Abra's. "Fred didn't meet Tammy for a lunch date yesterday. Thinking I was the last person to see him alive, Sheriff Dixon brought her over. She had a picture of her husband." She shuddered and, again, Shane steadied her with his embrace. "I didn't meet with Fred." She left Shane's hold and went to the opposite side of the porch from where Dalton and Sheriff Dixon's conversation was ratcheting up into an argument with Daniel Dixon's hands on the cuffs attached to his belt.

"He's dead. I'm sure he is. I think I knew it from the moment I saw the sheriff's car in Tammy's driveway. I had a feeling yesterday, and I pushed it away." She turned to face the cousins. "I've pushed a lot of feelings aside throughout the years, ones that counted for something. Warning bells—Beau's inability or outright refusal to share his past with me, Pap's murder, choosing to believe it couldn't have happened. Yesterday, gut instinct told me I was in danger, and I walked right into it. I'd seen the same man outside the toy store." She stared up at the bright blue sky. "I met with Beau's killer, and I think the only way he could have taken Fred's place is to have killed him." She gritted her teeth so hard pain set in her jaw.

On the other side of the porch, Sheriff Dixon leaned in. He poked Dalton in the chest three times, and Dalton's face reddened. But he nodded. Whatever Daniel said, Dalton wasn't arguing. Then Dixon pulled back. "Anything else you want to let me know so I can add them to the scale when I'm weighing the balance to determine if I'm going to arrest you for obstruction of justice?"

Randa rushed to him. "Daniel, what …? Dalton hasn't done anything. We're as clueless about Fred's disappearance as you are."

"Talk to your husband, Randa. Let him tell you what he's done." He moved to Abra. "I'm not giving up hope that Fred is conveniently being held somewhere. Don't you give up either. Tammy Colbert needs to have hope that God has spared her husband. If he hasn't been, we'll deal with the aftermath." He pointed at Dalton.

"What do we need to do?" Randa asked.

"Dalton's going to find a photograph and bring it to me. Randa, since time is of the essence, I think you might want to help him look." He started down the steps. "I'm going back to my office and make a call to Mazzie Harris."

"Mazzie …" Abra started after him. "What would Mazzie have to do with Fred's disappearance? She's been in Florida."

"According to Dalton, she's either on her way or planning to make her way to Amazing Grace. If she arrives, she's not to leave here."

Tears filled Abra's eyes and washed down her cheeks. What had her best friend done now?

Finn turned to his side and fluffed the pillow. His headache had subsided, and all he wanted was his release from his confinement.

Yeah, he could walk out, call a cab—if this small town even had a cab company—and get back to that hovel he called a home.

A hovel he'd begun to like the more he worked with

it.

Who was he kidding? He missed the pounding surf, wanted more than anything to feel the sand between his toes, to wake up in time for his beautiful woman to arrive with a cup of coffee from Tuttle's Grocery and sit outside his cabana watching the sunrise.

He missed the little things.

He longed for the most important.

He hadn't heard from her since his phone call begging her to find a way to him. But Abra said she was coming.

In the silence of the room, he'd gotten used to the footfalls in the corridor. The ones coming toward his room were heavier than most of the nurse's steps. Probably someone visiting another patient in a room down the way or a doctor—not his. He'd seen his thirty minutes ago when the old man told him he wanted to run a couple of more tests to check the extent of the nerve damage and then he could be sprung.

The way Finn's luck was running Dalton would be caught up with his family and unable to drive him home.

"Finn Osteen?"

The voice that met his ears was unfamiliar, and Finn didn't realize until too late that he'd bounded upward at the address.

A good-sized man in a brown uniform shirt and jeans stood with his hands on a leather holster.

Abra ... his sister's name swirled in his brain. She'd betrayed him. Something he never thought she would do.

"Finn Osteen?" the lawman asked.

"Jeb Castor." Finn held out his hand.

The sheriff didn't budge.

The leather of his holster stretched. "Son, if I haven't arrested your cohort yet, I'm not gunning for you unless you tell me one more lie. Let me give you another chance to get this right." The sheriff hiked a brow. "Finn Osteen, brother of Abra Carmichael, brother-in-law of the deceased Beau Carmichael, uncle to Peter and Paul Carmichael, partner in crime with one Dalton Rylander?"

Finn swallowed hard. "Yes, sir."

"Mighty fine work you did on the windows, son. My mother loves her decorations and the fact you used her inventory around town."

Finn dared let his gaze drop from the lawman's face to his nametag. Dixon.

"Ms. Grace? She's a sweet woman."

"The way she's been talking you up, I meant to hunt you down and say hello. I didn't get a chance. Now, I find out that you're the same man who's been on the lam for how long?"

Finn didn't answer. He had an idea that Sheriff Dixon knew exactly how long it had been since Beau's murder.

"So, are you going to tell me you didn't do it?"

"Kill Beau? I didn't do that."

The sheriff huffed and shook his head. "How about the kidnapping of Peter and Paul Carmichael?"

Finn's body jerked. He pushed the covers aside, looking for his clothes. "Someone took my nephews? I have to get to Abra." He opened a cabinet and slammed it shut. "Where are my clothes?"

"Calm down, son. I didn't mean today. When Beau was killed, did you kidnap them and keep them away from your sister?"

Finn fell back against the bed and sat, his heart rate lessening. "No, sir. I didn't kidnap them, but from what I understand they were away from their mother until Beau's funeral. And that was because of me."

"What about the recent disappearance of Fred Colbert?"

Finn shook his head. "Who? I know the name, but I don't know how I know it." Since the shooting, his brain did that to him on occasion. Was Fred a part of this nightmare, and had Finn forgotten him?

"Local realtor. He was supposed to meet with your sister yesterday. She met with someone who pretended to be him, but your sister verified that the man she met was not who he said he was."

"Colbert? I've seen his name on real estate signs." A heavy weight of fog lifted from Finn's brain. "Sheriff, I've never met the man."

"Dalton told me some things I should have known before now. Do you have anything to say about that?"

Finn shook his head. "Not without my lawyer present."

Dixon chuckled. "And let me guess. Rylander's your man?"

Finn nodded.

"I'm still deciding whether or not I should charge him. What good's a lawyer if he's facing disbarment?"

"We did what we did, Sheriff. That's all I can tell you. If Dalton spilled our wrongful misdeeds to you, then you realize that we're probably responsible for Beau's death. There's nothing more I can add to the story."

Dixon walked to the window and stared out beyond the glass.

A nurse walked in, stuttered when she got sight of the uniform, but moved forward. For the twentieth time, his temperature and blood pressure were taken and she asked him if he needed anything. And for the twentieth time, he declined.

The lawman's large shoulders sagged. "Beau Carmichael was a good man."

"Yes, sir."

"He didn't deserve to die, shot down in front of his boys."

"No, sir. He didn't."

"But I'm sorry he visited all of this upon you and your sister and their two children."

Finn jerked his gaze upward, and the sheriff turned. "Jeb, you do as the doctor says. I suspect he'll order you home to bed rest. You lay low. Don't let your sister come around you. Keep away from any of the children—hers and Shane's—until I say otherwise, and when I call you for a meeting, you come running. You hear?"

The dull ache began to return, and Finn placed his hand at the back of his neck.

"And don't leave town." The sheriff reached in his pocket and held out a card.

Finn took it and read the sheriff's contact information.

"If Mazzie Harris comes into town, you tell her to stay put at Abra's home. Do you understand?"

"Mazzie? Sheriff, she …"

"She's missing. I have someone on the Bodacious Cove Police Department looking for her. She was supposed to be en route from what her assistant told me. Detective Bastion informed me he'd spoken to her briefly before she got on the road."

Finn's head throbbed. His heart literally ached.

"She's had plenty of time to get here. No one's seen her since."

Everybody's Broken

Chapter 18

Shane stood beside the school's playground. Abra had been running late and asked him to wait for her. He'd already seen Taffy into her classroom, and Abra was doing the same for the boys. The principal, office staff, and the teachers were asked to keep a close eye on the children and instructed that no one but Abra or Shane could check them out of school. Since the sheriff had called an impromptu meeting, Shane had asked him to follow up with the school so they would understand the importance of keeping the kids safe, and he had advised that deputies would patrol the area between Abra's house and the school.

Abra hurried toward him. She'd done something with the long brown mane of hers, a loosely wrapped braid that left enticing tendrils of softness around her beautiful face. Blue eyes peeked out beneath her bangs. He'd love to push the strands back, hold her close, and kiss her lips …

Whoa! His heart was galloping faster than his brain. That couldn't happen again. Not now. Slowing down was prudent, but everything except common sense told him his first dive into love was deep.

He held out his hand, and she grasped it in hers.

Beau no longer kept him at a distance, and if Abra felt that Beau was a deterrent to their relationship, she never said. Shane's hope soared one moment and plummeted the next.

He was keeping a secret from her, and after all of Beau's manipulation, Abra didn't deserve this from him.

He'd tell her today. He'd invite her to lunch. Spill his guts. Tell her she had a stepdaughter. After the meeting at Dalton's office per order of the sheriff.

"Let's park at Manna and get some coffee. We can slip out the back to Dalton's office."

She nodded, and for the first time, her silence sounded an alarm in him. He wouldn't push. Perhaps Beau's ghost did linger. He didn't want to think of that.

She slipped into her car and drove away. The early morning hour left them with two parking spots in front of Manna. He exited his car, opened her driver's door, and followed her inside.

The line was small, and they slipped through, and out the back door quickly then hurried down the back road, past all the back entrances and loading docks of the Main Street businesses.

Steps followed. Shane turned and tucked Abra behind him.

A woman stepped toward them. "Hey, Shane."

Shane eyed her. He'd known her and had avoided her most of his life because of her reputation. Besides being the town prostitute who'd lied about Beau, she was the mother of two of the Jordan River kids he'd hung with in high school. "I don't have anything to say to you."

"Well, I ain't here to talk to you. It's her I want to see." The woman brushed her once raven hair, now peppered with gray, from her face.

Abra pressed against Shane's back. "Me?" she whispered.

"Yeah, you." She shook a trembling finger in Abra's direction. "I got something on my mind, and it needs to be said."

"She doesn't have to listen to your lies," Shane said.

"Well, I ain't lying about this. If you don't know it, I done retold my story, and I gave Daniel the truth."

Abra slipped to Shane's side.

The woman's brown eyes looked them over. "Well, ain't that nice. You losing your husband and gaining another one."

"Listen." Abra narrowed her gaze. "You don't pass judgment on me, and I'll withhold it on you. What do you have to say to me that's so important you'd follow me down this back alley."

Shane didn't dare smile, but this side of Abra attracted him.

The woman waved her hand in the air, moving her body like a piece of taffy in a pull. "Honey, I accused that man of yours—I'm sorry—that *other* man of yours of compromising me."

Abra winced at the words. "And ...?"

"He never did. He never would. Beau was a straight arrow. Treated me nice enough every time he arrested me. He didn't look down on me. Even took me to rehab a few times, but it never took—won't ever take, but I know I needed to apologize to him. Then I heard he was killed."

"So you're apologizing?" Abra said. "Thank you. I'm sure Beau didn't hold a grudge. I'm glad you realize words can ruin a person or scar them for life. Your lies affected many lives."

The woman held out her arms as if there were more than liver spots there. "You don't need to tell me about no scars. I got plenty. But I'm sorry I never got to tell him. This man, he paid me to lie. Paid me real good. He didn't have to tell me he hated Beau. One man hating another means nothing to me."

Abra took a deep breath. "What's your name?"

The woman's face froze for a fraction of a second, as if no one had ever cared to ask her. "Magda."

Abra's lips twitched, and Shane imagined she had caught the awful irony on the woman's name. "Magda, I accept your apology on Beau's behalf."

Magda reached into her bag and pulled out a bottle. She drank deeply of the Kentucky Bourbon Shane could smell from where he stood. "Thank you."

Abra started past him, but Shane held out his hand. She pushed by and wrapped the woman in her arms. "Thank you for your kind words about my husband. I needed them more than you could know." She stepped back. "Mr. Browne and I have an appointment, and we need to go. I hope to see you around. Don't hesitate to say hello, and I won't either."

Magda nodded. "Well that's right nice. More than my own daughter will do for me."

"Well, I'm sorry about that, but sometimes we let things get in the way of our relationships. Secrets came between me and Beau. He didn't want to tell them. I didn't want to ask." Abra pointed to the bottle in Magda's hand. "Maybe your daughter would be more receptive if you did your best to get rid of that."

"Don't know." Magda staggered. "But you be careful now. You, too, Shane. That man who paid me ... I've seen him back here. He don't look none too happy, but I stay out of his way. He's dangerous."

Shane pulled Abra back toward him. "Where have you seen him?"

"In town on Saturday. I see him walking sometimes up by that big gray house where Mrs. Carmichael lives."

"Magda, lay low," Shane warned. "I suspect Sheriff Dixon would like to hear from you."

"I already talked to him this morning. That's how I knew to wait, but I thought I'd see you out front, not back here."

Abra pulled at Shane's arm. "Let's go. We need to find out what's going on. Thank you, Magda."

The woman nodded, and with a turn that almost planted her face in the asphalt, she moved away.

"Daniel has some explaining to do." He led Abra down the street.

A set of old iron steps, hardly ever used, led to the second story above *Count It All Joy*. Shane had to knock on the back door.

Dalton opened and held it while they entered. He nodded to the coffee in Shane's hand. "What? Not interested in my brew?"

A pfftt and a cough sounded from inside Dalton's conference room.

Abra stopped dead in front of Shane, and he had to recover quickly to keep from scalding her back with his drink.

Dalton smiled. "I was ordered to sneak him in for this occasion."

Abra pushed past him without a word.

Shane entered behind her and stopped. Finn, of course, would be here. Since Peter's outing of his uncle Saturday night, Dalton had asked Shane to delay any questions about the man and his sudden arrival in town.

With all that occurred yesterday, he hadn't given Jeb—or Finn Osteen—much thought.

"Come on in." Daniel sat at the head of the conference table, a bulging file folder in front of him, as if this were his place of business. He hadn't shaved, and circles under his eyes announced loud and clear that he hadn't slept much, if at all. He reached into the file and pulled out two evidence bags, holding them up for Shane and Abra. "Shane, your call is untraceable and the carrier impenetrable this side of a court order, which requires probable cause and involvement with the prosecutor's office. I'm not ready for them yet. Abra, Chief Herman was checking on you. He confirmed the dropped call and apologized for the scare."

Dalton squeezed behind Abra and Shane to take his place at the other end of the table. The sheriff and the lawyer were vying for alpha male.

Randa sat on the opposite side of the table, Jeb on one side, and Dalton on the other. Her back was ramrod straight, and the frown on her face was so intense, Shane feared it might set in permanently. Her hands were clasped on the table in front of her.

Dalton placed his hand over his wife's.

Randa tensed even further, if that were possible.

Shane pulled out Abra's chair and waited for her to sit. Then he sat beside her. She reached for his hand, and Shane held to it.

"Are you feeling better?" Abra asked Finn, her tone flat.

"I'm fine. Don't worry about me."

The tight hold Abra had on Shane's hand lessened. "Finn ... I'm sorry about ... I love you, and I'm so thankful to God that you're alive and here with me—with us."

Finn held Abra's gaze and then gave her a slight nod, his face tense.

Randa stared straight ahead, past Shane, and to the wall. His cousin was hurting, probably feeling as left out by all of this as he did.

He looked back to the man across from him. "You lied to us."

Everybody's Broken

"We lied to you," Dalton confessed. "And you're about to hear more things that we've done. I'm asking only that you withhold judgment until we're done here."

Daniel cleared his throat as if to gain their attention. "I have one question to ask each of you before we continue here."

The room fell silent; everyone faced the lawman. "How'd Beau's lies and silence work to protect any of you?"

No one spoke. One by one, Daniel looked each of them in the eye before continuing. "Okay, everyone here has some level of understanding about the danger that's going on around you. I've been awake for more than twenty-four hours searching for a missing man and trying to decide if I should charge one or two of you with a variety of crimes."

Randa lowered her head and tears fell. She pulled her hand from Dalton's and placed them in her lap. Dalton stood and retrieved a Kleenex from a credenza behind Shane. He handed it to his wife, and she nodded her thank you—as a person might acknowledge the kindness of a stranger.

"Shane ...?"

Shane tensed. Why would Daniel single him out? Probably because in light of Finn's disappearance and the appearance of the bogus evidence, he was still the main suspect in Beau's death.

"I want to know when you last saw the gun owned by your grandmother."

Shane closed his eyes, thinking back. "I have never laid eyes on the thing."

"How do you suppose a gun you never saw ended up as evidence in your cousin's murder?"

This was Florida all over again. The only exceptions were a larger room and a bigger audience. "I have no idea."

"Randa?"

Randa jerked her teary gaze to Daniel. "I don't know."

"You don't know what?"

"How Grandmere's gun got to Florida."

"Have you seen the gun? Dalton, did you?"

"Dalton and I saw it together. Once. Beau found the combination to Grandmere's safe. We opened it, and the gun was there. Beau did a safety check and wasn't too happy to see that Grandmere kept it loaded. He unloaded the gun, did a cartridge check, and put the ammo back into the safe with the gun."

"And where did you last see the safe and the combination to that safe?"

"On the top shelf of Mrs. St. John's closet. The combination is tucked underneath?"

The sheriff turned to Abra. "That so?"

Abra thought for a minute. "Big white box?"

Dalton nodded. "That's it."

"The safe is still there."

"And let me guess," Daniel leaned back in his chair, the tips of his fingers together. "You haven't looked inside."

Abra huffed out a breath. "No, I haven't looked inside."

Daniel didn't seem to notice Abra's ire. "Is it safe to assume that if Beau didn't take the gun when he left here, someone who had access to the house took that gun to Florida at the time of Beau's funeral?"

Dalton cleared his throat. "Nope. Not going there, Daniel. That wasn't us. I told you what we did at Beau's instruction and why. The gun wasn't a part of it. I'd never do anything to implicate Shane. We had this discussion."

"What discussion?" Shane demanded. "Is this what you were talking to Daniel about yesterday?"

A light knock sounded on the door. "Not now,

Chrissy!" Dalton demanded.

The secretary opened the door anyway. "Sheriff, there's someone out front who said you asked for him to meet you here."

Daniel nodded. "Thank you. Tell him it'll be a few minutes."

"Now what?" Dalton slammed his hand on the desk. "Are you slowly torturing us? You want me to spill everything I know?"

"Shut up, Dalton."

Silence followed Finn Osteen's command.

"What do you want from us, Sheriff?" Finn asked.

"I thought I made that clear from the start. I want the truth. How deep are the two of you involved in this thing?"

"Involved?" Abra cried out the word.

"Abra," Daniel calmed. "Let them tell their side of things."

Dalton stood and paced in the corner, his cool lawyer exterior gone. "After the allegations that got him suspended from the department, Beau came to me. He was undone. Jasmine had asked him how he could have done something so heinous, how he could have jeopardized their health."

Shane closed his eyes; he winced, tightening for the blow that was about to unearth his tightly held secret.

"His health?" Randa caught on too quickly. "They were ... they—"

"They were two people planning to marry, babe." Dalton said.

Abra's gasp brought Shane's eyes wide.

She held her fingers to her lips, saying nothing.

"He said he needed to leave, that the allegations brought by Magda weren't as cut and dry as everyone thought. Someone else was behind them and since the two women ..." Dalton looked to his wife "... that he loved the most thought him capable of doing the unthinkable, he needed to leave because we were all in danger if he stayed."

Randa sobbed into her hands. "I knew I was the reason he left. I always knew, but Jasmine ...?"

Abra inhaled so deeply, Shane felt her body rise. She slowly pulled from his embrace. Tears vanished and her face took on granite hardness.

"Jasmine never said in the few months she remained here," Dalton continued, "but she must have found out Beau had fallen in love with Abra. Something else happened to her, something horrendous. I saw the bruises. I begged her to tell me or to go to you." He nodded toward Daniel. "She never told me who did it to her or what had happened. She went from being frightened for several weeks to being angry. I told you where I found her, how I got her keychain."

"I told her about Beau and Abra," Finn cut in. "Jasmine called me, and she said someone had hurt her. I thought she meant Beau—by leaving—but she said no. I hated to hear the hurt and pain in her voice. That's when I said that things probably worked out for the best for her. I was angry with Beau at first. Then I saw how happy Abra made him. I fooled myself into thinking that everything had worked out for the best for everyone."

"If I'd known Jasmine had hurt him, I'd have never accused him like I did." Randa cried. "I said horrible things to him." Her face paled. "I lost faith in who he had always been, and I know I hurt him after he'd done so much ..." She sobbed into her hands. "Beau, I'm so sorry."

Dalton bent down and slipped his arms around her.

"Randa." Shane remained seated, allowing Dalton to comfort his wife. "I thought he might have left because he lost faith in me. Daniel said that wasn't so. Let's put away our guilt and realize we can't change the past. Perhaps we

Everybody's Broken

need to start sharing everything we know." Shane stabbed himself with his words. He'd dodged a bullet, and he needed to tell Abra the truth before she recognized him for the hypocrite he was.

Randa continued to cry, but she nodded.

Daniel pointed to Dalton and then to Finn. "One at a time. Tell me what Beau shared with you."

"He kept me in the dark until he learned of Jasmine's murder," Finn admitted. "He didn't believe Daniel when he called to tell him she'd committed suicide. He wouldn't let it rest."

Shane's blood ran cold. He closed his eyes and breathed in and out. "Beau had known about Jasmine? When everyone else thought it suicide, he knew she'd been murdered, and he never told anyone?" Anger roiled like a tempest inside of him.

Finn nodded. "Several months after she died, he received a picture with a taunting note written on the back. He never understood what it meant, but he pointed out evidence in the photo that pointed to murder."

"You've seen the picture?" Daniel leaned back in his chair.

"Yes, sir," Finn said. "I thought you knew I had. I'm the one who sent for it, and I gave it to Dalton to leave on Abra's porch. I didn't tell Dalt what it was, only that it would keep Abra here."

"You?" Abra gasped.

"Did he know about the baby?" Randa asked. "Shane's baby. The affair Shane and Jasmine had."

"There was no affair!" Shane shot the words out.

Randa smirked. "Then the one-night stand you had with his girlfriend?"

Shane started to rebuke his cousin, but Abra's cold, blue gaze settled on him.

"How long after Beau left did Jasmine leave the area?" Daniel tilted the lid that would expose Shane's lie.

275

"Three months," Randa said. Then her eyes widened. "And six or so months before Shane came home with Taffy."

"Okay, folks. Listen. We're off track here." Dixon shot Shane a pensive gaze then opened his file and slid the picture of Jasmine's hanging onto the table. "This the picture Beau received? The one you had sent to you?" He narrowed in on Finn.

Finn looked away. "That's it."

"Who sent it to you from Bodacious Cove?" Abra rasped the question. She pulled away from Shane. "Was Mazzie involved in that?"

Finn ignored her.

"And, Finn, did you give your keychain with your Five H whatever to Dalton for any reason?" Daniel pressed on.

Finn nodded.

"And what was that reason?"

"To send it to Abra."

Abra tilted her head and gazed at the ceiling. Then she leveled it at her brother. "You didn't think I was hurting enough?"

"We needed you aware, Abra." Finn leaned forward. "You walk through this world with bullets flying all around you, and because you come out unscathed, you close your eyes to the danger and the reality around you. Pap was murdered. Your husband was murdered. I was shot and—" He clamped his mouth shut, slamming back against the chair. He winced and put his hand to the back of his head.

"Is that why Mazzie kept my children from me?" She ground out every word. "So I would face reality?"

"That wasn't the reason. She needed to keep them safe. I called Mazzie after I'd been shot. I don't recall much about the scene after that. I woke up in one of her rentals. Mazzie and the boys were there. Things were put

Everybody's Broken

into play so I could hide out. Herman was looking for me. He would have charged me with the murder. Mazzie and others kept that from happening, but we would never have taken the boys from you. Mazzie had to bring them back when she could. At a time when everyone would accept the lie we put into place."

"What are you saying?"

"Beau had someone out to get him for a long time. He thought that by leaving here, he could wait it out. He'd let his guard down until Jasmine's death. You were already married, and he was always on alert. You had just learned you were pregnant with the twins, and he literally had everyone keeping watch over you. When the boys were born, you didn't realize how protective he'd become."

"He was a good husband and a wonderful father. I never took that for granted."

"But you never saw beyond that, never saw his fear."

"But you did." She leaned forward. "I may not have seen the danger, but no one ever told me to look for it, did they? Perhaps if someone had mentioned my husband's previous lover had been murdered or even before that, if you'd told me I needed to force Beau to talk about his past life."

"You wouldn't have listened!" Finn slammed his hand on the table. "You wouldn't poke your head out of the sand long enough for me to point those things out to you. Tell me. Why did you marry the man if you were so afraid to broach his past with him? You didn't need me to tell you to do that. You were afraid he'd leave. You're always afraid someone will leave."

Abra stood and placed her palms on the table. "Because someone did!"

Finn's jaw clenched and then he released it. "Abra, one person—one thoughtless, self-centered person left her children. She had a choice to leave Pap or to stay with him. She didn't have to leave us, too. She could have stayed in town, could have been a part of our lives, but she didn't. What you've failed to see all these years is how many people stayed. How many of us loved you: me, Pap, Mazzie, that crazy bunch of misfits who settled in a town our father created—they all loved you. How many showed up at your birthday party every year. They didn't do that because of the holiday or the costumes or to see Pap. They did it because they loved you. Mercy and Zeb, they loved us so much that after Beau's murder, they broke the law by watching after the kids. You focused all your life on one person's abandonment, and you forgot how many of us stayed."

Abra sank into the chair. Her body seemed to deflate.

"Are we done here, folks? I'm glad we're clearing the air, but the problem still remains. Beau's failure to report his suspicions caused things to go terribly wrong. Did anything happen that made Beau nervous after Jasmine's death?"

Finn heaved a deep sigh and let it out. "That's what was strange. Years passed after the murder. Nothing happened. Then a realtor—Fred Colbert, I bet—contacted Beau about the house here. He had someone who wanted to purchase it. Didn't take much for Beau to get the name from the realtor and force our old pal to admit he wanted the The Gray Lady."

"Who?" Daniel asked.

"The old college acquaintance I told you about the other day," Dalton answered.

"Then Pap died," Finn said. "Beau got real tense. We conferenced with Dalt. For some reason that Beau never told me, he was sure this friend of ours killed both Jasmine and Pap."

Daniel held up his hand to halt Finn from continuing. "Dalt do you know the reason? Why would he suspect anyone of killing two people from two different parts of his life?"

Dalt swallowed hard. "I think he suspected him of Jasmine's death all along, but I only deepened his conviction with a theory I shared during one of our later calls together—the call he made to place everything in trust for Abra."

"Go on," Daniel motioned.

"I said Jasmine had been hurt, physically. Russell Price had been in town. He didn't come to see me, but I think he saw Jasmine."

Daniel nodded, sparing Dalton from spelling out his theory. "Do you think him capable?"

"Yeah, I do," Shane answered for him. "He was the jealous and greedy type. He wanted anything and everything someone else had. He was a creep."

"When Dalt and I conferenced with Beau, we cooked up a plan to draw him out. Beau hedged on the house sale, giving in and having seller's remorse, hoping to get him to show his bad side. Apparently, he did. We just weren't ready for it when he did."

Dalton released his hold on Randa. He stood his head back, staring at the ceiling. "Oh, God, forgive me for ever thinking I could handle these things."

Randa stood and pulled Dalton into her arms. "No, baby. Beau did this. Not you. If he hadn't tried to fix this himself, he wouldn't have torn our worlds apart. He wouldn't have left. Jasmine would be here. We would all be okay."

Ice could have frozen at the glare Abra shot toward them, then her brother, and finally at Shane. The woman was haunted by the truth that they were making her face, and part of that truth was something Shane should have already shared with her.

"Abra," Daniel slid another picture out of his file. "Is this the man you met at Colbert's office yesterday?"

Abra looked down at it. With one finger, she slid it

toward her, stared at it for a long second. Then she nodded, stood, and pushed her chair under the table. She leaned on the table, her attention riveted on her brother. "Are you going to answer me about Mazzie's involvement in all of this?"

Shane blinked at the odd question.

"What?" Finn asked.

"Was Mazzie involved in keeping any of the truth from me?"

"The only thing Mazzie knew was Beau's suspicion that Pap had been murdered accidentally, and that Beau was the one who should have been the victim. As I recall, she tried to tell you, and that's exactly why Beau shared as little as possible with her in an attempt to have her stay close to you."

Abra glared. "Regardless of what any of you think of me, I'm not a shrinking flower. I'm Dashell Osteen's daughter. I'm as strong and unwavering as kudzu. I've stuck with you, Finn. I did my best to help Pap see that you weren't cut from his cloth. When he realized how good you were at what we did, he was so proud of you. We built a highly successful business. I was married to a police officer, and I realized the dangers he faced every day. I never shrank from being a daughter, a sister, a mother, or a friend, but you never saw that part of me. You only saw my weaknesses, and right now, I don't care if I ever see any of you again."

"Abra!" Finn shouted.

Abra turned.

"After I'd gotten shot that day, I called you, too. I told you Beau was murdered. Mazzie is the one who came. She's the one that protected your children, who sheltered me."

Abra stared at him for a long moment, no emotion on her face. Then she nodded, looked to Shane, and left, closing the door softly behind her.

Everybody's Broken

No one moved to follow her.

Dalton and Randa held to each other.

Finn stared at his hands.

And Shane peered down at the picture and at the face of a man he had never liked or trusted. The fifth member of the Five "H" Society, the one Jasmine had invited into their lives, the one who followed Beau home time and time again, the man Shane always despised.

Russell Price.

"Trace Bastion!" Abra's surprise rang throughout the office. "What are you doing here?"

Bastion's response was muffled.

Finn's was not: "Mazzie's got to be dead."

Chapter 19

Only Shane and Randa remained in the conference room after Finn and Dalton rushed out.

Daniel had gathered up his materials, taking his time. As he left, he closed the door.

Randa stood and pushed the chair under the table.

Shane remained seated. "Are you okay?"

Randa shook her head. "No. I'm not."

"I know you're hurting, but Dalton did what he thought best. Beau could be persuasive—"

"Shane." She stopped him. "Put yourself in mine and Abra's places, will you? Just for a moment."

"I'm on the outside of all of this, too. I feel like the kid brother who never gets let in on the secret—even yours."

She huffed a small, false laugh. "You sound like that little boy who got his feelings hurt when Beau didn't want you tagging along. You kept a whopper to yourself, too."

Randa slapped him with the truth. She came to stand behind him, placing her hands on his shoulders. "You love Abra."

He shook his head. Even if he could admit it, he'd ruined his chances by lying to her—like Beau had done.

"She loves you."

He didn't look up. "I think I watched any feelings she had for me die when the truth came out before I could tell her. Randa, my little girl is her stepdaughter."

"No, she's the daughter of the man she loves." She shook him. "Give her time. Give me time. I'm reeling from a lot right now."

"And I'm sorry. I wish I had the words to tell you how much it hurts me for you and Dalt to learn that you can't have any children. Taffy ..."

"My possible infertility is a little personal, and I've been emotionally raw." She pulled out a chair, sat beside him as if he were a small child who needed an explanation, and took his hands in hers. "Dalton has been wonderful. He says we can adopt a houseful of kids if I want."

Shane looked up. He started to smile, but the sadness in her green eyes stopped him.

"I want my own child, and I'm throwing a temper tantrum with God even though I know I'm the reason we can't have kids. I understand your heart. You thought I'd be upset that Jasmine didn't choose Dalton and me." Randa brushed Shane's hair back. "The truth is, Jasmine wasn't my friend. We never were. Beau loved her. Dalton adored her. You liked her. I couldn't stand her. Back then, I wouldn't have gone to get Taffy even if I had known the truth. But I'm so very happy that you did."

"You've done the testing ...?"

"No. I don't want to know for sure. If there's any hope, I want to cling to it."

"What do they say is wrong?"

She tightened her hold. "I had an abortion." She bit her lip for a second and released it with a sigh. "Only

Dalton knew until I told Abra. I didn't want to burden you. Shane, I know you blame yourself for the things we got into in high school. I didn't want you carrying a weight that belongs on me."

She had him there. The weight of the load she'd just placed on him held him down.

She released his hands but placed hers on each side of his face. "I did it. Me. I got myself into trouble. Even in a drunken stupor, you told me I needed to avoid the baby's father like the plague. I didn't."

"I would have helped you with the baby."

"And that's why I love you so much, why I loved Beau, and it is definitely why I love that man who is in so much hot water right now with Daniel.

"Dalton helped me through the aftermath. Despite my deplorable action, God gave me that man out there. He loves me—loves you—and he loved Beau. That man who adores Abra and her children and who thinks Taffeta Browne is the most precious child in the world. Just like I do. Despite my feelings for Taffy's mother, she holds my heart in my hands."

Shane remained silent.

Randa shook his head from side to side. "Some people think Dalton's a high-IQ goof. They don't know the man who loved Jasmine enough to meet with her when she was hurting over Beau's stupidity, who found me outside an abortion clinic, who risked our livelihood with the things he's done trying to keep us safe."

"I'm sorry I never told you the truth about Taffy."

"I think Jasmine must have loved that little girl so much to put her into your hands. I've been listening to all of this, and I think Beau's pride left her easy prey to Russell Price while she was here and later when she died in Colorado."

"I'm not sure I can forgive Beau."

Randa forced him to look at her. "If you can't forgive

him, then you shouldn't be able to forgive me either. Unknowingly, I sided with Jasmine when I questioned his character. I've thought about why I would have been so mean to him. I can be spiteful for no reason on occasion. I've done it with Abra and you. I'm going to have to learn to watch my tongue. I don't want to open the door for evil to attack."

A thought slithered its way into Shane's mind. He startled.

"What's wrong?"

"If he raped Jasmine ..." he ran his hands through his hair "... Russell threatened me." Shane shot up from his seat and rushed out into the front office where everyone stood in conversation—everyone except Abra—who remained alone in the waiting area, staring out the window at the street below. "Taffy," he said. "The call I received—the one I thought was Beau—"

"Settle down," Daniel said. "You told me about the call."

"Russell was the caller who threatened me over Taffy." The words had melded to his conscious. "He said, 'She took the baby away from me, and she gave it to you. Hid it from me, and I want my little girl.'"

Dalton lifted his eyes to the ceiling. He closed them tight. "Abra nailed it."

Abra stumbled forward. "What do you mean?"

Dalton continued to stare upward. "You asked how long it had been from the time Beau left until Jasmine went away. Within that time is when I suspected Russell had harmed her."

"And ...?" Daniel asked.

Dalton stared at the sheriff. "Price might have reason to believe Taffy is his child."

"No!" Shane shouted the word. "DNA proved Beau was her father."

Abra tensed but said nothing. What he'd just blurted

out couldn't be misconstrued or taken back.

"You doubted?" Randa asked.

"Never, but Jasmine had wanted me to be sure."

"You don't need the DNA," Abra said. "She looks just like her dad—both of her fathers."

He wanted so badly to wrap the woman in his arms, to apologize to her for making her find out this way, but his daughter needed protection.

A throat cleared, and everyone turned their attention to Trace Bastion. "This investigation is a little more complicated than you thought."

"It's Price. He's the only one it can be. Abra identified him." Dalton moved to the center of the small group.

Finn pressed his hand to the back of his neck. "You don't understand, Dalt. One person can't be in two places six hundred miles apart. Either two people working individually wanted Beau dead, or we have two killers working together to destroy us."

"That makes no sense," Randa said.

Dalton held up his hand, index finger in the air. He paced in a circle for a moment then stopped. "We have two missing persons. One here and one in Florida. The timeline is too close together." He shook his hand. "We do have two killers."

"Mazzie …" Abra said her friend's name almost as an exhale.

She moved to wrap her brother in her arms, but he stepped away from her.

Abra pushed past Shane and stormed into the conference room. Before he could reach her, she returned with her purse, knocked him out of her way, and hurried out the office door.

Mazzie stirred, feeling the grit against her face and the gag in her mouth. Something else covered her eyes.

A slight tickle crawled up her leg. A bug ... or worse. She jerked to brush it away. Pain sliced into her shoulder and down her arm. She was tied. Hands behind her back.

Sweltering heat blanketed her.

She leaned back, getting her hands to touch whatever she lay on. Her fingernails scratched wooden planks; her only clue to where she was didn't offer much.

As the fog vacated her brain, fear settled inside, deep, threatening to pour out with her sweat.

She lay back on her side, attempting to alleviate the ache and fought against the moan her lips wanted to peal. Someone might be here with her.

She allowed her muscles to relax, let her head lull, and stayed motionless.

How'd she get here?

She'd gone to the police station, her last stop out of town. Trace needed to know where she was going, or he'd have the town searching for another missing person. They'd met in the conference closet—even joked about it. He'd told her to be careful. She'd been very cautious so far. Even then, they never mentioned Finn. "I need an Abra-fix," she'd told him.

When she left the station, she'd gotten on I-95 northbound.

She almost shook her head, forgetting that any movement could alert someone to her consciousness.

She'd made another stop. Finn's house. She'd already checked on Abra's place, and Finn's bungalow had been on her way to the causeway that led to the mainland and toward the interstate. She'd waited to do that last.

She'd been in his closet, digging for some clothes to take to him.

Beneath the blindfold she closed her eyes.

That's all she could remember.

No sounds alerted her to someone's presence. No fear.

One minute she'd held Finn's shirt to her nose, breathing in the scent of coconut that always reminded her of him on the beach, and the next minute ... was just a moment ago when she'd awaken in this predicament.

She remained still for several more minutes, listening, taking in the scents around her, making sure nothing else crawled on her body.

Waves pounded the shore. Not too far away. Salt tickled her nose. She was near the beach. Maybe a lifeguard's shack.

She had to take a chance or every bit of hydration in her body was going to seep out as sweat. She moved. A bit at first.

No reaction stirred from anyone who could be watching her.

She pushed to an upright position.

Her arms were numb, her legs fine, but she decided to walk on her knees until she found a wall or a table, something that would give her a point from which to begin exploring her surroundings.

The rough wood made the going harder than she imagined. She scooted forward. Something stuck into her kneecap. She cried out in pain and backed up. A large splintered piece of board had probably punctured her.

Several knee-steps later and her forehead hit wood. She fell back, the curse in her heart muffled by the gag. Sweat poured from her hair and down her face.

The pain in her knee and on her head vied for pity, but she shrugged them away. No one could get her out of this. Trace thought she was gone. Mazzie had told her assistant she was taking an impromptu vacation.

Unless someone ventured here—wherever here was—her body wouldn't be found until it started to smell and ruin the tourists' vacations. Mazzie had no intention of leaving this world as a smelly corpse—at least not while she was six feet above the surface. She'd lost her mother early on, but her crisp sweet Southern giggle and her charm flowed across Mazzie's memory, "Darlin', southern ladies don't sweat. It's not in our genes, and if it was, it'd spoil our makeup."

A muffled cry floated out with the sudden memory. *I want to see Momma, Lord, but not like this. Please get me out of here.*

She sat down against whatever it was she'd run into and leaned against it, trying to stifle the emotion. The tears might be the last bit of moisture keeping her alive.

The cloth in her mouth was dry and rough.

Her lower back was supported by a thin shelf, and then nothing—except familiarity. She used caution as she turned left, leaned back, and lifted one leg in the air. The shelf was longer than her legs, so she moved forward before trying again.

Pay dirt.

The old S.S. Osteen lifesaver still hung on the nail at the end of the rustic table in Finn's non-air conditioned and shuttered cabana. Who needed A/C? The wooden slats on each side and at the back could be held open with poles, and opening the double doors to the Atlantic Ocean brought in a nice breeze. Often they'd enjoy morning coffee or would sit for hours during the weekend in between swims or volleyball games. This space was mapped in Mazzie's mind and it had one lifesaving convenience for someone trussed up inside.

Mazzie pushed to her feet, wobbly at first as if she'd been drugged. She gained her equilibrium and her bearing in the cabana and shuffled diagonally across the room. Someone could have placed something in her way—maybe another body.

She shivered at the thought.

Everybody's Broken

The plastic curtain brushed her shoulder. Now, if the contraption wasn't too high ... She backed into the smaller space, feeling the tile wall. The metal spindle rested just above her tied wrists. She stretched on her tiptoes, grasped the knob, and turned.

Ice cold water poured over her from Finn's cabana shower head. She turned toward it, drinking in the water that seeped through the gag and letting it wash the sweat from her. Then she pivoted again, bringing her wrist against the metal. The rope caught the sharp edge of the star shaped knob. She tugged to loosen it, all the while enjoying the refreshing coolness.

If she could only ... Get. The. Rope. To. Give.

Someone slammed into her, knocking her back against the tile and to the floor.

The water stopped.

The person held her down. "Tsk. Tsk. Tsk."

Mazzie struggled to get away.

Hot breath brushed across her face. Then something soft and just a bit damp pushed against her nose. She turned her head, but her captor grabbed a handful of her hair. She held her breath for as long as she could. A mistake she realized as soon as she coughed and gasped for air—it came with a hint of sweetness.

Her eyes drifted closed; her body was lifted, the sounds of the person's grunts faded away, but the warm breath still touched her face.

Mazzie slid into darkness with one last thought: *spearmint*.

Chapter 20

Abra sat on the swing in her backyard staring at The Gray Lady's backside. When they were children, Finn would push her on their swing at their home in Bodacious Cove until she thought she'd fall from the seat. "Hang on," he'd warn.

Hang on. That's what she needed to do now. The only difference was Finn no longer wanted to push her and keep her going. She swung her legs up and back, reaching higher and higher. Then she gripped the chain and held on while she leaned back, her body almost a perfect incline as she let the swing slow.

Every one of them thought of her as a fragile child. Trying to see herself through their eyes, she looked back over the past: her mother's leaving, her father's death—no, his murder—Beau's murder, her babies' abduction—no, they were hidden from her—Finn's disappearance.

No wonder she didn't like to deal with things. Someone else always carried her burdens.

Pap and Finn had tried to make her feel loved after

her mother's abandonment. Beau had tried to protect her from the truth about Pap's murder, and Mazzie must have been manipulating a lot of people behind the scenes to keep Finn and the twins safe during the two weeks before Beau's funeral.

And Beau—she wondered if anything with him had been real. His secrets had morphed into phantoms of death. First they'd come for Jasmine, then Pap, and then for Beau himself.

She shuddered at the thought that Fred Colbert might be dead. Mazzie might be among the victims as well.

Who would be next: Dalton, Randa, herself ... Shane?

Shane. She'd believed he was the only one who had not hidden things from her. She'd trusted him, but he hadn't returned the kindness.

"He loves you, you know?"

Abra startled, nearly falling backward out of the swing. "Trace!" she screamed. "Don't do that!"

He fought against the smile, but it played on his lips. "I'm sorry."

"No, you're not. Creep." She sat up, stopping the swing with her feet. Then she covered her mouth. "I'm sorry," she spoke through her fingers.

"No, you're not," he fired back.

"No, I'm not." The kids had created a bare spot by playing on the swings so much. Abra dug her toe into the dry red clay.

She seldom saw Trace in jeans and a t-shirt and jacket, but the man wore them well. "Are you here because Mazzie's dead?"

"I'm here because Mazzie was supposed to arrive, and she didn't. Sheriff Dixon called to ask about her, found out how long it'd been since I'd seen her, and ordered me to get on a late-night plane and take a vacation day. I have several, and I took them."

Everybody's Broken

"So Herman's looking for her?" Abra stared up at him.

"No." He sat on the other swing.

Abra tilted her head at him. "You didn't tell him what was going on?"

He shook his head.

"I promise I won't shatter into pieces if you tell me the truth. Is no one looking for her because she's dead?"

"I don't know anything except she's not where she told me she'd be. And you're stronger than you think you are. You held up under some rough interrogation."

"Someone had to help Mazzie with Finn when he was shot. Was that you?"

He gritted his teeth and swayed a bit as if admitting to aiding Mazzie with anything hurt. "Yeah."

She narrowed her eyes. "Did Beau tell the others that you were involved?"

"Nope. On the plane, I had time to think. Neither Mazzie nor I knew about Beau's family. He strategically told me only about Jasmine's death after he received the photograph—the one I believe Finn had sent to you."

"Not by you?"

Trace smiled. "Zeb. Mazzie had taken the spare key from where Finn kept it. Finn called and asked him to send the photograph. He had to break in."

Abra could imagine Zeb sneaking around Finn's place. "It's a wonder he wasn't caught in the act, but why didn't he call you?"

"See, I'm beginning to learn something about Beau. He only told a person what he thought they needed to know. Finn's connection with Jasmine wasn't something I needed to know because that connection led to this place he didn't want me, or Mazzie, or you to find out about."

"I'm beginning to think I'm the only one who knew nothing real about my husband."

Trace's lack of response was answer enough.

"Any more brilliant deductions," she pressed.

He studied her for a minute. "Beau never told Mazzie or me about this place and the people he left behind. He never told Mazzie about Jasmine, and he allowed his family to think she'd committed suicide. Finn was the only one that had Beau's every confidence. After Beau was killed Finn was a little delirious with pain. I pieced a lot together from his rambling. The one thing I'm sure of is that Beau suspected only one individual—Price. He'd been caught up in keeping you and the boys safe, and even after your father's death, he wouldn't listen to me. He kept looking at Price. I have another suspect in mind, and after he killed Beau, I couldn't let him find out Finn was alive."

She widened her eyes. "What you told me about Shane and the planted evidence. All the ugly interrogations, and you knew none of us were guilty?"

He twirled the high school ring around his finger, the blue stone turning around and around, reminding her of Beau's taunting him over the habit. She'd spare him today.

"I hated to do it, but it was good for me and Mazzie," he said. "We've been at odds for years—since that day I knocked her off the monkey bars in fourth grade. Don't tell her, but my dad left bruises on my behind when he learned I'd done that."

"As I recall, once Mazzie got the air back into her lungs, she had you on your backside, whaling on you. You had a black eye to go with the bottom bruises."

"For such a dainty belle, she has a nice right hook. She's a good friend to have, Abra. She went out of her way to keep Finn safe and to harbor the boys. She loves Finn. She didn't tell me he was here, only said she was coming to see you. Now that I know what made her leave home so suddenly, I think she got careless because he called and needed her, and she only wanted to get to him."

Abra swallowed hard. "I asked her to come, too."

"I know you're feeling a little betrayed ..."

Abra wiped at the tears. "Tell me what happened the day Beau died, and maybe I won't feel so betrayed."

Trace nodded and let the swing go a little bit. "Finn said they drove up on the shooting. Beau's coward killer wore a mask. He shot Beau and turned the gun on the truck. Finn's first instinct had been to push the kids down. It probably saved all their lives. The bullet grazed the base of his neck. He remembered falling on the boys and telling them to be still while he played dead. He waited, and when the killer didn't come to the truck, Peter looked up and said the killer had gone. Finn managed to sit and dial Mazzie and then you before he passed out. Mazzie called me and got to the scene first."

Tears clouded Abra's vision before spilling over his face. "I didn't know what to do. I didn't go to him. I called the department, frantic. Mazzie held herself together and got there."

"Abra, don't beat yourself up over that. Not too many women have nerves of steel. Mazzie's one in a million."

Abra laughed and wiped her eyes. "Gee, thanks."

"She took the picture of the scene as I'd asked her to do. I wanted to make sure the murder scene wasn't contaminated."

Abra widened her eyes. "She enlarged a copy of the picture at her office because she believed we were in danger and wanted to scare us out of town."

"Yeah. That night after she did that to you, she was so shaken up about it, she cried on my shoulder. That should tell you how badly she hated doing it."

Abra would have laughed at his joke if her heart hadn't been left filled with holes of regret, shame, and fear. "How did she hide Finn and the boys?"

"I couldn't leave the scene once I arrived. We had to

work fast. I don't know how she managed to get him and the kids out of the truck without being seen or leaving a trail of Finn's blood, but she took him to one of her empty rentals. I'd warned her not to call for emergency help, but she called a retired EMT to the house."

"Zeb?"

"Yeah, the old man still knows his stuff. He patched up Finn as well as he could."

"Where did you hide his truck?"

He smiled now, almost as if the memory was a fond one. "Mercy Tuttle put it into one of the locked warehouses at Zeb's marina. Then she and Zeb stayed with Finn and the boys to allow Mazzie to help me make the investigation of you all look real. Zeb helped Finn get out of town on the morning of the funeral. Mercy helped get the boys dressed and ready for Mazzie to bring them to you."

Abra missed those two old conniving souls. "And you were able to convince Mazzie to do all this with you, how, when as far as I know she's despised you since the fourth grade?"

"Because Beau wasn't having anything to do with my gut instinct after Dashell died. We learned fairly early on that he'd been poisoned, but Beau kept to his original theory. His inability to listen to my reasoning is what got him killed. Beau let Mazzie in on the truth about Dashell because he wanted her to stick to you as much as possible. Mazzie was infuriated that he wouldn't tell you. She's not stupid, Abra. She knew as well as I did that Pap's murderer, and I believe the same person who killed Beau, was closer to home."

"And you think someone else killed Jasmine?"

"And possibly the missing man." Trace nodded. "I think everything that's happened proves my theory. While Beau was loved by many, he had two enemies who were willing to harm him—one enough to kill him. Finn, who again, was the only insider to everything, is upset that he didn't realize what was going on until today's meeting. That's why I needed to see you to tell you that he's not angry with you, but he is angry with himself, and that's a new emotion for your brother, don't you think?"

The cry that left her lips surprised Abra.

Trace didn't move.

The chilly wind that she'd failed to notice earlier picked up and wrapped icy tendrils around her. Her brother had always been there for her, and when he couldn't, she'd gotten angry and left him alone.

"Beau loved you, too, Abra." Trace pushed from the seat. "He was enamored with you, with your innocence, and your beauty, with your creativity. I used to have to tell him to shut up because I'd get envious that he'd found the perfect woman."

Warmth fanned Abra's neck and cheeks.

Trace turned toward the house. "He loves you, too, you know?"

Abra followed Trace's gaze.

Shane stood beside the solarium door, studying his shoes, and looking like a little boy who'd got caught in a huge lie and was very sorry for either getting caught or not having told the truth in the first place.

She shook her head.

Trace bent to his knees and grasped the chains of the swing. He peered up at her. "If you thought someone could take your children away from you, would you be so willing to tell anyone they weren't your flesh and blood? Shane was protecting his little girl." He raised his brows. "I suspect from the moment he took Beau's baby into his arms, he began to fear that Beau would find out and take her away from him. He told no one. Rylander's a good lawyer, and he has quite a poker face, but I hit a nerve with a question I didn't think would bother either of them in an interrogation in which I knew the man wasn't guilty."

Abra nodded her understanding. "Beau ..."

"Beau's gone, sweetheart. That man there, he's nothing like Carmichael. Oh, your husband was a good guy. His biggest flaw was that in trying to protect you and everyone he loved, he left you all vulnerable, and from what I see, pretty broken in spirit. That sheriff ..." Trace tapped his forehead "... he's a thinker. He got us together to get us all to the same conclusion he'd already reached. Beau had two different enemies either working together or separately."

"Did Finn have an idea of who shot him?"

"No. At least not that he's confessed." Trace stood again. "I'm going home to find Mazzie. I've talked Finn into waiting here. If he goes home, he'll be arrested."

"But you said you know he's innocent."

"I have a boss who wants the case closed." Trace touched a stand of her hair that had fallen out of the messy braided bun she spun it in earlier. He pushed it behind her ear and tucked it in place. "We shouldn't be calling him Finn. Russell Price knows who he is."

Abra stood. "Russell's here. He's the killer. I need to take the boys home."

Trace held her by the shoulders. "No."

"He's the killer in Amazing Grace. He killed Jasmine in Colorado and he might have killed Fred Colbert."

"But there's another killer at home, Abra. You need to stay here with your family. Mazzie might find her way here. Who knows? Our Lady of Steel might be an idiot with directions, even with GPS." He winked at her.

Abra threw her arms around Trace's neck. "Find her. Please find my best friend. I need her."

Trace kissed her cheek. His phone chimed, and he pulled away to read a text.

He pressed his lips together, pivoted one way and then back. Finally, he shook his head. "Listen, I need to get to the airport. I'm pushed for time, but I wanted to come see you. I don't think you realize what it does to the people who love you when we see you hurting."

"I'm sorry."

"No, you're not. You're wonderful."

She smiled at his play on words. "You're sorry."

He winked at her. "Yes, I am. Now, go mend some fences with that guy. I feel about as bad for him as I do for you. Throw the mopey puppy a bone, why don't you? I gotta go. Dixon said he'd be back in a minute. He's probably waiting for me." He left, waving as he went around the side yard and out the gate.

In Russell's hiding place at the back of the garage where the ivy-covered fence kept him out of sight, he listened to Abra and the man who should not be here. The phantoms swirled around him, taunting him with their self-righteousness and we-told-you so's, nearly making it impossible for him to hear the conversation.

Russell swatted in the air, trying to get them away from him. He twisted and turned, but their invisibleness kept them just out of his reach. He started to screech but stopped, as if their ghostly hands had clamped his mouth shut.

The soft whine of a car engine told him that someone had turned down the side street. He leaned out from behind the garage to look.

The sheriff.

Tires crunched on Frieda's driveway, and a car door opened and closed.

Russell crept to the fence on that side and pulled back enough ivy to see.

Dixon looked around him as he stepped onto Frieda's

porch and knocked.

He could pound on that door. Frieda wasn't going to answer, not with the drugs he'd fed her this morning. Lovely old dear, smiling up at him with eyes so glazed she probably didn't remember who he was.

He hadn't killed her.

Not yet.

No, not yet.

But soon.

He grasped his thundering head and yanked at his hair. He wasn't going to kill her. They couldn't make him.

Frieda was asleep ... a deep and restful slumber.

Still, he'd have to move on soon. Frieda's son had been calling her. She'd started to mention Russell during their last conversation but got sidetracked—a good side-effect of the drug. Next time, he wouldn't be so lucky.

He wanted to have one more try at the treasure. Then if he couldn't find it, he'd have to give it up. Not like he could hold anyone hostage and ask them what it was. The old dame had recited the riddle for all of them. No one seemed to know—except Beau. He'd seen the smile on Beau's face, a knowing wink at his grandmother.

Russell had been so close to being able to get his hands on that house. He'd dreamed of living here, legally, while waiting for the moment when he could leave, taking his daughter with him.

He wasn't stupid. He'd hoped sending the gun to Florida would have planted enough suspicion for Abra to stay away from here.

The fault belonged to his three friends: Wicked, Sick, and Twisted. That's what he'd named them.

They hadn't liked the name calling, but Russell didn't care. They were going to get him into trouble.

To spite him, they'd ruined Russell's brilliant plan moments before the realtor would have probably closed the deal for him with Abra. Russell didn't remember acting on their taunts, but Fred Colbert was dead all the same, and he'd had to wing the meeting with Abra.

The phantoms wanted him to fail.

Now, everyone was hot to find the realtor. Hot. He'd have laughed at the irony. Fred was anything but hot where he was today, thanks to the fiends and their—well—their pretty good idea.

The sheriff knocked on Frieda's door again and only waited a second. He walked to the carport and looked in Frieda's car. Then he made his way back to his vehicle and drove away.

Good.

Russell hid behind the garage until the sheriff passed. Then he stepped with light feet to the other side of the garage and listened.

Beau's detective partner stood in front of Abra. "We shouldn't be calling him Finn. Russell Price knows who he is."

Russell tensed. They knew who he was. Anger flamed inside.

They know you.
They know you.
Oh, boy, they know you.

Bastion had spoken of Finn in the present tense. Finn had to be alive. Russell had been informed Finn was dead.

He's alive.
He's told them about you.
You're in trouble now.

Russell tried his best to push the taunting phantoms away from him. The lying, cheating ... Russell promised he'd let everyone know the truth if the cops came for him. No problem, he'd been told. Finn was dead. And when the body wasn't found, he'd been told that despite the sloppy evidence to scare Abra, they'd pin the murder on her brother.

If Russell got caught, he'd sing like an opera singer during a coveted aria, and the mutual keeper of secrets would go down with him.

"Russell's here. He's the killer. I need to take the boys home."

Russell jerked his attention back to where it should have been.

Abra had gotten up from the swing. "He's the killer in Amazing Grace. He killed Jasmine in Colorado and he might have killed Fred Colbert."

Abra was too smart for her own good.

"But there's another killer at home, Abra. You need to stay here with your family."

He'd have never guessed it, but that guy was pretty intelligent, as well.

Smarter than you.

Doesn't matter who you killed. You're in a lot of trouble.

They'll stick a needle in you now.

The phantoms and their consistent chatter kept him from hearing more of what was said.

Russell straightened, and taking caution, walked toward Frieda's house. "Yeah, and if they kill me, you can go drive someone else mad."

His phone vibrated in his pocket, and he pulled it out. His eyes widened at the name on the text and narrowed when he read the message. Was this a trick?

The phantoms seemed to think so. They screeched so loudly that he almost went to his knees.

Kill the fool.

You better. Bury the only person who knows your truth.

No one ever keeps secrets, even when they have something to lose.

"Shut up," he snarled. "I'll make that decision when I see what's going on." Instead of heading into the house, he checked the area and hurried down the street to where he kept his car hidden. If nothing else, this was going to be a very interesting meeting.

Inside the car, he sent back a text. He'd meet the guy, do what he asked, and then he'd set him up real good. Russell Price was in control. Not the phantoms. Not some idiot from Bodacious Cove.

The treasure was lost, but he could still get out of this mess, take his daughter with him, and put the killings on the fool who'd ruined all Russell's plans.

Including the one last murder he needed to commit to seal the other man's fate.

Chapter 21

Someone pounded on something. Mazzie rolled over with a groan. "Go away," she yelled into the softness she used to cover her face.

"Ma'am. Asheville Police Department. We need you to open the door."

Mazzie opened her eyes. A dull headache threatened to erupt into a full-blown migraine if she didn't close them. She lay for several seconds, trying to get her faculties without sight.

"Ma'am, are you okay?"

Thump. Thump. Thump.

Cold air blew on her skin. Refreshing, if not goosebump producing.

She lay on softness and not hard concrete with gritty sand.

And the smells.

A motel room.

"She not okay. I saw men fight. You need to get in."

Mazzie sprang to her feet as the door burst inward.

She screamed at the men in blue, their guns pointed

at her. "Where ... where am I?"

"Ma'am, are you okay?"

She'd believe they were more concerned for her welfare if they'd put their weapons down.

"She okay?" an Asian woman asked.

Mazzie held her hands up and turned to look around her. "Where am I?" she repeated.

"You're at the At-a-Way Motel in Asheville." An officer advanced cautiously.

She stepped back.

"Have you been drinking? Doing any drugs?"

"No," she screeched and rued the action. Seemingly of their own free will, her hands fell to her head to protect her from the pain. "I was ... someone kidnapped me."

The officer patted her down. One picked up a suitcase and placed it on the bed. "Yours?"

Mazzie blinked. Yes. All her luggage lay on the floor at the bottom of the bed.

"Ma'am?" the officer pushed.

"Yes, but I don't know how." The mirror made her flinch. No wonder they thought she was on a bender. "I was taken from a home in Bodacious Cove, Florida. Someone put a cloth over my face. That's all I remember until you ..." She waved her hands at the door. "May I sit down?"

The officer stepped back and motioned for his buddies to lower their guns. "Go ahead. What's your name?"

"Mazzie Harris."

"And you're from where, you said?"

"Bodacious Cove, Florida."

Another officer came close, and she stared up at him.

"I haven't been drinking. I was taken."

"The motel's owner reported two men fighting outside your door. Do you have a husband and a boyfriend that might have caused trouble here?"

Mazzie closed her eyes for a second and waited for the room to stop spinning on her. "My boyfriend is ..." She shook her head. If she lost it, she'd get Finn in real trouble. "My boyfriend has been missing from home for six months. The authorities presume he's been murdered. His brother-in-law was found murdered." She swallowed hard. Not a lie spoken, so why'd it feel as if she'd told several of them? "I have no idea who the woman saw."

A small woman, her hair cut in a bob, pushed her way in. "Two tall, good-looking men. One, he drove in with car outside. He checked you in. Acted strange. Said you'd sleep for a while. He was in room with you. Other man walked up from somewhere knocked, and he open door. Next thing I know, two men outside the door. They fight. I call police. Men fight until the sirens come near. Then they run away."

"Who are you?" Mazzie snapped. The woman's peal could skin an armadillo.

"She called in the report, Ms. Harris. She was worried for your welfare." An officer folded his arms over his chest, reminding her of Beau.

That did it. Mazzie couldn't hold back the tears. They spilled over. "I'm sorry. My head is killing me. I'm seriously confused."

The woman sat beside her and patted her leg. "You okay now."

Mazzie nodded. "Two tall, good looking men, huh?" She swiped at her tears. "And here I thought I was dealing with only one psychopath."

"Any idea who?" an officer asked.

Mazzie shook her head, continuing to wipe the confounded waterworks off her horrid-looking, pale face. If Abra ever saw her like this, she'd never let Mazzie live it down. "Do I get a phone call?"

The officers chuckled. "You're not under arrest. According to Mrs. Lui, you were unconscious when the man carried you inside. She thought you could be dead."

Mazzie looked around her again. If her luggage was here, her purse had to be, too. Yes. She tugged it up from the floor and placed it on her lap. She pulled out her phone charger she'd placed inside because she planned to plug it into the car while she drove. Her wallet caught on the cord, and she tugged it out, opening and looking inside. She handed it to the officer who was not staring at her, arms still crossed over his chest. "I wasn't robbed. My ID's inside." Next, she dug for her phone.

Her shoulders sagged. The thing was as dead as Mrs. Lui thought she had been.

"Who are you trying to reach?"

She hadn't thought that far ahead. Certainly not Abra. "You know, I'm sorry. What day is it and what time?"

"Tuesday, 9:00 a.m." The officers looked to his partners. "What day do you last remember?"

Mazzie's head had cleared a bit, though the pounding had receded. "Saturday."

The woman beside her tsked and shook her head. "You raped, honey?"

"What? No." That was about the only other thing she was sure of. "I was in my boyfriend's home when someone apparently got me from behind. I woke up to find my hands tied and a gag in my mouth. I thought I'd been left to die inside his beach cabana, but I managed to get to the shower. I was trying to get untied. That's when someone took me down again. That's the last thing I remember."

She stared down at the awful turquoise carpet. Her mind whirled.

"You often go in your presumed dead boyfriend's home?" Folded Arms asked.

"Not often. I was making a trip up here to see his sister."

"Is that who you want me to call?"

Everybody's Broken

Mazzie had to think herself out of this one. She faced the woman. "Mrs. Lui, is there any detail you can give me about the man who checked me in?"

"Mrs. Lui reported one detail. Perhaps that will help you. The man wore a silver school ring with a blue stone."

"He twirl it round and round. He very nervous. Kept looking behind him whole time he check in."

Mazzie fought to keep her surprise from showing. The dirty, rotten, lowdown rat. She should have killed him the day she knocked him off the monkey bars at school—in fourth grade. Saved them all this horror.

The gears in her mind clicked together. She stared up at Folded Arms and his companion. "Attorney Dalton Rylander in Amazing Grace. Can you call him for me?"

Russell stared out over the rushing stream while the man with him kept himself busy setting up camp.

Years ago, Beau had brought him here a few times to fish. Russell hated fishing, but Beau and Shane enjoyed it. Beau never allowed Russell to stay alone with Jasmine, so it was fish or go home.

Russell never had a home. He'd had welfare housing or a bed in a shelter, sleeping beside his pathetic parents. Then he'd lucked into a scholarship and learned he could charm his way through school funding. Then he'd charmed a lot of old ladies and foolish women out of a lot of money—money he kept to buy The Gray Lady.

Saving money meant living sparingly because he couldn't get involved with any of the women around here and call attention to himself.

A year ago, Russell had set up camp here, careful to keep out of Shane's sight. He'd discovered a rarely used path out of sight of anyone in the vicinity. This place, Mount Tabor, belonged to Shane, who nearly stumbled over him and the campsite on one of his hikes with the little girl in tow. Now, Russell knew the little girl was his.

He knew because Beau had left Jasmine alone permanently, and Russell had taken what he'd always wanted from the woman Beau had loved.

Russell hadn't realized he'd given her a gift in return—not until Shane brought the beautiful child here. Anyone could see she belonged to Jasmine. And because Beau had left Jasmine, Taffy could only be his.

If it hadn't been for a speeding ticket in Colorado, he might never have found Jasmine to punish her for leaving him. He hadn't been able to figure out the smile that stayed on Jasmine's face as the noose choked the life out of her. Then he'd seen the little girl, and he'd known. Jasmine thought he'd never learn her secret.

Russell leaned against a tree and watched the man set up the tent. The bundle laying on the ground struggled within and tried to speak. He was trussed up and covered too well for that to happen. But he did know who they were, and he would have to die—eventually. Russell hadn't figured out the timing of that yet. The implications had to all point in one direction, away from Russell.

He only watched as the man hammered in the last tent peg. He'd made his accomplice carry up his quarry and his camping equipment by himself. Two trips. Quite a hike, but Russell wasn't leaving any more DNA for the cops to find. Nope. The fight he'd gotten into at the hotel was as close to the cops as he planned to come. The fool doing all the work would eventually pay for everything they had both done.

Tent up, the man leaned back, arching his back. He wiped sweat from his face. "You sure the owner doesn't come up here?"

Russell smiled. No use telling him he was on the land

Carmichael gave to his stupid cousin. "You'll be fine. Stow the idiot in the tent. I want to show you some things that will help with the plan I have to get us out of this mess you've made."

Finn paced Dalton's office. He'd taken a chance coming here again, but sitting in that rundown trap of a place and worrying if he'd ever see Mazzie again drove him near to madness.

"Sit down," Dalton ordered. "Shane and Randa wouldn't appreciate you wearing through the floor and falling into the store on top of some unsuspecting kid."

"Shut up!" Finn growled. "I'm not in the mood for your banter when I know you're as afraid as I am."

"Listen. You shouldn't have come to town. If Price sees you, the gig's up. And if we lose one of Daniel's prime suspects—and the reason we broke every one of his cardinal rules for propriety within his department—he's going to put us under the jail."

Finn slapped his hand down on Dalton's desk. "My sister is in danger. Mazzie might be dead."

"You think I don't know those things. I'm convinced he's found a way into The Gray Lady. We've planned for Abra to sleep behind a closed, locked, and blocked door in the kids' room every night. We got her out of there this morning as soon as we could get the kids ready for school. Shane stopped by to drive them. Staying away from home each day is going to wear on her, and you treated her pretty bad."

Finn blinked. "What'd I do?"

Dalton peered up at him. "Don't tell me you're not angry with her."

"I'm not. I love her. I had to open her eyes to

everything she's pretended hasn't happened. That broke my heart."

"And you snubbed her, Finn. Why do you think she left the meeting so abruptly?"

"She was angry at Shane. I kinda got the idea that the little girl of his is actually Beau's. That would make her Abra's stepdaughter, a half-sister to Peter and Paulie."

"Oh, she's plenty upset with him, but she was reaching to you for comfort."

Finn stepped back, slapping his hand against the pain at the base of his skull. Would it every go away? "I didn't realize. I need to see her."

"Well, you could've done that at your place. She's spending the day at Shane's."

Dalton's office phone rang, and a moment later, Chrissy intercomed him. "Dalton, Officer Morgan, Asheville P.D."

"Which case?"

"No case. He says he's calling regarding a Mazzie Harris."

Finn tensed.

Dalton picked up the call. "Officer Morgan. I understand you're calling about my friend, Ms. Harris." Dalton raised his brows. "Yes. Yes. No, I understand. You'll need to keep it. Yes, I'll be there. Tell me. Is she okay?"

Finn had forgotten to breathe. He let out the pent-up air and folded forward. *Please, Lord, let her be okay.*

"That's great. Yes, we've been very worried about her. That's right. She was coming to visit my sister-in-law. Mazzie's been missing since Saturday. Yes, Abra's husband was killed earlier this year. Yes, his brother-in-law is presumed dead."

Finn motioned for him to hurry the call.

"Silver ring with a blue stone?" Dalton jerked his gaze to Finn. "He checked her into the hotel?"

Everybody's Broken

Finn straightened. Trace Bastion. But how?

"Is that the only thing the woman could tell you? And Ms. Harris doesn't know anyone who wears that type of ring?" Dalton nodded over and over. "Yes. I appreciate your taking care of her. Please tell Mazzie that I'm approximately thirty minutes away, and we're glad she's safe."

He hung up the phone.

Finn started toward the door.

"Where you going?" Dalton grabbed his coat from the back of his chair.

"With you. To get my girl. Where do you think?" He opened the door.

Dalton shut it before he could go through. He leaned close to Finn, his voice low. "Mazzie's a smart gal. She had them call me for a reason, *Jeb*. Go home and wait for us and look out for your friend, Detective Bastion. I hear he's not left the area after all. In fact, very early this morning, he got into a fight outside the room he checked an unconscious Mazzie Harris into."

Chapter 22

Shane stepped out of the garage and stared at the motionless waterwheel. Abra stepped down off the porch and met him in the middle of the bridge.

"Done. Now all I have to do is live through a few restless nights until Taffy gets used to life without the flowing water."

"The boys and I had the same problem when we first arrived. The pounding waves were replaced with bug sounds."

He started to smile, but Abra's face held no humor. She leaned her arms on the railing, peering down at the trickling creek beneath them.

Shane's comeuppance had arrived. He'd half-expected her not to join him today, but when he'd arrived to drive the kids to school, she'd been ready. With their children tucked safely behind the walls and fences of the school, they'd left. He'd suggested they drive to his home to allow him to get some chores completed, and then they'd do whatever she wanted.

She'd only shrugged. He figured she'd just learned how not to speak her thoughts without putting her fingers to her lips as a reminder. This probably meant that whatever lay inside of her would sting him if it ever got loose.

"Abra, I'm very sorry I didn't tell you about Beau, Jasmine, and Taffy."

Abra straightened and pulled her jacket tighter around her. "And you think I'm angry about that?"

"Furious, probably, and rightfully so."

Her gaze traveled up into the trees. Her lips trembled for a second, and she caught her bottom lip in her teeth. Then she turned away from him. Her shoulders rose with a heavy inhale, and the coolness in the air frosted her breath as she exhaled. "I love you, Shane Browne."

He blinked, tried to replay her soft whisper, and prayed his heart had recorded the information correctly, and if he hadn't that she'd take his declaration well.

He opened his mouth to speak, but she spun toward him. "I'm sorry. You don't have to respond. Stupid thing for me to say."

"Abra," he breathed her name. "Be quiet." He pulled her toward him, wrapping her in his arms. It didn't matter to him that she was Beau's widow and that she might knock him down.

She was the first woman he'd ever loved. He'd been immature in the past, but his heart had grown immeasurably since those days when he'd tried to ruin his life.

Abra pressed to him. She kissed him deeper. Her luscious strands of dark mane tickled the back of his hand tangled within their softness.

She sobbed within their kiss, and he pulled away, touching her face.

Tears ran down her cheeks. "I love you so much," she whispered and sobbed at the same time. "And I'm scared to death of loving you because you are so much like Beau and so different."

"I love you." He kissed her tears, tasting their saltiness. "I promise. I won't hurt you. No more lies. Everything you know about me is all there is to know. I was an idiot in high school and afterward. Beau took me under his wing; he was always picking up after me until I learned to stand with God on my own two feet, trying to be righteous, failing some, but mostly going forward in His strength. Taffy is Beau's by blood only. From the moment I laid eyes on her, she was my daughter." He smiled. "Do you know when I fell in love with you?"

She shook her head.

"When you stood over me the day the kids knocked me—Billy the Kid—to the ground."

"That's funny." She swiped at her eyes.

"Really? Why?"

"I knew I loved you when I looked down at the goofy fellow who'd so easily fallen into play with two little boys who needed that distraction and with his daughter who expected nothing less from him."

He pulled her to him, and she laid her head against his shoulder. All felt right and comfortable. He closed his eyes and imagined endless nights of her laying in his arms, the children asleep in their beds. "Yours, mine, and ours ..."

"What?" She leaned away.

He tugged her back to him. "Just dreaming aloud."

"Sounds wonderful," she mumbled into his neck.

Somewhere above the towering maple and pine and dogwood, geese flew over, honking their congratulations. A chipmunk stopped at the edge of the walk, sat up briefly, and seemed to say, "You're a lucky fellow."

He was a lovesick goner if animals could turn him into such a sap, but he didn't care. He hated to break the moment, but he had to know. "You've been so quiet, and

I thought you were angry with me. I suspect someone has you upset."

She broke their hold and stood with her back against the bridge railing. "Beau probably thought he was doing the best, but instead, he's left us all broken inside and out. We're fighting more enemies than he may have suspected. Beau's silence left everyone he loves in danger, and I'm angry at him for it."

An oak leaf twirled downward, and she reached to let it fall into her hand. "What surprised me most of all is the fact that he had known about Jasmine's death, but he never let on."

Shane scooped the strands of hair that fell over her shoulder, lifted them back, and let them fall over her back.

"And I realized something last night, as I lay awake listening for the sounds that never came."

Shane leaned forward and kissed her. "What's that?"

"The thought of his mourning her, didn't hurt."

He shook his head. "I don't follow."

"For six years, Beau was wonderful to me. I'll never be sure of his depth of love because his past actions have turned him into someone I didn't know. I'm absolutely certain I loved him. But when I think of Beau, he's become a machine—a computer developing strategies based solely on fact. I'm not like that. I …" she struggled to keep it together "… I love."

"And you do it so well."

"No." She placed her finger to his lips. "I do it terribly. Beau died trying to protect me; Finn was injured trying to keep Beau's secrets from me, and now he hates me; Mazzie is missing because she was forced to stand on both sides, mine and Beau's; and in all of this trouble, I thought God didn't care when He was the only One who never lied to me and had faith in me."

Finally, they came. The words with the sting of a

Everybody's Broken

hornet, but they were filled with truth. He'd let her down as badly as Beau. But that wouldn't happen again. "If you give me one more chance, I'll never let you down again."

She laughed, a mocking but humor-filled glee.

He stepped back. Double sting. "Ouch."

"Oh, Shane, you'll hurt me. I'll hurt you. All I'm asking from you is that you realize that even if my heart is the thinnest of glass, even if it might shatter into a million shards, the pieces that are able to be saved will be stronger because of the truth. My brother isn't wrong about me. I never wanted to face anything, especially pain. Now, that I've been forced out of my pseudo-shell that never really protected me, I know I can endure whatever the Lord sends my way."

"Let me endure it with you."

"On two conditions ..." She grasped his coat and yanked him to her.

"Anything." The word had to rise from the depths of his heart and when it touched his lips, it floated out in a whisper.

She leaned toward him, her lips touching his. "Don't ever lie to me."

"And ...?" her lips tickled his as he spoke.

"And," she leaned back and stared into his eyes before again softly touching her lips to his, "let me endure your burdens, too."

"I will." He would have agreed to anything at that moment, but that promise was one he meant to keep.

She pressed against him, their kiss lingering as he drank in the sweet aroma of her strawberry scented shampoo.

"If I only had a brain" lilted in the air between them, and Abra giggled, reaching into her pocket for her phone. Then she stopped. "That's not funny." She pressed her fingers to those sweet lips that had just been evoking feelings in him, one's he'd never experienced with love attached to them, and held out her phone for him to see.

Finn.

He laughed then stopped. "No, I guess that's not funny."

"I'm terrible."

"I think you should answer it."

She swiped to answer. "Finn, are you okay?"

Car tires crunched leaves on their way toward the house. "Let's get inside." He motioned for her to head up the steps.

"What is it? Is it Mazzie? Please don't tell me she's gone." Abra wouldn't budge.

The car came into view, and Shane breathed relief.

Daniel climbed from the driver's seat.

Abra hung up. "He wants to take me down to Finn's and let you head to my house." Abra pulled her keys from her coat pocket and handed them to him. "Dalton's going to bring me home later."

"What happened to us enduring together?" Shane asked before Daniel met them.

"I was trying to be brave alone, I guess." She slipped the keys back into her pocket. Will you come to Finn's with me? I think I'm going to need you, especially if the news is bad."

Shane nodded and moved to lock his door. "We'll follow you," he told Daniel.

"I don't want your car seen at Finn's." Daniel looked at his watch. "You've got time. If you want a ride, get in."

Shane didn't ask any questions. He opened the door for Abra and climbed in with her. Daniel didn't say anything as he backed the car out, drove the short distance down the mountain, and pulled well behind Finn's claptrap.

Daniel exited the car, and Shane followed, going around and opening Abra's for her. The sheriff took the lead, placing his hands on the rickety railing and placing

Everybody's Broken

his feet cautiously before putting his weight on them. Abra followed in his steps, and Shane didn't dare place his foot anywhere they hadn't.

Abra slipped into the door ahead of him.

Her ear-splitting scream shook Shane to the core.

Abra screamed and covered her face with her hands. Sobs, great throat-wrenching emotion poured from her. She hadn't admitted it to anyone else, but she'd been sure she'd never see her beloved Mazzie again. Instead, to Abra's great relief, Mazzie walked to her and hugged her tight.

Abra fell against her, no strength left.

God was good. Very, very good.

The fears poured out of her with her continued cries. "I thought you were gone," she managed.

"Nope. I just enjoyed the sauna-like atmosphere in Finn's cabana and a drive to North Carolina I don't remember taking, only to wake up in Asheville. I hear I missed two men fighting over me outside the motel room."

Abra clung to Mazzie for a second longer then pushed her away. "Shut up," she said and backed up.

Shane placed a hand on her shoulder.

"Abra?" Mazzie tilted her head.

Abra wiped her eyes with the back of her free hand. "Look, I know you must have been scared. You don't have to act like it wasn't frightening for you ... for Finn ... for me." She sobbed again. "I thought you were gone. I didn't want to have to face my life with another one of the people I love taken from it."

"I'm here."

"I know you are, and you're doing what Finn so

clearly explained he and you and Beau always did. You're helping me hide from the truth." She stared at Mazzie for several long seconds. "No more. Tell me. Who did this to you?"

"Did what?" Mazzie held out her hands and twirled. "Nothing wrong with me."

"You're so full of crap." Abra narrowed her eyes. "Nothing this side of sheer terror would make you go out in public without an ounce of makeup."

Finn laughed, a full hearty guffaw. Then he grabbed the back of his head.

"You okay?" She'd not seen him before, but Dalton rushed from the kitchen toward Finn.

Finn leaned back against the wall. "Are you kidding? This is the medicine I need. My two favorite gals doing what they do best."

Mazzie planted her hands on her hips. "And just what is that, mister?"

Abra didn't care. Finn was … well, he was being Finn. Her Finn. He loved her after all.

He raised his hand up and down as if sizing up a view for a painting. "This … no one does it better than you and Abra, and I've missed it so much."

"So, Ms. Southern Belle," Abra baited, "what scared you so badly you forgot to put on your perfect face?"

"This is my perfect face," Mazzie hitched her hip and turned to Finn. "I have to wear makeup to add some flaws."

Sheriff Dixon laughed now, and Dalton joined in.

"Margaret Zelda Harris …" Abra spoke through gritted teeth.

"I was rudely awakened by Asheville's finest and a motel owner who thought Trace Bastion had left me dead in the room."

"Trace?" Abra spun toward the sheriff.

"I'd tell you it wasn't possible, but I have it on good

authority that Trace Bastion checked Ms. Harris into that motel. I don't know how. I can't get the timeline to work. I picked him up at the airport early yesterday morning. Except for the time he walked around town waiting to meet with us and when he was with you, I can account for his movements. I picked him up at the airport and that's where I dropped him off. He went through security."

"Maybe he parked the car at the airport and left me in it. I wouldn't know. I was out cold," Mazzie said. "Perhaps when you dropped him off at the airport, he pretended to go through security for a flight and double-backed."

Dixon bit his lip for a long moment. "Young lady, you ever think of a career in law enforcement? That or a fiction writer. You're pretty good at figuring out plots."

"Is he back in Bodacious Cove?" Abra asked.

"The chief was out of the office, but I caught him on his cell. He confirmed Bastion had taken some time off to do some fishing."

"Trace said he was going back to look for Mazzie."

"A big fat lie," Mazzie said.

"Did you see your abductor?" Abra asked.

"Nope. The coward got me from behind twice. He drugged me with something, but I didn't have to see him. A camera did."

Dalton nodded. "APD had me identify him from security video. Trace is the one who checked her into the motel."

"Abra," Finn pointed to his ring finger. "We don't need the video to be certain. The motel owner said the man wore a blue-stoned high school ring, and he kept turning it."

She'd never believe that the man who'd sat and talked with her yesterday could have been so calculating. "Where's your car?" she asked Mazzie.

"They left it in Asheville. APD's working the case as

a possible abduction. They'll be going over the car and the motel room."

"Trace didn't do this."

"Abra, this isn't the time to pretend." Mazzie held up clawed hands, as if she wanted to strangle Abra.

"No," Shane said. "She's right. If Bastion is the killer, he implicated himself. He confessed he'd been the last person to see you at the station. He blew his own alibi. I'm not a fan, but he's not that stupid. And what about the man you said he fought with. Any security video of that?"

Dalton shrugged. "I had someone ringing my phone off the hook." He pointed to Finn. "I got distracted. Sue me."

"I'll find out," Dixon said. "If we find out it was Price, we can link them together."

Abra shivered. "So we need to ferret out Russell Price. As soon as we can. Time isn't on Fred Colbert's side."

The sheriff remained by the opened back door, his attention drawn to both what was outside and inside the house. "I know a few of you have already made up your minds as to Bastion's guilt or innocence, but I need you to think outside the box."

Mazzie drew closer to Finn, and Abra reached for Shane's hand.

"While I liked the man I met, I can't put the pieces together to completely alibi him. I may have trusted him too much. I left Finn vulnerable. If he and Price are working in tandem, we need to be very vigilant."

Finn sat on his couch, which was covered with a light blue Chenille blanket tucked into all the right places—Finn Osteen style. "No matter what Beau thought, Russell Price has no connection to Bodacious Cove."

"That you're aware of," Daniel eyed him. "When he was here, Bastion claimed he had a suspect, was pretty sure of it, but he wouldn't give me any idea who it is."

"Didn't you think that odd?" Mazzie asked.

"No," Daniel said. "Because I was sure he had a very good reason for remaining silent, a reason he didn't have to give me because my speculation traveled the same path, still traveling that path, actually."

"The video ..."

"Ms. Harris, what possible reason would the man have for kidnapping you and bringing you to North Carolina when he knew you were already coming this way?"

"I don't know. Why would he kill Pap and Beau? Why would he link up with a murderer from Beau's past? Nothing about this makes sense. He's the one you need to arrest."

"Tell us the description of this man again," Daniel lifted his head just a bit, his attention riveted on Mazzie. "Your description of the man who abducted you?"

"Ms. Lui said he was handsome with short brown hair."

"No, I want your description of your abductor. Not hers."

"The video ...?" Mazzie repeated, hands flailing. "He was on the video."

"Checking you into a hotel. When another man joined him, he pushed the man from the room and got into a very loud and public fight in a room near the office, which one of the officers, with whom I spoke, said Mrs. Lui indicated he specifically asked for."

"You think he started the fight on purpose?" Mazzie's eyes widened.

"I don't know what to think, but Dalton said he didn't hide his face from the video. He made a show of twirling the ring. He asked for a room near the office, and when a man walked into that room, Bastion pushed him away."

"And," Dalton said, "they found you alive and well.

What Daniel wants us to do is to question everything but act according to what we know."

"Exactly," Dixon looked at his watch. "School's letting out in about an hour thirty, but I want to make some suggestions. Just in case Trace is our man, I'd like Finn to stay at your place, Shane. He's not to show up in town again. I'm suggesting the buddy system."

Under normal circumstances, Shane would never allow danger this close to his daughter, but Abra needed to know her brother was safe. "Glad to have you, Finn. I'd appreciate the extra security for Taffy."

"For the rest of you, life continues as normal. But, Dalton, Randa needs to be kept close. I have a deputy loitering outside the store. He's not doing anything to make anyone believe Randa's got security. He's fine there for another hour just talking to folks, keeping an eye out. I think Finn and Mazzie need some time, but Mazzie will need a ride home."

"Home?" Mazzie asked.

"You're staying with Abra," Dixon said.

Abra smiled. She liked the sheriff. The man could read people well. Even Mazzie wouldn't argue with the stern look on his face.

Abra clenched Mazzie's hand. "You get to sleep on the floor with me in the boys' room. They'll love it."

"Do what you normally do? Stay and visit with your brother and Mazzie. Dalton, you wait and drive the girls back to town after Shane returns. Shane, I have a job for you and Randa."

"Randa?" Dalton lost all semblance of ease.

"Yep, Randa. Nothing dangerous, Counselor."

"You need to tell me—"

A smile slid across Dixon's face. "Like the way you told me all the pertinent information I needed to know after I needed to know it? Oh, and the way you called me to go with you to Asheville. Obstruction of Justice can be

Everybody's Broken

a bear when you're fighting to keep in good standing with the North Carolina Bar Association."

Abra handed Shane her keys, and Shane jingled them. "When I finish with the chore Daniel has for me, I'll pick up the kiddos and turn the twins over to Randa's keeping when I leave."

Abra stood and walked to him. She touched his face and kissed his lips. "I love you."

Like a chameleon crossing pink fabric, Shane blushed. "I love you, too."

Chapter 23

Shane stomped his foot on the rug as he entered. Behind him Randa moved slowly, as if afraid, and Shane didn't blame her. Daniel's mission was not for the faint of heart.

She took a deep breath then said, "I don't know where Grandmere—"

Shane pushed his hands down to indicate she needed to lower her tone. This charade had to come off as believable if Price was inside the house.

If Price found a tunnel or secret entrance, he was smarter than any of them had ever thought.

"The book has to be on one of the library shelves, don't you think?" Randa continued, putting her best into her performance.

Shane put a finger to his lips and moved through the downstairs. He started in the living room, met her back in the foyer, and together, they searched the dining room, the laundry, and the kitchen. The French doors were locked, and the solarium was empty, its shades pulled down. Nothing lingered there, so he edged to the library. "You look in here. The story was one of Beau's favorites. Maybe he kept it upstairs." Shane headed in that direction, careful to hit the squeaky step.

He stopped at the threshold of Abra's room. The bed was made, and a flicker of wonder slipped into his mind. Had she ever slept in Grandmere's high-backed mahogany with the feather-perfect mattress he and his cousins used to jump on until they were caught and punished severely with milk and cookies? Or had she spent every night on the floor between the twins?

The smile quirked his lips. Grandmere would have approved of Abra, but would she have approved of his falling into love with her favorite grandson's widow?

Yes.

The word floated through him, making him peer deeper into the room. He'd never forgotten the Southern lilt of Grandmere's voice, and his thoughts had pulled it from the very deepest place in his heart where he leaned upon it in the bad times and in the good. Grandmere's essence, the one he kept so close to his heart.

Shane shook the cobwebs from his head. "Thanks, Grandmere. I love you."

He waited in the doorway, wanting one more time to pull up the memories of the woman that left such a mark on him. *I know, but you could never love me as much as I love you.*

Enough. He needed to get to it. He opened the closet door and almost laughed at the neatness within the space where he used to hide while Beau and Randa sought him. No one but Shane dared to climb inside the mountain of clothes that etched Grandmere's scent into his brain forever, still lingering here amongst Abra's sparse belongings.

The safe where Beau had kept the gun was on the top shelf. He pulled the latex gloves Daniel had given him from his back pocket, put them on, and lifted the heavy

Everybody's Broken

metal box from the shelf. Nothing rattled. Of course, the gun wasn't inside. The Bodacious Cove Police Department was holding it for evidence. How they'd gotten it was clear: Russell Price.

He placed the safe on the bed and went back to the closet. The paper Randa said the combination was written on was not on the shelf or on the floor.

"Did you find it, Shane?" Randa called. A hint that she may have stumbled across something.

"Nope," he said. He slipped from the bedroom, the safe under his arms. He placed the safe to the side of the stairwell so he could carry it out and give it to Daniel. He kept on the gloves.

In the library, Randa stood with her hands folded over her middle, her hand over her mouth. She held up her hand and rushed to the half bath under the stairwell.

Randa wretched behind the closed door, and he rushed there.

"You okay?"

"The book is green with gold lettering." Her voice was muffled by running water. "Give me a minute, okay."

Shane shrugged and turned his attention to the wall of books before him. He started his perusal at the book on the shelf fitting Randa's description, the one on the edge of the middle set, fourth shelf from the bottom of six. Tilting it toward him, he half-expected it to create an opening in the wall. He stood back, book in hand.

Nothing. Bookshelves that turned around in a wall were movie made. There wasn't enough room for that to happen here. The stairwell ran up the wall on the other side of the library with the small bathroom built into the area underneath.

The configuration of the shelves made it impossible for them to slide back and forth. Grandpere had known how to build with excellent craftsmanship, but his passion had been as a concert pianist and a teacher of music.

So, if the shelves weren't moving, had it been Price or the twins who'd shoved the furniture?

He stood back and examined the area.

Abra's boys had been around furniture and decor all their lives, much the same way Taffy had enjoyed the wildlife. If their mother told them something was valuable, they weren't going to touch it any more than Taffy would disturb the nature around her or attempt to pet a wild animal.

Price had definitely done the moving, but why?

Taking care with his grandmother's first edition collection, Shane took them one by one from their place and sat them on the end table. Nothing appeared abnormal. He ran his hand over the wood until he felt a hole. He pulled back and squinting, looked closer at what appeared to be a natural knothole in the wood, but Grandmere's library had been built of nothing but the finest and smoothest craftsmanship, a labor of love from her husband.

Shane slipped his finger into the knot. The circle left space for him to bend his finger and pull, and he did, listening for even the slightest of movement. Abra had heard a door shut in the library. If so, the shelves were the natural place.

He studied the hole again. The sides were smooth. He ran his fingertip over the bottom. Even with the gloves, the rim at the bottom was evident. He pushed downward.

The gasp behind him nearly covered the sound of a latch clicking open.

Shane spun around.

Randa pointed to the floor, dead center in the room where the hardwoods showed a gap.

Shane stepped to her. They smiled and gave a silent high-five.

Shane knelt and shivered at the cold air coming up from underneath. He listened. Then he lifted the wood until the approximately four-by-two-foot opening revealed smooth concrete steps going down. When opened, the back of the hatch fit smoothly into the lines of the floor. The hatch was heavy, and when closed, no one would suspect it to open to a cavern beneath.

"We need to follow this? You okay?"

Randa nodded. "Hold on." She left, returning with two flashlights. "I left a note on the refrigerator in case ..." She didn't need to continue her thoughts.

This was dangerous, but if it meant they were closer to discovering Price, Shane was willing to take the risk.

"Good thinking." Shane turned on his light and started down the five concrete steps that stopped and took a sharp left angle. Randa's beam bounced from behind him as she followed.

The stench of years of dirt hidden from ventilation assaulted him. Randa stayed with him, shining her light beside his onto the walls of each side of the stairs.

"There." He pointed to the wall halfway down the first five steps to a niche on the left, placed his finger inside, and found the slender telltale bar. "This is how he gets into the library. But he's getting in from the outside somehow?"

At the bottom of the steps, the beams of light barely cut through the darkness.

Shane shined the flashlight around the space. Randa kept her beam with his, giving them a larger field of vision.

A ten-by-ten room with sturdy walls, reinforced with planking squared around them. A ratty old desk, discarded possibly a quarter century before and one folding chair sat in the room littered with papers, as if someone had thrown a temper tantrum.

A string hung from a dangling light, and Shane pulled, illuminating the dank hold.

Randa bent down, picked up a few of the papers, and

examined them. "These are copies of Grandmere's probate and other files. Decades of warranty information and other personal papers. Randa grabbed up a book and thumbed through it, holding it for Shane to see. "Grandmere's diary."

Shane turned around, looking at the mess. He bent down and picked up another book, and another. "These are all her journals. I never knew she kept anything like this."

"He's looking for something." Randa stood, a book in her hand. "And from the look of things, he's mad because he hasn't found it."

"He's mad all right. We need to leave everything as we found it" Shane shot his beam along the rafters. "We'll get these all out of here eventually. The key is not to clue him into the fact we've discovered his secret." He motioned for Randa to work with him once again.

She complied, and from one corner of the room, they worked their way around.

"Look for any type of niche. That's Grandpere's MO," he whispered.

"It's chilly down here. I'm glad we didn't take our coats off. I don't think he stays here long."

They scoured the walls, pouring over each inch. On the far side of the room, across from the steps, Shane studied a piece of wood running diagonal from the horizontal planks. He attempted to push it downward. No luck, but it was the only abnormality.

He had to think like a man building a safe refuge for those seeking safety. Someone inside would need to easily know how to get out once any danger was over. The trick was to make it hard to get inside not out. So, this should have worked.

"Move it up," Randa whispered.

Shane did. With a click, a portion of the beamed wall opened a crack.

Everybody's Broken

"Duh," Randa used the word she usually saved for her problematic moments.

He smiled and pushed it back.

The aroma of damp North Carolina dirt and clay assaulted him.

Randa sneezed. "It's a tunnel."

"Any doubt where it runs?" Shane stepped inside. "It's not as reinforced as the area under the house. If you want to wait here—"

"Are you kidding?" She started to push past him, but he put his arm out. "Stay behind me."

Their lights bounced off compacted dirt.

Shane ran into a spider web. Time stood still as he swatted at it. "Is it on me?" He shuddered. "I can deal with anything if it doesn't have eight legs."

"So octopuses make you scream like a girl, too." Randa snickered.

"Did I scream?" he asked.

Randa laughed. "You couldn't hear it? The pitch was so high the neighborhood dogs are barking."

So much for the element of surprise. "If Daniel heard me, I'll be kicked out of the stealth squad for ruining his investigation."

"Maybe he'll arrest you instead of Dalt," Randa's laughter vanished.

"He's not arresting any of us." Shane continued on. "When Daniel's jabbering at us, he's on our side. When he's silent, that's when we're in trouble."

They traversed the area a little slower. Dirt sifted down on them. This was definitely not a place he wanted to be caught in should the old beams break and crash. The dirt ended, and concrete lay above them. "We're under the driveway," he said.

They reached the tunnel's end where five steps made of compacted dirt led upward. The space was too tight for both to look, so Randa acted as light bearer while Shane searched. Finally, giving up on finding another niche, he pushed upward against the cold rough concrete. It didn't budge.

Ten minutes turned to twenty, and all Shane had for his efforts was a neckache and a pressing need to get out of the space. He had to pick up the kids from school, and he was cutting it short. "Something has to move that floor."

"Unless this is a trick or an illusion Grandpere made. Look at this tunnel. It's not like the room."

"But the tunnel isn't meant for anyone to stay inside. It's a passageway. I'll bet that whatever moves this is something amazing." Shane wiped his hands on his jeans.

They made their way through the space that closed up on Shane with every second he remained under the earth.

They entered the square room and closed up the tunnel entrance.

A white sheet of paper on the old desk fluttered with the slight breeze created by the closure. He leaned over and studied the scribblings on the page. One large printed word sat alone in the middle of the page: *treasure*. Around the word, as if penned by several different hands were words and phrases, some written on top of others. *Jasmine smiled as she dangled. Taffy is mine. Beau knew the secret. Old lady dead. Killed her.*

As hard as it was to pull himself away from the scribblings of a madman, he focused on one set of fragmented words scrawled over the other notes in dark ink as if someone repeatedly penned the words.

More treasure than all the treasure of the world at my fingertips. All mine. All mine. All mine. All mine.

Mixed with the other words, the paper brought several things into focus for Shane. The truth sank in deep. Shane fell back a few inches toward the wall. "We need to get out of here."

Randa looked down at the paper. She stared up at

Everybody's Broken

him, her face pale. "He killed Grandmere, too." She placed her hand over her mouth. "No ..." She moaned. "Shane, no. Poor Grandmere."

"I knew you always loved her." Shane smiled, trying to keep his cousin calm. "But I need to get out." He pointed to the three words that had shaken him to the core. *Taffy is mine.* He grasped the light's cord and pulled, leaving them only the beams of their flashlights.

They climbed out of the hold. Shane pushed it shut. "There's Abra's closing door," he said, turned to the bookcase, and smiled.

"There's nothing amusing about anything here," Randa turned off her flashlight and took his from him.

"You're right. Let's get the books back on the shelf."

"Then tell me what you were smiling about."

"Whatever Price has been doing, Abra's been in his way. He hasn't been able to search for his treasure." Shane sobered. "None of this makes sense. Why is someone else here? Russell Price isn't one to share. He's always taken and hoarded, used and abused the people who dared get close to him."

Randa wrapped her arms around her stomach. "I feel as if we're living a nightmare."

Shane turned to the bookcase and back to the floor. "The key to the garage entrance has to be distance. The floor isn't moved by any machination close to it."

"I don't understand."

"Grandpere placed the latch in here where it would be hard to locate, but not too hard if you learn how he thought. But the entrance outside, he'd really want to make it difficult to find, place it nowhere near the opening."

"Like outside the garage."

Shane smiled. Randa was showing the St. John spirit of ingenuity that ran through Grandpere's three grandchildren. "Grandpere's family hid Jewish refugees, and they never got caught. They had to have a way for them to get inside a building—somewhere their pursuers would correctly suspect. It had to seem easy, but not too easy, but in reality, that door was exactly what it seemed. An entrance and nothing more. But something triggered another entry from elsewhere. Something that would be opened when they entered and easy to close to avoid the rapid advance of the enemy. And once inside, it had to be harder for anyone to determine where the refugees took shelter." He shook his head. "I always wondered why he separated the garage from the house with the fence and then the vines."

"And you think you've figured it out."

"I bet Grandpere's family farm in France had a tunnel from an outbuilding, and I bet the barn or whatever was the first place the enemy searched unsuccessfully." He snapped his fingers. "And I would bet my last dollar that an old pump well sat somewhere near the same type of building in France."

"That old rusty thing ..."

Shane smiled. "I can't look for it now. It's too risky. Russell can't suspect. We have to deal with what we know." Shane placed the books back on the shelf.

"Russell either spent a long time learning the secret or he's smarter than I ever gave him credit for being," Randa said.

"The creep only used his resources on what was important to him. He may know how to get in from the outside. But I don't think he's learned how to get this floor moved if he accidentally gets caught in the house. We need to make sure that entrance is cut off from him."

The ornate baby grand, the one only the most serious of musicians were allowed to touch—translated Shane—was a master of carved oak, but it weighed a ton, and its age meant it had no wheels.

"No?" Randa's eyes went large. "Grandmere would

not like that idea."

"Grandmere and Grandpere would want us to do whatever it takes to keep anyone in this house alive."

Randa nodded. "You're right." She positioned herself on the other side of the beautiful instrument.

She pushed, and he pulled, and with deep scratches etching the inches that the front of the piano was moved, they had it in place. Russell Price wasn't getting in the house unless he crawled through a window or opened a door.

He peered around the room deeming it safe for Abra.

"Shane, don't you let anything happen to my precious Taffy. She's the treasure for me," Randa said.

Shane kissed her cheek. "I love you for loving her so much, but do you know what else amuses me?"

"No? What?"

Shane lost his smile. "I can't tell you."

"Shane, we're not supposed to be keeping secrets any longer."

She had him there, but he didn't want Russell Price to ever learn the secret. He wanted him to stay tormented by the riddle that cost Grandmere her life.

He pulled a book from the shelf and opened the pages, flipping them with his finger. "More treasure than all the treasure of the world at my fingertips." Our Grandmere was a very wealthy woman.

Randa's eyes gleamed with her tears. "I miss her, Shane. I'd give all the treasure of the world to hear here say, "Randa, darlin', I love you, but ..."

"That but was always followed with loving advice. I heard it every time I walked through that door drunk or high, and you know, she never sent us away. She loved us despite our failings."

Randa sniffled against him. "That's because Beau was perfect enough for all of us."

"True in her eyes, and now I need to make sure our

three perfect little treasures are brought back here safely to your keeping."

Randa started out with him but stopped. She turned back and waved at their grandmother's portrait. "Love you, Grandmere."

Shane listened, and from deep within his heart he heard Grandmere say, "I know, but you could never love me as much as I love you."

Chapter 24

Abra laughed as the boys jumped and played in the semi-darkness of the church parking lot, chasing after each other, not fazed by the cold temperatures. She stuffed her gloved hands into her pockets and bumped against Mazzie as they followed after the boys to her car.

Mazzie's cheeks were rosy from the cold weather she wasn't used to, the weather Abra was learning to love. Of course, a few good night's sleep in her own bed did wonders for her disposition, and the hard work of preparing for the church's Harvest Festival kept her busy during the day.

Until now, absent from her thoughts had been Russell Price, the missing Fred Colbert, and the suspicion surrounding Trace Bastion, whom no one could locate. The dispatch at the Bodacious Cove PD told her only that Chief Herman was unavailable, and Trace was still out fishing. The fact Trace claimed he was hurrying home to find Mazzie made the story a little fishy to Abra, but she wouldn't admit that to her friend.

Time moved swiftly, especially after Abra had picked up the children from school to return to finish up. She and the other volunteers had worked to make sure the Harvest Festival games and the other materials lay sorted inside the church sanctuary for easy transport to their designated spaces in the parking lot for tomorrow night's festivities. Dalton finished up research for a hearing and a couple of depositions before showing; Randa arrived after closing the store, but Shane had worked all day with her and the other volunteers to mark those designated spots, to do the heavy lifting, and to prepare the outside stage for the storytelling and music.

They'd begin again tomorrow morning with the setup of the balloon houses, food prep, and everything that could be done before the hordes arrived for the early evening fun.

Shane would be singing some well-known Christian songs throughout the evening, and Pastor Moxley would stop the games and the food court to tell a brief story with a biblical message.

The old wooden white chapel by the creek was the perfect autumn setting for the event. Perhaps it was the chilly air or the aroma of wood in nearby fireplaces that made the place feel so special that she could almost forget the danger.

Poor Finn. He had been placed in solitary confinement by Sheriff Dixon, sitting alone at Shane's house. Abra smiled when she considered God was in the details. Finn needed his rest, and if given the go-ahead, he would have been in the thick of everything.

"Hey!"

Abra turned at the call.

Shane and Taffy ran toward Abra and Mazzie.

"You want me to follow you home and make sure everything's secure?" Shane asked.

Apparently, he hadn't been able to forget their

problems the way she had.

She looked to Mazzie who shrugged. She'd been exceptionally quiet most of the afternoon.

If Abra only had herself to worry about, she'd probably tell him no. Even though the noises had stopped, fear still mingled in the house, and she and Mazzie and the boys stayed in her room now, locked behind the door.

With the sudden quiet in the house, Abra would almost wager Russell had not slipped inside the secret passage only he had found. But why? If he'd not gone inside or tried to come out of the place Shane had described to her, where was he? If she could hear one sound that would alert her to his presence, she'd be able to call Sheriff Dixon, and at least one trap would be set.

Funny how the lack of noise disconcerted her more than the rustling in the walls had ever done.

Abra clicked her keys and the car lights flashed. The boys jumped in the backseat and Mazzie in the front. Paulie rolled down his window, and the boys jabbered with Taffy.

"I would love to have you and Taffy stop by." She tilted her head and smiled. "I pray that one day soon we can stop walking this tightrope where danger looms and get on with our love affair."

Shane turned and faced her, even in the dusk the red showed on his face. "Did you really mean it?"

She peered up at him, batting her eyes. "Whatever do you mean?"

"You don't do coy well." He wrapped his arms around her. "Do you really want to take this farther?"

She closed her eyes and leaned against him, feeling his strong arms around her. "Yes, Shane Browne, I love you terribly."

He leaned back and tipped her chin. "You love me wonderfully." He bent down and pressed his lips against hers. "And I'm a blessed man." He kissed her again then tilted his head toward the car. "The kids are watching. Peter put his finger in his mouth and gagged. Paulie punched him, and Taffy has that look in her eyes she gets when watching a little princess movie."

"You have a keen eye, Mr. Browne."

"I'm always attentive. I don't want anything to happen to any of Beau's—"

"Our children." She touched his face. "Yes, Beau's, too, but they're in our keeping, and they belong to us."

"So noted. Here's the plan. If you'll tuck Taffy in the car with you and wait outside the house until I get there, I'll go grab us a pizza-to-go and be there in a minute."

"You think it, too, don't you?"

"Think what?"

"Price is close and up to something."

"He hasn't gone away. That much I know." He rubbed his hands up and down her arms. "He wants his treasure, and it's been in front of him the entire time."

He'd told her the answer to the riddle when they'd talked on the phone, insisting he'd never figured it out until he'd come out from the tunnel he and Randa had found. Grandmere's treasure of first edition books were truly a treasure.

She stood on her tiptoes and kissed his cheek. "We'll wait outside for you."

"You got it." He walked to her car, opened the door, and ushered Taffy inside. "Okay, you three, I'm in love with your mom. You okay with that?"

You three. The two words ran deep. Shane had given him her entire heart, and that included the tendering of his daughter into her care.

Paulie clapped. Peter put his finger in his mouth, faked a gag, and then smiled. "Grownups! Yuck!"

Taffy stared up at Abra, and the street lamp caught her large smile and the tears in her eyes. Taffy would be a motherless daughter no more. Abra would do everything

Everybody's Broken

she could to keep Taffy from that pain.

Abra backed out of the spot and drove the few blocks to her house.

Clouds covered the moon and left the neighborhood streets in the dark.

"Let's drive around and not wait in the driveway," Mazzie suggested.

"Good idea." Abra drove past the house and turned down the side street where the garage sat.

Frieda's house on the other side of the garage had one light shining from deep inside.

"Mommy," Peter asked. "Where's Ms. Frieda been?"

Abra slowed as she passed the property. "That's a good question. I haven't seen her out in a while."

"I think he has her." Peter sat back, arms crossed.

Abra glanced to Mazzie. "Who?"

"The guy who killed Daddy."

Abra pushed her hand against her chest as her heart pumped so hard her muscles ached. Now or never. Now or never. "Baby, your daddy's killer isn't here," the words whispered between her lips. But there was a killer among the citizens of Amazing Grace. He'd killed Jasmine Roy and possibly Fred Colbert. And poor Ms. Frieda. Had he killed her, too?

Even in the pale moonlight, in her look at him through the rearview mirror, Paulie clearly blanched. "Then why did Peter get the note?"

Peter leaned over Taffy and punched him. "Stupid."

"Stop that!" Abra pulled the car around the curve, driving slowly. "What note?"

"That day we were playing. Ms. Frieda handed me a note. She said to be careful, that we were being watched.

We've seen a man come out of her house, but we never see her anymore."

"Was this man the one who shot your dad?" Mazzie turned.

"We told you before, Mazzie. We can't tell who shot Daddy," Peter said.

"But the person stepped over the dune. He wore a mask. Daddy didn't see him. He shot Daddy. We told Uncle Finn what we saw, and he told us not to tell anyone."

Abra made her way completely around the block and pulled into her driveway. She undid her seatbelt and turned to look at the two, traumatized boys and the little girl who sat between them, her eyes wide. "What did he look like in his mask?"

"A dog. He wore a rubber mask, and Uncle Finn cussed. He told us to get down. We didn't do it right away, and Uncle Finn yelled at us. He never yelled at us before." Tears filled Paulie's eyes.

"We ducked," Peter jumped in. "And the glass shattered. Blood hit us. Uncle Finn's blood. Paulie started to scream, and I put my hand over his mouth. We waited, Mommy. We did, and the dog-faced man didn't come to the window. So, I peeked up, and Paulie did, too."

Abra clutched the back of her seat. She'd never thought that, short of a heart attack, she could ache so deeply.

"He was gone. That's when Uncle Finn whispered for us not to move, and we knew he was alive, but he said he was hurt, and he needed a minute. Uncle Finn told us not to look at Daddy. He was sorry, and Uncle Finn cried. He called Mazzie and you, and he told us not to get out of the truck no matter what. Then we thought he died. He didn't move. He wouldn't answer us. Mazzie came, and when she pulled up we didn't know it was her, and we were scared. She said everything would be okay, but she had to take a picture. Then Detective Bastion came."

Abra knew this side of the story. The boys had corroborated everything Abra had learned from Trace.

"Mazzie found a towel behind the seat in the truck. She wrapped it around Uncle Finn's neck and got him to an old car and told us to get in. Officer Bastion stayed there, and Mazzie drove us to one of her places. She told us to go inside. She had a hard time getting Uncle Finn inside. Then Ms. Mercy and Mr. Zeb showed up."

Abra dared to glance at Mazzie. Her friend stared straight ahead, tears falling down her face. "I could have put them in more danger, but Beau said Bastion could be trusted."

Lights pulling into the Rylanders' driveway next door illuminated the wide eyes of her sons, but beyond the window to Peter's right lay the hay wagon. Abra blinked. Something was very wrong.

"What are you doing?" Dalton tapped on the top of the car. "You all partying in the car?"

"Where's Shane?" Abra pushed open her door. She grabbed her keys and bent back in to make sure the children caught the seriousness on her face. "Stay!" She slammed her door.

"He pulled out of Slice of Heaven and was right behind me. He got stopped by the light. Why're you waiting out here?"

Mazzie climbed out of her side of the car. "Abra, what is it?"

Abra's body trembled as she made her way to the back of the vehicle. "Did Randa go inside?"

"Yeah." Dalton turned to look up at his home. "She said to make sure we got invited for the pizza, and she'd join us." He smiled. "We have some great news to share."

"The boys and Taffy need to stay with her."

"What's going on?" Dalton tensed.

Shane pulled his car into the drive behind Abra's

vehicle.

Abra turned to Dalton. "I need you to take the boys and Taffy to Randa. Make sure she's alone in your house, and come back here."

Dalton shook his head as if trying to clear his thoughts.

Abra clicked her keys and unlocked the car door. You three, follow Uncle Dalton."

"But we want pizza." Paulie complained.

Abra met up with Shane and took the pizza from him. "Aunt Randa has plates. Now, do as I say. Take the pizza."

Dalton didn't ask another question.

"Hurry …" Abra begged.

"Don't tell me we have to share," Shane teased.

Abra's breath hitched as she drew it in and let it out. "Look at the hay wagon." She touched his arm.

"What is it? You're quaking."

"Shane, please." She stared up at him, unable to make herself look again. Having an over the top imagination right now would be a gift from heaven.

Shane stepped away from her, and she latched on to him.

He drew back, his gaze still on the wagon as he pulled out his phone, hit three numbers, and waited.

Mazzie stepped toward the scarecrows but scurried back, her hand over her mouth. She hurried after Dalton and the children.

"This is Shane Browne. Please tell Sheriff Dixon Fred Colbert's been found. He needs to come to Abra Carmichael's home with his investigators and an ambulance, but don't sound the sirens. Fred's wife lives across the street, and I don't want her to find out that way. He's dead." He hung up from the call, and Abra burrowed into him, muffling her scream with his coat.

Everybody's Broken

Abra shivered in the darkness.

Headlights turned onto the road, moving slowly as if searching. Then Sheriff Dixon pulled his car to the curb.

Shane kept Abra wrapped in his embrace.

"Sheriff!" Tammy pushed opened her front door and ran down the porch steps to the road. "Have you heard anything?"

Shane released the two women in his arms and intercepted her.

Sheriff Dixon turned his gaze from them to Abra.

Abra nodded toward the hay wagon.

Dixon looked, closed his eyes, and stepped to talk to Tammy. His voice remained low, just the sound of it comforting Abra. It had to be soothing the poor woman who was about to find out that she was a widow.

Abra didn't have to turn to look at the scene to know that Fred Colbert had died a gruesome death, his head was almost severed completely, and bits of hay sprang out around it. No blood.

How was that possible?

Tammy's wail hit the air, and Dixon caught her before she hit the road.

"Mommy!" Melissa tore out the door, and Shane hurried to her. He picked her up, whispered to her, and carried her to the waiting arms of Randa who ushered the child into the Rylander home with the kids and Mazzie.

Dalton joined them. He spoke to Randa, and when she nodded he ran across the yard.

He came to stand beside Abra, and his gaze fell on the murdered man. He gagged and turned away, vomiting onto the driveway. He straightened and wiped sweat from his face. "God, please, no." He looked to the heavens.

Abra took several deep breaths. "God, please be with

Tammy."

Randa came from her house with two bottles of water. One she handed to Tammy, the other to Dalton. "Bad news?" she whispered.

"Yeah, babe." Dalton coughed. "The kids need you right now. I'm going to ask Sheriff Dixon to let me walk Tammy over as soon as she's able. Fred's body's been found."

Randa gasped. "How? When? How did you know?"

"Baby, believe me. You don't want to know right now." Dalton blocked Randa's view of the wagon. "Trust me." He choked out a sob. "Please just take care of yourself. I need you to do that, but Tammy and Melissa are going to need us, and right now, you're the one who has to be with her first."

"Okay."

"Randa," Sheriff Dixon called. "I've asked Mrs. Colbert to go with you. Her mother went home today, and I don't want her to be alone. Is that okay?"

"Definitely." Randa stepped forward and slipped her arm around Tammy's shoulders.

Tammy turned to look at the wagon and stumbled forward.

Randa jerked her gaze there, and if she saw anything, she didn't act surprised, but when she faced Abra, tears pooled in her eyes. "Come?" She motioned for Abra to join her.

"They need Abra," Dalton said. "They'll be asking her some questions."

Randa nodded. "Let's go inside where it's warm, Tammy. Melissa needs to see that you're okay. She's had a rough few days." Randa continued to talk to Tammy until all that Abra could hear were murmured words.

Abra embraced Dalton, placing her mouth to his ear. "Did Finn ever tell you that the man who murdered my husband wore a mask that made him look like a dog?"

Everybody's Broken

Dalton pushed from her hold, stared at her, and stumbled back. He leaned over and vomited once more, this time in the grass.

Chapter 25

No one had gotten much sleep the night before, with police lights flashing, interrogations, investigators milling around the yards. Still, weather-wise, the day was going to be a nice one, sunny with a little chill, but rain would move in later in the night. Hopefully, the moon's glow would shine before the deluge and dispel the lingering fear that settled over the town following last night's discovery of Fred Colbert's body and the rumors spun by the gossip mill.

Abra stood in the parking lot of the church and took in the registration table she'd decorated with miniature hay bales.

"Much better without the ..." Mazzie's bracelets jangled as she waved her hands indicating the decorations "... you know."

Abra had found small scarecrows within the church decorations and had planned to place them around the table. Instead of bringing them outside, she'd found a box and stuffed them all away. She never wanted to see another scarecrow in her life. Those in her yard had been bagged, tagged, and confiscated for evidence along with the wagon. A blessing really. If Tammy had to come home for anything, she wouldn't have to look out her door or window to see it sitting there, a reminder of the gruesome scene. Comforting Tammy, sitting with her and letting her cry and share her memories of Fred had nearly done Abra in.

Very early in the morning, they'd helped Tammy and Melissa pack a few items before her parents came to take her back to Asheville where she and Fred had roots and where the arrangements for the funeral would be made. The commute was less than half an hour if the police needed her for anything, and Dalton had promised to look after her house.

Tammy had hugged Abra tightly, telling her none of this was her fault, but haunting doubts balanced precariously up and down as Abra leveraged her guilt on one side and her anger with Beau on the other. After all, he could have prevented everything if he'd only … *wham!* … the scale of remorse slammed down on her side.

If only she'd shown him she was stronger than they all thought.

"You okay?" Shane walked toward her and Mazzie carrying three coffees loaded with caffeine-fueled energy for the day ahead. "The kiddos are fine," he whispered as he got closer. "They're watching over Uncle Finn, who was happy to have his solitary confinement invaded by the munchkins."

Mazzie reached for the coffee Shane held out to her.

"Daniel called," Shane said as Abra took the warm cup from him. "Two things: Fred has been dead probably from the day he went missing. He died of blunt force trauma to his head and not the …" he ran his hand across his throat "… that was done after death. He was frozen

Everybody's Broken

and had to have been kept nearby. That's why there was no blood. The coroner says the body hadn't been there long before its discovery."

Abra gasped and shared a look with Mazzie. In all of the horror of finding Fred's body, she'd forgotten to tell Dixon what the boys had said about the man at Ms. Frieda's place.

Shane narrowed his eyes. "Why do I get the feeling this isn't good news?"

Abra sighed. "The boys mentioned they'd seen a man at Ms. Frieda's house. Peter said she'd given him a note and warned him. I saw Peter with the paper, and it never occurred to me that she would be warning us. Peter seemed angry at whatever he'd found. He tore it up before I could have asked, and I didn't pry." She took out her phone and dialed Dixon.

When she confessed her forgetfulness, the sheriff sighed. "That's understandable. Trouble is, I've been trying to get into Frieda's house for days. She never answered the door. I found her today?"

"You found her?" Abra closed her eyes.

"Is she alive?" Mazzie grabbed Abra's arm and held on tight.

"She's extremely disoriented. She was already starting down a road to dementia."

Abra nodded to Mazzie who sank back against the table, almost upsetting it.

"She's been drugged beyond belief. She has bedsores, appears to have been fed only canned soup. She was laying in filth. It's a wonder she survived physically. Mentally, not so well. She did have a moment of clarity, and she asked me about the young man who'd stayed with her. She said she'd been worried about you because he seemed so interested in the house. She's been taken to the hospital. Her son will arrive soon, but I'm keeping a deputy there with her as they examine the deep freeze where we believe Price kept Colbert's body. Act normal as we said, but be careful."

"Thank you, Sheriff. I'm so sorry." Abra choked on her regret as she ended the call.

She covered her face with her hands.

Shane stood behind her and rested his hands on her shoulder. "This is not your fault. I won't even blame Beau. He couldn't have known how this would affect so many others." He turned her toward him. "Listen to me. I've met Price. I hated him. That's a hard thing for me to say, but he never sat right with me. Beau shrugged it off. So, did Dalton. Jasmine saw the good in everyone. I spouted off during our meeting with Daniel, but I never thought him capable of murder."

"But, according to Bastion, Beau did," Abra said.

"But he didn't suspect Trace of anything," Shane reasoned.

"Beau knew the poison Pap drank was meant for him," Mazzie said. "I think he put his faith in the wrong person trying to connect Price to that murder."

"Daniel says he's still trying to locate Bastion and talk to Herman again." Shane said. "All he's gotten is assurances from the department that the chief and the detective are okay."

Abra still couldn't reconcile the man who shared his heart with her at her home the night before she left Florida and then again in her backyard here in North Carolina with a cold-blooded killer?

Shane kissed her cheek. "I better get busy. I got teased yesterday for hanging out with one particularly beautiful woman."

Mazzie fluffed her hair. "Well, I'm glad to know what they think of me."

Abra laughed and waved Shane away.

Mazzie straightened. "If I get my hands on Trace Bastion, I'll kick him so hard and so far, he'll be burned up in the outer atmosphere."

Abra paced back and forth for a moment. "I still don't think Trace is our man."

Mazzie didn't speak.

"What? No argument?"

"Every time I spout off like I just did, I remember what Sheriff Dixon said about his actions at the motel."

Abra laced her arm with Mazzie's. "Trace is who he has been the entire time. He is Beau's grieving partner on the force. He failed to protect Beau. He's feeling the pain of it. He's done his best to protect you, Finn, me, the boys, and everyone and everything Beau loved. He did not kill Pap nor did he murder Beau. Someone else did. But one thing bothers me."

"He's not home yet," Mazzie deduced. "Which means what?"

"After finding Fred's body, I can't shake the thought that Trace Bastion is dead, too," Abra admitted.

"I don't know, and that's what frightens me so much." Mazzie squeezed Abra's arm to her.

"Ladies, you look a little too serious." Pastor Moxley joined them. "Is this a private party, or can anyone join?"

Mazzie released Abra and walked with the preacher. "Is this your way of telling us we need to get to work?"

"Exactly. I haven't seen Shane. I'm wondering how the music's coming along for tonight."

"I haven't heard him sing a word," Mazzie teased then took a drink of her coffee.

Pastor Moxley stopped, bit his lower lip, and then smiled at Abra. "Think there's any chance we can get Dalton in that chicken outfit again?"

Mazzie coughed. "Dalton in a what?"

Abra couldn't help it. She laughed. Had the pastor known how the Lord had used such a silly thing to draw her back to Him? Probably not, but God did, and he'd just lightened her heart a bit. "You had to be there."

"Oh, I hope we have an encore." Mazzie raised her cup in the air. "Lead me to the work, Pastor." She skirted away from them but turned. "Come along, girlfriend. You're not hanging around outside by yourself. I'm not only helping with this fine festivity, but I'm planning the best birthday party this side of your—how many years is it?"

"Enough years to know that there's not going to be a party. One man is dead, Mazzie, and another is missing."

Abra's words were lost on her friend as she and the pastor walked inside the church.

Abra peered around her and hurried after them.

Abra thought Sheriff Dixon would have his deputies lined everywhere. This unincorporated town had enough of them to spare, but the parking lot of the church was filled with little kids excited for a chance to show off their costumes before Monday's trick or treating.

Children were dressed up as anything from Captain Jack Sparrow to characters from *The Lord of the Rings* to Disney princesses. The boys were policemen; Taffy had donned a flannel shirt and blue jeans with a rope for a belt. With a tiara tucked inside her hair, which Shane had braided into pigtails, she called herself a cowboy princess. Only a few of the kids, older ones and most likely not ones from the church, had some gory things going on. One taller kid carried a very real looking sickle, stomping it on the ground as he walked around with the dark cloak and a black fencer's mask shadowed to appear as if his head were a skull.

Abra shivered when he looked her way. The church wouldn't turn anyone away. This was what the event was about: taking the evil out of something cultures had

Everybody's Broken

placed Satan into for centuries. If you turned those who were drawn to the darkness away, how would they ever get a look at the Light?

Abra had never minded the costumes or the going door-to-door. Perhaps she and Finn had participated in it before their mother left, but Abra had no memory of it.

The grim reaper brushed past her, and Abra pulled away. She needed to concentrate on other things like keeping the children beside her and safe. Her decorating and helping the ladies set up the snack table completed, she had the responsibility of the kids while Dalton, Randa, Shane, and even Finn and Mazzie worked. And Mazzie was having a grand time. Finn, however, was not.

Randa was running a game booth for the smaller kids. She'd sent someone to ask Abra to relieve her once, and Taffy and the two boys had done a fine job helping the toddlers catch a magnet fish with a make-believe metal hook. When Randa returned, her face had been flushed, but she wore a smile and ushered her family off for more fun.

Dalton was minding the sound equipment and working with Shane. They'd had a few problems with the mics. Shane was on break and working out the kinks with Dalton. CD music filled the church lot as the children played the games or bounced in the houses or ate in the makeshift food court.

At the front of the crowd, a big white emaciated rooster greeted kids with tickets for a free snack. Beside him walked a woman no one would ever recognize as Mazzie Harris. Somehow, she had managed to find one of Grandmere's old dresses, one Abra imagined she'd worn while gardening, and Mazzie had put together an ensemble that made her look like Ma Kettle. She'd snapped a picture of herself and sent it to Randa, who arrived with an old lady's gray wig styled in a bun to complete the transformation. Randa had also loaned her one of Grandmere's shawls. The air was chilly, but Abra, for the first time, hadn't noticed it until she sent up a prayer of thanks that Finn was truly not roasting inside his outfit.

Pastor Moxley milled about the crowd. On occasion, he'd stop and talk with an adult or child.

Now, he talked with the grim reaper who nodded with his whole body as he spoke. The guy was good at his role, but could anyone be so clueless not to realize that the entire town was on edge because of a man's death?

Abra's cell phone buzzed in her pocket. "Hang on, guys." She held up her hand to stop the kids from moving any further. Then she placed her hand to one ear and the phone to another. "Hello."

"Aabbrraa …" If not for the intensity in the voice, she would never have been able to understand the whisper.

"Who is this?"

"Danger. You."

"Mr. Price, I'm not afraid of you." Before speaking them, the words had been a lie, but once through her lips, calm overtook her.

"No. Loyal. Danger. You." The voice grew weaker. "Sorry."

"Hey!" Another voice yelled and cursed. The call ended.

Abra looked at her phone's face. Loyal Herman's personal mobile. Like a hen to Finn's rooster, she ushered the kids to follow her.

"Ah, Mommy, we haven't had any fun yet," Peter complained. "Can we just go in the bounce house?"

Abra glanced that way. With no police presence, she wasn't about to let them out of her sight, especially now.

"Go ahead, Abra," a familiar voice said from behind her. "They're fine."

Abra spun around. Sheriff Dixon tipped a Stetson hat.

Everybody's Broken

"My team's in plain clothes, and they've been given the order to watch out for each of you." His jaw clenched. "Not one more murder in this town if I can help it."

"You're sure they're safe?"

"I'm positive. If anyone makes a move toward them, my deputies will be on them in a moment. We're trying to be discreet, and the grim reaper, he's a kid that works for my mom. Brain dead but harmless."

Abra let out her breath. She needed to share the call with the sheriff, and she didn't want them to hear. "I'm glad. Go on kids, but you stay there or come back here. Nowhere else. Do you understand?"

They nodded, ran, and cheered their way to freedom.

Abra held up her phone. "I received a call."

He took it from her.

A little boy ran to him, tackling his arms around his legs. "Sheriff Daniel." He hugged tight.

"Hey there, Cade. Where're your mommy and daddy?" Daniel picked up the little boy.

Cade pointed.

Daniel focused his attention in that direction for a long moment. "You're having fun?"

"Lots of fun. Daddy helped me win a stuffed animal."

Daniel's face seemed to lose some of its tension. "Well, I'm glad. You tell them I said hey, okay?"

Cade ran toward his parents.

"Your grandson?" Abra asked.

Daniel narrowed his eyes then smiled. "Cade's my good buddy. He lives across the street from my mother. I heard you met his grandma?"

Abra shook her head. "Not that I'm aware."

"Magdalene."

"Magda—the pros..."

Daniel winced as if she'd belted him and held up his hand. "She's a hurting soul. Always has been. Some of us have hurt her more than others, and she ends up hurting everyone she knows. The day she caught up with you had to be a very rare good one. She was feeling for more than herself."

"I'm sorry to hear that."

"Well, if her son can't get through to her, I doubt anyone else will be able to do it."

"Her son? She mentioned a daughter."

Daniel tilted his head first toward little Cade and his parents. "Her daughter." Then he motioned to the man standing on the other side of the woman.

Abra's gaze met Quinn Moxley's. He nodded and waved at her and Daniel before turning away.

"He's such a nice man," she said.

"Tell me about it. He's always been a good kid. Raised his sister."

"Sheriff, why do I think that you are and have been a surrogate father to a lot of kids in this town? If not father, then a good friend?"

"I suppose because God placed it in my heart. I wouldn't do it otherwise." He held up her phone to her. "Get me in this thing."

She did as he asked. He studied the number then pulled out his iPhone. Thumbing along, he stopped then held both phones for her to look upon. "I saved it when I spoke to him about his previous call to you."

"Yes," she said. "Herman—Loyal—he's the one who called. He's in trouble, but he said I was in danger."

"Everyone will be gathering around the stage in a bit. Story time should commence. Get yourself and the kids up front so Shane can keep an eye on you while he leads the song worship, and Dalton can safeguard you from behind. I need to phone into the station, see if I can get them working on finding that police chief. I thought he was avoiding my last few calls. Maybe that's not the case." Daniel's brisk stride took him to the street where his car was apparently parked.

Abra headed toward the bounce house. The phone in her hand buzzed. She stared at the unrecognizable local number on the caller ID. "Hello?" she said through clenched teeth.

"Abra?" the tiny voice cried into the phone. "He's going to hurt me if you tell the police he has me?"

"Who, baby?" Abra stopped and looked around her, cautious not to alert any of the officers hidden in the crowd to her terror.

"I—I don't know." Taffy sniffled. "I want my daddy."

The slap was so hard that Abra flinched. "Taffy?" she begged for an answer.

"The grim reaper's waiting for you, Abra."

Abra looked around her again. The costumed attendee was nowhere in her sight. "Where are you? Don't hurt her. I'll do whatever you ask?"

"Follow my directions to the letter. I'm watching you. Tell Randa that the kids are still in the bounce house, and you need to do something inside. Go into the church, walk out the back door, and get down to the stream. Head to the left, and you'll find yourself in familiar territory. Come to The Gray Lady." The phone went dead.

Abra stared at it for a moment as if waking up from a nightmare. She peered into the bounce house until she located the two bobbing heads of her sons among the many kids inside.

She'd done this. She'd allowed them to go, but Daniel had said they would be safe. He'd promised her the grim reaper was no one to fear.

She kept her gaze on the inflatable until she was certain Taffy was nowhere inside. She couldn't approach. If the boys saw her, they might notice Taffy's absence. Lost in the mix of kids, they must not have noticed. If they realized she was gone, their actions would alert the officers.

But how had he gotten her?

She shook the fear off. Taffy needed her. With determined steps, she made her way to Randa. "The kiddos are in the bounce house. Daniel said there are deputies all over the place. I need to go inside to help with something."

"A few of them left after Daniel did. There was a little bit of confusion for a minute, but I think the remaining deputies have settled back into place."

Confusion? Price must have done something to give himself an advantage.

Abra nodded and turned but spun back around. "I understand that the show's about to start. If I'm still inside, will you gather Taffy and the boys? Daniel wanted them seated front and center."

"Will do," Randa promised with a bright smile.

Abra headed toward the church.

Mazzie and her gangling chicken were the hit of the crowd, and just as Dalton had done, Finn entertained the children. Abra stopped for a moment to see her brother and her best friend one more time. Would her last look at Finn be in the chicken suit that God had used to bring her back to Him?

She looked toward the stage. Shane was watching her. She pried a smile into place for him and pointed to the bounce house and then to Randa.

He winked.

Abra went inside, empty except when the volunteers came in for supplies. She walked down the aisle and stopped at the altar. Taffy needed her, but Beau and Mazzie and Finn had always been right about her. She was a weakling when it came to facing her fears. She fell to her knees and stared up at the cross against the darkening night outside. She had to believe that God cared, if not for her, for that precious girl. "Dear God in Heaven, take me, but be my strength. Use me to free that little girl. You have some good people who will see to Peter and Paulie, but Taffy's alone, and she's Shane's world. He could live without me." She cried into her hand. "But I could not live without any of them. So, use me to be Your arms." She sat with her eyes closed, garnering her strength. The words began to form in her heart, and she listened as the prayer poured from her. "I'm not a David, Lord. I need your miracles. Help me to see that I mean something to You—if only for me."

The front door of the church swung open, and Abra jumped to her feet, running to the door on the left that would lead her to a corridor and an exit that opened up to a beautiful deck along the creek.

The water gurgled past, sending an even deeper chill into the dropping temperatures. Abra took the steps from the deck to get to the muddy bottom. She slipped and picked herself up, clinging to tree limbs and to vegetation to stay upright on a steep slant.

Something rustled the leaves ahead, and Abra stopped.

"Relphh," the muffled cry reached her. "Relphh me."

She stepped slowly. The creeping darkness making it hard for her to see. Against a maple already bare of its leaves, a man wearing only a t-shirt and jeans struggled. Abra bent down beside him. He was tied to the tree with a heavy but thin filament. His struggles left him bleeding, and a rag in his mouth, held firmly in place by the same line was sure to be cutting into the corners of his lips. Pinned through his t-shirt and into the tree was a knife, keeping a note in place.

"Geatt me offa here," the young man struggled.

Abra ripped the note from beneath the knife and did her best to read it in the dark. "Leave him here. Do not set him free. The little girl's life depends upon it."

Abra stared down at the man.

She tugged the knife free of the tree and had him lean

forward. With a nick of the knife to the rope, he was able to spit the gag free. He started to speak and cried out in pain.

"Listen to me," Abra touched his shoulder. "I can't let you go. I know you're in pain, but you have to stop struggling."

"He told me he would come back and kill me. You have to let me out of here."

"He lied to you. Were you the one wearing the grim reaper costume?"

He nodded. "I left the festival, walking down the street. He stepped out of a car, offered me a lot of money to buy the costume from me, but he wanted to change, so I followed him. We got down the road, and he ..." the young man hung his head. "I'm an idiot."

"He pulled you into the woods, stole the costume, and tied you up?" Abra needed to make this as brief as possible, but she needed to know how Price had done what he'd done. "Tell me. After he left, did he come back this way?"

"I think it was him, but he wasn't wearing the costume, just a dog mask and his clothing had changed. All black, but not the costume. He took out the knife. I thought he was going to kill me with it, but he stuck the note through my sleeve."

"Did he have Taffy Browne with him?"

"No. He was alone."

She had the answer to the question they had all pondered. The two men were obviously working in tandem.

Abra laid the knife down at his dangling hand. "Free yourself." She pushed off the tree.

"Lady ... help me."

Abra closed her eyes. This was someone's son, on the cusp of manhood. She imagined Peter and Paulie at his age—hopefully a little brighter. She stooped back down

Everybody's Broken

beside him. "If I let you go, you need to help me. Will you do that?"

"Whatever you ask."

"You need to wait here ten minutes. Don't move."

"But I'm cold."

Abra shrugged out of her jacket and dropped it at his feet. "Listen to me. Give me ten minutes to get to Taffy. If you don't, I can't be sure she'll be okay."

"I'll wait."

She slid the knife across the rope and flinched when he cried out again in pain. She folded the knife, slipped it into her pocket, and pushed the note into his lap. "Ten minutes." She ran along the creek to a path that ran to her right. Climbing upward, she found herself on familiar territory near town and not far from her home.

The cold bit at her as she made her way through the streets. Somewhere children played in their yards. Someone barbecued even in the bitter cold.

All these things that should have warmed her heart left it untouched, the cold springing up like twisting vines, overtaking every part of her. "Please, God," she whispered as she walked past the Colberts' empty home, crossed the street, passing her front walk to follow the sidewalk around the corner.

She stopped in the street and looked back in the direction she'd come. The caller said only to go into The Gray Lady. What if he'd gone through the garage and learned he couldn't lift the hatch in the library?

She stepped to the corner of the yard, contemplating. Movement at the back of the garage caught her eyes. "This way."

She made her way around the building. Darkness now enveloped her, but she could make out the figure standing by the open door. "Where's Taffy?"

"Get inside," he demanded.

Abra jerked from him. "Where is Taffy? Your

messenger said you didn't have her with you when you left the note."

Silence greeted her. Then hands grasped her and pulled her inside the pitch-black building. "I'm not playing games."

"You didn't take her, did you?" Abra taunted.

"She's inside. Get on your knees."

"Why?"

"Follow directions or you won't get a chance to say your good-byes."

"What are you planning?"

"We'll have this conversation, but first you have to listen." His words were innocuous, but the fury in his tone was enough. She got on her knees. A shadow of something lay before her. She thought back to the day they'd been inside with the sheriff. The shadow was a leg of the work table.

"Now turn and face me and back up slowly. There's an opening behind you. Once you slide into it, you'll feel the stairs beneath your feet. Five of them. Go down and stand against the wall."

"But it's dark."

"Do. As. I. Say."

Abra turned her body and backed up until she felt a cavernous area beneath her. She dangled her right foot for a second and then the left, afraid that he had set her up for a very deep and deadly fall.

With her stomach against the garage floor concrete, the security of earth met her tennis shoes. She found her footing and with her back against the wall, made her way down five steps.

Price followed her without closing the opening. Had he learned that Shane had closed up his entrance to the house and could he think Shane learned the secret to the garage? Why else would he leave it open? Unless he expected his cohort.

Everybody's Broken

A flashlight shone in Abra's eyes. "Good girl. Taffy was a good girl, too. Good to see you again." Russell Price lowered the light. "Let's get inside the heart of The Gray Lady and have a talk before Shane comes to your rescue. He'd never reveal the treasure. Too much like Beau. But I'm done with that. I've got what I want from him." He grasped her arm and pulled her down a long tunnel, his light bouncing off the gray dirt walls.

His fingers dug deep into her skin as he brought her into a large opening. Then he placed the flashlight on a table, bottom side up. The heavy torch thudded against the wood. Price grasped a string and the room filled with light from a single dangling bulb. He turned off the flashlight, standing before her in the grim reaper costume.

Abra shuddered.

He removed the mask.

Shane had shared with her and the others the dimensions of the room. He'd even shown her how he'd learned to get inside from the library.

But if Shane got the note and suspected Price was inside, moving the piano would alert the maniac to the arrival he seemed to anticipate. And the open garage entrance bothered her. Price couldn't be sure Shane found that access. Was it left open for Shane or someone else?

No avenues of escape existed for her and Taffy unless Abra took care of Price.

Taffy cowered in a corner, tears flowing down her face, which held a large whelp that would leave a bruise. Abra yanked her arm from Price's grasp and scurried over papers littered around the floor to hold Taffy against her.

"I want my daddy. I want my daddy," she cried.

Abra stroked the child's hair, afraid to make promises she couldn't keep.

Price laughed. "Honey, you don't know it, but you've got your daddy right here."

Taffy stared up at Abra with green eyes so like

Beau's that Abra's emotions would shatter if she didn't hold tight rein on them. She gave a slight shake of her head and tucking Taffy behind her, turned to the man. "Why don't we leave her out of this conversation?"

"She's my daughter, you know."

Cornered. No way out of the room or the conversation with a man who seemed so normal but whom she knew to be utterly mad.

"You told me not to tell anyone I was coming here."

"But you did." He shrugged. "Human nature. Women's nature. Look to their knights in shining armor." He paced toward the stairs leading up into the house. "Beau was too easy to read. First I paid the prostitute to ruin his good name. Pride comes before a fall, right? That pride moved him on, just like I planned it. He never let me near Jasmine when he was around. I made sure he abandoned her. I gave her reason to doubt. I had plans for us."

Abra held in the gasp.

Russell picked up the flashlight. He stared at it.

Abra's fingers itched to get to the knife in her back pocket, but she didn't dare hint that he'd been so careless as to leave her with something to defend herself.

But ... he hadn't. A man in a dog mask had. Trace? But why would he have killed Beau and not some dumb kid or Mazzie? The more she reasoned, the more confused she became.

Abra kept her attention on the light turned weapon. She turned to the child who shrank back as far as she could into the space she'd found. Had Price hit her with the light?

Abra pushed her glare to him. "You hit a child who did nothing wrong? Are you mad?"

She'd spoken without thought and brought her fingers to her lips.

A sick smile crossed Price's face. "Abra. Abra. Abra.

Always saying the worse thing at the worse possible moment. Beau told me about that. Said you had a mouth that could skin a cat if he didn't help you keep it under control."

Anger flamed within Abra. How dare Beau betray her? She lowered her head and pushed back the tears.

"Does that bother you?" Price taunted.

Abra hadn't noticed the cold until the blaze inside her died down a bit. She wrapped her arms around herself and lifted her head.

The smile she offered him was genuine. "No. Because Beau didn't say anything like that. You heard me in the house telling Randa when she asked about my habit. You're adding your own twisted version to Beau's action of love by helping me to overcome a bad habit I admitted to him I had."

He tilted his head and looked at her with a demonic sneer.

She didn't care. She'd tell this man the truth. "You live in this world where you fancy you're owed everything, and you don't care who you hurt to get it. That's probably why Beau didn't like you. I thought for a while that I didn't know my husband. You made us all doubt who he was, but one thing we're all certain about is you might be the only person on this earth Beau Carmichael hated. And he always knew you were his betrayer. I thank God Beau died never knowing the truth of what you did to Jasmine. A badge wouldn't have stopped him from putting you in the ground."

Russell brought the flashlight down hard on the desk. "He knew nothing. I had Beau right where I wanted him until the idiot accidentally killed your daddy and then to correct matters blew Beau's head off."

Abra flinched.

"Beau was getting close to letting me have this place. The closer he got to you and the boys, the easier it was to talk to him about buying it."

Abra laughed. "How does a man who barely got through college, who has no job to speak of, buy a home as beautiful as The Gray Lady."

Russell raised his hand and moved his index finger back and forth. "Sweetheart, you don't know me. That's why you're speaking so freely, but that's okay. I use my wit and my charm to get by."

"No, you use your murderous mind to get what you want most of the time, but Beau was leading you on, Russell. Beau was sure you'd murdered my father, and taunting him with the picture of Jasmine ... not a good move."

"I didn't murder your father." He paced in front of the desk. "And I didn't kill Beau either. I would have rejoiced at seeing his head explode if he hadn't been planning to meet up with me to sign the deal. He was too stupid to guess I killed Jasmine." Price moved to the entryway they'd used and listened there for a minute. Then he came near. "You're going to meet the man who murdered your father and your husband. You might be very surprised, but you'll never live to tell anyone it was him. He's going to take the rap for everything. But he'll never see it coming."

His body jerked backward as if someone touched him. Then he turned his head one way and then another before whirling around, the flashlight in his hand. "Shut up!" he screamed.

"I didn't say anything?"

The man startled. Then he turned to look at the stairs that led up into the house. "I know. But not now. The time has to be right."

Abra's breath hitched. Who was he talking, too?

"I'm not going to do it. I tell you. Not until Shane's here. He's getting Shane here. And the girl. She's mine. I would never ..."

Voices? Were they prodding him to do something unthinkable?

"Shane has to die." Russell stormed toward the stairs. "Now, leave me alone."

Taffy tugged on Abra's shirtsleeve. "He talks to people I can't see," she whispered.

"Russell," Abra called him back. "Who killed my father and Beau?"

Russell stared at her. If possible, his features had grown more demonic. "I'll let you meet him. When he gets here, I'll kill all three of you." He grasped his head.

Abra took a tentative step forward, her fingers on the knife in her back pocket.

He jerked away, turning and banging her in the arm with the heavy light. Pain burst into her arm. Taffy had not been hit with that. She would be dead.

Russell stared at her arm, his fingers still grasping his head. "I'm sorry. I'm sorry I have to kill you, but I can't help it. He has to take the blame."

Abra moved cautiously to the only chair in the stark room, and rolled it to him. "Here. Sit down."

He stared from her to the chair and back to her. "They want me to kill you now, but it's too early. Shane's got to die with you."

"Who? Who wants you to kill us?"

"I don't know who they are. They talk to me. Sometimes they win. I don't want them to win. I have to do it after—" He clutched his head and bit his lip hard. Blood dripped down his chin.

"Then why don't you leave me and Taffy here. Get away from us so they can't win."

"I—I wouldn't hurt Taffy. She's mine."

"I am not!" Taffy pushed up from her corner. "My daddy is Shane Browne. And when he finds you, he's going to hurt you because you hurt me."

Russell dove across the table.

375

Abra released the knife and jerked Taffy back. "She doesn't know, Russell. Leave her alone. Shane's all she's known. He's Taffy's father."

Russell backed away. He huddled in a corner, talking incoherently to the unseen.

Abra bent down and held Taffy by her shoulders. "He's lying and confused," she mouthed. "You are Shane's little girl. Whatever happens, you don't forget that. Your daddy loves you so much, baby. I can't tell you how important you are to him."

Taffy wiped at her tears. "I want my—"

Abra covered Taffy's mouth.

Taffy looked beyond her, her eyes widening. "Look out, Abra!"

Something was wrong. Very wrong. And Shane should have noticed it before now.

He looked out over the crowd, and the only face of those he wanted to see was Dalton's, and even Dalton looked concerned.

The crowd murmured.

Shane had forgotten his song. He'd stopped in the middle of it.

Something deep within told him to keep going, to let God handle things. If anything was wrong, Randa would have told them by now.

He took a deep breath. "Sorry, folks." He strummed for a second before relaunching into the hymn with Bluegrass flavor. Finishing the song, he waited for Quinn to step up.

The preacher stepped on stage. "Thank you, Shane." Quinn backed Shane away from the microphone. He placed a firm hand on Shane's shoulders. "Dixon needs

Everybody's Broken

you inside the church. Take Dalton with you. The others are inside waiting."

As if he were on a plane that plummeted hundreds of feet before being able to rise, Shane stumbled toward the steps and off the stage, waving Dalton with him. He ran into the church and stopped in the foyer.

Finn no longer wore the chicken suit. His hair was damp from sweat. Mazzie was clinging to Finn. The fear in Randa's eyes was all Shane needed to see to know that the news wasn't good.

Then he saw Timmy Slayton. The boy had several rows of slices and bleeding cuts that were dripping onto the tiles of the floor. His mouth was cut and made him look a lot like one of Batman's nemeses.

"What's going on?" Shane demanded.

"Abra's gone." Dixon held his Stetson in his hand. "Timmy stumbled out of the woods a bit ago. Abra untied him from a tree where a man had left him after stealing his costume. The grim reaper ..."

"You moron," Dalton muttered to the kid.

"We're suiting up to go get her, Shane. I thought you should know."

"Where is Abra?"

"She went after the man." The sheriff handed Shane the note.

"Leave him here. Do not set him free. The little girl's life depends upon it." Shane stared up at Daniel for a second then reread it. "Do not set him free. The little girl's life depends upon it."

Shane stumbled back. "Taffy? I thought she was with ... where are the boys?"

"They're in one of the classrooms with one of my deputies. She'll keep them there until we have Abra and Taffy safely back with us."

"Price?"

"All we know is the man wore a hound's mask."

"I'm sorry, Shane." Timmy could barely open his mouth. "Your friend read the note. She's determined to save her."

"Timmy's going to need some stitches, I believe," Daniel said and sent the boy toward a silent deputy. "Shane, let me handle this."

Shane backed away from them.

"Shane, I said I have deputies suiting up."

"If he's got them in Grandpere's secret room ..."

"Let us handle it." Daniel demanded.

"If you barge in the only way I know to get in there, you're going to ..." Shane's pocket buzzed. He reached inside and stared at the message. "Oh, baby." He held up the message from his daughter. "Daddy im skared he kilt her." Shane scrubbed his hand over his face and tried to get his mouth to move while keeping his heart inside. "Something's happened to Abra. He won't kill Taffy. Right now, he must still think she's his, but he'll leave with her, and we'll never find her."

Daniel walked away and stepped back. "Call Abra's cell phone."

"What?"

"Call Abra's cell phone. Get him to answer. We need to negotiate."

"They aren't in the room," Randa said. "How could they be? Taffy couldn't send a text without a signal?"

"Abra's home wireless might have pulled a signal." Dalton nodded. "Do it. Call the phone."

Finn cleared his throat. "Shane, do what the sheriff says. If Abra's dead, I don't want her to have died in vain. She went there to save Taffy. Let's help her do that."

Shane fumbled with the phone and dialed the number. He put it on speaker phone. "Daddy?" his little girl cried. "I'm scared."

"Let me talk to the man, Taffy."

"I can't."

"Did he leave you there alone?"

"He's dead. Another man came in after he hit Abra. That man shot the man who killed Abra."

Mazzie gasped, turned, and buried herself against Finn.

"That man left. Abra's so cold, Daddy. I think she's dead. Peter and Paulie ... Daddy ..."

"Do you know who the other man was?" Shane had to keep her on track.

"No ..." Taffy's voice held the desperation of the world in it. "Help me, Daddy."

"We're coming, baby. We're coming. I want you to put your head down and don't look at them. Listen to me." Shane started for the door.

"Shane!" Dixon jerked him around. "We don't know where the other killer is," he said softly. "We have to be sure."

Shane stopped. "Taffy, are you sure the man left?"

"Yes. He put the thing back over the hole. The dead man left it open, but he put it back. I tried to get out, but I can't."

"Don't worry, baby. I know how to get you out. Listen a moment and tell me if you hear noise upstairs."

Silence lingered. Then Taffy's scream filled the air.

Everything went quiet.

Chapter 26

Russell stared up into his little girl's face. He'd heard her scream, but now she wasn't there.

Beau stared back at him.

"You're dead." Russell laughed and reached up to slap his hand against Beau's face.

"You killed Abra! You killed her!"

The voice faded for a moment.

He must have shut his eyes.

He awoke and looked not into Taffy's face or into Beau's. Abra stared down at him. Her hands pressed into his stomach. "Russell, stay with us. Stay with us," she repeated.

You're dying, you fool.
And she's trying to save you.
Who's more foolish, you or her?

"No," he moaned.

"Lay still."

Russell tried to rise, but he was tired and cold. Though he could feel her touch, Abra seemed far from him. Why was she doing this?

"Russell, do you know the Lord? I hope you know Him."

"The Lord?"

"He wants you to know Him. Can you hear me?" Abra winced and put a hand toward her head. Red ran down onto her shirtsleeve. She didn't seem to notice that it got into her hair. "Would you like to know Him?"

"Don't know ..." His vision blurred.

"Russell, I'm losing you. Don't let the voices win. Call out for Jesus. Ask for Him. He'll chase those voices away. I promise. Ask Him to save you."

His head seemed to have a mind of its own as it rolled to face the wall. "Don't deserve it." He could barely keep his eyes open.

We're taking you away now.

You'll be with us forever.

Always.

Russell took a deep breath and tried to lift his head back to Abra. He couldn't move. "Jesus ... Save ... Me."

"Thank You, Lord." Those three words seemingly spoken by three different people: Abra, Beau, and ... Jasmine ... were the last three words on earth he heard.

Abra held Taffy against her side, shielding her from the gruesome scene. Taffy had cried, telling her about the man who'd come into the room from above only to shoot Price. Now, she'd gone quiet, and with the blood on Abra's hands, she didn't dare touch the hair over Taffy's forehead to see if she was sleeping. Instead, she leaned her head against the wall and fought off the exhaustion that seemed to fall from nowhere.

Maybe it was an adrenalin crash or she had a

concussion.

Either way, she couldn't drift off to sleep. Taffy needed her.

Her phone lay in a pool of blood, and she had no stomach to fish it out. Taffy said she'd talked to her daddy, and Shane said he was coming.

Taffy's soft breathing fell into the rhythm her boys had when they slept. "Thank You, Lord," Abra breathed the words and with them came her sobs. This man had done horrible things. He'd killed Taffy's mother and Fred Colbert. Yet, the compulsion to get him to accept Christ had been one she could not fight. Perhaps the thought of the voices speaking to him brought pity.

Abra closed her eyes and started to drift off to sleep.

"Abra ..." someone called.

She looked around her. A man had called to her, but Taffy was still asleep beside her, and no one else was in the room.

Tiredness bowed her head.

"Abra, I'm here."

She looked up again.

Russell had heard voices. They'd driven him mad. Was this place filled with something she'd rather not know about?

Taffy moved in her hold, and Abra allowed her to slip down with her head in her lap.

The fact that Abra was cold seeped into her brain, but she didn't care. She was alive.

Again, she settled back. How long had they been here? Russell had hit her hard with the flashlight. The knot on her head was large and sore. Somewhere she thought she'd heard that if there was a knot, at least the blood wasn't building up in her brain. She sure hoped that was truth and not wishful thinking.

She looked toward the wall where the tunnel entered the room. Taffy said that the person who'd shot Russell had closed them in. But how?

She continued to look at the dark crevice, but her body refused to move. She only needed to rest her eyes for a second. She'd be stronger then, and she'd go look.

She let her eyes fall closed.

"Abra ..."

"Go away," she muttered.

"I'll never leave you."

"I just want to sleep." She kept her eyes closed and swatted at the air.

"I'm not a gnat, Abra Carmichael, and neither are you."

The words, like springs, opened her eyes. "God?"

She listened hard for His voice and heard something else instead. Rustling from above. Hard sole shoes, plundering her house, books hitting the floor, the push of something heavy on the floor, and then the opening of a door.

Steps pounded down the stairs and men in uniform, wearing Kevlar vests and holding rifles swarmed into the hold.

Abra closed her eyes. "I'm not a gnat, Lord. I'm not a gnat. I don't believe that anymore."

"Mrs. Carmichael?"

Abra worked to open her eyes. "Yes."

"Stay awake." A female officer was beside her. Her hands plundered Abra's body. "Are you shot?"

"No ... My head. He hit me with the flashlight."

She heard rummaging. "With this?" an incredulous voice broke through the haze. "Keep her awake. Don't let her go down."

"Mrs. Carmichael ..." the female cop slapped her face. "Stay awake."

Abra again found a way to force her eyes open. "I'm so tired."

"There're a lot of anxious folks up top, and they think

you're dead."

"Not dead. Tired."

"But you need to stay awake. Get the EMTs here stat!" the woman yelled.

"Taffy."

"The little one's just fine," a male voice said from the other side of her. "I'm going to lift her up and carry her to her dad. He's very anxious."

Of course, he would be. Abra's eyes flooded with tears. "My brother ..."

"Which one is he?" The female officer slapped Abra's face again. "Come on. Stay focused."

"The big white chicken."

Snickers broke loose, and Abra snorted. She put her hands to her face, smelled blood, and put them down. "Did I snort?"

"Yes, ma'am, you did." The woman laughed. "Pretty loudly, too."

Abra giggled. "Can't I just sleep?"

"Goodness," a man spoke and then metal clanged. "I guess he doesn't need the gurney. Not until the medical examiner gets off her backside and gets here to do her job. This must be the little lady in need of a ride."

"I can walk," Abra declared.

"Sure you can, honey," the cop laughed. "Why don't you just sit there and let these men do their job. You're going to give them a lot to talk about. You can't brag about carrying a damsel in distress out of the dungeon of her home very often. Joe, I'm going to hand her over to you. If any of this blood is hers, I think it would come from her head, but I don't see a wound. I suppose it's all the alleged perps."

"I saved him," Abra muttered.

"I'm pretty sure he's gone. Probably a good thing, especially if he's wanted for two murders in two different states. Saved the people a lot of money."

"He's in Heaven."

"Abra ..." At first, she thought the voice was Joe's.

Then she recognized it, even if she was imaging God talking to her outside of scripture, she was grateful. "Thank You for doing what I asked, but I saved him."

Abra sobbed. "I'm sorry. Lord. I'm sorry."

"You're gonna be just find, little gal," Joe said. "The officers had to hold two young men back when they learned you were alive. They're anxious to see you. Who might they be?"

Abra felt lighter than air for a moment and her back was no longer pressed into the cold floor. A blanket was laid over her. She snuggled into it. "My brother ..."

"That could be, but the other one, I've knowed him since he was a little boy. Always getting into mischief. A good kid, though. I prayed for him for lots a years when I watched him struggle. The good Lord, He got that boy through, and in watching him, there's something I never saw him do, and he sure has gone and done it now. I can tell."

Abra opened her eyes and stared into the gentle dark eyes of the man readying to take her upstairs. "What's that?"

"He's done gone and fell in love. Hard, too, if I had my guess."

"Oh, I hope so," she said. "Joe, where are my boys?"

"I don't rightly know."

Abra held up her finger, pointing it at Joe's face. "You have got to meet my friend, Mazzie."

"She single? 'Cuz my wife, she don't cotton to me meeting single ladies."

"You'd like her. You and her ... you got that same southern-fried sass she loves."

"Southern-fried sass. Now, I like that." Joe smiled down at her. "You hold on. I got you tucked in and tied up pretty tight, but that's a tight squeeze and a turn."

Abra's eyes closed.

"And stay awake!" Joe shouted.

Abra sprang awake. "Yes, sir."

She turned her head as they moved. The deputies stood around Russell Price's body.

Abra bit her lip. *I forgive you.*

The gurney lift was a bumpy one, but the smell of the fresh air inside her home was heaven.

Mazzie was by her side in a moment. "I thought you were dead."

"Now you know how I felt for months and months, not knowing where my brother was." She put on a brave face. "We're even."

Mazzie touched her face. "You're a mess. An awful mess, Ms. Abra Carmichael. We need to get you cleaned up."

Joe leaned over. "Mazzie?"

Abra nodded.

"Well now, you might be right about that southern-fried sass."

Mazzie continued to follow the gurney. They passed Dalton and Randa. Beau's sister held Taffy in her arms as Taffy cried.

"Where're Shane and Finn?" The tiredness seemed to be easing.

"They went to get the boys." Mazzie held to her hands. "They'll see you in a bit."

"The boys. I need Peter and Paulie."

"Sweetie, Shane's gone to get them," Mazzie cooed almost too sweetly. "You let them take care of you. We'll meet you at the hospital. He'll have them there."

Abra laid back on the gurney. She was no longer tired. For a second, she'd been hurt that Shane and Finn weren't waiting for her. Then her heart soared. Shane had gone to get the boys for her, wherever they were. He'd taken Finn with him to make sure they were safe.

Lord, I love that man. Can I have him?

Everybody's Broken

Chapter 27

The church parking lot was almost empty when Shane pulled into it. Finn had held to the dashboard most of the way.

Dixon had asked him what the rush had been, and Shane hadn't been able to tell him.

Abra needed her boys more than she needed him. That feeling had washed over him like a bucket of ice water as he stood there inside The Gray Lady beside Finn, holding Taffy and wanting only to see Abra's beautiful face.

He'd thought her lost to him forever.

And he still quaked with that fear.

Still, he'd never felt such a jolt that sent Taffy into Randa's arms and him out of the house. Finn had followed without asking questions, and they'd rushed back to the church.

Quinn walked around the parking lot cleaning up bits of trash missed by the volunteers. Shane waved and moved through, Finn on his heels. Volunteers called greetings as he pushed through the side door to the Sunday school corridor where Daniel said he'd find the boys with one of his deputies.

He looked into the windows of each door on the left while Finn did the same on the right. Nothing. Nothing. Nothing.

Shane stepped back, shook his head, and peered through the glass again.

No mistake. He'd seen what his brain relayed to him. "Finn." Shane opened the door and stepped inside. "We have a problem." He leaned over the woman's prone body. Taking her wrist, he felt for a pulse.

The female deputy was alive but out.

His phone rang, and he answered Dalton's call. "Get Daniel on the phone, Dalt."

"Get to your house, Shane. Bastion's there with the boys. With Herman, too. He wants you."

Shane ran his hands through his hair. "He's threatening to kill the boys if you don't get there."

"Where's the sheriff?"

"Getting his men in place."

A groan brought Shane around.

Finn bent beside the deputy. "Are you okay?"

"The boys?" she startled. "Where are the boys?"

"Did you see who did this to you?" Shane asked.

The woman took a long moment to gather her thoughts. "Dark clothes. Head to foot."

"His face?"

"Behind a mask."

"A grim reaper?"

She shook her head. "No. A dog."

Finn muttered something Shane was glad he had not heard from the tone of it.

"He walked in?" Shane asked.

"I didn't see him. The boys and I were reading one of the stories. Their little faces turned ash white, and when I turned, I saw the dog mask. He put me in a strangle hold and placed a cloth over my face. That's all I remember."

Shane gripped the phone. "We're on our way. Tell Daniel his deputy's been injured. Tell Abra I love her."

"Shane, be careful. Randa wants you to be here for the birth of our first child."

Shane swallowed hard. "Low blow, Dalt. Now, I'll have to be careful." He hung up the phone, emotions warring inside him. "Like it or not, we're about to face Trace Bastion." He motioned Finn to follow him.

Outside Finn rushed toward the preacher and asked him to see after the deputy until help arrived. Then he ran to the car and climbed inside. "If that man hurts the *phews*, I'll kill him myself."

The ride seemed to take forever. Shane pulled up the drive. His place was dark against an even inkier night. He and Finn climbed out of the vehicle, and Shane scanned the timberline. No sign of Bastion or anyone else for that matter.

He crossed the bridge, looking hard for any shadows on his porch. Nothing jumped out at him.

Finn followed him up the stairs as Shane pulled his keys from his pocket and stopped. A note was taped to his door.

Finn reached and pulled it free. "Mount Tabor. Come alone. That's not happening."

Shane snagged the note and retaped it to the door. Then he turned to look into the woods around his home.

Something niggled at the back of his mind. He stood against the railing for a long moment trying to comprehend all that had happened since darkness had begun falling.

He didn't even know the time, but it had to be late.

"What is it?" Finn asked.

Movement in the distance caught Shane's eye, what he'd been waiting for. Several men moved into place.

"The cavalry's in the woods." He'd bet Daniel was among them and sending a text or phoning the sheriff would be too risky.

Daniel would have to trust him.

He unlocked his house and went inside.

Finn stood at the door.

Shane reached into the cabinet. "You prefer a rifle or a 1911?"

"Neither," Finn said.

Shane turned and stared. "You can't go up there unarmed."

"I have to. I'm not letting you go alone, and if Bastion sees me with a weapon ..."

Shane pulled out the rifle, refusing to listen to Finn's reasoning. "I've got a holster you can hide under your coat—well, another coat. That one isn't warm enough."

"Shane, I've never owned a gun. I don't know how to shoot."

Shane nodded. "Thanks for your honesty. You're right." He left the rifle in the cabinet but unlocked the drawer beneath and picked up the magazine. "Wait here."

Upstairs, he reached under the bed and pulled out his safe. Unlocking it, he held the gun out and checked the barrel. Habit, something Beau had taught him long ago. He inserted the magazine and did checks on his safety, another habit that came from shouldering a gun—either the 1911 or the rifle—when Taffy or the boys were with him on hikes.

He slipped off his coat, tugged on his holster, placing the gun securely inside. The temps were dropping, and even at slightly higher elevations the chill would wear them down quickly. His heavier jacket went on over the holster. He grabbed another one for Finn and headed out the door.

Outside, he stopped and pulled the note from the door, letting it fall to the ground. "Stay behind me." He told Finn before rushing downstairs and around his house, behind his garage, and up the trailhead to the mount.

"Did you see the boys' jackets in the Sunday school room?" Shane kicked himself for letting that get past him. If Bastion had taken the kids out without protection, they could be in serious trouble.

"I didn't see them." Finn's breath hitched.

Shane stopped. "Are you up for this?"

"I was in great shape before getting shot. I'll be a little winded, but, like you, nothing's keeping me from the kids."

The hike up the trail was steep at one point, but after a half mile it leveled out.

The place wasn't well known. People had to ask for Shane's permission to be on the land or risk trespass charges. Those he knew to be hunters were not granted permission. Experienced hikers and campers were free to enjoy the pristine beauty of his little corner of the Appalachians.

Shane drew up short.

Finn stopped a step behind him. "See anything?"

"Only someone who's been around the area would refer to this place as Mount Tabor."

"Price?"

"He used to fish up here with Beau sometimes. He could have led Bastion here."

Shane's phone buzzed, and he ignored it, moving forward.

If someone was following, they'd know, and if the caller happened to be Abra, he didn't know how he'd explain to her what was going on. "Lord, let them give Abra some good medicine to sleep, and let us be there with her in the morning with her boys—and if You aren't planning for us to get out of this, then let the boys be there. Please protect them from harm. Warm their bodies. Give them protection."

"Amen," Finn agreed.

"Bastion didn't kill them before. Maybe there's some shred of decency in him."

Finn didn't respond.

Shane stopped again. "Somehow, they'd met and planned to kill Beau. The mask said it all: Hound Dog. There has to be a connection between Price and Bastion."

"Remember. We act on what we know. But I'm not sure," Finn warned.

Shane's phone buzzed.

And once again he ignored it.

He pressed forward. He wouldn't stop until he reached Mount Tabor, not the top by a long shot, but a leveled area where the stream rushed down. This was his favorite place to bring Taffy—and the boys. Bumblebee liked the area, too.

Shane gave a quick look around. "Be vigilant. Humans aren't the only killers in these woods."

The breeze kicked up, and for a second, the sound of the rushing water he'd become so used to, faded behind the rattling leaves which floated down around him. Dark clouds roiled in the sky. The scent of rain came with a gust of wind. "The storm they predicted is closing in. When the wind kicks up this quickly, you can bet the skies will open up soon. We need to make sure the boys have on some kind of protection."

As if in answer to his words, a flash of light flickered across the blackness in the distance and several moments later, the thunder rolled.

He turned to Finn. "Not good."

"Also, not good." Finn pointed.

"Shane!" The man was on them in a moment. He could have taken Shane down if Finn hadn't been on the lookout. Shane reached under his jacket, his hand on the gun.

"It's me. Loyal Herman. Chief Herman." He stopped

short. He wiped his hand over his balding head. If Herman had been from the area, he would have known the necessity of wearing head cover. "Finn? You're alive. Son, I can't say how glad I am to see you."

Shane kept his hand on the steel, summing up the situation. "What's going on here? I was told this was a rescue of you and the boys."

"The boys are safe. Bastion's here. I overtook him. Finally. I got the chance. Follow me." He stepped toward Finn who said nothing as he held his ground.

"Hold up. Don't take another step." Shane pulled his gun from the holster.

The police chief's eyes widened.

"Where are the twins?" Shane asked.

"Safe. I've got Bastion bound. I wanted them to stay near the tent."

"Then head up. I don't want them out in this weather for longer than they need to be."

Herman didn't ask another question. He trekked upward, and Shane and Finn followed.

After five minutes had passed, Shane stared up into the angry heavens and then through the timberline, hoping not to give any detail away if Daniel trailed with his team.

Something didn't smell right, and he wasn't thinking about the rain.

Abra had tired of waiting. If someone didn't tell her what was going on right now, she would have a full meltdown, and they would all realize that she wasn't the fragile little woman they wanted her to be.

Dalton had his phone to his ear. Mazzie huddled close. Dalton punched the phone a little harder than Abra thought necessary.

Dalton clenched his phone and entered the room.

"If my boys aren't here with Shane and my brother by the time those test results are back or by the time I can walk on my own, I'm outta here," Abra told him.

Mazzie came to stand beside her. She straightened the bed sheet, and for the first time in her life, Abra found her look rather sheepish.

"Where are my children?" She pushed the sheets away and pushed to her feet. Only to find herself face down on the floor.

"Good thing that's a wrap-around gown," Mazzie said.

Dalton apparently had the good sense not to snicker.

A nurse ran inside.

They helped her back into bed.

The nurse looked at her watch. "The doctor said I could give you a sedative thirty minutes ago. I've been holding off. I think it's time." Her shoes squeaked across the floor and out the door.

"Now," Abra demanded. "Mazzie, tell me now, or I'll bring down this hospital with my screams."

"Bastion has them," she confessed. "He told Dixon the boys would be safe if he allowed Shane to meet him."

"Dixon sent a civilian in to do a deputy's job?"

"Two actually. Finn's with him." She leaned toward Abra, tears in her eyes. "And there's something they need to know."

"What?" Abra pleaded.

"I recalled something about my abductor." Mazzie's face paled. "He smelled of spearmint."

Abra stared at her friend. "That's a pretty big detail to leave out of a story, Mazzie, especially one in which you're adamant about a man's guilt."

"I forgot, Abra. I couldn't remember. I was drugged. When we walked in here, the hospital smells reminded me of whatever he pushed in my face to knock me out and

Everybody's Broken

that reminded me of the spearmint."

"So Shane and Finn are heading into an ambush thinking they're going to talk one man down, but another one is going to kill them, and then he'll kill my boys."

Mazzie's eyes filled with tears. "We've tried to contact Shane. He's not answering."

The nurse returned, hypodermic in hand. She went for the IV cord.

Abra yanked the needle away from the tape, her hand smarting, and blood flowing. Again, she got her feet on the ground, careful to stay upright. "I'm going to my boys. No one is going to keep me from them again."

The nurse blubbered for a few seconds before turning on her heels.

Mazzie slipped off her beautiful, long coat. She walked around and put it around Abra, helping her to slip in her arms. "I'll get a wheelchair and be your legs from here to the car."

"Wait." Dalton slipped out of his coat and thrust it at Mazzie.

"Thank you," she told Dalton then turned to Abra. From the car, you're on your own."

Abra hugged her. "No. Actually, we have Someone else watching over us, and He hasn't let us down so far."

Chapter 28

Shane kept his hand on the gun and his attention on the man leading him through the dense overgrowth.

Deep, dark clouds covered the moon.

He held his hand out to stop Finn and waited, listening and looking around him to get his bearings in the darkness. The wind howled now, keeping the sound of the water's rush at bay, but Herman was leading them up stream.

A bolt of lightning cracked the sky with a loud crack. Shane and Finn ducked. Ahead of them, Herman hit the ground.

High on the mountain a ball of flame erupted.

Had the world around him gone insane while he strove to live a life of simplicity, free from drama? "Get us out of this, Lord, please." He spoke into a freezing gust that knocked him on his backside.

Finn reached out a hand and pulled him upward. "Again, amen."

He refused to remain fearful. Vigilance in this type of

situation was required, but God was in charge.

Shane kept his thumb on the safety of the 1911 and pointing it to the ground as he rushed forward before Herman got to his feet, leaving Finn to catch up.

Herman eyed the gun but wisely kept his mouth shut.

"Let's go," Shane ordered. "This storm is bearing down on us."

"Sure thing," the man said without moving.

"Step forward, Chief. Stay outside of arms' length, and we'll do just fine. You should have brought those boys down the trail with you."

"The boys are fine. I told you. I have Bastion tied up. I wouldn't have left them with him if I didn't think so."

"They're five years old. You don't leave them on a mountain!" Finn's angry words brought vulnerability to Shane's plans.

"That begs the question, Chief. How are you so familiar with my place?" Shane motioned with his gun for Herman to get a move on.

The man turned toward him. "Your place?"

Shane again moved the gun to command he move.

Herman walked ahead of him, waving his hands as he spoke. "Trace must have known this was your place. I didn't. He's had me up here for days. He's pushed me around. I'm nearly dead, man. Can't you tell?"

"Then tell us how you overcame a man half your age?"

Another bolt sizzled across the sky. Herman ducked.

"Move," Shane yelled.

The older man stopped, putting his hands on his knees. "I can't go much further."

"We're not asking you," Finn said. "Those boys are in danger and afraid. They've been through too much already."

"I'm telling you. I'm exhausted."

Shane circled to the right of Herman. "Stand straight.

Everybody's Broken

Hands in the air. Don't think of lowering them. And watch your step. If you stumble, my finger might twitch." He'd apologize if the guy was straight, but right now, he had no idea what to think.

Herman's clothes were caked with mud. When the wind was right, his ripe odor drifted Shane's way. The possibility did exist that the man was innocent, that he'd rescued the boys from Bastion, but Shane had to keep up his guard. "Get!" he demanded. "Or I'll shoot you here and work out the details later."

The chief glared, but he raised his hands and continued up the mountain.

Rain pelted down on them, stinging Shane's already cold face. Herman wasn't dressed for the weather. The man struggled up the steep trail, and Shane stayed behind him.

They reached Mount Tabor. Shane stopped and allowed the man to keep going. He looked around him for a sight of anything that might indicate danger.

Herman continued on. Shane kept his eye on him. "The only reason someone with law enforcement training wouldn't survey their surroundings is if they know the situation to be clear," he said over his shoulder. "Either he's telling the truth and he contained Bastion, or he's always been contained."

Again, a bolt brought a momentary light as bright as the sun to the plateau.

Herman stopped, and Shane's feet froze. He put out his hands for Finn to halt.

A figure, tall, on two feet, loomed between them and the smaller figures and what appeared to be a man sitting on the ground in the distance.

"Is that a—" Finn started.

"Yes, it is."

As if having trouble standing, the figure moved forward and a fierce growl, unbuffered by the wind bellowed toward Shane.

He caught Herman's movement.

"Drop it, Chief!" Shane ordered. He held his gun with two hands moving it between the advancing figure and Herman.

"You going to let it kill me?" Herman backed up.

"Stand your ground! Drop the gun. Don't move. If you shoot at her, you could hit one of the boys."

Brightness swung across the sky once more. Bumblebee, the bear Shane had come to love, fell onto all fours.

Shane held his breath.

The bear shook her fur, whether to dispel the rain or readying for a charge, Shane couldn't tell.

"What do we do?" Finn asked.

"Stand still. Last ditch effort fall down and play dead. Whatever you do, don't move."

Herman lifted his gun.

"You heard Shane. Drop it!" Daniel moved out of the timberline from the stream bed, his gun pointed at Herman. When he got into clear range of both Herman and the bear, he halted.

Behind all of them, two other men moved with caution into the campsite. One raised a hand and seemed to motion toward Herman as if in answer to a question.

Daniel trained his gun on Herman; Shane kept his on the bear.

He didn't want to, but if Bumblebee threatened, he'd have to take her out. "Please don't make me do it, BB," he whispered to the bear.

"Shane?" Daniel shouted over the wind.

"Stand your ground," Shane answered back. "I'll take her down if it needs to be done. Bumblebee, go!"

"My men have the camp secure. I have my bead on our suspect."

"What are you talking about? The boys will tell you

..." Herman turned his gun toward the sheriff.

Daniel fired.

Herman dropped his gun and screamed out in pain.

The sheriff pointed his gun back and forth between bear and man. "You should know better than to turn your weapon on law enforcement, Chief Herman."

Bumblebee lumbered forward a few steps.

"Shane," Finn's wariness cut through the charged air around them. At least the rain had stopped.

"Stand still," Shane warned. At this range, he could put a bullet in Bumblebee's head most days, but his hands were cold. He'd rather not rile the beast, but he was very afraid one of the deputies might not be so cautious.

Herman continued to wallow in his pain, crying out.

"Shut. Up. Lay. Still. She's. Going. To. Kill. You," Shane spoke to the wailing Herman.

Herman quietened.

"Shane ..." Daniel shifted position but never took his aim off Herman.

"The boys, Daniel. Not after everything they've been through. They need Bumblebee to go on her way."

"Well, Bumblebee might not think that's a good idea. In fact, I'm not so sure it is either, and as much as I'd like to let her have this fool, that would cause her to be put down as well."

Bumblebee turned her entire body and ambled a few feet back.

Great. Now, if the bear charged the boys, the deputies would riddle them all with bullets.

The bear swiveled her large head and stared at Shane for a very long minute.

Shane didn't breathe; he kept his hand on the trigger.

"Rumphrff," the bear seemed to mutter before she turned and ran off away from them.

Shane inhaled the cold into his lungs and let his gun fall a bit. If he didn't know better, he'd think the bear knew what she was doing. The gunshot alone should have sent her either charging or scurrying. She'd done neither.

Herman's screams again filled the air.

Daniel ran toward him, pinning him face down. "Not one more death. Not one more death in this town caused by you or anyone you may know." Fury lit the sheriff's face.

Herman struggled as Shane approached and kicked the man's gun out of reach.

In what seemed like one swift move, Daniel had the man in cuffs and lofted him up to his feet.

Herman struggled to stand. Blood poured down his pant leg. "What are you doing? I lost my head. The bear—I'm not the one you want."

Finn's gaze remained on the man for a long while, drifting over the figure and seeming to rest on the hand covering his wound. Finally, he gave his attention to the campsite. "Can I?"

Daniel grabbed Herman up and trudged forward. "Yeah, we need to get the kids out of here and to their momma." He thrust the chief to the ground and looked to the skies. "Until I sort this mess out, you have the right to remain silent ... you can recite the remainder for yourself. Time is precious here. The storm is a quick mover but dangerous in these temps nonetheless."

Herman said nothing. He looked to the man sitting against the tree. "I know my rights."

"So, you're saying I won't need to repeat them to Detective Bastion?"

Herman remained silent.

"Not so easy getting these two down, I think." A deputy approached. "We have him awake. I thought for sure he'd been beaten to death." He pointed to a mess of a man dressed in black, leaning against a tree, his face a massive swell of purple and blue. "The EMTs are driving as far up the trailhead as possible. They'll hoof it the rest of the way up with the gurneys. I'm not sure he'll be able to walk down either. I asked them to secure more blankets. The kids and the two men aren't dressed for this weather."

Daniel took quick strides to where the boys stood beside Trace Bastion. Finn tucked the blankets around them that a deputy took from inside the tent. "You boys okay?"

The twins shivered but nodded as one.

"You were pretty brave." Daniel dug into a bag, pulling out clothing. He stopped when he pulled out a dark shirt and a pair of dark pants. He lifted them to his deputy. "Evidence. They're surprisingly still warm in contrast to the other clothes here." He ripped another shirt and used the strips to tie off Herman's wound.

Shane checked his gun's safety, tucked it back into his holster, and bent to his knees. He motioned for the boys.

They ran into his arms, crying against him.

"Didn't Taffy and I teach you anything? Where's the worst place to stand in an electrical storm?"

"Under a tree, but we couldn't leave Detective Trace. He's hurt bad."

Shane leaned in. "Boys, do we have the right man?"

"You have him," Finn clenched his jaw then held his hand out to Trace. "You saved Mazzie's life, man. I'll never forget that."

"I'd do it again." Trace lifted his arm slowly and winced when Finn simply grasped his hand.

"How are you so sure?" Shane asked Finn.

"I'll let the boys tell you. They've been very good to keep quiet this long to keep their mommy safe for me. Go ahead, *phews*." He gave each a warm smile.

"He shot Uncle Finn," Peter accused, but both boys pointed to Herman in unison.

"He shot our daddy. He wore the dog mask," Paulie

said.

Shane hooked his gaze to Daniel and back to the boy. "But the deputy at the church said the man who took you wore black clothes and had on the mask. The description fits what Detective Bastion is wearing."

Though obviously hard, Trace smiled. "They're pretty smart kids—just like their dad."

"Uncle Finn said we shouldn't tell anyone because he couldn't remember, and he didn't want him to hurt us, but the man who shot daddy had a silver ring on his pinkie finger. The sun caught it when he came over the dune."

Shane looked to Herman's hand. Underneath the blood, he could see the silver. That's what Finn had focused on.

Peter moved closer to Shane. "The man who came to the church and brought us here had on dark clothes, but he wore that ring. He disguised his voice. When we got here, he told us to stay outside the tent."

"And did you?"

"We were going to run away into the woods, but Bumblebee stepped out, and you told us never to move if she paid attention to us. Bumblebee stayed while the man in the tent moved around a lot. Just before Chief Herman came out, she went back into the trees."

"We were fooled when Chief Herman said he'd beaten up the guy who'd taken us, and he needed to go for help," Paulie rushed in.

"What made you think you were being fooled?" Daniel stood over Herman.

"When he left, we went in the tent, and we saw it was Detective Trace wearing dark clothes, but he wears a ring, too." Peter pointed. "He twirls it when he talks sometimes. We figured out that Chief Herman was moving around so much because he was changing his clothes to match Detective Trace."

"The boys probably have it right. The bag there was

Everybody's Broken

inside the tent. I moved it out when I saw we needed room to help the detective out."

"And he's still wearing the pinkie ring," Paulie pointed to Herman.

"And the man who took us from the church was Chief Herman because he always smells like spearmint."

Trace nodded and cleared his throat. "I received a text from a blocked number that turned out to be Herman's. I had no idea at the time, but he told me if I got on the plane and headed back to North Carolina, he'd kill her. I guess he overheard Mazzie and me talking at the station the day she planned to leave. He knew she was coming here. He must have gotten hold of my notes on my investigation ..." he placed his hand against his jaw "... and knew I was gunning for him. Mazzie was a last-ditch effort to set me up as the Florida murderer since he had no idea Finn was even alive. I let the sheriff drop me off at the airport, and I doubled back out of security. I had to wait hours for his arrival, but he finally texted me to meet him in the parking garage where he wanted me to meet him." Trace leaned his head back; the effort to talk had to be hard for him. "He led me to Mazzie's car. She was completely out, laying in the backseat. From the time we left parking, I noticed we had a tail. We drove to a gas station beside the motel, and Herman got out."

"Why didn't you drive away then?"

"I thought I could get us out of our situation and bring Herman's head home on a platter. I checked Mazzie into the motel. I asked for a room near the office, and I did things to draw the woman's attention. She had a shrewd look about her, and she was wary of me from the start. I made a show of getting Mazzie out of the car and into the room. I was going to lock her inside, safe, and do my best to find out what Herman and the person in the other car were up to. Before I could get out, Price came in. He was angry at the room I'd gotten. The two idiots

407

had forgotten to think, assuming I'd be given a room away from prying eyes. When the sirens wailed and drew nearer, Russell took off, and I followed after him, again thinking I could save the day. I soon learned I was a bigger idiot than both of them. Where is Price, by the way?"

"Dead." Daniel moved to Herman, and after a short tussle, held the man's hand up. He tugged at the ring, but it didn't budge. "I don't think that's been off your finger in a long while. Probably not before you killed Abra Carmichael's father and gunned down one of our own."

A deputy approached. "EMTs are close by. Their on foot. Two gurneys. In light of the bear, I think we should walk together in a group."

Daniel raised a brow at Shane, and he nodded. "Good idea."

Daniel turned his back on Shane for a moment, and when he looked back, Shane saw a shine in the man's eyes. He was holding back emotions. "Beau didn't deserve to die like he did." He turned to Herman and back to Shane. "Your daughter can identify him as Price's killer."

Herman looked up. "What are you talking about?"

"Why didn't you kill her to keep her quiet? Could it be your conscience stopped with the killing of small children? I thank God for it," Daniel said. Then he snapped his fingers. "Or you were so certain of the detective's death and your safe identity behind the mask."

"There was no child in that room. I knew Price had taken the little girl, but I thought he'd put her somewhere else. I left the note with the stupid kid Price tied to the tree to help so that someone would know she was in danger. I went in to save Abra, but Price had killed her already."

Shane jerked his gaze to Daniel. The sheriff had known what he was doing. He'd tricked the fool into a near confession.

Daniel grasped Herman by the collar. "She was in that room. Abra was knocked out cold, not dead. You probably thought Price had killed her or you would have put a bullet in her, too."

"There was no kid in that room. Price and Abra were there. I would never shoot Abra. I didn't go there to kill him, but I heard him tell Abra he planned to kill her, Browne, and me, and set me up for it all. When I saw what he'd done to my precious girl, I had to kill him."

"Your girl?" Finn clenched his fist. "You killed our father, her husband, and shot at her sons and me ..."

"And you're the one who shot at Dalton and me." Shane glared. "I think we can leave off attempted murder. You're going to get the death penalty anyway."

Herman's lips tightened. "I'm not saying anything more."

"Then let me fill in the blanks for the authorities here," Trace said. "I'd already learned enough to solve two murders he's responsible for in Florida, and I have enough to connect him to the disappearance of another person."

"Who?" Finn startled.

Trace tried to stand but didn't quite make it. "I guess Beau thought I needed protection as well. I located some research he'd been doing on long ago missing person's case." Trace closed his eyes and leaned his head back. "Herman lived for a long time thinking Abra was his daughter."

"That's ridiculous," Finn said.

"Yeah, but he must have had some reason to get a sample from Abra during Beau's murder investigation to try to match it to him. Trouble was, he learned that Abra was your father's daughter after all, and his testing told me all I needed to know as to one of the reasons he wanted Beau dead. Beau still never got it in his head that

Herman was Dashell's murderer. He went to the chief and told him he was looking into Abra's mother's disappearance, to give Abra and Finn closure."

"Is that true?" Finn demanded. "Did you kill our mother?"

Herman's eyes narrowed. "Your mother was a liar and a cheat, boy. When she wanted me to take her away from the cove, she told me Abra was mine. Then she changed her mind, and she planned to go back to your *pap*."

"So you killed her? That's why she never came home, why Abra suffered all these year? Why we thought she hated us?"

Herman shook his head and remained silent.

"He didn't mean to kill Dashell," Trace continued, his voice growing weaker. "As Beau knew from the start, the poison was in the can he opened. Dashell's mistake saved Beau's life and cost him his own."

"You said the investigation was one of the reasons he killed Beau. What was the other?" Daniel stepped around Herman.

"This could have been lipservice from Price, but the rest comes from what I overheard them say when they thought I was unconscious. It's hearsay, but I think his miscues here will be enough to take him down for the murder of Price, even if he did the world a favor where Price is concerned."

"You have anything to say?" Daniel prodded the chief.

The man's shoulder's sagged, but he remained silent.

"Price was supposed to meet up later with Beau. We had an investigation on the dune, and Beau was sure he could find something we needed," Trace said. "The dune was on Beau's way to the restaurant where he planned to meet up with Finn and the boys. He stopped and was looking around for the evidence."

Trace coughed and took a few deep breaths. "Do you know what the odds of Price being in that area at the same time would be? But he was. And he saw the shootings. He saw everything, and Herman never saw him. From what I gather, that's when Price met up with Herman. He was still angry here because he thought Herman had literally killed a deal for the sale of that home Abra's living in now. And despite his efforts with the gun he sent to Herman to scare her off Beau's family, she ended up here."

Trace coughed again, and blood spewed from his mouth.

"Steady." A deputy leaned down while the other ran off toward the woods. "Maybe we can go over this later, Detective."

"No. In case something happens ..." Trace managed. "Two things set Price off: Abra returned here, and apparently when Price met with the chief, Herman told him about Jasmine and Beau's baby. Price thought she was his; they even argued about it out here. Herman told him he wouldn't have killed Beau if the little girl hadn't been his, but Beau had cheated on Abra, and he had to die. He said he had letters from Jasmine Roy to Beau, telling him about the impending birth, and another one stating that Jasmine had done with the baby what they both had agreed was best. I think that was secondary to the fact that Beau was digging into Mrs. Osteen's disappearance, but he wouldn't tell Price that. Instead, he told the man the one thing that could unhinge him more." He looked to Shane. "Price, who was already a little left of center, went rogue, and Herman had to find a way to rein him in or pin everything on him. Price killed the realtor. Herman ended up kidnapping Mazzie. Both attempting to frame the other and working together to do it." Trace tried to laugh but moaned instead. "There are copies of everything related to the Florida investigations in the hands of one of the officers at the station. He was told not to open it unless something happened to me." Trace coughed again, this time covering his mouth. Blood covered his hand.

"No more," Daniel said. "We have everything we need."

The EMTs entered the campsite. Shane nodded to his buddy, Old Joe. He passed Shane. "Why ain't you with that pretty little girl down at your place? She's worrying herself to deff, you know. Heard she walked right on out of that hospital with a never-you mind."

"We're going down together, Joe. Take good care of our friend, Detective Bastion. He's family."

"Why the dog mask?" Finn bent down and glared at Herman. "How'd you know?"

"Know what?" the chief shot back.

"That Price's nickname was Hound Dog."

Herman shook his head. "I have no idea what you're talking about."

Shane moved beside Daniel as the EMTs set to work on both men. "Thanks. I know you told your deputies not to shoot Bumblebee." Shane held out his hand and Daniel shook it.

Shane picked up both boys to hold them as long as he could as they headed down to the trailhead seconds ahead of the EMTs. "Let's go find Mommy."

Abra moved over so Mazzie could sit beside her on Shane's couch after snooping around Shane's studio. "Impressive. Who knew the man was so talented ... and rich?"

"He's not rich." Abra leaned back, her hand over her aching head.

Everybody's Broken

"Abracadabra, the boy has written songs for the best. He has golden records on his wall. That translates into royalties which translates into mon-ney."

"I don't care, Maze, okay. I just want my boys back so I can take whatever prescription it is that Dalton's gone to get."

"The only reason he left is because you look like a mess. The pain is all over your face."

"Not pain. I'm scared I'll never see them again."

"Then open your eyes."

The voice didn't register for a moment.

"Abra?" the worried tone seeped deep into the emptiness that had been growing inside her.

A boyish giggle filled the hole with happiness. She opened her eyes.

Peter and Paulie were in front of her. She grabbed them to her and held them close. "Oh, you two, what am I going to do with you? You're always finding trouble."

"No, Mommy. Trouble finds us."

"Yes." She laughed until the sobs of joy found their way to the surface. "Yes, you do."

A soft touch lighted on her forehead and she looked up into eyes of deepest blue, and beside Shane stood Finn.

"I thought I'd lost you all," Abra cried.

Mazzie gathered the boys in her arms. Then she practically sent Finn sprawling with her embrace.

Abra stood. "Shane, I ..."

"I love you, Abra." He lifted her hair over her shoulder and let it lay down her back. With frigid cold hands, he caressed her cheek. She didn't care. He was alive.

"A wise man once said, 'Plan a little; live a lot.' I'm asking you now to follow his direction. Plan a future with me." He tilted his head. "If everything that's happened this year has taught me anything, it's that our future might be one minute, one hour ..."

"One day ... one week ..." She brushed her lips across his and pulled back. "One lifetime."

He placed his hand on the back of his head, the motion she loved, but when she winced and sucked in air, he pulled back. "Sorry. Sorry. So sorry."

"I don't care." She kissed him long and hard. "Marry me, Shane Browne. Marry me, and let's join this family that God has made possible."

"Very soon," Shane agreed, teasing her with his lips.

Mazzie jumped to her feet. "Monday." She slapped Shane on his shoulder. "You'll never forget your wedding anniversary?"

Abra moaned. "No. No. No. You're making my head hurt worse."

"Mommy's birthday," Paulie cheered.

"Mommy's birthday," Shane took her by the shoulder. "I love the idea. If you're feeling up to it."

"Oh, I'd crawl down an aisle to meet you there, but the license ... Not going to work."

"Same day. We go Monday morning. We get married Monday afternoon."

"And who's going to come? Shane, we've just been through so much ..."

"What better reason to turn the corner? Dalton and Randa are pregnant, and we're getting married. Thank You for the blessings, Lord."

"In the middle of kids ringing the doorbell?"

He stopped for a second, seemingly stumped. Then he smiled. "Leave everything to me. No ringing doorbells but one grand party."

"A murder was committed in my house. The kids were taken from the church. I don't like the idea of—"

"Abra!" Mazzie stood and stomped her foot. "Stop making excuses."

Abra smiled wide and held her hands out to Finn. He held to her.

Everybody's Broken

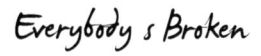

"Let's make Pap proud," she whispered in his ear.

Everybody's Broken

Chapter 29

Abra stood in the open meadow where Shane said her boys had been held by Loyal Herman. All traces of that night had been erased.

After church the day before, Abra and Mazzie sat in the hospital waiting room for hours until Trace Bastion was allowed visitors after surgery for a myriad of internal injuries. During that time, Sheriff Dixon cleared the crime scene for use by Shane, who had gotten men together.

They had set up this place with eight chairs, set in the grass, which had thawed in what rays the sun had reached through the cold to warm. Four chairs set only a few feet from a beautiful arch covered with plastic flowers.

A little cheesy, but she didn't care.

Further back a large white tent, its sides buffeting the chilly breeze stood like a beacon. She'd asked Mazzie what it was about, but for her other southernisms, letting go of a secret wasn't one of them, and Abra wasn't allowed to enter.

But a scent of some tantalizing food drifted to her

from there.

After Abra and Shane obtained their license, Mazzie had driven her to a bridal store in Asheville where Abra found a soft mauve gown, almost imperceptible from white.

"It's for a winter wedding. Look," Mazzie had pointed out the long trained coat trimmed in faux pure white fur. "Abra, you will be beautiful."

Now, Abra stood back from the arch. She reached down and tucked Taffy's hand in hers. "You sure?" She winked at the beautiful little girl wearing a dress of light pink, her little matching patent shoes shining in the sun.

Abra had spent the early afternoon with the girl who would be her new daughter. She'd brushed and tied Taffy's curls into a French braid.

Taffy now looked up at her and smiled, her green eyes wide. "Are you sure?"

The question shocked Abra. "What do you mean?"

"You really want to be my mommy?"

Abra bent down and touched a curl that strayed from the braid. "Oh, baby, I can't think of anything I'd like better."

"I can." Taffy smiled.

"What's that?"

Taffy turned and looked toward her father. "Daddy's wife." She giggled. "Right?"

Shane stood at the center of the arch with Quinn Moxley, who agreed to officiate the ceremony. Peter and Paulie fidgeted in front of Shane, and Dalton loitered to the left of them.

Peter and Paulie bounced with excitement.

Abra closed her eyes and bit her lip as if weighing her answer. Then she smiled. "Oh, I think they're both equally important to me. I wouldn't have one without the other."

"And Daddy wouldn't have you without the boys."

"Think you're going to like having brothers?"

"I think I'm going to like living in three houses most of all."

Abra laughed. "So, your daddy told you."

"Yeah, and Paulie said he'd teach me to surf."

Abra stood. "That should be interesting, since he doesn't know how to surf yet himself."

"I know, but it'll be fun to let him try to pretend."

Abra looked down at the little girl, who looked up at her.

A camera clicked.

"Perfect," Mazzie exclaimed and hurried off.

"Ready, girls." Finn was handsome with his dark hair trimmed nicely, his beard gone, and dressed in a dark suit borrowed from Dalton. He held out his right hand to Taffy and hooked his left arm into Abra's right. "He's a good man." He leaned toward Abra.

Abra nodded. "You understand?"

"You didn't ask me until now, but yeah. I've seen you two together before you knew I was here. I think you probably loved him from the start."

"No." She shook her head. "Or if I did, I didn't realize it, but now that I do, I know we were brought together through tragedy so that we can be happy."

"Then be happy."

"Finn, are you okay about Momma?"

Finn shrugged. "She left. I haven't thought much about her except for the hurt she caused you. She's been gone from us forever. No matter how she went."

"You're lying for me, I know, but thank you." She hugged herself against him.

"I didn't do anything to deserve your gratitude."

"You told Shane he could share the truth about her and about the letters Herman read from Jasmine. Shane could have kept it from me, and he probably would have except he said he talked it over with you."

"You're stronger than I ever knew." He kissed her cheek. "Now, let's get you two down the aisle. I checked in on Trace. He says to give you his love and his congratulations."

Abra smiled. "I didn't doubt him for a minute."

"Or me." He smiled. "Or Shane."

Abra shifted her gaze to her man. He stood straight and tall, his left hand clasped over his right wrist. He smiled at the boys who turned to look up at him.

Click.

"Perfect," Mazzie exclaimed once again.

"You had to make her the camera girl, didn't you?" Finn teased.

Abra stopped, halting Finn, which halted Taffy. "Finn," she whispered, "this is so different from my wedding to Beau."

"Abra, it's good. It's all good." Finn kept his voice low. "Are you having cold feet?"

Abra shook her head. "No, just thinking how different Shane is from Beau."

"Good different."

Taffy fidgeted, looking toward Shane.

"Taffy," Abra winked, "What say we get this family put together?"

"Yes, ma'am," Taffy said.

Abra clasped Finn's arm closer to hers and stepped forward. "This is going to be fun."

Finn stopped when he got to Shane's side. "Hectic, terrifying, but fun …? I'm not sure, but I know that it will work." He kissed her cheek once again.

"Who gives this woman to this man?" Quinn asked.

Finn held her hand up and taking Shane's put them together. "I do." He stepped back to take his seat.

Abra placed Taffy in front of her, and Shane had the boys facing their sister … their flesh and blood sister.

So much needed to be decided. Would they tell the

Everybody's Broken

kids? Would they wait until they were older? Shane told her that they would pray about it daily together, and they'd know when the time was right, even if it were a minute later.

Abra fell into Shane's azure gaze as he repeated the vows Quinn said. His voice was so soft, so reverent that it chased away any chill of the day. She was warmed by his love.

Quinn turned to her, and she found her heart lifted as she promised to love and honor her husband until death did them part.

Her heart sank for only a moment as the word *death* fell from her lips. *Please, Lord.* Her soul whimpered as she kept her voice strong and steady.

She barely registered the words Quinn spoke before Shane stepped to the side of the boys and cradled Abra's face with his hands, now much warmer than the night when he'd rescued her boys. His lips touched hers, lingering, kissing her so deeply and so passionately, that she had to wrap her arms around him to stay on her feet, but once she held him in her arms, she never wanted to let him go.

"Okay, Mr. and Mrs. Browne, I think you should save a little for the honeymoon."

"What honeymoon?" Dalton chided. "They have kids. I'm not babysitting."

Shane turned to face Dalt. "I'll remember that, Papa."

Abra peered out over the landscape of her wedding, trying to remember every aspect of this chilly autumn day so that in years to come, she could use the memories to warm her heart.

"Shane." She grasped his sleeve. "We have another guest."

Shane spun in the direction she stared transfixed with fear.

The bear lumbering along the timberline pushed up

on two feet. She raised her paw as if saying hello, lowered herself, and turned back into the woods.

"Bumblebee's just letting us know she's happy we're a whole family," Peter declared.

Shane and Abra bent down and wrapped their arms around their children. "A whole family," Shane agreed.

Click.

"Perfect." Mazzie held her camera to one side then turned.

One person had been missing from the ceremony, and Abra hadn't wanted to ask, but now, she saw him coming over the rise with several people, she'd gotten to know since her arrival in Amazing Grace. Daniel Dixon's mother clung to his arm, chattering away. Behind her, the stream of church family coming up the trailhead warmed her as if the wedding had taken place on Bodacious Cove.

"We're home, Mommy," Peter said. "Wherever we go together, we're home."

"That's what you said," Paulie chimed in.

"And we're not broken any more." Shane touched her cheek tenderly and kissed away one of her happy tears.

"And next year ..." Mazzie proclaimed. "We'll have a masquerade ball for your anniversary."

Abra opened her mouth to protest.

Click.

"Perfect," Mazzie scooted out of Abra's reach.

Everybody's Broken

Note to Readers

Dear Readers:

I have always found great pleasure in words. Many times, the writing of them has been my comfort and my escape. Yet when I get to the end of my storytelling, I have always found that God has used the story to speak into the issues of my life that I might be failing to acknowledge or willfully ignoring. When God works with me through the issues, I feel as if God has allowed me to write a story that will speak to issues in the readers' lives as well.

Our emotions are often like the sails of a boat. They cast us adrift on a sea of lies and misconceptions. God, though, is never changing. He is always with us no matter how far emotion tells us He has moved away. We are the ones at sail, but God is the wind. Romans 8:28 is my life verse both for the simplicity and the complexity in the words: "And we know that all things work together for good to them that love God, to them who are called according to His purpose." The truth of this verse can be found in every book I write. It can be found in every part of our lives. On the surface, God is saying to us, "I'm in the details."

When God is in the details, we can rest. We can lose our fear of what is to come. We can let go of the guilt that settles over us and reminds us of the wrongs we have done, the dangerous paths we may have veered upon. Nothing has taken God by surprise in our lives. When things go wrong for whatever reason, rest assured. God is not caught unaware, and His plans are to make all things work to our good, specifically for those who know Christ as Savior.

My desire for you is that you learn of, or are reminded of, God's undying love and realize that we can do nothing to be worthy of it. And as a child of God, there is nothing that we can do that would make Him take His arms from around us. He holds us tightly. If my stories can bring that truth to the reader, I am more than blessed.

And my prayer is that you will be blessed as well.

Fay Lamb
October 2016

Everybody's Broken

Chapter One of Stalking Willow
Book One of the Amazing Grace series by Fay Lamb

In the growing darkness, a maniac waited for Willow Thomas.

Outside the high-rise office the dusky blue sky gave way to the night. With a shudder, Willow turned away from the window and started her computer.

Tap-tap-tap. Her pencil eraser hit the oak desktop. Dare she risk going home?

The monitor cast a bright glow into the semi-darkened outer office. The desks there, all lined up in neat little rows, represented the rungs on the ladder she'd climbed to become a junior executive for Peterman and Bruin Advertising. Today she'd hooked a lucrative account with Anglers' Fishing Lures, Inc. Another step up.

What did she have to show for ten years in New York? A college degree, a growing career, and now, peril. Not one friend she could call, no one to walk her home, not a single somebody to watch her back.

Tap-tap-tap. She'd rather risk running into the madman with a camera than open up to anyone. She shook her head. Never again.

Somewhere on the vast floor of offices, a vacuum hummed. A hint of ammonia filled the confined air. The cleaning crew had arrived. At least she wasn't alone. Dropping the pencil, Willow clicked on the e-mail icon.

She needed to concentrate. Had anyone in a crowd of strangers looked familiar to her? Did she recall someone looking at her through a camera lens?

She sat back in her seat. As she suspected, the mysterious e-mails waited in her inbox, the font of each subject line printed in bold.

Watching You!
Watching You!
Watching You!

Only three. Since lunch. After she'd changed her address. How could he get her new e-mail so fast? She'd notified only her father, the office, and the bank.

She clicked on the first one and opened the attachment. He'd caught her walking down Fifth Avenue. The image captured a side view of her face. Of course, she wasn't looking straight ahead.

She'd been alert, constantly scanning the crowd.

Something to the left of her path must have drawn her gaze.

And she'd missed seeing him.

"Come on, Willow, think." She picked up the pencil, slammed it down on her desk, and looked to the ceiling above, studying the rectangular patterns on the fluorescent light covers.

"Who can it be?"

"Talking to yourself?"

Willow jumped. "Jeffrey, you frightened me."

Jeffrey Peterman crooked a finger under his dark blue tie to loosen it and unbuttoned his white dress shirt. He leaned his medium-sized frame against the door.

"Anglers' Fishing Lures liked the artwork, signed the contract. I'm relishing the victory. You should be happy I'm working, boss." Not exactly a lie. She was working to discover the identity of a maniac.

"I heard. When you showed me the drawings, I knew they'd take the bait."

"Ha." She smirked at his pun.

"Go to dinner. Celebrate with friends, but don't stay here."

"In a few. Night, Jeffrey."

"I'm cleaning up my desk. Be gone before me." He snapped his fingers and pointed at her before moving out of sight.

"Yes, sir." She saluted.

What a show. As if he really cared. Jeffery was good at acting the part of the concerned boss, but he never put his words into action. She closed her eyes. A friend right now would sure be nice.

Willow's cell phone rang. She frowned when she saw the caller's name. "Hi, Scott."

Her father cleared his throat.

She hadn't given him the respect he wanted. Willow would never call him Dad. A man who stayed with a woman like Suzanne Scott—what kind of father was he?

"Checking in," he said.

"I'm fine." Why had she told him about the e-mails? Now he'd have an excuse to call her every day.

"Have you gotten any more notes from your secret admirer?" His familiar deep timbre and his false jovial demeanor did more to soothe Willow's nerves than she wanted to admit. Maybe he did care—a little.

A smile played at the corner of her lips, but she pushed it away. After all, his famous lifestyle probably made her the target of this stalker. Just as it had done ten years ago. "I think it's more serious than that."

"I'd like to send a bodyguard, kiddo."

"And alert the press? Forget it." That's all she needed. She waved her left wrist back and forth to straighten the simple silver bracelet she always wore—a gift from Granny. Her gaze lingered there. Granny would know what to do.

"Your mother and I would feel safer if you'd let us send someone."

Willow cleared her throat and closed her eyes. "How is Mommy Dearest?"

"Willow ..."

Her lips trembled. More than a friend, she longed for a mother's embrace and soft, soothing words telling her she'd be safe. She missed Granny and Quentin—her real mother and her only friend.

Willow picked up the pencil and the ever-present sketchpad from her desk. Her hand flew across the page, the lead rasping against the paper with each stroke—drawing the scene she'd been trying to recreate for years.

"I've seen this type of thing happen with your mother. Sometimes it's nothing. Other times, kiddo, the person is berserk."

Willow closed her eyes. If she could call the police without the press hearing about it, what would she tell them? So far, the stalker had merely sent photos of her by e-mail. They came through at an alarming rate, but taking pictures wasn't against the law, especially if your parents were celebrities.

Her father rambled on as Willow continued to draw.

"Willow, are you listening to me?"

She hadn't heard a word. "Sure."

"Then go. Get away from the office. Don't you miss the lake? You haven't been home since Granny died."

She bit hard into her lip. Scott did care about her. She'd spare him any further sarcasm today.

"Got a question for you. Would you have given up one minute of your life in Amazing Grace to live in Hollywood?"

Maybe her silence was harder for him to take than her unloading the dump truck full of bitterness upon him. "You never gave me that choice." Her hands continued to fly across the paper, making the memory concrete. "Scott, it's late."

"Go home. To North Carolina."

"I'll think about it." Not. "'Night."

"'Night, kiddo. I lo—"

Willow hung up and gave her full attention to the drawing. Long minutes passed before she finished. She held up the picture: seventeen-year-old Quentin McPheron sitting against the post of her Granny's dock with a fishing pole in his hand. Not quite as good as the original, wherever it had gone.

She placed the sketchpad on the desk and stared at his handsome face. No matter how Quentin had treated her, Willow would always care for him.

"Come on, Willow. Walk out with me." Jeffrey called as he stepped out of his own office.

Willow held up her hand. "Give me a minute, Jeffrey. Can I trouble you for a lift?" She closed out the open e-mail.

A new e-mail landed in her inbox, taunting her.

Surprise.

The subject lines never varied—until now. Her hand shook as she clicked on the attachment. The picture sprang onto the screen.

With a gasp, she turned in her chair, stood, and backed away.

"What's wrong?" Jeffrey rushed to stand behind her, resting his hands on her shoulder.

Willow turned in his arms. Jeffrey wrapped her in the embrace. Would he let her stay here, safe and warm?

"What is that? Who sent that to you?" The tender touch of his hand against her head, cradling her, sent shivers down her spine. How long had she craved a caress, someone who truly cared?

But the cost was too high, more than her momentarily ransomed soul wanted to pay. Willow pulled from his hold and ran the back of her hand over her eyes. "That's my place. Someone trashed my apartment. Jeffrey, I need to get home."

※

Willow paused as they walked the hall leading from the
elevators and around the corner to her apartment. Jeffrey ran into her and mumbled an apology.

"My door's open," she whispered.

Noise came from inside the apartment, and her heart hammered. Had her stalker expected her to arrive home alone? Didn't he think she'd call the police?

Jeffrey edged down the corridor, his footfall soft against the beige carpeting. He peered inside. "Excuse me," he spoke to someone.

"Who are you?" a male voice demanded.

"You're in a home that doesn't belong to you. Maybe you should tell me who you are." Jeffrey held up his hand, a silent command for Willow to wait.

"Detective Bob Hominski." A man in an unremarkable blue suit and a too-skinny red and blue striped tie peered out and down the hall at Willow. "Ms. Thomas?"

Willow stepped forward. "Yes, sir."

"We found the door opened and the place a mess."

Willow nodded and stepped inside. She shook hands with the detective.

"Jim's my partner." He motioned toward a tall lanky fellow in a similar unremarkable suit and tie.

"So I take it this isn't your usual state of disarray," Hominski raised his brows.

Willow covered her mouth with her hand and shot him a narrowed-eyed glare. How dare he joke when everything she owned appeared to be in ruin.

Pictures she'd drawn lay in ripped pieces throughout the living room. Broken glass and frames covered her wood floor. The shards would never come out of her oriental rug. Her curtains hung in tatters. The drawers in her kitchen alcove had been dumped. Silverware littered the floor. At least the creep hadn't topped the whole mess off with food from her refrigerator.

She stepped out of the large area and down the short hall to her bedroom. Hominski followed. The space was a complete disaster. She opened her mouth to cry, but no sound came.

"Sorry, ma'am. I probably should have warned you."

Willow lowered her head and made her way back out into the living room. She bent down and grabbed the insides of her favorite throw pillow. The cottony smoothness in her hands did little to soothe her nerves.

Tears filled her eyes, but rage pushed them away. She paced back and forth across the small living room until the crunching beneath her feet frayed her last nerve.

"Do you have a boyfriend?"

"How about an ex-husband?"

"Have you made any enemies?"

Like corn in hot oil, the detectives popped, popped, popped the questions.

"I have no boyfriend. I've never been married. I don't have many friends, and I certainly don't go out of my way to make enemies."

She'd had enemies once, but she doubted her cousin, Laurel, and that hideous Tabitha Cowart had anything to do with this. She hadn't seen them in over ten years, and surely they'd grown out of the high-school bullying stage by now, even if Willow hadn't healed from the taunts they'd unceasingly thrown her way.

Willow tugged out her laptop, booted up Outlook, and showed them the pictures she'd received from the beginning—one month earlier to the last one of her destroyed apartment. This time a picture wasn't worth a thousand words, just one—*enemy*. "Whoever is responsible for all of this isn't a part of my world."

A crash sounded in the powder room. Detective Jim bolted back into the living room. "Just being thorough."

How much longer would the detectives stay, walking over and destroying what was left of her personal property?

"Willow, why don't you come home with me?" Jeffrey touched her arm.

She'd forgotten he was here. He'd stayed. Maybe she'd been wrong about him all this time.

The softness in his mocha eyes beckoned her to take refuge.

She turned away from him. "I can't do that."

He tugged on her sleeve. "C'mon. Grab something to wear, and let's go. You'll be safe at my place."

Safe from the stalker but not from the press who, if they found out, would love to report that Suzanne Scott's daughter was in a tawdry affair with her boss. She needed to protect Jeffrey from the bad publicity. "No thank you, but I appreciate it. People would talk."

"Let them. I've been trying to get the nerve to ask you out for a long while. I can think of worse rumors to fly around the office."

Did he think her so easy that a date meant she'd stay overnight with him? Her granny brought her up to know right from wrong, and, well, that was wrong on so many levels.

"Willow, I have the extra room. You'll be safe from your stalker and from me."

She shook her head. "Thank you, Jeffrey, but I can't."

He frowned. "Now that you know how I feel, I'll definitely ask you out when you return. If you won't stay at my house, I suggest you get out of town. Do you have a place to go? Somewhere outside the city? Parents' home, anything, where you'll be safe? If not, I have a house in the country. It's yours for as long as you need it."

Scott and Suzanne had a chalet in Switzerland, beach houses at Martha's Vineyard and Malibu. They probably had a home in Tahiti. Right now, Tahiti would be a nice change of pace.

Jeffrey's fingers pressed lightly on hers. "Willow?"

"I have a place." She stepped away from him. The lake house Granny left her would do, back in her hometown of Amazing Grace, but she never intended to return there the same way she'd departed—on the run from a stalker.

The two detectives shared a look, the meaning lost on her.

"You've earned a vacation." Jeffery closed the distance and placed his hands on her shoulders. "Take it. Just let me know where you are and how you're doing? Work remotely on the Anglers' account. Make it your priority. You did a great job reeling them in."

She would smile at his lame attempt at humor if the detectives weren't still stomping all over what little the stalker left for her to recover. "Thank you, Jeffrey. For everything."

He kissed her forehead. "I mean it, Willow. When you get back here, you save a date for dinner. I'll call you tomorrow to check in." He strode out the door.

Detective Jim followed him.

Detective Hominski studied his notes and walked around the place once more before stopping in front of her. "I know these questions seem tedious, but I'm hoping to jog your memory. Is there someone you crossed?"

"Detective, I haven't crossed anyone. I don't like conflict, avoid it like the plague." True. She avoided it. Somehow, though, it always found a way to seep into her life. Still, she didn't believe Aunt Agatha would leave North Carolina to do something like this. No, Aggie was a vindictive prude, but she wouldn't hurt her—not this way.

"So, you have absolutely no idea who would want to do this to you?"

Detective Jim returned. "We have a problem, Bob." He stepped inside.

"What?" Hominski looked over his shoulder.

"We got dirt chasers outside. They're asking about Ms. Thomas."

Detective Hominski cocked his head to the side and raised his eyebrows.

Willow cringed. He probably wasn't the type to take lightly the lack of information from a victim. She wished she'd gone with Jeffrey.

But if she had, the tabloid reporters would have been all over them, and Jeffrey would have learned her secret. Surprise. Your life just got as complicated as Willow Thomas's—daughter of Scott Thomas, and his lovely, but aging wife, actress Suzanne Scott.

"Ms. Thomas, why would the paparazzi have an interest in you?" Hominski scrutinized her too closely.

More importantly, how had the vultures circled her carcass so quickly? She'd been able to live in relative peace, keeping to herself. One call to the police station and they were crawling all over her like this?

Could that be the stalker's plan? Draw her out in the open? Make her vulnerable? If so, that person knew too much about her already.

Willow pinched the bridge of her nose. "My father is Scott Thomas." She prayed they'd recognize the name so she wouldn't have to admit her relationship to Suzanne. She couldn't stomach putting that truth into words.

"Scott Thomas." Hominski tapped his index finger against his temple as if evoking a memory. "Screenwriter. Director."

He'd forgotten to add producer, but Willow wouldn't remind him.

Detective Jim gave her his full attention. "The last I knew, those devils aren't interested in kids of directors and writers, not unless the kids make spectacles of themselves." He leaned in, peering at her like an eagle swooping down on its prey. "Have you given them any reason to take interest in you?"

Hominski shook his finger at her. "You're Suzanne Scott's kid. The one they did all the reporting on several years back. Pretty sly of your mother using her husband's first name as her stage name." He cleared his throat. "Oh, sorry. Must be a touchy subject with you, her never wanting to see you at all."

Willow shook her head. Touchy, no. Heart wrenchingly painful, yes.

So, Detective Hominski had an ear for Hollywood gossip. Maybe she could work with him. Willow motioned him away from Detective Jim.

In the kitchen, silverware clinked as she pushed it aside with the toe of her shoe. "I've worked hard to put the past behind me. You can see why."

"If I were a betting man, I'd say a Suzanne Scott fan is looking to gain her attention."

"It's important to shut this down quickly. They think I'm the door to a sensational story about Suzanne. Their interference is making it easier for the stalker."

The detective scratched his chin.

Willow waited, her breath caught somewhere between inhale and exhale.

"You say you got a place to go?" Hominski asked.

She had only the lake. Would the stalker know about Amazing Grace? Not many people knew the small town existed—at least until the truth broke ten years earlier.

She'd have to take the chance. "I think so."

"What about your father hiring a bodyguard?"

"He's suggested that, but that brings attention."

"It also brings safety, young lady." He motioned around the room. "Does this look like you're safe?"

"Not an option. I just want to get out of town. Can you help me?"

Hominski stared at her for a long moment. A heavy sigh lifted his broad chest. He shook his head.

Willow fingered Granny's bracelet.

Hominski's eyes were drawn to it. "Mean something to you?" The detective obviously didn't miss much.

"A gift from my grandmother."

He continued to stare at it.

"Well, what do you say?" Willow leaned in. "Can I count on NYPD to help me flee the city?"

Detective Hominski scratched his temple with his pen. He pressed his lips together, and took another look around the ruins of her apartment.

The odds didn't look promising.

His arms fell to his side, and his pale blue eyes met hers. "Jim, disperse the maggots. Arrest them if they don't disband." He shook his finger at her a second time. "Wherever you go, I expect you to take precautions."

"Scout's honor."

"You ever been a scout?" Hominski smiled.

"No, but I'll hold to the creed."

"I can arrange to get you out, but that's it. They're going to be able to get the facts as soon as our report is complete. I'll try to bury it for a while. Leave me a contact number."

Willow looked around her living room and kitchen. A stranger had invaded her sanctum. Jeffrey, her father, and the detective were correct. She had to leave.

"Get your stuff. You'll have to clean up this mess some other time. Before you go, I'd like to show you a trick to keep you one step ahead of this nut job."

Willow didn't argue. Instead of a bodyguard, Scott could send a cleaning crew. She moved down the hallway toward her bedroom and stood looking at the devastation. Her sheets, her mattress, her pillows were ripped to shreds. The table lamp was broken and laying on the floor beside the broken shards of her dresser's mirror.

She climbed over the clothes the intruder had strewn across the path to her closet and pulled out the shirts, slacks, and skirts he'd been kind enough to leave in one piece.

Since her dresser and chest drawers were turned upside down and some of the clothes under them shredded as well, she had to dig through to find jeans and other incidentals. She piled them on a corner of her mattress and reached under her bed for the musty suitcase that had remained there since she'd moved to the apartment many years before. After stuffing her clothing inside, she zipped the suitcase and leaned on it for a second.

Who knew she'd feel a loss at leaving the four walls she'd despised when she'd first arrived in New York—alone, angry, and afraid? She shrugged off the emotion, lifted the suitcase, and trudged down the hall and back into her living room.

"Jim's dispersing the crowd," Hominski took the suitcase from her.

Willow nodded. Cut and run. She'd done this before. She always thought she'd return to Amazing Grace a much different person, but no, she was still alone, angry, and very much afraid.

Also by Fay Lamb

Better than Revenge
Book Two in the Amazing Grace Series

Michael's fiancée, Issie Putnam, was brutally attacked, and Michael was imprisoned for a crime he didn't commit. Now he's home to set things right.

Two people stand in his way: Issie's son, Cole, and a madman.

Can Michael learn to love the child Issie holds so close to her heart and protect him from the man who took everything from Michael so long ago?

The Art of
Characterization
How to Use the Elements of Storytelling to Connect Readers to an Unforgettable Cast

Ties that Bind Series

All of Fay's books are available on Amazon.

About the Author

Fay Lamb is an editor, writing coach, and author, whose emotionally charged stories remind the reader that God is always in the details. Fay has contracted three series. With the release of *Everybody's Broken*, three of the four books in the Amazing Grace romantic suspense series, which also includes *Stalking Willow* and *Better than Revenge*, are currently available for purchase. *Charisse* and *Libby* the first two novels in her The Ties That Bind contemporary romance series have been released. Fay has also collaborated on two Christmas novella projects: *The Christmas Three Treasure Hunt*, and *A Ruby Christmas*, and the Write Integrity Press romance novella series, which includes *A Dozen Apologies, The Love Boat Bachelor,* and *Unlikely*

Merger. Her adventurous spirit has taken her into the realm of non-fiction with *The Art of Characterization: How to Use the Elements of Storytelling to Connect Readers to an Unforgettable Cast.*

Future releases from Fay are: *Frozen Notes*, Book 4 of the Amazing Grace series and *Hope* and *Delilah*, Books 3 and 4 from The Ties that Bind series.

Fay loves to meet readers, and you can find her on her personal Facebook page, her Facebook Author page, and at The Tactical Editor on Facebook. She's also active on Twitter. Then there are her blogs: On the Ledge, Inner Source, and the Tactical Editor. And, yes, there's one more: Goodreads.

Anyone interested in learning more about Fay's freelance editing and her coaching should contact her at fay@faylamb.com.

Everybody's Broken

Questions for Bible Study

1. Abra Carmichael had what appeared to be a perfect life. She clung to her own false perceptions and did not understand the dangers around her because of her fear of losing those most precious to her.
What does God's Word say to those who live in fear?

> **2 Timothy 1:7**
> **1 John 4:18:**
> God does not give us a spirit to fear for what may happen to us. Rather, those who know Christ as Savior are given a spirit of power, of love, and of sound mind. Because God's perfect love does cast out fear, when we allow fear to rule our lives, we show a lack of maturity in our Christian faith.

2. After the death of her husband, Abra struggled with feeling unimportant to the Lord. She still attended church, but her relationship was lacking because she felt herself unworthy of God's love.
What do we know about our unworthiness before God?

> **2 Samuel 7:18-19**
> Just as David stated humbly in this verse, we are not worthy, but God does bestow blessings despite our unworthiness

> **Psalm 18:3 (also) 2 Samuel 22:4**
> **Matthew 8:8**
> Despite how we feel about our own unworthiness, God is always worthy of our praise and our trust.

> **Colossians 1:10**
> **1 Thessalonians 2:12**
> **2 Thessalonians 1:11**
> We should always walk in this life so that our God will count us worthy.

3. Can you think of any scripture that, if Abra had tucked them into her heart, may have helped her to see that although we can do nothing to be worthy of God's love (our worthiness comes through what Christ has done for us-**John 3:16)**, He does very much love us and cares about even the most insignificant problems in our lives?

> **Psalm 139:14**
> **Matthew 10:29-31**
> **Jeremiah 29:11**

4. *Everybody's Broken* is about lives shattered by tragedy. However, the roots of this tragedy are born in lies and unsaid truths that continued to destroy each of the lives of those Beau Carmichael had loved. His death caused the lies to begin to unravel and for his loved ones to realize their wrongs as they continue to harbor secrets. The characters each believed that in keeping their secrets and by telling lies, they were protecting one another. What does God say about lying, and is there ever a good lie or a reason for even a "little white lie"?

> **Proverbs 12:22**
> **Proverbs 13:5**
> **Proverbs 6:15-17**
> God abhors lying under any circumstance. In fact, Jesus is clear in John 8:44 that Satan is a liar and the father of lying.

5. Abra did not lean upon scripture as she struggled with her own problems, yet we find that God still used her to speak truth into the life of her sister-in-law when Randa reveals the devastating event in her life. How did that Truth come to Abra, and what is the importance of studying and memorizing scriptures?

John 14:26
John 16:13

God has given those who have accepted Christ as Savior the Holy Spirit, not only as a comforter but a teacher. We are told that the Holy Spirit will bring scripture to remembrance. However, if a believer does not read the scripture, study the scripture, or memorize scripture, he or she should not expect the Holy Spirit to give what the believer has ignored.

Write Integrity Press

Thank you for choosing
Write Integrity Press.
Find more of our books
at our website:
WriteIntegrity.com.

If you enjoyed
EVERYBODY'S BROKEN,
please leave a review
for the author
on Amazon.